Black Tom: Terror on the Hudson

Black Tom: Terror on the Hudson

Ron Semple

**TOP HAT
BOOKS**

Winchester, UK
Washington, USA

First published by Top Hat Books, 2015
Top Hat Books is an imprint of John Hunt Publishing Ltd., Laurel House, Station Approach,
Alresford, Hants, SO24 9JH, UK
office1@jhpbooks.net
www.johnhuntpublishing.com

For distributor details and how to order please visit the 'Ordering' section on our website.

Text copyright: Ron Semple 2014

ISBN: 978 1 78535 110 5
Library of Congress Control Number: 2015936227

A CIP catalogue record for this book is available from the British Library.

Design: Stuart Davies

Printed in the USA by Edwards Brothers Malloy

We operate a distinctive and ethical publishing philosophy in all
areas of our business, from our global network of authors to
production and worldwide distribution.

To Traci, Mookie & Elena,
you can never be further
away from me than my heart.

Love,

Pop

To Jane Guarascio Semple, the joy of my life, and to
Devin and Warren Murphy without whom this book would
never have been written. And to the Society of Jesus and the
United States Marine Corps. One formed the boy, the other
made the man.

The All Highest

The "All Highest," Kaiser Wilhelm II, the German Emperor, King of Prussia and Supreme Warlord, was inspecting himself in a full length mirror. He liked what he saw. From his brilliantly polished cavalry boots, to his gilded sword, to the blaze of decorations on his chest, to the top of his spiked helmet, he looked the epitome of a Prussian warrior.

He particularly liked the bayonet tips of his upturned martial moustache, kept perfect by the daily visits of a highly skilled barber.

His eyes lingered on his crooked and withered left arm, mangled at birth, the hand resting atop a dagger. The foreshortened sleeve was perfected tailored.

No one will notice, thought the Kaiser. He was wrong. Everyone noticed, no one looked.

The All Highest was in a particularly good mood. The old man, Otto Von Bismarck, was gone and he, the All Highest ordained by God to lead Germany to greatness, was free to do just that. The first piece of complicated nonsense negotiated by the so-called Iron Chancellor to go was that ridiculous secret treaty with Russia. The Kaiser let it lapse.

Let Cousin Nicky take care of himself, the Kaiser thought at the time. The Czar did. His government negotiated a mutual aid treaty with France, something Bismarck had considered imperative to prevent. From such small things, catastrophes can spring.

The Kaiser turned and looked in the mirror again. There was a bare spot on his chest that could use a decoration. Maybe his grandmother, Queen Victoria, would give him one.

His mother, Victoria's daughter, was so English that when she died she was buried wrapped only in a Union Jack. Her son considered Great Britain his potential enemy.

Unlike his late, courageous yet peace loving father, none of Wilhelm II's medals were for combat.

While the Kaiser was admiring himself, a book that would influence the fate of nations in two World Wars was being published in America in 1890. It was "The Influence of Sea Power Upon History, 1660-1783" written by Captain Alfred Thayer Mahan. Stripped down to its essentials, Mahan argued that whichever naval power that controlled the sea lanes would dominate the world. He, in essence, urged the United States to revive its Manifest Destiny by expanding overseas. That meant American defensive bases and coaling stations in the Caribbean and the Pacific as well as the acquisition of Hawaii. In a decade, this would be so.

When Mahan was head of the Naval War College, he struck up a friendship with the assistant secretary of the navy, Theodore Roosevelt, who later, as president, would implement many of Mahan's ideas.

American industry and agriculture were already the most productive in the world. Exports, which would benefit from Mahon's brand of protection, included one-fourth of its crops and half of the petroleum America produced.

Mahan's influence on foreign navies was extreme. The Kaiser ordered that copies of his book be placed in the ward rooms of all of his ships. The Japanese studied Mahan assiduously and ultimately were defeated by an equally informed but more powerful Navy—ours. Even the British admired Mahan probably because they had perfected the naval practices his doctrines were based on.

Captain Mahan, unquestionably the most prominent naval strategist of his time, was not much of a seaman. Ships under his command often seemed to run into things they should have avoided. The Navy prudently kept him ashore during most of his career.

His book set the stage of America's emergence as a world

leader and ultimately a superpower which frequently has had the unwelcome role of policing the world thrust upon her.

Mahan's theories would have a direct effect on a knob-shaped protrusion on the Jersey City waterfront called Black Tom.

Millions of immigrants arrived at the Port of New York before and after the Statue of Liberty was opened in 1886 to greet them. Many of them—Irish, German, Italian, Jewish, Russians, Slavs and others—never moved inland more than a few miles away, if that, from her golden lamp. There they lived, worked and died in the shadow of her promise. Some forswore the old country, others did not.

Such was Jersey City, an improbable place for this improbable story. It is a story that intertwines the daily lives of the ordinary and extraordinary people of this otherwise forgettable place with war, militarism, America's rise to power, sabotage, railroads, greed, politics, profits, nationalism, intrigue, assimilation and a search for really good tomato sauce.

Black Tom was to be part of a worldwide cataclysm that would kill millions and would affect all of us to this very day more than a century later. Yet the few who knew or suspected what actually happened at Black Tom said nothing at the time.

Why?

Do You Renounce Satan?

Amelia McGurk shouldn't have been in church. It wasn't done. Not here in Jersey City. The mother should be at home getting ready for the party with her husband while the godparents took the baby to be baptized.

But Amelia couldn't resist. She slipped into the back of St. Michael's and watched as the monsignor went through the ancient ritual of cleansing her baby of original sin. Not that she understood a word of the Latin that echoed through the church, empty save for a few pews up front crowded with family and friends. Amelia was in the back with the handful of ubiquitous old biddies.

All she knew was that her baby, her Michael—named for her brother as well as the archangel—was now safe from the grasp of the devil. Of course, Amelia's friends would have argued that it would have been Satan who would have been in jeopardy had he made his presence known. Amelia was celebrated for her quick temper in a neighborhood where common brawling was unremarkable.

Baby Michael howled when the monsignor poured cold water over his head and baptized him: *In nomine Patris, et Filii et Spiritus Sancti.*

Amelia all but grabbed the infant from his godmother's arms at the front door of the church.

The monsignor couldn't help but see her. He ignored the breach of local protocol.

"That's a fine boy you have there, Amelia, God love him," he said.

"Thank you, Monsignor," answered Amelia. "He's a gift from God that's going straight back to him. Michael will be a priest just like you, Monsignor. Mark my words."

"Now, Amelia," said the monsignor with more patience than

he felt, "the priesthood is a vocation. Either God calls you to it or he doesn't."

"Don't worry, Monsignor. Michael will be called. I'll see to that."

Michael, infant and boy, lived on Cork Row in the Horseshoe, the 2nd Ward at turn of the 20th century Jersey City. He was surrounded by his own kind: Irish Catholics.

The Republican legislature of New Jersey created the Horseshoe in an attempt to cram all the Democrats possible into one legislative assembly district and thus limit their political influence. On a map it looked like an upside down U—a horseshoe. It looped around the vast property of the railroads which dominated the Jersey City waterfront.

The limitless flow of immigrants, Germans and Irish first and then Italians, Slavs and others, would not cease until the newcomers overwhelmed those who came before until Republicans—except in presidential years—would be hard to find in Jersey City. The Horseshoe became and remained the heart of the Democratic Party.

The Horseshoe was a place of railroad tracks and trestles, docks, piers, cobblestone streets, gas lights, horses, wagons, dirt, noise, streetcars, trucks, motor cars, Catholic churches and forty saloons.

It was a place of poverty and privation. But it was home to thousands of Irish immigrants and their children who crowded into its wooden and brick tenements and its shanties. Kneaded by their brogues, that name "The Horseshoe" was slurred to "The 'Show." Elsewhere in Jersey City it was still called The Horseshoe.

The men worked for the railroads, on the river, on the waterfront or in any factory where there was not a sign that read, "Catholics Need Not Apply." Their women grew old much too swiftly caring for their large families in conditions that would make a serf weep.

It was squalid and disease was a constant. Especially feared was tuberculosis. Sure it would kill you in the end but the real threat was that the health authorities would come and ship you off to a sanitarium. Take you from all you knew and loved.

Children grew up on the streets in the 'Show. Their flats were too dark and dreary. The streets were exciting and inviting. Mickey was a happy child and a tough one.

You learned to fight in the 'Show immediately after you learned to walk. It was either fight or flight and small children can't run very fast. It was better to stand and fight. With luck, an adult—almost always a woman—would intervene if you were taking too much of a beating.

If the streets were dangerous, it was more because of the traffic and the railroad tracks spearing through the place rather than boys dukeing it out.

If your family lived in a cold-water flat, you had to heat it yourself. If you were lucky, you heated with coal. Coal was free, at least to most people in the 'Show. That's not the way the coal owners in Pennsylvania planned it, but that is the way it worked.

Coal bound for the great city of New York entered Jersey City from the west—"back of the hill." From that moment until the coal cars entered the safety of the yards on the waterfront, boys of all ages and sizes swarmed all over them with burlap sacks pilfering coal.

All of them promised their mothers never to jump on a moving coal car. They were only to pick up coal which had fallen onto the rail bed. None of them kept that promise. More than a few of them ended up crippled or dead under the wheels of a coal car.

The railroad police worked hard to keep the thievery down. But if they caught you, all you got was a nightstick across the back of your legs. All you had to do to escape more punishment was to run away. No railroad dick was going to jump off and chase you down the street. Not in Jersey City. Certainly not in the

'Show. The railroad bulls weren't suicidal.

No one had ever heard a sermon that held it was a sin to steal coal from a Pennsylvania robber baron. The souls of the "Molly McGuires," long since hanged in the coal fields, could be heard chortling in the laughter of the kids mocking the railroad police.

Thus it was that the baby Michael became the boy Mickey on Cork Row in the Horseshoe. Mickey's father was dead—crushed between two boxcars. The Erie railroad gave Amelia McGurk $200 to compensate her for her loss.

Most of the kids in Mickey McGurk's neighborhood spent more time than they wanted to in church. Mickey didn't feel that way. He assumed he was to be a priest. Everyone assumed that. Amelia McGurk, mother of five, made sure that they knew that her youngest was destined for the cloth.

In time, Mickey became an altar boy at Saint Michael's which wasn't as easy as it sounds. You had to memorize all the Latin responses to the priest's prayers during the Mass. You had to learn the choreography of the Mass. When did you take the missal from the epistle to the gospel side of the altar, when did you ring the bells? You had to ferret out all the little idiosyncrasies of the pastor and his three curates. Which one wanted a drop of wine, which one a chalice full.

The priests were not patient with stumbling altar boys.

"Don't you know what an honor it is to be an acolyte? It is a minor order. It leads directly to the sub-deaconate, the deaconate and then the priesthood. Do it right, you numbskull."

Mickey rarely had to be told twice. He was an acolyte. He was on his way to the priesthood.

He even took a swig of the sacramental wine with the other boys when the priest was not in the sacristy. Just to see how it tasted, mind you. It was awful. Cloyingly sweet. Sickeningly sweet.

But Mickey thought that was just another sacrifice priests must make for the privilege of turning ordinary bread and wine into the body and blood of the Savior.

He was an altar boy when his neighbor, Frank Hague, married Jennie Warner. Frank was a well-respected man on 9th Street. He was the Democratic precinct leader and he had a great job as a deputy sheriff for the county. Frank gave each altar boy a silver dollar before the ceremony. Never was there a more pious recitation of the Latin responses at a nuptial Mass.

Mickey was an altar boy when his older brother married the girl next door, Frank Hague's younger sister. Frank Hague was the fourth of the eight children his mother, Margaret, delivered on the kitchen table of her tenement flat.

It was Frank who gave him another silver dollar, this time after the ceremony and said to him, "I guess this makes me your Uncle Frank."

"You bet it does, Uncle Frank," answered Mickey McGurk who was considered one of the brightest lads in the parish.

Mickey was still an altar boy when his insistent mother managed to get him into St. Peter's College High School on a full scholarship which the Jesuits offered since they reckoned the family was penniless anyway. The Jesuits, impressed with his intelligence, thought of him as a possible candidate for their own ranks. The thought of Mickey as a Jesuit brought his mother close to swooning.

Mickey could see both Ellis Island and Bedloe Island from his 2nd floor classroom window. Miss Liberty, as would be noted by many during the coming decades, had her back turned to Jersey City. A nearby third island, Black Tom, connected to Jersey City by a causeway, now had a long wharf, piers and warehouses serviced by many railroad tracks. It looks nothing like the uninhabited island it once was.

It is Black Tom that will have the most effect on Mickey—and so many more—in the not too distant future.

Mickey was still an altar boy and a third year student at St. Peter's that summer night in Van Vorst Park on Jersey Avenue when his best friend, Jimmie Cribbins, introduced him to Marge the Barge.

Mickey, who had four sisters and lived in a crowded flat, needed no anatomy lessons. But he had no idea just how soft and warm female flesh could be even when it came in a package that outweighed you by ten or twenty pounds.

Still less could Mickey imagine exactly how it would feel when the generous Marge let him go all the way like the small squad of neighborhood boys that preceded him.

Jimmy spent the rest of the long evening trying to persuade Mickey that he was not desperately in love and that he didn't have to marry Marge.

The priesthood was another matter.

The confrontation came during his retreat at Manressa House on Staten Island. It took two ferryboat voyages to get there since they were still digging the Tubes, a subway tunnel that would link Jersey City to Manhattan.

Most of his classmates had finished their retreat and were going home in the morning after a week of total silence, sermons and meditation. Several were asked to stay for another week. Mickey realized that all who were to remain were probably seminary bound. He panicked and asked to see the priest from St. Peter's who had accompanied them to Manressa.

"What's this all about, Mickey?"

"I can't stay for the second week, Father. I've got that job delivering groceries after school. I give the money to my Mother. We need the money, you know."

The Jesuit stared at Mickey for a second and then said softly, "Mickey. Do I look like an idiot? Stop tap dancing. What is this all about?"

The boy almost cried. He took a deep breath and blurted it out. "I can't be a priest, Father. I just can't."

"Why not?"

"I just can't. That's all."

"That's most certainly not all," said the Jesuit. "What's her name?"

Mickey was stunned. "What do you mean?"

"You know what I mean. What's her name?"

"I can't tell you that, Father."

"You can and will. What... is... her... name?"

Tears flowed now but Mickey was not sobbing. "Marge O'Brian," he whispered.

"Ah, yes," said the Jesuit, "Marge the Barge. Well, at least you can't be accused of corrupting an innocent."

The tears stopped.

Marge the Barge? How in hell does he know that? He doesn't even live in the neighborhood.

A concise summation of the life of St. Augustine followed but Mickey who had inherited no small part of his mother's stubbornness soon ended it.

"It's no use, Father. I'll try to control myself. I know it's a sin. But I'm not taking any vow of chastity. Not now. Not never."

"Not ever," corrected the Jesuit educator. "Avoid double negatives. All right, Michael. That's enough talk for now; you can go home tomorrow with the rest of your class.

"How old are you, son?" asked the priest.

"Seventeen, Father."

The priest took a good look at the boy. *Tall for a Jersey City kid, maybe five feet nine inches. Make it five foot ten in his shoes. Around 145-150 pounds. Solid. Good carriage. Good looking enough. Blue eyes, light brown hair.*

"Good. You'll be doing mostly college work in a couple of months. How does that strike you?"

Mickey didn't have any idea. He had thought he was going to the seminary. But now that was out.

"I don't know, Father."

"Do you want to go on to graduate?" The course at St. Peter's was six years. You started with high school subjects and rapidly proceeded to college work and ended up with a bachelor's degree. The idea was to provide leadership for the Catholic working class.

"No," he said quickly. He already had more education than anyone he knew except for the priests. He didn't know what he wanted but college was not it.

The priest looked thoughtful. "You know, Ignatius was a soldier before he realized that God was calling him to greater things," said the Jesuit. "Maybe that's what you need. We Jesuits have friends, you know. It could be arranged. You're big enough, you're strong enough and God knows you are smart enough. How'd you like to see something of the world? Serve your country. Learn that there is more to life than the transitory delights of the flesh. How'd you like to be a Marine? A United States Marine. I know the recruiter in Manhattan."

Mickey startled himself when he didn't hesitate. "I think I'd like that just fine, Father."

"Good. I'll talk to your mother."

Thank God, thought Mickey McGurk who would much rather face his country's enemies than his mother.

The White Man's Burden

"You may fire when you are ready, Gridley."

With those words, Commodore George Dewey doomed both the Spanish fleet off Corregidor and its colonial rule in the Philippines and propelled America into an unfamiliar role as an imperial power.

When the smoke cleared on the morning of May 1, 1898, the Spanish fleet had been destroyed and Manila had surrendered to the Americans.

Dewey had been at Hong Kong when the USS Maine blew up in Havana harbor in February, killing two hundred and sixty sailors and Marines, and the American press began to beat the drums of war. America's sympathy had been with the Cuban rebels and now, by jingo, she was going to do something about it.

While Dewey was defeating the Spanish in the far off Philippines, America was readying an invasion of Cuba which lay just ninety miles off Key West, FL.

The first landing was made on June 6 by Marines at Guantanamo Bay and was unopposed. The Navy was busying itself cutting telegraph cables and shooing off puny Spanish gun boats. The Marines moved inland drawing fire and casualties. The Leathernecks proved apt pupils for their Cuban allies who gave them instant lessons in how to fight the guerillas who were loyal to the crown.

The prize the Marines sought was the Cuzco Wells, the only source of fresh water in the area and the site of the Spanish headquarters. The Marines requested supporting fire from the USS Dolphin but the gunboat's shells dropped in the direct path of fifty Marines trying to flank the Spanish position. Up jumped Sergeant John Quick with his back to heavy enemy fire. He used a large handkerchief on a crooked stick to signal the Dolphin and have its fire shifted. For this, Sergeant Quick received the Medal of Honor.

Wrote a correspondent who witnessed his bravery under intense fire, "I saw Quick betray only one sign of emotion. As he swung his clumsy flag to and fro, an end of it once caught on a cactus pillar, and he looked sharply over his shoulder to see what had it. He gave the flag an impatient jerk. He looked annoyed."

The United States leased forty-five square miles at Guantanamo Bay as a coaling and naval station in 1903. A century later it contained a notorious military prison holding terrorists from around the world.

Meanwhile in 1898, Lieutenant Colonel Theodore Roosevelt, on horseback, led his Rough Riders and other units to victory on the San Juan Heights. He had resigned as assistant secretary of the navy to fight first hand. His courage, charisma and vision led to the governorship of New York, the vice presidency and, after an assassination, to the presidency of the United States itself.

Another unexpected result of the outbreak of war was the dash of the USS Oregon from San Francisco around the tip of South America to Florida to join the fleet in time for the Battle of Santiago.

It took sixty-six days and virtually ended the debate on whether to take over and continue the work of digging the Panama Canal. That now was considered a strategic necessity for a potential world power such as the United States which now possessed the Philippines, Guam, Puerto Rico, Midway, Hawaii and, of course, Alaska.

But the lot of an imperial power is not always an easy one. Now we were responsible for "our little brown brothers" in the Philippines, Puerto Rico, and Guam. Some of said little brown brothers were less than grateful and we found ourselves mired in a nasty insurrection in the Philippines, an unpleasant occupation of Cuba, troubles in the Caribbean and instability in those parts of Mexico we hadn't bothered to steal a half century earlier.

We had taken up, in the words of Rudyard Kipling, the poet

laureate of imperialism, "the white man's burden." We didn't like it much, but there it was.

The Philippine Insurrection was supposedly over in 1902 but for almost ten years after that soldiers and Marines tangled with "Irreconcilables" and Moros swapping gunfire and atrocities.

The hostilities gave rise to a strong anti-war and anti-interventionist movement which has continued to exist in one form or another to the present day. The isolationists would protest but, in the end, lose even when they were right.

One of the arguments for continuing to occupy the Philippines was that if we didn't, some other imperial nation would. One such was Germany which had strings of islands nearby which contributed little to the Fatherland other than the occasional coconut and a place to stockpile coal.

But with warfare petering out, Kurt Jahnke, an agent of Section IIIb of the German General Staff, had been ordered to leave the Philippines and get to Panama to report on how progress on that canal was going.

Marine Private Jahnke was standing before his first sergeant.

"So do you think you can get me a transfer to Panama, First Sergeant?"

The first sergeant's answer was immediate. "Of course I can get you a transfer. I could probably have you taken out and shot if I felt like it. I'm a first sergeant.

"But I think you're making a mistake, Yankee. I think the old man is going to make you a corporal. You go to Panama and you are going to have to start all over again. Why the hell do you want to go to that pesthole anyway? Aren't the Philippines miserable enough for you?"

Jahnke laughed. "I joined the Corps to see the world, First Sergeant."

"Yeah, and I joined the Corps to forget what's her name. Well, if you want to be a thickheaded kraut, I'll not interfere. I'll get the paperwork going."

"Thank you, First Sergeant," said Jahnke as he turned to leave.

"Yankee. You've been a good Marine. You even speak good English which is more than I can say for some of the fucking foreigners in this company. I'll write up a little note you can give to your new first sergeant when you get to Panama. It'll help. We all know each other."

Marge the Barge, a Tragedy in One Act

The night was hot. Stifling.

Young Marge, her plump body clad only in a thin nightgown, had gone to sleep covered with a sheet. That had been thrown off as she drifted into sleep.

She was having a recurring dream. A wonderful dream.

Marge could see herself and her dream-husband as clearly as if she was floating over her bed looking down.

Of course, her dream-husband's face was fuzzy. She couldn't quite make out his features but she knew he was handsome, he was very tall, very strong and, without doubt, he loved Marge beyond all calculation.

They were going to make love. Marge was always thrilled when that happened.

She could feel him caressing her breasts under her nightgown. She felt the nightgown being lifted up.

Marge held her breath. She felt him penetrate her and heard his sigh. Marge felt his weight upon her and was content. She wrapped her arms around him.

She smelled the whiskey on his breath.

In between sleep and awakening, Marge thought, *Something's wrong. My love doesn't drink whiskey. He doesn't drink.*

Marge opened her eyes. It wasn't her dream-husband thrusting inside her.

Oh, my God!

It was her father.

Marge pulled her arms back.

"Dad. Da..."

"Shush. Shush, sweetheart. It'll all be over in a minute. Just a minute..."

He kept thrusting. Marge wanted to shove him off her but she didn't.

16

Dear God! It feels good. Better than any boy. She met his thrust, her hands on his shoulders.

"Oh, there's a good girl. Help your father. It'll all be over in a minute. Soon. Ah! Ah! Oh! There, there. That's a good girl. Good girl."

Her father collapsed on top of her. Muttering.

Marge lay still. She said nothing. He was still inside her.

Her father rolled off her. Marge saw him stand, pull up his underpants, put on his trousers which were hanging from the doorknob and stumble into his slippers.

When he was at her door, he looked back. Marge didn't look at him, she squeezed her eyes shut.

"Go to sleep, Marge. Forget what happened. It was just a bad dream. We won't tell your mother about this."

Marge heard him shuffle down the hall, open the front door and then climb the iron rung ladder to the roof. He hadn't closed the door.

She got out of bed and padded barefoot down the hall to her parents' bedroom, the front of her nightgown stained.

She had no idea what she was doing.

Her mother was lying there snoring. Passed out. Dead drunk. As usual.

This was the first time but not the last. *He'll be at me every night. That can't be. It's wrong. Oh, God, what's the matter with me? I enjoyed it. God help me! Please.*

Marge headed back down the hallway and up the ladder.

She had to talk to him. Tell him it was wrong. Tell him to stop.

Marge felt the soft black tar under her bare feet.

Her father was at the edge of the roof, smoking a cigar. She could smell the smoke.

He didn't hear her approach.

At the same time she pushed the small of his back—hard— she said, "You bastard."

Her father waved his arms trying to regain his balance. The

cigar flew out of his hand.

He failed. Without a word, without a sound, he went over the edge still waving his arms.

A second later she heard him hit. Marge looked over the edge, her hand over her mouth.

Her father was lying inches from the curb, his head at an odd angle, an arm under him.

The street was very still. Not a light went on. No one was about. It was long after the saloons closed.

Is he dead? He looks dead. Suppose he's not dead. Should I help him? Call for help? What should I do?

Marge looked over the edge again, careful to keep her balance. Her father had not moved.

He's dead. Dear God, I've killed my father. I murdered him. What will happen to me? What will they do to me? They'll hang me, that's what. No, I'll get the electric chair. They'll run a million volts of electricity through me and fry me like a sausage.

The street remained silent.

Then Marge remembered what her father had said. *Go to bed. Forget about it. It was just a bad dream.*

She did and fell asleep at once, her thumb in her mouth.

The milkman found the body, ran to the corner and saw a policeman two blocks away. He yelled and jumped up and down waving his arms. The cop came running.

The two of them stood by the body. The cop made the Sign of the Cross and said, "Jesus, Mary and Joseph."

He turned to the milkman and said, "Be a good fellow and stay here while I go to the call box on the corner. I got to get some help here."

The milkman had no intention of leaving until he was chased away. This was the most interesting thing that had ever happened on his route.

"I will," he said, "Do you think he jumped?"

The cop who normally wouldn't speak to a civilian—except to

say "Get the hell out of here"—needed the milkman so he answered.

"I don't know," he said, "we'll let the detectives figure that out."

It didn't take the detectives long.

"Do you think he jumped?" asked one.

"Nah," answered his partner. "You see that big cigar butt there? A guy doesn't smoke a cigar while he's committing suicide. Nope. He lost his balance and fell. He had a snoot full, too. You can still smell it on him."

"That makes sense," said his partner.

The lead detective stood up and looked across the street to where the beat cop was controlling a small crowd of neighbors and passersby.

"Cover him," he said.

He walked over, pointed back and asked, "Does anybody know who that fellow is?"

"I do. That's Bob O'Brian. He lives up there on the third floor."

"Thanks."

Marge heard the knocking on the door, knew who it was, and knew that her mother wouldn't—couldn't—answer it.

She put on a bathrobe and slippers, feeling the tar stick to the heel of her right slipper.

She opened the door part way.

"Yes?"

She could see the detectives' badges pinned to their civilian jackets.

"I'm Detective Scanlon and this is Detective Scully. Can we come in, Miss?"

"I guess so."

Marge tried to look puzzled which wasn't hard since no adult had ever addressed her as "Miss" before.

Scanlon spoke.

"And you'd be?"

"Margaret O'Brian."

"Can I call you Margie?"

"Yes, sir."

"Now Margie, do you know where your father is?"

Marge looked towards her parents' bedroom. "Sure. In bed with my mother."

"Would you go get him, please? Your mother too."

"Okay."

Marge went into her parents' bedroom closing the door behind her.

She tried to rouse her mother who opened and closed her eyes, rolled over and started snoring again.

Marge left the room and stared at Scanlon. "My father isn't there and I can't wake my mother."

"What's wrong with your mother?" asked Scanlon, instantly alert for more trouble.

"Nothing," said Marge, "I think she had a bit too much to drink last night."

Scanlon relaxed. *Early Sunday morning with the piss-in-the-sink Irish.*

"When did you last see your father?"

"I don't understand. Where is my father? Why are you here? What's going on?"

Scanlon put his hand gently on Marge's shoulder. "We're trying to sort that out, Margie. What you tell us may help."

"All right. We all had supper together around six o'clock. We did the dishes and then my Mother and Father went out."

"Where?"

"I don't know. I went out too, saw some friends and came back at about nine o'clock. I went to bed when it got dark."

"Were your parents here then?"

"No."

"Does anybody else live here. Brothers, sisters, a lodger?"

"No. I'm an only child. My mother had, you know, plumbing problems."

"I see. Now Margie, Detective Scully is going to stay here until your mother wakes up. He has to talk to her. Do you have anyone you can stay with?"

"You're scaring me, Mister; I don't want to stay with anybody. I want to know what's going on. Where's my father?"

Scanlon thought about it. *She's old enough and it's a hard world down here. They grow up fast.*

"Okay, Margie. Sit down.'

She did.

"I'm really sorry to have to tell you this, but we think your father is dead."

"Oh, my God in Heaven."

"We're not certain, mind you, but we're pretty sure. Your mother will have to identify the body."

Marge was crying now. The tears were real. "Where is he? Where is my father? At the undertakers?"

"Not yet."

"What happened?"

"We think your father fell off the roof."

"This roof? Here?"

"Yes."

"I didn't hear a thing."

Marge started sobbing. Genuine sobbing.

Scanlon put his arm around her. She tried not to stiffen.

"There. There," he said. "Did your father go up to the roof often?"

Marge struggled to catch her breath. "Yes. Yes. He liked to smoke cigars up there. My mother hates cigar smoke."

Case closed. Scanlon left.

"Mama! Mama!"

Marge rushed into her mother's bedroom and tried to wake her again. Her mother kept snoring.

Detective Scully shook his head in disgust and settled into a kitchen chair. Marge emerged still sniffling.

"Do you know how to make a pot of tea, Margie?"

"I do."

"Then please do. I think both of us could do with a cup right about now."

Afterwards, Scully said, "Get dressed, Margie. I think I hear your mother stirring. It would be better if you weren't there when I tell her."

Margie scraped the tar off her heel with her fingernails and then cleaned them with her teeth. When she went into the kitchen to embrace her mother, Scully stopped her.

"Margie, I don't think your mother understands what's going on. Are there some neighbors or relatives you can get?"

"Yes. The lady downstairs. My aunt lives in the Heights."

"Give me her name and address and I tell her what happened."

Marge did.

With that, the word spread and the Irish women nearby eased into their well-practiced choreography of death which was as traditional and unchanging as a kabuki dance.

Neither Marge nor her mother went to Mass that Sunday.

But the next day, while her father's body was yet to be delivered to the undertakers, Margie pounded on the door of the rectory.

It was the housekeeper who answered, a thin, purse-lipped, crone whose meals gave the pastor and his curates a foretaste of purgatory.

"I need to see the pastor."

"The pastor's busy."

"I need to see the pastor now," said Marge.

"I said the pastor is busy."

A voice intervened. It was the pastor. "What's all the ruckus, Mrs. Houghton?"

"I told this young lady you were busy, Monsignor."

"I am that, but maybe I can spare this poor girl a minute or two."

The pastor knew Marge and knew that her father was dead. In fact, he and his curates were discussing whether Bob O'Brian had fallen or if he jumped. If it was suicide, he couldn't be buried by the Catholic Church.

Mrs. Houghton left trying to look very dignified but annoyed that the monsignor had reversed her ruling.

"How are you holding up, Marge?"

"Not good, Monsignor. I need to go to confession. Now."

"Ah, there's time enough for that come Saturday, my girl."

"It can't wait, Monsignor. I can't wait." Tears were running down Marge's cheeks.

The monsignor's interest was piqued. Any priest would tell you that the worst part of the job was hearing confessions. Boring. Very boring. Listening, week after week, to those ghastly, trivial, banal sins repeated time and time again:

"I stole a candy bar, Father."

"I had bad thoughts about my sister-in-law, Father."

"I got drunk and smacked the missus, Father."

What could it be that propelled this poor thing towards the confessional on a day when confessions are not regularly heard? He knew Marge well enough. He had already dealt with her escapades with some teenage boys. Gave her three Rosaries for her penance last time.

Penitents think that the screen in the confessional protects their anonymity but few realize that priests get very good at identifying voices.

No. It's more serious than another boy. I doubt that she wants to be saying Rosaries for the rest of her life. It's something more serious.

"All right, child. Let's go into the church. No matter what the sin is, God will forgive you."

"I hope so, Monsignor. But I'm not sure."

So Marge told him. She left nothing out. Told him about her dream. Told him about her real life nightmare. Told him about her father lying there, still inside her.

The monsignor was not shocked. Incest, especially incest mixed with booze, was an old, evil story.

"That wasn't your sin, child," he said. "It was his. Mortal sin requires full consent of the will. And you did not give him full consent."

Marge was sobbing. "Monsignor. I know you can't lie in confession or your sins are not forgiven. Monsignor, I'm sorry, I'm sorry but I enjoyed it. God help me, I enjoyed it."

"You did not enjoy it, my child, your body did. Your body betrayed your soul as it so often does. It was not your sin. It was his. There is nothing to forgive."

The sobbing continued. "It's worse than that, Monsignor. Worse."

Worse? How?

"Tell me, my child."

"I murdered my father, Monsignor."

Step by step she took the monsignor through the act until she was back in bed with tar on her heel.

"Marge, did you climb that ladder intending to go up there to kill your father?"

A pause. "No, I don't think so. I don't know what I was thinking. I just had to make him stop."

"Of course, my child. Now when you pushed your father and called him a 'bastard', did you want him to fall off the roof and break his neck?"

Marge realized she was horrified. "No, Monsignor. No. I didn't want him to die. But I did want him to stop."

"Again, my child, lack of full consent. Your father may have died as a result of your push but your intent was not to kill him. Again no sin. At least, not to the church. The civil authorities— the police—may think otherwise."

"I lied to the police, Monsignor. I don't want to die in the electric chair."

The monsignor smiled. "I doubt that it would come to that under any circumstances, child. Were the lies deliberate?"

"They were."

"Then there's your sin."

"Are you going to tell the police on me, Monsignor?"

"Marge, the seal of the confessional is sacred. No one, not the police, not the Pope, can compel me to tell what I hear here."

I can't even tell my fellow priests who would love this story.

"Monsignor, did my father go to hell?"

The monsignor thought for a moment. "Marge, the theologians are divided as to whether Judas went to hell. And he betrayed Our Lord and then killed himself. We don't know whether your father was sorry for his sins. For all we know, he was up on that roof saying a Good Act of Contrition. But I think we do know this. If Satan didn't claim his soul, then Bob O'Brian will spend a lot of time in purgatory washing it clean.

"All right, Marge. Say an Act of Contrition."

She did. Monsignor blessed her and said, in Latin, that ancient rite that begins: *"Te absolvo…"*

Marge waited for her penance.

"For your penance say three 'Our Fathers' and three 'Hail Marys.' Go and sin no more, my child."

That night, after a typically horrendous supper, the monsignor said to his curates, "It looks like Bob O'Brian gets a Christian Burial after all. He fell off that roof."

"How do you know that, Monsignor?"

"Policemen gossip too, you know." *A neat little evasion, that. Maybe I should have become a Jesuit.*

* * *

They were back from the cemetery and at Aunt Agnes McCann's

house on Irving Street.

"Where's my mom?" asked Marge.

Aunt Agnes took both her hands. "You know this better than I do; your mother's not well. She hasn't been for a long time. They waited until after the funeral but they took your mother to the hospital."

"Which hospital, Aunt Agnes?"

"The one on Snake Hill, sweetheart."

The insane asylum was on that rock pile in the middle of the Meadows. Many people went there, but few came back.

"We'll visit. Uncle Jim will take you and me out there and we'll visit."

"Will she get well, Aunt Agnes?"

"Who knows? Probably not. But they'll take good care of her. We can't. But Uncle Jim and I can certainly take good care of you, Margie. You know we never had children. You'll be like the daughter we never had."

Marge felt at peace, maybe for the first time ever.

She blurted out, "Can I call you Momma Agnes and Poppa Jim?"

"Certainly, my love. You're our family now," said Momma Agnes who had prayed for years for a child and had, finally, given up hope. And now, when she least expected it, her prayers were answered. And she was Marge's flesh and blood too.

Marge threw her arms around Agnes and kissed her. Both of them cried.

"So, you won't miss the 'Show?" asked Agnes, who had grown up there.

"Not a bit," said Marge.

After supper when the three of them were sitting around the kitchen table, Marge brought up something she had been thinking about for hours.

"Momma Agnes. Poppa Jim. This is going to be a new life for me. I want to scrub myself clean in the tub. I want to wash all my clothes. I want a new name."

"A new name. What a thought. What do you want to be called?" asked Agnes.

"Peggy," answered her new daughter. "I want to be called Peggy McCann."

"I like it," said Agnes, "Peggy. I like it. I never did like Marge."

"Me either," said Jim McCann.

Poppa Jim, who was close to being tone deaf, clasped his hands over his heart and sang "Peg of My Heart."

Fortunately, the words were loud and clear even if the melody wasn't.

"Peg of my Heart
I love you
Right from the start
I love you
Dear little girl
Sweet little girl."

Then the words trailed off to "la-la-la" which, when sung by Poppa Jim, sounded like some sort of death rattle.

They burst into laughter, the first of thousands of such bursts around that kitchen table. They were to be a happy family.

Apparently love and tender care is a remarkable recipe. Peggy grew tall. Shed many ugly pounds. And became the lovely Peggy McCann. Bold, confident and—to Poppa Jim's chagrin—daring.

Still, she didn't care much for boys. Or men. Poppa Jim was the exception until she ran into another man years later.

Peggy McCann kept her secrets. Even Momma Agnes and Poppa Jim never learned just what she really had been through.

The monsignor went to his grave, the seal of the confessional intact.

HMS Dreadnought and the Great White Fleet

"What do you mean my five new battleships are obsolete? Four of them haven't even been launched yet."

Admiral Alfred von Tirpitz, who feared little, had dreaded this meeting with Kaiser Wilhelm II. The "All Highest" was easy enough, though fickle, to deal with when things we were going the way he wanted. But when they didn't, petulance quickly turned into tantrums which often ended very badly indeed.

"The British have launched their all 'big gun' battleship, HMS Dreadnought. It is heavily armored, its 23,000 horsepower engines drive it through the water at twenty-one knots, and its twelve-inch guns are more powerful and have greater range than anything afloat. If our five battleships were to meet Dreadnought alone in battle, she would likely sink three of them in the time it took the other two to turn and run. Then, using her superior speed, she would catch and sink them too.

"Dreadnought has made every other battleship in the world obsolete, All Highest."

"I don't care about the rest of the world, I care about Germany. How long will it take for us to catch up?"

Tirpitz was known to evade, but he never lied to the Kaiser. "We will have to start from the keel up. We can do it but by the time one is launched, Great Britain might have half-dozen dreadnoughts. There is another problem too, All Highest. We shall have to deepen the Kiel Canal before we can move any big gun battleship between the Baltic and the North Sea. I regret to say; we may never catch up, Your Majesty."

The Kaiser covered his mouth with his good right hand. Then he spoke. "If the Royal Navy is unbeatable, how can we avoid being strangled by a blockade?"

The only possible answer to that question was unfolding in

America.

* * *

The United States Navy was training, experimenting and improving the submarines invented by an Irish immigrant to northern New Jersey, John Phillip Holland, who grew up in County Clare speaking Gaelic.

Funded in his early days by Irish republicans in America, the Clan na Gael, his first working boat was called the "Fenian Ram" and was launched in 1881. The United States Navy commissioned a very much improved USS Holland in 1900. Six more were built in Elizabeth, NJ.

Germany commissioned its first submarine, SM U-1, in 1906. By the time war came, the German Navy had forty-eight submarines in service or under construction. It would be the All Highest's most lethal weapon at sea.

In 1907, President Theodore Roosevelt sent the American battle fleet on a circumnavigation of the globe.

Called "The Great White Fleet" because of its peacetime paint color, sixteen pre-Dreadnought battleships and their auxiliaries left Hampton Roads, VA in December, 1907, and returned in February, 1909, after cruising more than 43,000 nautical miles.

The Great White Fleet showed all the world, friend and potential foe, that the United States was a formidable sea power not easily reckoned with. It was obvious that American power could be dispatched even from East Coast ports to defend its possession in the Philippines and the Pacific, let alone in the nearby Caribbean, once the Panama Canal was built.

The epic voyage also unpleasantly displayed America's need for more coaling stations in the Pacific and uncovered serious design flaws in our capital ships which were corrected in subsequent classes.

Not corrected was the need for many additional auxiliaries

such as colliers, supply ships, refrigerated ships, tenders and the like to support the battle fleet. It took World War II to adequately address that naval need.

All in all the cruise of the Great White Fleet was a triumph for America and its imperial president, Theodore Roosevelt.

Our chief executive also had a triumph in 1905 when he mediated an end of the war between Russia and Japan. The Japanese had launched a sneak attack against the Russian Pacific Fleet at Port Arthur in Manchuria and destroyed it.

The Czar then sent an aging and inadequate Baltic fleet stumbling more than half-way around the world to the Straits of Tsushima where the Japanese navy crossed the "T" and annihilated it.

But despite their victories, the Japanese couldn't win a land war and Russia couldn't win by projecting power over water.

Enter Theodore Roosevelt who invited both to a conference at the Portsmouth Naval Shipyard in Kittery, ME, and intervened personally to get the parties to agree to a peace treaty.

For his efforts, he received the Nobel Peace Prize and much adulation.

As he said, "It's mighty good thing for Russia and a mighty good thing for Japan, and a mighty good thing for me too." America was a global leader and its chief was center stage.

There can be no doubt that the president of Princeton University, Woodrow Wilson, the man who would become Roosevelt's nemesis, took note of his winning the Nobel Peace Prize. Wilson's efforts to cast himself as the peacemaker who would end World War I in Europe would be continuous until America was dragged into it.

Down in the Horseshoe

"Please, Frank, you've got to help me. I've nowhere else to turn. Sure, Tommy's had a bit a trouble before. But down deep, he's a good boy. You know him, Frank. You know he is a good boy."

So spoke Delia Dugan as she sat in the kitchen of Frank Hague's new home on Hamilton Park sipping hot tea on a cool autumn day in 1904.

Hague, who rarely smiled, because he, unlike most of his Irish neighbors, lacked humor, smiled now.

He knew Thomas "Red" Dugan all right. Red was sitting in a Boston jail awaiting trial for swindling a bank out of $500.

There but for the grace of God go I, thought Hague, not for the first time.

Red had balls. Imagine, dressing up a pal as a Protestant clergyman, the two of them strolling into a bank, bold as brass, with a phony check for $955 to open an account. Then they persuaded some imbecile of a bank president to let them walk out with $500 in cash. Think of it, $500 when a skilled workman made less than $2 for a ten-hour day.

Hague actually chuckled, startling Mrs. Dugan.

"What's wrong, Frank?" asked Mrs. Dugan.

"Nothing at all, Mrs. Dugan. I was just thinking of the good times Tommy and I had as kids."

"You see," concluded Mrs. Dugan incorrectly. "You know he's a good boy."

Hague knew a lot about Mrs. Dugan's little boy who was now approaching the age of thirty. Red had been out on parole after doing four years in the penitentiary for breaking into a real Protestant clergyman's house and then shooting the parson's wife in the head when she caught him in the act. She survived and identified Red who was sentenced to fourteen years in prison. Hague hadn't heard Red was out of prison.

The Jersey City cops had sent up an expert to identify Red in

Boston, too.

Red was a burglar, a con artist, and an all-round bullyboy. *His only saving grace*, thought Hague, *was that Red was reliable when a ballot box needed stuffing. Still, you were going to have to dive real deep before you found any other measurable good in Red Dugan. Still, what Red lacked in brains he made up for in moxie.*

Without irony, Hague said, "Of course, Tommy is a good boy. Everybody in the 'Show knows that."

Tommy's mother was smiling now.

"He has friends too. We'll do our best for Red, Mrs. Dugan, we'll do our best."

"That's all I can ask," said Mrs. Dugan, rising. "I knew I could count on you. And you can always count on me and me men."

Good, thought Hague, putting another ten votes or so into his political vault.

Deputy Sheriff Frank Hague was on a train to Boston with another deputy from the Horseshoe to supply Thomas "Red" Dugan with an alibi when the telegrams started to zip back and forth between the Boston and Jersey City police departments.

The defense attorney had to inform the prosecutor than he had two alibi witnesses who would swear that Red Dugan was enjoying the August sunshine in a Jersey City park on the day he allegedly swindled the bank in Boston. They were deputy sheriffs, added the delighted defense attorney.

A deputy sheriff in Hudson County wasn't exactly Wyatt Earp of the Old West. Frank Hague, when he wasn't serving the occasional writ, might have to escort some forlorn character to prison in Trenton. Hague was an unusual deputy in that he usually treated the convicted felon to a good meal before he turned him over to the warden. Even felons had men folk who voted. Mostly, Deputy Sheriff Hague hung around the new City Hall and talked politics. Hague was already building his organization.

The Boston cops told the Jersey City police chief that they had an unshakable case against Dugan and if Hague and the other deputy tried to give him an alibi they too would spend some time with him in a Massachusetts prison, the laws of perjury being what they were.

The police chief made this public and a friend telegraphed Hague at his hotel. *Forewarned is forearmed.*

Hague took the stand. "There's no question. I saw Thomas Dugan in Van Vorst Park in Jersey City on that Saturday in August," testified the dapper Frank Hague who always dressed better than most bank presidents.

He was an impressive witness. Tall for his time, almost six feet, pale blue eyes, already balding a bit, trim but powerful and with that grace and agility that marks most boxers.

The prosecutor rose for the kill on cross-examination. "Mr. Hague, are you absolutely certain you saw Thomas Dugan in the park in Jersey City on Saturday, August 15...the third Saturday in August?"

Hague hesitated. "I think so... You say August 15 was the third Saturday in August?"

"Yes."

"I know I saw Dugan in the park on a Saturday in August. But I really can't be sure whether it was the second or third Saturday. I'm sorry."

The other deputy's testimony parroted Hague's.

Dugan was doomed. It was the pen for him. But he gave his friends a big smile when they left the courtroom. They had done their best. The Dugan family vote would stay in Hague's possession for close to a half century.

Thus the young deputy sheriff evaded the pitfall of perjury but he lost his job anyway.

Frank Hague had gone to Boston instead of testifying in a case after he had arrested some Afro-American Republicans for alleged illegal registration as voters.

Judge John A. Blair was not amused. He found Hague in

contempt of court and fined him a whopping $100. The judge also ruled that Hague could no longer serve as an officer of the court. Hague was finished as a deputy sheriff.

No matter. Frank Hague was a hero in the Horseshoe where loyalty was prized far beyond legality.

Hague was not an articulate man though he came from a people who bathed themselves in words. They might not be able to read or write but they certainly could talk. And talk they did.

As a sage once said, "A thousand years ago, England and Ireland made a trade. They gave us their language and they took our land. We got the better part of the bargain. We've given them back their language much improved. The trick now is to get the land back."

Hague liked to make speeches though. He ambled and rambled, confusing and perplexing, all the while torturing syntax almost beyond his audience's capacity to endure. Yet somehow, when he spoke, his people understood what he meant.

He incessantly used the phrase, "My friends." They believed him.

Usually, he just attacked somebody or something. They enjoyed that, nudging each other in the ribs, howling for more.

Even by Horseshoe standards, Frank Hague was poorly educated.

On his first day at Public School 21 on 10th Street he crawled out a basement window and scampered off. That set the pattern for his educational experience. By the 6th Grade, the school had had enough. He was expelled for chronic truancy, bad behavior and poor performance. Frank Hague was thirteen.

That certainly wasn't the end of his education. He walked incessantly and took in a unique knowledge of his city and its people with every step.

For a while, he ran with a tough gang. Maybe not as bad as the Red Tigers that had terrorized the ward years before, but bad enough. Two Hague brothers had been Red Tigers.

Young Hague tried his hand at becoming a blacksmith like his father had been. He was taken on as an apprentice blacksmith by the Erie Railroad. He didn't like that hot, hard, filthy job any better than his father did. His father was now a bank guard thanks to a political favor.

Hague quit the railroad. In fact, he was later to become the railroads' worst enemy in the state of New Jersey.

Tough as an anvil himself, Hague thought about being a boxer. But he always insisted that his robust health was actually frail. He took to wearing high collars to protect his throat. He didn't drink whiskey, wine or beer for fear of upsetting his gurgling stomach. He would smoke the occasional cigar but he gave that up years later too because of his fears of collapsing health. Hague had never heard the word hypochondriac.

The ring was out but it still attracted Hague. He tried his hand at managing the career of another tough kid from the neighborhood. His fighter was game enough but his jaw was far more delicate than his manager's health.

What next? Politics.

It came naturally in the 'Show where the women found solace in church and the men turned to the saloons and politics. Hague passed on the booze but found politics much to his liking.

Hague was just twenty-one when he was elected ward constable in the Horseshoe. He had the backing of Nat Kenny, a powerful saloonkeeper who was on the outs with the local Democratic leader. Kenny gave the impoverished Hague $75 to campaign with.

But it was Monsignor John Sheppard, pastor of St. Michael's, who turned the election. The monsignor endorsed Hague in the parish bulletin. Hague and his mother, Margaret, were devout Catholics. Frank Hague did not attend Mass just to be seen and the monsignor knew it.

Hague's rise had been rapid but once again he was out of a job. *So what.* He would concentrate on building his organization in the 2nd Ward. A smart young man could always find enough money to get by.

The people of the 'Show admired and respected him. He was no glad-hander, he slapped no backs, but he always came through when you needed help.

You need a job? See Frank Hague.

You need food? See Frank Hague.

Is your kid sick? See Frank Hague.

You need a ton of coal? See Frank Hague.

Is the kid in trouble? See Frank Hague.

Are you having problems with someone at City Hall? See Frank Hague.

Don't worry about paying him back. Frank Hague will come to see you on Election Day. There is more than one way to repay a debt. He considered every vote valuable. Your vote was valuable. Your family's votes were priceless to him.

Frank Hague got jobs and lost them. Hague made alliances and broke them. Then he made new ones. If there was a political scrap, Hague was in the middle of it and usually he ended up on top. All the while, he was slowly building a political organization like no other.

Like the time when the county Democratic boss tried to replace him as 2nd Ward Leader with a man named John Sheehy.

"We'll see about that," said Frank Hague rallying his supporters at the 2nd Ward's Tammanee Club four days before its annual election. He was checking the membership roster to see just how much support the popular Sheehy had.

"Well, looky, looky, look who hasn't paid their dues," said Hague. "You can't be a member in good standing and vote if you haven't paid your dues. Now, can you?"

"A lot of our people haven't paid either," said one of his allies.

"Oh, yes they have," said Hague, reaching for his wallet.

Hague's people arrived for the meeting a half-hour early and glued themselves to every available seat.

A squad of Hague's hard men were at the door controlling admission.

"Sorry, you're not a member in good standing. You haven't paid your dues," many of Sheehy's people were told.

Several tried to pay on the spot and were firmly informed, "Forget it. We're busy. Come around tomorrow. Now move out of the way like a good fellow."

At one point, some of those good fellows milling around outside attempted to rush the door and break up the meeting. Hague's men easily and happily beat them back.

It was too late anyway. The Tammanee Club voted to keep Frank Hague as ward leader by a modest 432-18.

He was custodian of City Hall in 1910 when Joseph P. Tumulty came to see him. Hague had turned "a job for a janitor" into a real power base using all the jobs he controlled as political patronage, civil service rules notwithstanding.

Hague got to know Assemblyman Joseph P. Tumulty very well during his time as sergeant-at-arms of the State Assembly in Trenton. Joe was three years younger and had been a lawyer since 1902. They were both Jersey City Democrats and they liked each other.

Tumulty was now in Hague's splendid City Hall office.

Joe Tumulty knew that Hague didn't like to be called by his first name but "Custodian" didn't seem like much of an honorific. There were even those in Trenton that called him "Sergeant Hague" and laughed. Tumulty never joined in the laughter.

No one in Jersey City laughed at Frank Hague. It was a bad mistake.

Ah well, "Mister" will have to do.

"He's going to win, Mr. Hague. It's time to get on his bandwagon."

He was Woodrow Wilson, the president of Princeton University who was running in the 1910 Democratic gubernatorial primary as a reformer against Jersey City's own Mayor Otto Wittpenn. The mayor had been Hague's champion when the county Democratic boss soured on him.

"I can't do it, Counselor. I'm committed to the mayor. For Christ's sake, he got me this job."

"Wilson will win, Mr. Hague. The party is uniting behind him. Times are changing. He'll be in a position to do good for his friends. Perhaps even I will be in such a position."

Hague had no stomach for logical arguments. He preferred to attack.

"Why in the hell are you backing that prune faced preacher's son anyway? You're from Jersey City."

"He's a good man, Mr. Hague, and he is going to be a powerful one. The people are ready for change. He's going to give it to them. The day of the "Progressive" has arrived. As for him being a Presbyterian, I wasn't aware that his opponent, our good mayor, had secretly embraced our Holy Mother Church."

Hague didn't smile. He just shook his head. "I can't do it. I just can't do it, Counselor."

Tumulty rose. "I fear you will regret this decision, Mr. Hague. But there is still time," he said with a smile. "The church always allows for late conversions."

Tumulty offered his hand. "I am sure this is not the last time we will speak, Mr. Hague. I wish you luck—but not in this primary."

Hague was grim when he shook the assemblyman's hand.

"There will be other elections, Counselor. Other elections."

"I hope so, Mr. Hague, I truly hope so."

Wilson buried Wittpenn in the primary. Hague delivered the 2nd ward to the mayor but that counted for little. The austere, coldblooded Wilson was elected governor. Now Hague had a political enemy running the state.

But Hague hoped he could deal with Joe Tumulty who was now the governor's secretary and chief political advisor. It was

Tumulty who would be handling the patronage not the professor who had written more books than Hague had ever touched.

But Tumulty wouldn't take his telephone calls. Apparently he was rarely in his office. Frank Hague knew better.

Agadir

France rushed to help the Sultan of Morocco in 1911 when one of his many brothers raised the flag of revolt in Fez. This did not please the Germans who had substantial commercial interests in the country and didn't relish the idea of it becoming a French protectorate.

What the Germans really wanted was the southern part of the country for themselves since some of their miners and metallurgists were convinced it was heavy with raw material.

So a gunboat was dispatched to Agadir, deep in southern Morocco, to protect German businessmen and interests there although no German managed to arrive there until three days after the gunboat Panther dropped anchor. Not much to look at, the short, squat, lightly armed Panther had been used to impress natives in the colonies, who most admired the brass band she carried among her one hundred thirty man crew.

The light cruiser Berlin with its ten four-inch inch guns and crew of three hundred, which arrived a few days later, was more impressive.

Instantly, mobs in France, Germany and Great Britain demonstrated in the streets which could have led to war.

Great Britain, allied with France, suspected the Germans wanted to establish a naval base athwart the sea lane to South Africa. The British had read their Captain Mahan, too.

The German High Seas Fleet was reportedly on its annual cruise to Norway. But supposing it wasn't? The British were alarmed.

Winston Churchill, Britain's home secretary, learned that his unarmed police were charged with guarding the magazines holding Royal Navy's reserve of gunpowder.

At a garden party, Churchill asked the chief commissioner of police, "What would happen if twenty determined Germans in two or three motor cars arrived, well-armed, on the scene one night?"

"Well, sir," said the commissioner. "They could do what they liked."

Churchill got on the telephone to the Admiralty and demanded Marines. He got a curt refusal. Unfazed, Churchill moved quickly to arm his police and got soldiers as back up.

Fortunately, the German High Seas Fleet, indeed, was in Norwegian waters.

Soon the Germans and French were deep in seemingly interminable negotiations while their inflamed populaces were demanding total victory. Great Britain made it clear that she intended to back France even if it came to war.

Germany, which was prepared to bully France, did not want war with Great Britain. She backed off. The Kaiser was humiliated.

Germany, in essence, recognized Morocco as a protectorate of France. France, in turn, ceded 100,000 square miles of worthless jungle in the French Congo to Germany which joined it to the equally worthless Cameroons next door.

The crisis ended. War was averted. For now. France had won and Germany had lost.

President Theodore Roosevelt kept eight battleships in the Mediterranean just in case, as befitted a growing world power.

* * *

He had some difficulty in 1904 with Germany when she demanded a naval base in the Dominican Republic to satisfy a debt. Roosevelt, no doubt waving his big stick, forced the Germans to back off. This became the Roosevelt Corollary to the Monroe Doctrine. If European powers had problems with a less than solvent New World country, America would handle such problems without interference. This would lead to a number of

American interventions in the Caribbean.

Another consequence of Agadir was that Winston Churchill became First Lord of the Admiralty. Great Britain was worried about the future of the Royal Navy. Germany was fast building her own dreadnoughts.

In Sunny Tropic Scenes

Private Michael McGurk was lying on his canvas cot with his hands behind his head, eyes open, staring straight up. Not that he could see anything. The mosquito net overhead was blocking his view of the roof of his squad tent.

McGurk was off duty and he was about to go on liberty. He was free to do as he pleased, within well-defined limits, until shortly after sunrise the next morning.

Money wasn't a problem. A grateful nation gave him $15 a month to help protect it and he got an extra $2 a month "beer money" as a rifle sharpshooter. He hoped to qualify as an expert the next time he and his Springfield '03 rifle were sent to the range. That would mean an extra dollar per month.

Mike worked it out in his head. That would be almost a six percent pay raise.

Not bad, he thought.

It was "Mike" now since a sergeant at the receiving ship at the Brooklyn Navy Yard had told him Mickey was a "kiddie's" name and re-christened him "Mike."

Those first days, weeks and months as a Marine were absolute chaos. He had enlisted at seventeen for a "cruise" that would end on his twenty-first birthday.

Mike, who had three years of Latin, two years of Greek and two years of German at St. Peter's had to learn still another language; that of a seagoing Marine.

He most definitely learned that his rifle was not a gun. Mike still remembered his fellow "boot" standing there with his '03 in one hand and his crotch in the other bellowing, "This is my rifle. This is my gun. This is for work. This is for fun."

He thought his days on the receiving ship would never end but they did.

He was assigned as a rifleman in a floating battalion aboard a transport, the USS Dixie. He was part of an eight-man squad led by an Irish corporal. Mike felt right at home.

Once they had landed in Nicaragua to protect American interests for a day or two and Mike got to guard a coal pile. Mike did his duty cheerfully; he hadn't been in the service long enough to be cynical.

After a year, Private Mike McGurk was transferred ashore and joined Major Smedley D. Butler's battalion camped at Bas Obispo in the Panama Canal Zone. Major Butler had won the Medal of Honor during the siege of Peiping during the Boxer Rebellion. The press dubbed him "The Fighting Quaker."

The "ditch" itself was a very long way from being finished but as the newspapers said, "the dirt was really flying"–now that the Army's Colonel George Washington Goethals was chief engineer and the driving force behind construction.

Mike arose from his cot and donned a fresh set of khakis. They'd stay crisp at least until he passed his pre-liberty inspection a few minutes from now but they would soon wilt in the unrelenting heat and humidity of December in Panama.

His squad mate, Private Kurt Jahnke, was a German immigrant who spoke excellent English if you overlooked his turning a "w" into something halfway between an "f" and a "v".

Everybody in the platoon called him "Yankee."

Kurt was some years older than Mike and had seen active service in the Philippines before coming to Panama. He was moderately tall, with light eyes. A distinctive face. He was also an agent for the German General Staff but Mike didn't know that.

Kurt was intelligent and had an insatiable curiosity about the ditch and how it was being constructed. He had a good German camera and everywhere they went, Kurt snapped pictures. Even when they were assigned to guard the trains that crossed the isthmus, Kurt would take his camera from his pack and fire away.

But Mike had never seen any of the pictures. When he asked Kurt why that was, the German said a photographer in Panama

City gave him the film and developed the prints in return for keeping the negatives of anything he could make into a postcard for the tourists. Kurt said the photographer sent the photos home to his folks for him.

"Don't you want to see how the pictures turn out?" Mike asked.

"Not really. When you get right down to it, it's just a ditch."

"Right," said Mike, "who'd pay for a picture postcard of a hole in the ground?"

"You'd be surprised," answered Private Kurt Jahnke.

Mike adjusted his khaki field scarf and donned his salty fore and aft campaign hat which the major permitted enlisted men to wear on liberty because of the blinding sunlight. It provided a bit of merciful shade. His spit shined shoes were perfect.

"Okay, my friend Yankee. What say we go search for the transitory pleasures of the flesh?"

Kurt laughed. That's what Mike said every time they went on liberty.

"Some pleasures. A glass of lukewarm beer and a chance to flirt with the barkeep's mustachioed mother," Kurt said.

Bas Obispo was not a good place for liberty unlike Colon or Panama City, both of which were outside the canal zone. But the Marines would make do.

They were standing at attention looking like recruiting posters as they waited for the first sergeant to look up from his desk. They would not think of interrupting his concentration.

"All right, what do you people want?" asked the red-faced sergeant who didn't tan despite years in the tropical sun.

"Liberty, First Sergeant," answered Jahnke who was senior and a favorite of the first sergeant.

"Liberty? You want liberty? I'll tell you what you are going to get. Hammocks on a troopship leaving Panama City tomorrow morning. Get out of here and saddle up; we're shipping out."

The first sergeant turned to the company clerk. "Roundup all the NCOs. The old man's going to give them their orders in a half an hour."

"A couple of them are ashore already, First Sergeant."

"I don't care if they are on the far side of the moon. Get them here."

"Right, First Sergeant," said the clerk, who knew he wouldn't have much trouble ferreting them out of the two or three places they could be in Bas Obispo. He wouldn't bother to search the chapel.

"Where are we headed, First Sergeant?" asked Mike as Kurt sucked in his breath in dismay.

"Don't be a smartass, McGurk. Your squad leader will tell you what you need to know, when you need to know it."

With that, the two privates did a smart about face and hurried out of the first sergeant's tent.

"Where do you think we're headed, Yankee?"

"Who knows? It's probably someplace on the Caribbean side of Nicaragua since we're leaving from Panama City. Probably Bluefields or some shithole like that."

And so it was.

Nicaragua's dictator of-the-day was always fomenting trouble not only in Nicaragua but also in El Salvador, Honduras and Guatemala. The United States found him to be, as the diplomats say, a monumental pain in the ass.

He was one reason Butler's mobile battalion was stationed in Panama.

This time his heavy-handed ways had prompted the moderate Catholic party to rise in rebellion. The rebels were organized but so was the dictator. He had them cornered and meant to obliterate them. The United States couldn't tolerate that.

The USS Paducah, a gunboat, banged away at the loyalists without much effect.

So the battalion was back on a troopship headed this time for Bluefields, a squalid port town.

As soon as Butler's battalion came ashore, both sides took to the swamps of the interior. The Marines did not follow.

In Bluefields, McGurk's platoon was walking slowly in an open column formation down both sides of the street, with the lieutenant and his platoon sergeant in the middle.

Better them than me, thought Mike. *No shade there.*

The men were carrying their '03s at high port. Bayonets— almost as long as swords—were attached to the barrels. Their cartridge belts sagged from the weight of eight five-round clips, a canteen and a bayonet scabbard. They looked formidable. Menacing. That was the idea.

The street ended in a T intersection. In the middle of the T was their objective, the Hotel Nacional. Four stories high with a typical red tile roof, the hotel towered over the wire bearing poles whose crosstrees proved that Bluefields had some sort of electric power, maybe even telephone and/or telegraph service.

The point men detected some sort of movement on the hotel's wide, shaded, verandah. They held up their right hands halting the columns. The lieutenant and sergeant slipped into the shadows and moved swiftly to the front of the column.

"What's up, Marine?"

"I don't know, sir. There's people in uniform on that there porch. But I think they're just sitting around drinking and smoking."

"Let's have a look," said the young lieutenant, breaking out his binoculars and raising them to his eyes.

"Jesus Christ."

"What's up, Lieutenant?" asked the sergeant who was both his subordinate and his mentor.

"I'm not sure. There's about a dozen of them. They're just sitting there. They're all in the damnedest full dress uniforms you ever saw. But they don't look like Latins, they look like Europeans. Or Americans."

The sergeant turned from the lieutenant. "Corporal, send one of your people and get the old man down here pronto."

"Right, Sarge."

The lieutenant passed the glasses to his sergeant. "Jesus H. Christ," said the sergeant.

"Hmmm," commented the captain in turn after he arrived. "All right, Lieutenant. I'm going to go find out who those people are. I want your lead squad to escort me to the hotel. Have your sergeant take two squads and form up a line of skirmishers across the mouth of the intersection. If firing breaks out, you take the rest of your platoon back round the block and block the street fifty yards east of the hotel. First Sergeant, be ready to bring up the rest of the company if necessary. Understood?"

"Aye aye, sir," said just about everyone in earshot.

"Good. Corporal, uncase that guidon."

The company clerk took the khaki cover off and unfurled a small scarlet flag with a golden "A" in the center. He screwed the three pieces of the pole together and said, "Ready, sir."

The captain put his binoculars away and stepped into the center of the street. The clerk, looking nothing like a clerk, took his place three paces to the rear and one to the left of the company commander. Four Marines took up flanking positions on each side.

The captain softly gave his commands.

"Port arms."

"Forward march."

He didn't count cadence. Officers seldom did. The men were in perfect step. They could feel the first sergeant's eyes hot on their backs.

The guidon whipped in the slight morning breeze. The men on the verandah all rose. A few put down their drinks.

By the time the small party had halted at the steps of the verandah, the skirmishers were in place behind them.

A man strolled to the top of the steps and waited. He was in early middle age, sweating in a double-breasted blue uniform worthy of the opera "Carmen." Intertwined gold braid climbed up his arms past his elbows and golden epaulets, with two inches of gold fringe, sat on his narrow shoulders. This uniform climaxed with a high collar ringed with gold lace that flashed in the sunlight. He wore the rank of a brigadier general.

It was he who broke the silence. "Captain, do Marines no longer follow the custom of saluting when they are in the presence of a superior officer?"

"Sir, be assured that I will salute the instant I ascertain that I am, indeed, facing that situation. Now, sir. Who are you?"

Everyone on the verandah drew themselves up. Several actually sucked in their stomachs. All were dressed in some variation of that notable uniform.

"I, Captain, am Brigadier General Lemuel Starkey, currently attached to the general staff of the Provisional Army of Nicaragua."

"The Provisional Army?"

"Indeed, sir. That band of patriots who would have rid this beautiful nation of that pestiferous dictator, Zelaya, had you not spoiled our plan of attack by intervening."

The captain ignored the accusation. If the Marines had not intervened, the Provisional Army would have been annihilated by now. Everyone understood that.

"I take it by your accent and your coloring that you are not a native of this beautiful nation," said the Captain.

He waved his hand across the verandah. "Indeed, I suspect that you and your colleagues are countrymen of mine. You are Americans."

"Your supposition is correct, Captain."

"How many are you, sir?"

"Some days ago, there were fifty. But it is possible that some of them have resigned their commissions in recent hours and have left for parts unknown."

"I see. Might I request that that you draw up a roster of your staff or whatever is left of it, complete with names, ranks and assignments? For my commanding officer."

"Most certainly, Captain. I'll have my adjutant do that immediately."

"Thank you. I am certain that my commanding officer will have other questions for you. Meanwhile, for your protection I will post sentries round the hotel. No one will enter and, of course, no one may leave. I trust you'll be comfortable."

"No doubt, Captain."

"Then I'll take my leave, sir."

The Marines executed a smart about face, the guidon was posted properly and they marched off.

The general could not but note that the captain had not saluted.

Oh, shit, he thought.

Major Butler was incredulous. "How many of them?" he asked his adjutant.

"About fifty of them. We found a few of them hiding in the city. All filibusters. You know. Soldiers-of-fortune they call themselves. Recruited in New Orleans by some agent of the revolutionaries. The rebels knew Zalaya's regular troops would make mush out of them but they hoped these guys could train their mob to put up some kind of fight. Most of these Americans served in the Spanish War but only a couple of them were officers. One old timer claims to have fought in the War Between the States." The adjutant was from the South.

"Dear Lord," sighed his major.

"Most of them claim to be colonels now. There are a few generals and one or two majors. No junior officers or enlisted men. Terrific uniforms, though."

The adjutant fell silent as the major's eyebrow raised.

A few days later Mike and Kurt were part of the guard that took the fifty increasingly bedraggled men from what the battalion now called the "War College" to a tramp steamer that would get under way within the hour.

"Where are they headed, Yankee?"

"I hear they're headed back to New Orleans."

"I'll bet they call themselves 'Colonel' or 'General' for the rest of their lives." Both men laughed.

A few days later back in Panama, Jahnke walked up to McGurk and stuck out his hand. "Well, this is it, Bunkie. I'm out of here."

McGurk said, "I thought you were going to ship over."

"Nope. My cruise is just about over. I'm getting out."

"So where are you headed, Yankee?"

"Who knows. You know me. I just want to see something of the world."

In fact, Kurt Jahnke did not know where he was headed. His superiors at Section IIIb of the German General Staff would tell him that when he made his way back to Germany.

Shaking hands, Mike said, "I hope our paths cross again, my friend."

"Who knows," said Jahnke, "the world is smaller than most people think."

* * *

On his twenty-first birthday in 1911, Mike McGurk found himself standing in front of the officer commanding the Marine barracks at the Brooklyn Navy Yard.

"Are you sure I can't convince you to re-enlist, McGurk? You're a good Marine and I'm told you're a cinch to make corporal on your next cruise."

"I'm sorry, sir, but the private must respectfully decline."

"Too bad. What will you do, McGurk?'

"I think I'll join the police force if they will have me, sir."

"Well, the best of luck to you, Marine"

With that he handed Mike an envelope and small cardboard

box.

"Thank you, sir," said Mike as he did an about face and marched out. Marines don't salute indoors unless under arms.

The envelope contained his Honorable Discharge with the details of his service on the reverse side. The box held his Good Conduct Medal.

It was a handsome medal.

On the front were an anchor and a Marine in an old fashioned kepi serving a naval gun.

On the back were three words. Fidelity...Zeal...Obedience.

Frank Hague never saw this medal but those three words captured the values he wanted in instill in his growing political organization except they were to be centered on him and him alone.

Third Time's a Charm

"I tell you, Redmond is going to pull it off this time, Jack," said Jeremiah O'Leary, a leader of Clan na Gael in Manhattan.

He was enjoying a beer with Fat Jack Lynch in one of the innumerable saloons of Hell's Kitchen. Lynch, a longshoreman from across the river, was his counterpart in Jersey City.

"You know, Jerry, I've heard that bullshit since I was a little kid sipping tea from a saucer. First Parnell, then Redmond. Ireland's going to get Home Rule. She's going to be like Canada—a dominion—in charge of her own destiny. A nation once again. Bullshit. England's not going to get out of Ireland until we throw her out."

O'Leary bristled. "If I thought for one minute we could kick England's ass out of Ireland, I'd be over there right now instead of talking to the likes of you. We've tried that time and time again and we've gotten our ass thumped every time. England is too strong. I don't care how brave we are, England's too strong. Redmond is right, the road to Home Rule is through parliament and now his Irish Parliamentary Party holds the balance of power. Asquith needs him. He can't get his budget past the conservatives in the House of Lords."

"Who gives a shit?" asked Lynch.

"Listen to me for a change. Asquith needs to defang the House of Lords. To do that, he needs the Irish members. If Redmond goes along with Asquith and pushes the budget through, a Home Rule Bill will be introduced next year."

"It will be defeated like the first two," said Lynch.

"Aha! But the House of Commons passed Home Rule in 1893, it was the House of Lords that defeated it. That can't happen this time. Lords can only delay it, not defeat it."

"Then those fucking Orangemen in the North will kill it somehow. Do you really think they're sitting around saying, 'Oh, goody, now we can play patty cakes with the Catholics'?"

O'Leary laughed. "Yeah, I know. 'Home Rule is Rome Rule.' I'm told Redmond isn't worried about Ulster."

"Well, he ought to be."

Another Irishman, not yet introduced to these two, Roger Casement, had just been knighted by the King of England. Sir Roger was honored for his service as British Consul in Peru where he championed the cause of the pitiful Indians. Earlier he had been decorated by the Crown for his expose of the hellish conditions suffered by natives in Africa's Free Congo which was, unbelievably, owned solely by King Leopold II of Belgium since 1895. The king relinquished his private holdings after Casement's report.

Casement would resign from the Consular service in 1913 to devote all his time to the struggle for Irish freedom from England.

Then those three Irishmen would meet in New York.

Back in the 'Show

Brooklyn is only a few miles from Jersey City and easy to get to if you are a ton of coal. It was just a ride in a barge across the bay. You could look past the tip of Manhattan and see Brooklyn from Black Tom.

Other than coal, it meant a couple of subway rides, or maybe a ferry and a bit of walking. Say two hours from the Brooklyn Navy Yard to Mike McGurk's mother's flat on 9th Street.

Mike had no civilian clothes. He hadn't kept the clothes he wore when he enlisted. He had no need of them. They wouldn't have fit anyway. Mike had put on twenty pounds of muscle in the Corps.

He bought a second hand suit, a new shirt and tie, and a derby in a used clothing store on Sand Street. He thought he looked good in the derby. With his highly polished shoes and his sea bag riding easily on his shoulder, what he looked like was a man just cut loose from the service.

Mike was familiar with the subways. He took one to Manhattan.

He had seen the sign at the Downtown Manhattan subway station pointing the way to the Hudson and Manhattan Tubes.

Why not? The Tubes were being dug under the river when he left for the Marines and had expanded since then.

The Tubes seemed like the other subways but that peculiar underground odor was slightly different. Mike thought that it just might be the smell of home.

When he got out at the Grove Street Station, Mike was quick to note that his city had changed in four short years. There seemed to be a lot more people on the streets. More Italian faces, more Slavic faces. His time in the Corps had introduced him to the variety of immigrant groups who had abandoned the old world for the new. Newcomers didn't bother him.

Traffic was much heavier as well.

Cars had been rare in 1907. Now they were everywhere. Most of them were Fords. Lots of heavy trucks, too. There were electric trolleys where they hadn't been before and the telegraph poles virtually groaned under their heavy wire burdens. Still, horse and wagons outnumbered trucks.

But as he walked, things got more familiar block by block until he was back in the 'Show. There, nothing had changed. If anything, it was a tad worse. Like a homely pair of tattered slippers four years later.

People were smiling at him now with a slightly quizzical cast of face as if they were sure they knew him but had momentarily misplaced the name.

A man his age stopped and stuck out his hand. "Hot damn," he said. "It's Mickey McGurk, home from the sea."

Mike almost corrected him but then immediately thought, *No, I'm home. My name is Mickey. Nobody thinks it's a kiddie name in the 'Show.*

"Jimmy," he said, returning a firm hand shake that probably would have left indentations on an iron bar. "How the hell are you? How's Marge the Barge?"

"Still pining away for her one true love. She's no appetite at all. She's wasted away, crying buckets over you, bucko."

Jimmy Cribbins put his finger to his head as if he had had a flash of brilliance.

"I've got it! I'll take you to her this very instant unless you'd rather go to Hogan's for a nice, cold beer or a nice, hot whiskey."

"I think we better make it Hogan's. The thought of dear Marge might make me want to reconsider taking that vow of chastity."

"Personally, I think chastity is much overrated by our esteemed clergy," said Jimmy as they pushed open the swinging doors and marched into Hogan's.

The saloon was practically deserted at this time of day. The bartender, a couple of old rummies nursing beers and "Fat Jack"

Lynch hunched over a table reading an old edition of the Gaelic-American. It was an open secret that Fat Jack headed up the Clan na Gael in Jersey City.

The bartender walked over.

"Say hello to Mickey McGurk, Al."

The men shook hands. "You've filled out, Mickey," said Al English.

"You know, Al, three squares a day. It's a wonder I'm not the size of Jack over there."

Fat Jack looked up, knowing by the tone of voice that no slight was intended. He was among friends.

"Mickey," he said. "You're back. Let me buy you a beer."

"Nope," said Jim. "It's my shout. Three beers, Al, and one for yourself."

They settled in at the table with Fat Jack. Al brought the beers. He nodded to Jimmy, raised his short beer and made a toast.

"Here's to you, Mickey. Welcome home."

The men stood and drank from their schooners.

Then Mickey stood and held out his schooner. "Here's to you, my friends, and the old 'Show. It's great to be back."

It was a warmish day and it was not more than a few seconds before they set down their empty schooners.

"Another round, Al," said Fat Jack.

"Not at all. This one is on the house to celebrate Mickey's return," said Al.

"Aha," said Jimmy, "a blowback after a single round? Hogan'll have your guts for garters, Al."

"He will not," said Al. "If Hogan was here we'd be toasting each other with fine Irish whiskey, on the house."

Everyone, including the rummies, laughed. Hogan was a notorious skinflint. His standing orders were no blowbacks until the fourth round was bought and paid for. Then he would bitterly watch you drink it as if it was his children's blood.

Jimmy addressed Fat Jack. "No work today, Jack?"

"No. I made the shape all right but that son of a bitch wouldn't hire me. That's twice this week."

Lynch was a longshoreman. He and a hundred others would appear on the pier at seven o'clock in the morning and the boss stevedore would hire whoever he needed and wanted for the day. There was no appeal. If you weren't hired, you might rush off to another pier if it wasn't too late. Usually, you were done for the day.

"Why?"

"I don't know. He either doesn't like my face or my politics."

"Not much to choose from there, Jack," The men laughed.

Fat Jack pointed his finger at Mickey. "Maybe I should go over to his uncle," he said.

"You could do worse, Jack. In fact, you are doing worse," said Jimmy.

"I think I will. This longshoreman stuff is getting old. I'd like a nice cushy job like yours, Jimmy."

Again laughter. Mickey didn't know what they were talking about but since they were in the 'Show he figured it was politics.

Fat Jack stood and said, "Got to go. Good seeing you, Mickey ... Jimmy ... Al, tell Hogan I owe him a round."

"I will, if it ever comes up in conversation."

Fat Jack draped his cargo hook over his left shoulder and walked through the swinging doors as if he was parting the Red Sea

"So, Jimmy, are you in politics now?"

"I am that. I'm with your uncle."

"Who?"

"Your Uncle Frank ... Frank Hague."

"Of course," said Mickey smoothly, although he hadn't thought of his "uncle" in years.

"I helped him in his fights with Sheehy," Jimmy said. "Of course, he's beyond that now. He gave Sheehy the title of ward leader like he was giving him an old jacket from the St. Vincent de Paul. Did you know he's a commissioner now?"

"I didn't. Mom's letters were more about births, deaths and weddings than about politics."

"Well, he just got himself elected to the Board of Streets and Water. He's in charge of cleaning the streets."

That meant Frank Hague had a zillion jobs to give out. All his people had to do was pass a really simple civil service examination and wait for an opening. Cross Frank Hague and you became the opening.

"Are you on the payroll, Jimmy?"

"I am."

"What do you do?"

Jimmy looked perplexed. "I am a politician."

"No, I mean what do you do when you are at work? Do you sweep the streets?"

"God, no. I'm a fireman. I sit around the firehouse over on Grand Street playing pinochle waiting for a fire to break out. Then I hop onto the engine, jump off and save all the pretty girls and babies. But most importantly, at election time I remind you who to vote for."

"Supposing, you don't take that part of the job seriously. What happens? You're civil service, right?"

"Well, Mickey, my son, there are fire houses and then there are other fire houses," said Jimmy, holding his thumb and index finger in a circle as if they held a dead rat by the tail. Jimmy grimaced and shook his head.

Mickey laughed again. It was good to be home.

"I don't know. But I've got to do something. My mustering out pay won't last long. I was thinking of trying to get on the cops."

"Dear God," said Jimmy, "we're really shooting for the stars, aren't we? Mick, you're not fat enough to be a cop. You're too smart to be a cop. You've got too much of a conscience to be a cop. Go rob banks. You'd be better off. Hang out with a better class of people all together. Better yet, go see your uncle before you do anything."

"I probably will. Tell me, how is Marge the Barge?"

"Aw, to tell you the truth, Mickey, I haven't seen the poor girl in years."

"Why so?"

"Well, her father fell off the roof of their tenement and killed himself, her mother was sent to Snake Hill and poor Marge was shipped off to an aunt, God knows where."

"Well, wherever she is, I wish her good luck. She had no future in the 'Show," said Mickey.

"You are so right," said Jimmy.

A shrill voice came from just outside the swinging doors. A woman was standing on tiptoe trying to see over them.

"Mickey! Mickey, are you in there? Mickey McGurk, are you in there?"

A silent Al English looked inquiringly at Mickey. "That'd be my mother," said Mickey, rising.

"No need for Western Union in the 'Show," Jimmy said. "A waste of money."

* * *

Frank Hague's office in City Hall was splendid. He sat behind a polished oak desk. There wasn't a scrap of paper on it. Hague didn't believe in putting anything important in writing. He gave his orders in person or spoke to you over the telephone.

"You look good, Mickey. Your mother told my sister you were back. Are you registered to vote yet?"

"No, Commissioner, I've only been back two days."

"I'll have one of my people take you up the courthouse when we done with our chat. We'll sign you up for the Tammanee Club too. It's no trouble at all. And when we're alone, it's Uncle Frank, my boy."

"Uncle Frank."

Hague had what Mickey had learned was "command presence." When you were in a room with him, you knew he was in charge. He was almost six feet tall and he had that wiry build of a fighter. He was wearing a suit with jacket buttoned all the way up with a handkerchief peeping out of the jacket pocket. He wore a high collar and a conservative tie. His shoes were almost as well shined as Mickey's. If Frank Hague told you to do something, your instinct was to do it. When his eyes locked on to yours, it would be you who turned away.

"Now, Mickey. What are you going to do with yourself after you've had a bit of rest?"

"I thought, Uncle Frank, that I'd like to ask for your advice before I did anything."

"Very wise, Mickey. Would you like to be a civil servant?"

"I'm not much good at anything except hiking and shooting."

"Wonderful qualifications," said Hague. "But after all those years at St. Peter's with the Jesuits, I'd think you'd pass any civil service examination with ease."

Mickey smiled. "I certainly could give it a good try."

He hesitated and Hague, picking up on it, fell silent too. "You know, I've thought I might like to be a policeman, Uncle Frank."

"Now would you. That's surprising. They're a lazy, dangerous, corrupt bunch, you know."

"Does it have to be that way, Commissioner?"

"Only for the moment," replied Hague. "Maybe things will be different by and by."

"Could you help me get on the force, Uncle Frank."

"I could, Mickey, but I expect you to help me when I need it."

"You can count on me, Uncle Frank."

Hague counted on everyone in his organization without exception. If you produced good results, he was generous. If you were a slacker, he was vengeful.

"One thing, Mickey. I know it would be easier to be a cop in the 'Show where you know everybody and everything but you might be of more use to your city and me somewhere else, Say, up in The Heights—Hudson City. Do you speak any German?"

"Kind of … I studied German at St. Peter's for two years but I'm better at reading it than speaking it. I picked up some Oxcart Spanish in Panama too."

"Good enough. Aw, well, I expect you'll learn all you need soon enough. I hear a lot of those Dutchmen up there speak English pretty good too although maybe not in front of an Irish cop. Let me see what I can do, Mickey."

Hague was relatively weak in Hudson City. That was Wittpenn territory. He had people up there, of course, but he had to take what he could get for the moment. The day would come when they would be replaced with competent, loyal men. Meanwhile, Mickey could help watch them. Hague left nothing to chance.

A week later, Mickey was back in a blue uniform. This time he had to pay for it himself.

I Spy

Officers of the Royal Navy were expected to be versatile. Captain William Reginald Hall was certainly that. He had a distinguished career at sea before the First Sea Lord tapped him to head up the new Mechanical Training Establishments which would train enlisted sailors in engineering. That success was followed by an appointment as captain of the cadet training ship HMS Cornwall and Hall then was given an unusual assignment.

The Admiralty had determined that it was probable that Germany would be its next foe. Hall's training ship was to make goodwill visits to various ports including Kiel in Germany. Hall was to determine exactly how many ships had been constructed there to build large naval vessels.

While the cadets were ashore cavorting with their German cousins, Hall and three of his officers, all dressed as enlisted men, prepared to race around the harbor in a borrowed motorboat.

"Remember. We're supposed to be on a lark," said Leading Seaman Hall, who looked a bit old for his rank. "Look like you're having fun while Haverstraw here takes his photographs."

Then pointing to Haverstraw, he said, "But if we're nicked, quietly drop the camera over the side and look innocent like the rest of us. We stick to our story; we're just jolly tars out for a bit of a spin. Nothing more. Any questions?"

His peculiarly patrician looking crew had but one. "Suppose they look at our hands, sir?" asked one lieutenant.

Hall's answered at once. "We're captain's writers, of course."

Round the harbor they sped, stopping here and there to tinker with what seemed a finicky engine. No one noticed Haverstraw taking pictures. If fact the few that did notice them, smiled, shook their heads and thought, *Sailors! They're all alike.*

The mission was accomplished without incident and when

they were back aboard the Cornwall, Hall said, "Now that was bracing, wasn't it?"

Captain William Reginald Hall had just been introduced to the realm of naval intelligence. He enjoyed it.

Not so two of his officers who, later "on holiday" in Germany, were arrested and charged with espionage. The Admiralty disavowed any knowledge of their activities. They served two and a half years of a four year sentence before they were released in honor of King George's visit to Germany.

Meanwhile, Germany's ambassador to the United States was charming Washington. The handsome, mustachioed Count Johann von Bernstorff spoke perfect English, had an American wife and an American mistress. He was so popular he received nine honorary degrees. One was from the hands of the president of Princeton University, Woodrow Wilson.

Germany had but one sleeper agent in the United States. Dr. Walter Scheele, a German reserve officer, who was sent there in 1893 by Section IIIb on a mission of industrial espionage. He stayed and settled in Hoboken, a few miles from Black Tom.

The Heights

Ah, thought Mickey as he collected his new gear, *the impedimenta of a servant of the people.*

The complete uniform consisted of a high necked dark blue blouse and trousers, a belt, socks and stout brogans which would stomp a thousand miles before they needed any attention save polishing and a hat not unlike his old barracks cap. *Well,* he thought, *at least they ditched that old, foot-tall, leather helmet.*

He fingered the rubberized rain gear that would cover him from head to foot and a heavy wool winter great coat which he had already learned was referred to as "the bag."

The .38-caliber revolver fit in a holster on a gun belt, which was worn under the blouse and accessed through a pocket on the right side. *A bit awkward,* thought Mickey, *but maybe they don't want to make it easy to yank out and shoot up the neighborhood.*

The weapon of choice was obviously the nightstick. Heavy wood with a core of lead, it measured two and a half feet long and the only place you could put it to gain use of both hands was to hang it by its leather thong from your badge. The Irish were always fond of clubs. This was just the new world version of the shillelagh.

Mickey swung the nightstick in an arc bringing it down firmly into the palm of his left hand.

Ow, that hurt!

A black jack, as backup, slipped in a special pocket in the right rear of his trousers. Spare ammunition and handcuffs went onto the gun belt. A notebook and pencil went into a blouse pocket.

Mickey changed into his new uniform and hung his civilian clothes, his rain gear and "the bag" in a wooden locker built on the side of the wall. He snapped a lock on the hasp.

Just in case there isn't honor among thieves.

The new policeman looked at himself in the full-length

mirror. Everything fit but there was no mistaking him for anything but a rookie. Everything was as brand new as he was.

Mickey had to buy all this stuff himself; the cost would be deducted from his pay which was more than double what it was in the Marines.

Naturally, he now had to feed himself and put a roof over his head, too.

His mother would take care of that. He would room at home and pay his mother rather than a stranger.

It was only fair. Like most of the widows in 'the Show, Mrs. McGurk took in boarders. Greenhorns, from the old country, who would stay until they married and set up their own homes or moved in with the in-laws.

Mrs. McGurk had three boarders, her only source of steady income. Her grown children would slip her a dollar or a couple of quarters once in a while but she certainly couldn't live on that. Usually, they needed every dime they had for themselves and their families.

Her husband, Francis X. McGurk, had worked for the Erie railroad until he was crushed between two boxcars in the yard. The railroad, ever generous, had showered $200 on her for her trouble. Not quite enough to last her and her brood forever.

So she took in boarders. That wasn't so simple. She had to compete against every other widow in the 'Show with a spare bed.

A few of the youngest and prettiest widows were able to attract another man but it was dicey business trying to entice a man to the altar before he lured you into his bed. Even a greenhorn could figure out a widow with children was vulnerable.

Many a reputation had been ruined forcing the disgraced widow and her children to skulk away leaving the 'Show and its soul slicing laughter behind.

Mrs. McGurk was too old and too worn to attract much

attention along those lines although she did have to clout one or two of the less fussy boarders early on.

Still, one of the boarders was packed off to a neighbor when Mickey came marching home.

Mickey, who thrived on spicy tropical dishes featuring god knows what, was not looking forward to his mother's cooking.

Irish cuisine reached its apex when the water came to a boil. After that, it was all downhill.

"Garlic," she had replied to one of his first suggestions. "Why would I use garlic in my food? What do you think I am, one of those guineas stinking up the 5th Ward? No garlic for me or for you, boyo. You'll get good, plain, decent food like the rest of them and, by God, you'll get as much as you want. No one ever starved in my house." Mrs. McGurk was known as a grand feeder.

Your daughters, granddaughters and great-granddaughters don't inherit much in the way of culinary skills when all you had to cook—and eat—was potatoes. To this day, it's an odd Irishman who ever meets a potato he doesn't like.

But Mickey wondered if any of those Italians in the 5th Ward had started a restaurant. His mouth watered.

He emerged from the locker room into the cavernous main room of the Northern District precinct on Oakland Avenue.

The desk sergeant looked up from the blotter. He was a great ox named Ernst Schlager. Like Mickey's old bunkie, Kurt Jahnke, Ernst converted "Ws" into a mutation of "Fs" and "Vs" before he let them escape his mouth.

"Well, let's have a look at you, boy. Not too bad. Skinny though. We'll have to put some meat on you. Get some good German beer into you, hey, boy?"

McGurk, who hadn't been called *boy* since he left the receiving ship, let it pass. He knew he would have to pay his dues up here in Hudson City.

Those weren't the only dues he had to pay. He had to join the union.

"Ja," he was told, "we have a real union, an honest-to-god AF of L union. You pay your dues; keep your mouth shut and the union will take good care of you. We don't let the bosses push us around. No, by God, if there is going to be any pushing, we'll do it."

Most people who worked for the railroads were in a union too and Mickey was familiar with the American Federation of Labor and its cigar maker leader, Samuel Gompers. When Gompers was asked what labor wanted, he answered succinctly, "More."

His advice to his brethren was, "Reward your friends, punish your enemies." Mickey's "uncle" certainly understood that concept.

Apparently that went for downtrodden workers who carried nightsticks and packed pistols too.

"I didn't know cops could strike," Mickey had said.

"Who said anything about striking? Cops have ways of making your life miserable even if you think you're a big shot."

Schlager captured Mickey's attention again. "I'm going to send you out with another Irisher for a couple of weeks until you learn the ropes, hey? He lives over there in St. Anne's Parish. He knows his way around. You won't get lost."

Mickey knew most of the German Catholics in the Heights went to their national parish, St. Nicholas, on Central Avenue. There were several Lutheran churches as well; St. John's was the biggest. The platoon of German Jews were mostly shopkeepers who stayed out of the way of both groups.

Sergeant Schlager waved at one of the policemen forming a line for muster. "Hey, Paddy, come here, will you?"

A big, beefy, red-faced cop strolled up, smiling. "What's up, Sarge."

"Sergeant. You are to address me as sergeant. You Irishers have no discipline."

"Sorry, Sergeant," said the unrepentant Irishman.

"I want you to take McGurk here on patrol with you until I say otherwise. You are to teach him everything you know. That shouldn't take long, hey, McAlinden?"

Paddy McAlinden winked at Mickey. "Not long at all, Sarge."

"Sergeant, goddamn it."

"Sorry, Sergeant. Bad habits die hard."

McAlinden and McGurk shook hands. "Stand on my left during roll call, McGurk."

"Right."

"No, my left."

Mickey grinned. "Gotcha."

Mickey had never been in such a crooked line. The policemen didn't stand at attention despite the command from the desk sergeant. They scratched themselves and fiddled with their equipment. The closest they came to showing any respect for their sergeant was to stop talking.

The sergeant droned on but Mickey noticed that no one was jotting down what he said. He was soon in a packed horse drawn patrol wagon being taken to McAlinden's beat which was north of Bowers Street up to the West Hoboken line.

"It's pretty quiet up here," said McAlinden. "You'll get plenty of rest. Once in a while the Dutchmen howl on a Saturday night or a burglar from Hoboken tries his luck here but all in all the Germans are law abiding bunch. A lot of them spend Saturday night at home with the missus drinking a stein of beer and reading their German language newspaper."

"No, the Germans are not like us," said Paddy McAlinden. "They outnumber the Irish here about five to one but you'll have five times the trouble with the Micks. Especially on Saturday night. They're not afraid to take on a cop either. The German coppers have little tolerance for drunks disturbing the peace and they are a tough bunch themselves. You're going to find yourself helping the Dutchmen crack Irish skulls."

"If that's the case," Mickey answered, "I'm going to get a

thicker nightstick."

The men laughed easily. They were comfortable with each other.

Mickey watched McAlinden touch the brim of his cap in salute as he passed a pair of well-dressed burghers.

Then he stopped and pointed his nightstick at a young man lounging in a doorway.

"I've got my eye on you, O'Malley."

"Sure, I'm innocent as a lamb, Officer McAlinden, just taking the night air."

"See that you stay that way," McAlinden threatened.

"That's Billy O'Malley. He'll steal anything that's not nailed down and if he has a claw hammer in his hand, then nothing's safe. The O'Malleys are good people but the boy is bent. He's for the slammer soon enough."

"Speaking of family, McGurk, where are you from?"

"9th Street."

"Ah, the old 'Show." Most outsiders called it the Horseshoe.

"Are you from there yourself?"

"I am. My family moved up here about fifteen years ago. My mother hated Railroad Avenue. It was so dark and dirty. All that coal dust, you know."

Railroad Avenue lived in perpetual shadows cast by the railroad trestle that occupied most of the street.

"So my mother had my father drag us all up here. We live in a two-family house now on Griffith Street and my mother is out there every morning scrubbing the stoop with the other hausfraus. She thinks the Heights is the Promised Land."

"I'll bet. May I call you Paddy?"

"You may since we'll spend more time together than we do with our families."

"Thank you. I'm Mickey."

The men stopped and shook hands once more. "Are you married, Paddy?"

"Not yet but I've got my eye on a pretty one over on Hutton Street. Who knows?"

"If you marry, where will you live?"

"Somewhere in Hudson City. I'm not going back to the 'Show. Besides I'm used to the Dutchmen now."

McGurk asked, "Anyone else live in the Heights besides the German and Irish?"

"Indeed. There are a bunch Italians in St. Paul of the Cross. The Maresca Family, mainly. There are two Slovak families on my block but they go to St. Anne's since they don't like the Germans much. Got some Jewish businessmen here too. And of course, we have a few mixed marriages."

"Catholics marrying Protestants?" asked an incredulous Mickey.

"Of course not. Irish marrying Italians. It's always a greenhorn Irish girl marrying a guinea boy. They sing and dance and treat a girl royally when they're courting. A lot more romantic than we are. The greenhorn girls are easy pickings."

"Don't they have trouble after they marry?"

"No more than anyone else. The girls have to learn how to cook Italian before they marry. But the Italians are big on family. There's one other advantage. The Italians think only fools get drunk, so their women don't get banged up as much as ours. They produce good looking kids too."

"That's a comfort," said McGurk.

"So, Mickey, what were you doing before you got on the force?"

"I just finished a cruise in the Marines."

"No kidding," said McAlinden, inspecting McGurk once more. "See any action?"

"Not much. Mostly I floated around in the Caribbean and killed mosquitoes in Nicaragua and Panama."

"You should feel right at home around here. God knows the Meadows are the biggest mosquito factory in America. They'll eat you alive in summer and carry your bones off to suck on during the winter."

The Meadows were thousands of acres of swampland on both sides of the Hackensack River that formed the western boundary of Jersey City.

"Yeah. I remember those huge 'sketters," said Mickey McGurk.

"Well, you shouldn't have any trouble with our drunks. Just pretend they're sailors and club them just enough so they can repent on their knees. By the by, you know a nightstick is very effective when it's used like a bayonet. Jab them hard in the stomach or between the ribs. That'll take the starch out of them. If you have swing at somebody, aim for a joint. Wrist, elbow, knee or ankle. Not the neck though, that might kill him. The neck breaks easier than you think.

"Some of these boyos might balk at walking over to a paddy wagon. Let me show you a little trick. Don't worry, I won't hurt you."

McAlinden stood behind him and put his nightstick between Mickey's legs. He turned it parallel to the ground and lifted up.

The pain in Mickey's scrotum was excruciating but all he could do was stand on his tiptoes to escape it. McAlinden's left hand held him firm by the collar.

"Ow! Let me down, Paddy."

His grinning partner slipped the nightstick out from between his legs.

Mickey had all he could do to stop himself from grabbing his crotch. "Wow! That really hurt. I couldn't do anything but walk on my tippy toes."

"Exactly."

"But you said it wouldn't hurt."

"I lied. You know the Irish. No discipline."

More laughter. McAlinden knew the rookie wouldn't forget that lesson. "Let's walk over to old man McCann's. That's my local. We can get a shot of whiskey just to put the life back into us."

"Mr. McCann is my father's cousin although I haven't had too much to do with that side of the family," said Mickey.

"God love the Irish! Thick as thieves, so to speak." Both men laughed again.

McCann's saloon was on the corner of Congress Street and the Paterson Plank Road. It sat on top of the Palisades. Hoboken was directly below.

A group of loud men was emerging from McCann's and the old man stood on his threshold holding a heavy bung starter. "And don't come back until you learn to keep a civil tongue in your head, Honeychurch."

"Ah, stuff it, you old geezer," said one of the four men looking back at the saloonkeeper.

"Now, boys, quiet down. People are sleeping you know," said McAlinden in a conciliatory voice.

That was a mistake. Young Honeychurch mistook it for weakness."Sez who?" he slurred and hauled his right arm back to launch a fist at the bigger cop.

McGurk had instinctively moved a few feet to McAlinden's left when they stopped in front of the quartet. Now he swung and his nightstick caught Honeychurch on the right elbow a nanosecond before the punch was thrown.

Down went Honeychurch, screaming in agony and clutching his elbow.

"Now be quiet, boy. You've got another elbow, don't you know?" said Paddy.

Honeychurch knew and started a low moan instead.

None of the other three had moved. They hadn't had as much to drink as Honeychurch.

"Now, can you see how such a commotion is bound to end?" asked McAlinden as McGurk kept his nightstick at high port.

"Pick up your friend. Go home quietly and find your beds.

We'll say no more about this. Be sure to say your prayers!"

McAlinden turned towards his rookie partner and nodded. "You'll do, McGurk."

Insha'Allah

Mustafa Bey took a long drag on his aromatic Turkish cigarette as he peered placidly at the scene before him.

Two young Italian prisoners were kneeling, their hands tied behind their back, just feet from where he and Kurt Jahnke were standing.

One prisoner had his eyes tightly closed, his face oozing fear along with his sweat, his lips moving with no sound to be heard.

Probably praying, thought Jahnke.

Mustafa spoke in German. "Do you think Allah, the merciful, the compassionate, hears the prayers of infidels? No offense, my friend."

"None taken." Jahnke thought for a few seconds. He wasn't sure what to say since he would be considered an apostate, at best, by most of the major Christian denominations of the world and an "infidel" by all of Islam.

"If there is silence, what can be heard?" he said, not having the faintest idea what he meant.

"Hmm," said Mustafa. "You have either just said something very profound or I don't understand German as well as I think I do."

Jahnke chuckled. The second Italian prisoner stared straight at him.

Is that disbelief? Or anger? Or courage?

The Arab pulled the first man's head back with his left hand and slit his throat with his right. There was a spurt of blood, a bit of a gurgle and then his lifeless body slumped sideways, his eyes still closed.

His comrade looked at him and then back at Mustafa and Jahnke.

"*Cula di tua sorella*," he said softly in Italian a second before the Arab pulled his head back and slit his throat.

"What did he say?" asked Mustafa.

Jahnke, who knew only a few words in Italian, knew these. "I believe he said 'Up your sister's ass.'"

"Good for him. He died well. We all must die but the fortunate get to decide how to do it," said Mustafa. "Our Arab friends enjoy killing prisoners. They are implacable enemies when aroused. Me, I have no taste for it."

He ground his cigarette with his boot. "*Insha'Allah*," he said.

If God wills it, thought Jahnke.

Section IIIb of the German General Staff was the most efficient secret service on the continent and had no difficulty attaching Jahnke to the Turkish troops fighting the Italians in Libya.

But the Turks, badly outnumbered and poorly supplied, could not long resist the Italians whose fleet punished the Ottoman's most severely. Still, it was only the guns of that fleet that permitted Italians to cling to a narrow coastal strip of Libya.

When patrols ventured inland, they often ended up like the two men whose blood watered the sand in front of Jahnke and Mustafa.

The Turks withdrew and left the lifeless desert to the Italians and that Ottoman retreat emboldened the Christian nations of the Balkans.

The Balkan League—Serbia, Greece, Montenegro and Bulgaria—declared war on the Ottoman Empire in 1912 and virtually drove Turkey out of Europe, creating an independent Albania in the process, before they fell to fighting among themselves.

Austro-Hungary was not a combatant in the Balkan Wars but, when the battles ended with about a quarter of a million men dead, she faced a grave threat. A far larger, more powerful Serbia emerged to be the champion of the south Slavic peoples she wanted to join in one state.

This meant an inevitable clash with Austro-Hungary which intended to annex the Balkan provinces of Bosnia and

Herzegovina that she had occupied since 1878.

As Jahnke's colonel said, "The gun is cocked. All that is needed is a finger to pull the trigger."

Walking the Beat

Mickey McGurk loved being a copper.

He didn't like the uniform that much but he liked what it engendered — respect, comfort, admiration, relief and, yes, fear.

He loved the power the badge gave him. When he walked his beat in the Heights he wielded enormous power that could change people's lives in an instant.

It wasn't just that he could beat people senseless with his nightstick, which he sometimes did on Saturday nights, it was that he could often impose his will which didn't always coincide with the mandates of the law he was there to enforce.

Often McGurk served as judge, jury and sometimes as a bit of an executioner.

A kid caught shoplifting a toy at Cheap Sam's on Central Avenue might be frog marched home to face the wrath of his parents, a sentence Cheap Sam himself heartily approved of since he didn't want any would-be customers to shun his store from either anger or humiliation.

A hardworking man a schnapps or two distanced from prudence received nothing but patient understanding and a steadying arm to help him home.

Even a man who beat his wife might receive this counseling: "Ray, I know you gave Ellen that black eye."

"I swear, Mick, she asked for it!"

"I don't care if she did or not. If you do it again, I'm coming for you. And you know what — you'll resist arrest. I'll give you a good beating and then I'll run you in. Sure, Ellen'll get you off; she won't let her kids starve. But you'll be walking with a limp."

"Jesus, Mick."

"Behave yourself, Ray. It's not that hard." Such counseling usually produced good results. But not always.

Mickey McGurk was capable of considerable violence to go

along with his guile and charm. A number of men, and even a
few women, in the Heights were afraid of him.

Yes, there was some real crime in the Heights but the detectives dealt with that. It was McGurk's job to maintain order. To
keep the peace.

Mickey liked working nights best. Granted, Saturday nights
were taxing especially when the saloons closed—if and when
they closed. Most would stay open as long as they had
customers. But most of the men they served didn't have the
money to drink all night and besides momma would have them
in the pews on Sunday even if, for the Catholics, it meant the
"Drunkards' Mass" at noon.

Late at night, the streets were quiet enough except for the odd
horse's hooves on the cobblestones. The gas lamps gave off
enough light although street cops carried flashlights too. Big
ones, useful as another weapon in a pinch.

Of course his mother was right when she said, "Only rogues
are abroad after midnight." Or people who needed help.
McGurk was quick to handle both.

In between, Mickey walked. He liked to walk but it wasn't the
carefree, absentminded stroll of the innocent. Mickey walked, his
head and eyes in constant motion, looking at everything. If
anything or anyone was out of place, different or new, McGurk
focused in and, when necessary, either made a mental note or
took action. This is what good coppers did.

If McGurk made most of his enemies at night, he made most
of his friends by day.

He had a lot of friends. He was friends with all the storekeepers on Central and Palisades Avenues especially those who
could feed him.

He was friends with every saloonkeeper and bartender on his
beat especially at Pohlman Hall, the three-story German social
club. Sometimes he got complaints about noise—mostly singing
and ompa-ompa music escaping from its thick walls. He settled

these easily: "Were you here before the Hall was built? No? Well, then maybe you should stop complaining or move away." Most saw the logic of putting cotton in their sensitive ears.

He was friends with most of the doctors, nurses, orderlies and ambulance drivers at Christ Hospital on Palisade Avenue. That's where the seriously hurt, the dying and the dead went.

He was friends with every priest, nun, minister, deaconess and rabbi he met.

All his friends fed him information which, in turn, made him a better policeman—all the while feeding his sense of power.

He did have one particular friend and he hoped she would become more than that very soon.

Oddly enough, he did not meet Hannah Ganz on his beat although she lived just a few doors down from Pohlman Hall on Ogden Avenue.

Jimmy Cribbins, Mickey's best friend, owned a Ford Model T or at least he owned half of it. The other half was owned by another fireman working a different shift.

Jimmy explained, "We're never off duty at the same time. So it's like owning your own automobile for half the price. Smart, huh."

"How much did you pay?"

"$250."

"Where did a jerk off fireman like you get that kind of money?"

"Pinochle. The Dutchmen won't play against me but there are a lot of idiots in the neighborhood eager to give their money to me and Tommy."

"Tommy who?"

"Tommy Bobojanian."

"Bobojanian? That's Armenian. He's a fireman?"

"Nah. He's a photoengraver at the Jersey Journal."

"They're all photoengravers."

So it was that when Mickey finally got his summer vacation,

Jimmy was on vacation that week too. "Let's go to Lake Hopatcong," he proposed.

"Never heard of it," countered Mickey. "Let's go to the shore. Keansburg's great."

"You'll love it," said Jimmy. "There's a great hotel. The food's good. There's a beach. There's lots of girls. There's even an amusement park a couple of miles away."

"What kind of girls?"

"What do you mean what kind of girls? Girl girls. Jeez."

"Where is it?"

"Up in Morris County. About forty miles away. Couple a three hours. Four at the most. Some of the roads ain't too good," said Jimmy.

"Morris County? I've never been there. We'd be the only Democrats in the whole damn county."

"I don't know about you, but if the girls like Republicans, I'm a Republican."

Mickey asked, "You sure you know how to drive that thing?"

"Me? I'm a regular Barney Oldsfield."

The four-seat Model T made the trip in less than four hours including the time necessary both to change a flat tire and to decipher unfamiliar maps.

The Hotel Mount Arlington was a big, sprawling, two-story wooden structure with sheltered porches facing the road and the lake. A saloon, with a separate entrance, was at road level out of sight of the guests on the wide porch.

Mickey checked in. Jimmy took the flat tire to be repaired at a garage a few hundred yards down the road.

There were only a couple of rooms left. The hotel was popular with families that took the train from Hoboken to Netcong where a jitney from the hotel met them. Some other guests were motor car enthusiasts. Hotel Mount Arlington was an overnight destination for them.

Mickey and Jimmy were on the American plan which meant

they would eat all their meals at the hotel.

The dining room was crowded. Both young men discreetly looked around the room like young lions looking for antelope.

Mickey's eyes locked for just an instant with those of a pretty blonde who was maybe nineteen or twenty years old eating with an older couple and a boy about ten years old. Mother, father, brother and sister. *Perfect*, thought Mickey McGurk.

The courtship, because that what it turned out to be, began on the lakeside porch in the late afternoon.

"Pardon me. I'm Michael McGurk. I wonder if I might be permitted to get you ladies a glass of iced tea? So refreshing, what with this heat."

The mother, Sophie Ganz, made her appraisal in a nanosecond.

"Why, yes. That would be very nice, Mr. McGurk." She pronounced it "Mack Gook."

Hannah, who had been thinking of fetching a light sweater because of the breeze off the lake, smiled and said, "Thank you. It is hot."

Over iced tea, Mrs. Ganz, controlling the conversation, elicited enough information to be disappointed but not dismissive. *Irish, not Scottish. Catholic, not Presbyterian although her husband thought Calvinists were even worse than Catholics. Nice enough young man though. If nothing better came along, Hannah might enjoy a few days with him here at the lake. Good practice for her. She should be getting married pretty soon. Married to the right young man. Unhappily, Michael Mack Gook would not do.*

Billy (christened Wilhelm but re-named Billy in the first grade) was a perfect chaperone. He went everywhere with Mickey and Hannah. Jimmy had met a nice Irish girl named Barbara from Brooklyn. The Hamills did not see Jimmy as a threat, either. It took hours to get to Brooklyn from Jersey City. Two rivers were in the way.

When they took the Model T to Bertrand's Island, Jimmy told

both sets of parents, "Billy can sit in the back seat between the girls. There's lots of room."

Lots of room there was but Barbara got in the front seat and Mickey in the back as soon as they were out of sight. "Barbara has to show me how to get to Bertrand's Island," Jimmy said to an oblivious Billy who at ten knew less about life than the average six year-old in the Horseshoe.

It was a week of mounting frustration for the young men. A hurried kiss here, a hug there, a lot to imagine in none too revealing bathing costumes. The girls had a great time testing out the equipment.

When it rained, Jimmy would play three-handed pinochle with Mr. Ganz—Otto—and an elderly guest from Newark. Mickey would try to get Hannah alone, a ploy usually scotched by Sophie Ganz who would sit down next to them and cheerily say, "Here you are. Wonderful."

On their last day, Mickey ate with the Ganz Family.

Mickey took his best shot. "I hope to see more of you and your family, Mr. Ganz, when we get back to Jersey City."

Otto opened his mouth but Sophie answered, "All good things must come to an end, no? Sad but true. Like most families, Mr. Mack Gook, we are very busy. Now if you went to Bethany Lutheran Church over on Summit Avenue, we would see you every Sunday. Where do you go to church, Mr. Mack Gook?"

Mickey, who wouldn't dare to correct her pronunciation of his name, said, "I live near St. Nicholas Church but I usually go to St. Anne's on the Boulevard. I have relatives there."

Otto stiffened. This was bad news although it confirmed what his wife told him.

Sophie said, "How nice for you. At least you are not lonely."

Otto cleared his throat. "You know I think I remember seeing you at Pohlman Hall. I go there often. Maybe, we'll see each other there."

"I sincerely hope so, sir," said Mickey who knew he had been dismissed.

And I'll see her too. I don't give a shit whether you like it or not.

Such thoughts were left unspoken. Hannah smiled softly and squeezed his hand hard when they said goodbye.

Mickey was waiting for her the next Monday when she got off work as a clerk at Colgate's plant down by the river.

"Can I take you home, Hannah?"

A flushed Hannah looked at him for five interminable seconds. "Yes. To my corner—not home. I'm sorry, you understand why?"

They surreptitiously met on Mick's days off. But never on Sunday. On Sunday he went to St. Anne's with his aunts and his cousins and then headed Downtown to visit with his mother who was growing suspicious.

"What do you do at night when you're off? You never come at night unless it's Sunday."

"You know, Ma. I hang out with my friends."

"You're not drinking are you?"

"No, Ma. You know I'm not much of a drinker."

"Hmmm."

His mother's thoughts then turned to the only other thing most young men were interested in. But she said nothing.

Mickey and Hannah plotted, planned, schemed, lied and stole every hour they could.

Hannah's mother had asked, "Where do you go when you don't come home right away from work?"

Hannah was ready. "Oh, I usually go to the big library on Jersey Avenue or sometimes the girls and I go for tea on Newark Avenue."

The frugal Sophie was satisfied. Why would anyone buy a book when you could read it for free at the library?

"You know, that Heinsohn boy at church seems interested in you. Why don't I invite him and his family here for supper next Sunday?"

"That would be nice, Mama," said Hannah who was to endure a small procession of German and Scandinavian young men who came to supper. She did not encourage them.

Behind her back, they called her "The Iceberg." Yong Heinsohn said, "I think she sank the Titanic."

It all came to a boil one early evening when Hannah and Mickey were kissing in the deserted gazebo in Mosquito Park.

Mick's hand, not by chance, wandered up from her waist and touched the bottom of her left breast.

The fully clothed Hannah leaped up as though he had plunged a hot poker into her.

"I-I-I've got to go home now."

"Calm down, Hannah. I'm sorry. That was an accident. It won't happen again."

Tears were flowing from Hannah's eyes. "This has to stop. It can't go on. I can't stand it. All the lies. No more."

Mick, who had just wanted to cop a quick feel, said more than he intended.

"You're right, sweetheart. I can't take it anymore either. I love you, Hannah Ganz. I want to marry you. Will you marry me, love of my life?"

Hannah was speechless although the tears kept flowing.

Finally. "You're crazy. I know all the Irish are crazy, but you are really crazy. What's the matter with you?"

"Don't you love me, Hannah, or do you treat all the boys this way?"

"It doesn't matter that I love you, I can't marry you. I won't marry you. I haven't even met your mother!"

"Don't worry about my mother, she'll come around," said Mick who didn't believe it even as he said it. "Would you marry me if your father gave us his blessing?"

Hannah wasn't crying anymore. *Was it possible? Maybe a miracle?*

She looked straight into eyes. "Yes, Michael. I will marry you if my father gives us permission but I will not cross him. If he says no, then it's no and you and I are through. Love will not matter. Do you understand me?"

"Let's kiss on it, my love."

The New Freedom

Teddy Roosevelt wouldn't stand for it. His party—The Republican Party—refused him its nomination as president of the United States.

Granted, he had turned down the nomination in 1908. But that was to fulfill a much regretted pledge not to seek a second full term. A big mistake, but that was then, this was now.

It was the conservatives who were behind the nomination of William Howard Taft for re-election as president. Teddy Roosevelt was no conservative, he was a progressive and, by God, he intended once again to mount that "bully pulpit."

He formed the Progressive Party and took its nomination for president.

It took 46 ballots before Woodrow Wilson, the governor of New Jersey, won the Democratic nomination for president. That's when William Jennings Bryan, three time Democratic nominee and a three time loser, threw his support to the transplanted Virginian.

Thus Americans had three choices for president. Four if you counted Eugene V. Debs, the perennial Socialist candidate, which most people didn't.

The campaign was hard fought. Roosevelt railed about how the conservatives had "stolen" the Republican nomination, Wilson lectured on what he called the "New Freedom" and Taft conducted his low key effort based on his argument that judges deserved more power than elected officials.

The most dramatic moment of the campaign came in Milwaukee when a hostile saloonkeeper shot Teddy Roosevelt. The bullet had to go through his eyeglass case and fifty folded pages of the speech he intended to give before it entered his chest.

Roosevelt never faltered. He delivered the speech as the cops grabbed his assailant.

This was the first time that all forty-eight contiguous states got to vote. Arizona and New Mexico were admitted to the Union earlier that year.

Wilson walked away with the electoral votes of forty states but managed to collect only forty-two percent of the popular vote to Roosevelt's twenty-seven percent and Taft's twenty-three percent. Hardly a mandate. None of the candidates carried their home states.

The new president's inaugural address sounded more like a sermon than a speech but it spelled out the domestic initiatives he intended to pursue under what he called the New Freedom.

Woodrow Wilson devoted not one word to foreign policy.

He did however reward Bryan for his support. Wilson named him secretary of state. Bryan, the onetime "Boy Orator of the Platte", was a pacifist.

Bryan managed to negotiate and sign twenty-eight "Treaties for the Advancement of Peace" with countries that agreed to bring disputes to arbitration before going to war.

Despite his best efforts, Bryan was unable to get Imperial Germany to sign such a treaty.

The Commissioner

Frank Hague's big desk dominated the room. He had it made especially for him and it moved into his City Hall office just minutes before he did.

It looked like most desks but it had one unusual feature. A drawer in the center of the desk which could be pushed in as well as pulled out. When it was pushed in, it extended six inches or so and was easily reached by the person sitting in the chair in front of it.

That way if a person wanted to make a donation to Hague's "organization" it could be done discreetly and without embarrassment. Donations were frequent. Some were large.

There wasn't a sheet of paper on the desk. Frank Hague didn't believe in putting anything down on paper if he didn't have to and he was more than impatient if anyone gave him some paper to read.

"I don't have time for all this crap," he'd say—then, more beguilingly, "You tell me what's going on." Aides learned to master whatever was needed before they approached Frank Hague, the new city commissioner and director of Public Safety in Jersey City.

The truth was that the commissioner wasn't much of a reader. No one had ever seen him read a book. He was educated on Jersey City's streets, not in its schools. And as he was wont to say, "Paper always comes back to bite you in the ass."

The black telephone sitting off to the right on his desk was his secondary instrument of communications. He used it if he had to but it didn't ring very often and he picked it up to make a call even less frequently.

Hague preferred his conversations face-to-face. Not all of them, of course.

Hague vividly remembered a conversation, if you could call it that, with Woodrow Wilson when he was still the governor.

Hague and Mayor H. Otto Wittpenn were summoned to Trenton—"like fucking schoolboys sent to the principal's office" was Hague's description. Hague had had that particular educational experience more than once.

The onetime president of Princeton lectured them for what seemed like hours on the need for unity and the wonders of the new city commission form of government then sweeping the nation. What he didn't tell them was that he was going to try for the presidential nomination at the National Democratic Convention in Baltimore that summer of 1912.

Wilson converted Wittpenn, but not so Hague, who kept silent.

When Wilson finally announced his intention to run for the Democratic nomination for president Wittpenn and his Jersey City allies quickly endorsed him. Hague hesitated.

Wilson even came to Jersey City to get Hague's endorsement. Hague remembered that conversation too: "That arrogant son-of-a-bitch told me it was my duty to back him. My duty!"

Not only did Hague not endorse Wilson, he made sure the county Democratic Committee stayed silent while he actively campaigned against Wilson's nomination.

It didn't work.

It took two-thirds of the votes of the Democratic delegates to win the nomination.

Champ Clark of Missouri led on the first ballot with Wilson right behind him. On the 9th, New York—controlled by Hague's friends at Tammany Hall—switched to Clark. It looked like he had the momentum to win. But the votes dragged on until William Jennings Bryan, three-time presidential candidate, and an arch foe of the big city machines, gave his nod of approval to the pious Wilson. Wilson won on the 46th ballot.

Hague jumped on the bandwagon and once again the principal's summons, this time to Sea Girt and this time Wilson threatened Hague as well as lectured him again on the need for party unity.

Unimpressed, Hague fielded a full ticket against Wittpenn's slate for county offices in the September primaries. Wilson, furious, stormed into Hudson County and campaigned against Hague's people.

Wilson—and Wittpenn—rolled over Hague's candidates. Only the 2nd Ward in Jersey City, Hague's heartland, stayed loyal. Wilson went on to victory in November. Republicans split their vote between William Howard Taft and Teddy Roosevelt. Wilson was now president of the United States.

The hard-nosed politicians of New Jersey—Frank Hague among them—seriously underestimated Woodrow Wilson. They thought the professor-president of Princeton would be easy to manipulate. They were wrong. He was as crafty a politician as they come.

In fact, Wilson was closer to the truth when he characterized the politicians of New Jersey as "amateurs" when compared to faculty members who practiced campus politics in their spare time.

Wilson and Hague had one trait in common. They demanded absolute loyalty from their followers. Hague had not been loyal. Wilson would not forget.

Hague still talked to Joseph Patrick Tumulty, now secretary to the President, from time to time. But serious politics were not discussed. Each was just keeping a line of communication open. Just in case.

When Hague thought of Wilson it was, *Good riddance*. One useful thing had been wrought by that election though. Hague—like Wilson—became a "progressive."

Frank Hague, who appreciated sarcasm more than irony, was dubbed a "reform" candidate and endorsed by the Jersey Journal in the first election for the new five member city commission the following May.

There were ninety-one candidates on the ballot. The top five voter getters would be elected. He and his friend, A. Harry Moore, survived the cut and a very different Irishman, the young undertaker, the Republican Mark Fagan, was picked as mayor. Hague was named director of public safety.

Hague did it with the help of a growing organization that attracted men like Fat Jack Lynch, men who were ambitious and who saw Frank Hague as the key to their future.

* * *

Frank Hague expected his people to work diligently but Fat Jack Lynch was really tired.

It had been a hot, hard day on the docks and he was glad to come home to his small flat which was just a shade cooler in late spring.

Jack trekked over to the Hoboken piers in the early morning hours every day but Sunday. Longshoremen did not have steady jobs. The stevedore companies that loaded and unloaded cargo hired them on a day-by-day basis.

If you "made the shape" you worked that day. If not, you hustled over to another pier and tried again. Two piers were about as many as a man could get to before the stevedores were done hiring.

If you didn't make the shape that morning, you walked home or to a saloon.

It was hot, brutal work in the summer and cold, brutal work in the winter. If you got hurt, that was your problem and a longshoreman was bound to get hurt sooner or later. The money was not bad but unpredictable. It was no job for a family man, although many such grimly worked at it as long as they could.

Fat Jack thought himself lucky. He could see a way out and the very nature of the shape up would help him do it. He supported no one but himself so three days' work a week would be enough to pay for his rent, his food and the few bills he had.

One of those bills was for the Chinese laundry. Jack would wear his work clothes two days in a row but by the third day, summer or winter, it was time for the laundry bag.

Tonight his duds went into the laundry bag.

He needed a bath but the water closet and tub was down the hall and was shared with three families. It never seemed to be available. There were ten women and girls on the floor.

There was a big sink in his kitchen. One half, covered with a metal lid, was much deeper than the other. It was designed to wash clothes in and that's where Fat Jack washed his socks, underwear and handkerchiefs before he hung them out to dry on the clothes line.

Tonight that's where he would wash himself. He had no hot water but it didn't matter as the evening was warm. In fact the cold water helped him shake off his tiredness.

In the winter, he'd put the kettle on and heat up the water in the tub that way. Not that it didn't get cold quickly anyway.

Fat Jack sat on the porcelain divider between the tubs, the water up to his calves, sponging himself down with a dish cloth and brown soap. His body was red from scrubbing.

Jesus, I must be a sight.

Washed clean, Fat Jack dried himself with a long rough towel which got sent to the "Chinks" every other week. He drained and cleaned the tub. Then he turned to the shallow section of the sink where he washed his dishes, stood on his toes and urinated into it.

What the hell. That's why they call us "piss in the sink Irish." At least there were no dishes there.

The first thing Fat Jack intended to do when he landed that lovely job with the city was to move to a flat with its own bathroom.

Fat Jack would have liked nothing better than to stroll down to the stoop, get a growler of beer and talk with his neighbors.

He was a popular man and his company would be welcome.

But his work day was not at an end.

Fat Jack Lynch, longshoreman, a leader of the secretive Irish group, Clan na Gael, was now a block captain for Frank Hague's organization. He was determined to use the fast approaching election to propel himself within reach of a different, better life. One with a bath tub.

He had no more education than any other longshoreman who went to work on the docks as soon as he was big enough to swing a hook. But he was very intelligent, good with numbers, scrupulous with money, fair, tough and he had a flair for structure.

Lynch also had a prodigious memory, very useful since the Clan na Gael was wary of anything put down on paper.

Fat Jack Lynch, dressed in his only suit, tie, and his good shoes was off to visit with some of the forty-seven voters on his block.

His neighbors greeted him as he reached the stoop.

"There you are, Jack. You look grand."

"You're the man to get the votes out, boyo."

"Jack, I'm with you and so is my brother."

Jack was all smiles and cheery greetings. When he reached the sidewalk, an older woman called out, "Jack. Do you have a minute?"

"I do indeed, Mary," he said, taking her elbow and leading her towards the corner so they couldn't be overheard.

"I have a problem, Jack."

"Tell me, Mary."

"It's me daughter, Sheila. She's sixteen, you know. She's out of school and she needs work. Do you think you could help me?"

"If I can't, Mary, I know people who might."

"I know Sheila isn't the brightest candle in the room but she's a good girl. And she'll work hard or I'll break her back."

"Ah, Mary. Sure that won't be a problem. The Reehills are all known to be hard workers. Except your brother-in-law, Bobby, who's all but useless. Let me see what I can do, Mary. I'll try to get back to you in a week."

"God bless you, Jack. We'll all be with you. You can count on the Reehill votes."

"Thank you. Mary, I am counting on the Reehills. It's a tough election."

That's three Reehill men. She'll make sure they vote. If I produce.

When Fat Jack returned to his flat he picked up "The Book" while his memory was fresh and turned to the page with "Gerald Reehill" printed in the top left corner.

He made his entry.

Lynch had bought a common schoolboy's copy book. He devoted a full page front and back to each of the forty-seven voters on his block.

Every time he would talk to one, a valuable tidbit might be written on his page.

Not only the vital statistics on him, his wife, children and anyone else who lived with the voter, but the voter's interests or hobbies—not that many working men had one.

If Lynch helped out, down it went. If the voter had any political opinions, down they went. Some voters had a second page in the back of the book.

Soon a picture, not only of each voter but of his collective block, emerged. Lynch was sure he could produce results that would impress the organization.

Lynch studied that book like others studied the Bible. He was never at a loss for small talk when he ran into a voter.

He divided his voters into those who didn't work and could vote early, those who could vote at lunch time, and those who had to vote after work.

Lynch's job was to get every "reliable" voter to the polls, no matter what.

He was not sure of six of his voters. *Three of them were Reehills so let's try to add them to the side of the angels.*

Within a week, with the help of his precinct captain, Sheila Reehill had a job in a broom factory over on Sussex Street.

As Mary Reehill said, "The money ain't much but it's a godsend to us. If it wasn't for you...I don't know. We're with you, Jack Lynch. You've got the Reehill votes to a man."

He would decide between now and Election Day what to do about the other three.

One of them, he was convinced, was the political equivalent of the village atheist. His reputation was rooted in denial. But the man liked his bottle. Perhaps a visit to a saloon on Election Day. The other two would commit after a personal appeal accompanied by a basket of fruit. It was said you could tell who the "lace curtain" Irish were because they kept fruit in the house even when no one was sick. Fruit was a delicacy in Fat Jack's neighborhood.

The city commission campaign was in its last days and had grown in intensity until the big day itself.

The political organization Hague was building block-by-block, precinct-by-precinct, did not start an electoral campaign on Labor Day or any other set day. It started working on the next election the day after the last one.

The people—voters if you will—always had needs and the organization would perpetuate itself by filling, or at least ameliorating, those needs.

When you needed help, your block captain or precinct captain helped. Then on Election Day, you helped him with your vote. Ideology had nothing to do with it.

The debt the voter incurred was never fully repaid. You were expected to vote the right way in every election henceforth.

The organization also offered a sense of belonging to something bigger than oneself. Just like the church.

The organization worked to make campaigns fun. There were rallies, songfests, picnics, outings on the river, parades. Everyone was welcome even if only adult men could vote. The men would pay for the family entertainment with their vote.

People liked to belong and the organization understood that. In fact, everyone was encouraged to consider themselves as part of the organization. You probably would find yourself working for the organization sometime during the campaign or on Election Day. You belonged.

Probably the only national progressive concept that Hague truly yearned to see enacted was giving women the franchise.

"Think of it," he would say, "The size of our organization doubled overnight."

Hague knew full well that many of those women would not work outside the home once they married. When woman's suffrage became a reality he intended that women would stand co-equal with men at every level of the organization below ward leader.

That didn't mean women would get to drink in Jersey City's saloons. As Hague once said, "Women don't want to drink in a saloon and they sure as hell don't want their man drinking in a saloon with some other woman."

Voting was by secret paper ballot but given the usual chaos of the polling place how one voted was rarely a secret. Voting was a festive occasion in Jersey City where the saloons stayed long after the polls closed.

When the votes were counted Fat Jack Lynch had delivered all forty-seven of his voters to Frank Hague and the rest of his ticket.

Lynch's political bosses were impressed.

The Paterson Silk Strike

Peter Capparelli and his wife took in two of the strikers' kids as soon as their parents were arrested.

"We can't let them starve in the street," said the Italian born anarchist to his wife.

"Of course not," said his Irish wife, wrapping her arms around two skinny, scared boys. "Would you like a nice cold glass of milk?"

The older boy, ten, nodded.

"And a piece of toast to go along with it?"

The younger boy, seven, said, "Yes, lady."

Capparelli, who, unknown to his employer, carried the card of the International Workers of the World, lived in Newark but he wholeheartedly supported the strike of the silk workers in Paterson some miles away. So did his radical, syndicalist union—the Wobblies—led by William "Big Bill" Haywood. The IWW fought for a non-capitalist system where the workers would own and manage their industries. Not a very popular idea in capitalist America where millions dreamed of becoming tycoons themselves. All they needed was a piece of Horatio Alger style luck.

A Wobbly leader, Elizabeth Gurley Brown, "The Rebel Girl", was the first to be arrested as she delivered red hot oratory demanding an eight hour day, better working conditions, and a halt to the introduction of labor-saving multi-loom weaving systems that ate jobs while producing silk cloth.

More than 1,800 strikers followed her to the cells and hundreds of their children were farmed out to sympathetic families throughout Northern New Jersey. Many went to Jersey City to live with relatives. Most were as skinny as the Capparelli's kids.

The silk mills had changed during the past decades. More and more machinery replaced skilled weavers and more and more women and children replaced higher-priced male workers.

The IWW had won in Lawrence, Massachusetts, in 1912 and had exacted higher wages for the mill hands. Big Bill thought Paterson would be another big win for the Wobblies.

Paterson's police and civic leaders were very wary of the Wobblies because of their reputation for violence. The Wobblies did not disappoint.

It was a bitter strike that dragged on for six months and ended in defeat for the poor, penniless strikers. The bosses had to hold out. If they did not introduce the multiple loom systems, their competitors elsewhere would have destroyed them. But workers can't eat economic reality.

One of the Wobbly leaders in Paterson was Carlo Tresca, an Italian born socialist-turned-anarchist, who had joined the Wobblies in 1912.

Europe was beset by violent anarchists for three quarters of a century and while socialism made strong inroads there, it was despite the fear and hatred of the anarchists.

Socialism had little appeal for Americans and its successes were few and local. Anarchy's history in the United States was also violent but ineffective. All the bomb thrown on Haymarket Street in Chicago had done was to kill nine people. All the anarchist's bullet that killed President William McKinley had accomplished was to make Teddy Roosevelt president a couple of years ahead of time. No anarchist he.

Still, the anarchists' bombs went off with regularity.

Peter Capparelli was no bomb thrower. He never had that chance. But like most anarchists he hated policemen. He thought them traitors to the working class.

Capparelli was resigned when the two little boys, fatter now than then, went back to their defeated parents in Paterson.

His wife wept. She had grown to love those boys. She had no children of her own.

Rice Pudding Day

Mickey McGurk walked up to the police call box on the corner of Griffith and Central Avenue. *Time to call the desk and check in.*

This is how the sergeant knew where you were and could keep track of you. Find a cozy place to snooze, or "coop" as the cops called it, and nap a little too long and Sergeant Slager would turn on the sarcasm full blast.

"You're walking slow tonight, McGurk. What's the matter, your flat feet hurt? Or was you chasing an axe murderer down Central Avenue?" Such comments were invariably followed by a guffaw that most resembled a pig snorting.

McGurk's answer was always the same. "Minding the stores on Central Avenue, Sergeant. That takes time, you know."

"Ja, I know, Irisher." McGurk kept the cooping to a minimum.

So tonight: "Patrolman McGurk reporting in, Sergeant. All's quiet, no problems."

"Good. See me when you get off duty."

"What's up, Sergeant?"

"I said see me when you are off duty. I'm your sergeant, not your secretary."

That ended the conversation. *So I've got a message or something. Interesting. This is the first time that happened. Tomorrow is my day off and a big day it is. I hope I'm not being sent somewhere; I've got to have the day off.*

He had arranged to meet Otto Ganz at the German club after supper. He was going to ask for permission to marry Hannah and he needed the day to marshal arguments towards that end.

Mickey had some misgivings. Truth to tell, he didn't really want to get married right now. But he loved Hannah and he had dug this hole with his own big mouth.

Ah, well. In for a penny, in for a pound.

The sergeant motioned to him as he passed though the station house doors. "Come around, behind the desk. The whole world should hear what I have to say?"

That attracted everyone's attention. "Morgan! If you have nothing to do, I will find something for you to do." The would-be eavesdropper scurried off to the locker room followed closely by several of his ilk as Mickey reached the sergeant's side.

"I have a message for you, Patrolman. You are to report to the office of the director of public safety at City Hall at nine o'clock sharp. In uniform. Looking better than you do now, Irisher."

Three hours to clean up and get Downtown. Right. It wouldn't do to be late. Uncle Frank is not an easygoing man. I wonder what this is all about.

"McGurk, I don't know why he wants to see you. You're not a bad policeman. Better than most. You understand discipline. That comes from the military. Us Germans, if we didn't come here as kinder, we was in the army. That's why we like the police work so much. That Mr. Hague, he is a fire-eater, ja. I think he will change things very much. He has already broken our union. Gone. Kaput. Everyone is afraid for their job. Have you done anything I don't know about? Anything bad? Tell me now."

Mickey McGurk wouldn't pass for a corrupt cop in Jersey City. Sure he didn't pay to get on a trolley or get into a theatre. Sure most of his meals on the job were free. Sure store owners might give him some clothes, or groceries or the occasional pair of shoes to show their gratitude for his presence in their hard world. A little money even changed hands once in a while. That went with the job. But no one would call that corruption. At least, not in Jersey City.

"No. I don't think so, Sergeant. No."

"Good. I believe you. So, I will stand behind you, if I have to."

"Thanks, Sergeant." Mickey never called Ernst Slager, "Sarge". He didn't stick straws up horses' asses either.

Mickey McGurk, duly scrubbed, pressed and polished, stood in front of the commissioner's young secretary whose Irish mug seemed familiar.

"I'm Patrolman McGurk. I'm told the Commissioner wants to see me."

The young man stuck out his hand. "Terry Lynch. Fat Jack's brother. Yeah, the commissioner wants to see you. But don't worry; you're not on the griddle. I'll announce you." Such tidbits of knowledge were Lynch's source of power. It was easy and fun to pretend he knew more than he did.

"Patrolman McGurk, Commissioner."

"Good. Sit down, McGurk." Lynch made no attempt to leave. Hague looked at him and then at the door. "Thanks, Terry." Lynch left.

"Okay. How are you doing, Mickey?"

"Very well, Commissioner. Thank you."

"Commissioner. Doesn't that have a nice ring to it?" Hague came close to smiling. "Well, behind closed doors, it's still Uncle Frank, Mickey."

"Yes sir, Uncle Frank."

"I'm hearing good things about you, Mickey. You've got things under control on your beat. The Dutchmen even like you. And, I'm told you're a great help to the organization at election time."

"I try, Uncle Frank," said Mickey who knew that if he wasn't of help to the organization he wouldn't be a cop much longer.

Hague grunted approval. Mickey noticed his "uncle" had taken to wearing a small diamond stickpin in his tie. It went nicely with his high collar. All in all, quite natty.

Hague stared at the ceiling for a moment or two and then locked eyes with McGurk.

"Mickey, do you know how I ended up as the director of public safety?"

"No, sir. I do not," said Mickey as he thought, *Because they didn't want you for mayor?*

Hague pointed both index fingers straight up in the air:

"Because nobody else wanted the goddamn job! Nobody, that is, but me. Mention Public Safety and my fellow commissioners leave the room. No, they didn't want it. Can't say as I blame them. The fire department. A bunch of fat slobs sitting on their asses all day playing pinochle when they're not fast asleep. I'll bet that Roman guy—what's his name—Nero? I'll bet he had a fire department like that."

McGurk was startled. He couldn't imagine how his "uncle" came up with that comparison on his own. He suspected Harry Moore or, maybe, John Milton down in Trenton.

"And the cops. God help us... the cops. You know, we'd be better off to turn the city over to the crooks if they would only agree to steal less than the cops. More fat slobs. Only they carry pistols and are quick with the nightstick. Protect the people? They're a goddamn menace to the people. I'm going to put an end to that. By God, I will. I've already started. That stupid union's on ropes. Sure, they're suing but, you know what? I'll buy lawyers by the gross. I'll win, if not today, tomorrow."

Hague was showing real passion. His face was red. His right fist was pumping. His face contorted.

McGurk was vigorously nodding his head. "No doubt, Uncle Frank. No doubt at all."

The commissioner's right index finger darted out, straight at him. "And you are going to help me."

Dear God, here it comes.

Hague rocked back in his chair, his hands clasped on his chest as he searched the ceiling again. McGurk waited—seemingly calm— but silently reciting Hail Marys.

"I'm forming a new squad, Mickey. Handpicked men. Hard men. Fearless men."

McGurk listened, very afraid now.

"Men I trust. Men from the 'Show. You know a lot of them. Ray Reehill. Tommy McLaughlin. Bob Waldron. John Fitzgerald. The O'Shea brothers. Red Burke."

Mickey interrupted. "Is that Tommy Burke?"

"Yeah. There are two Tommy Burkes. This is the one with the red hair. The other one is going to be a priest."

Aha. I'm about to be appointed to Frank Hague's flying squad. Okay.

"We are going to clean up this city, Mickey. We're going to make it fit for decent people. No more whores. No more girlie shows. No women in the saloons. No more dope. No more bent cops. We'll crack the skull of every burglar in town. We'll stuff them all on the ferries and ship them to New York. To hell with the lawyers and the courts. If they come back, we'll break their necks."

Mickey wondered just how far his uncle was going to go. "What about liquor and gambling, Uncle Frank?"

"Booze? I'm not some old biddy with a hatchet. Do you want to try to get between a Dutchman and his beer? Or a guinea and his wine? Or, God help us, a mick and anything that's fermented? Forget it. If you want to drink—drink. Just behave yourself.

"And gambling? What's wrong with putting a couple of dollars down on a horse? I do it myself. I even play poker once in a while."

And I'll bet you never lose.

"You know what gambling is? Hope. It's the only hope most people have. No, we're cracking down on vice. Real vice. Not the few pleasures the workingman has."

Hague actually looked righteous. If Hague's agenda exactly mirrored that of the Irish Catholic clergy, so be it. Those were his people. McGurk understood that such an agenda would immeasurably strengthen Hague's organization. The priests would love it, some ministers would like it even if it didn't go far enough, and the women would endorse it wholeheartedly. Of course, women couldn't vote. But their influence was enormous. Some were even pushing to get the vote. Frank Hague didn't think that was a bad idea although he was no suffragette. He'd thicken his organization with women if he got the chance.

"I want you on that squad, Mickey. I know I can trust you. I know you'd just as soon turn on a lazy cop as a thieving bum."

"I'm your man, Uncle Frank."

"I know that, I'm your uncle. Okay, Mickey, as of today it's Sergeant McGurk."

Holy shit! Less than three years on the job and I'm a sergeant. That's faster than the Corps. A lot faster.

"Thank you, Commissioner. You won't regret it."

"Of course not. Now, you're going to have a lot of hard work to do. You're going to help train these new men and train them right. We can't have them cracking heads we don't want cracked."

"Right."

Mickey had a thought. "What are you going to call this new squad, Commissioner?"

"The Zeppelins," said the director of public safety in Jersey City.

* * *

Aloysius "Al" Murphy, Hague's leader in the 2nd Ward, was sitting at his kitchen table talking to Fat Jack Lynch.

"What I like about you, Jack, is that you're flexible.

"When persuasion is called for, you persuade. When action is needed, you act. Plus you got all forty-seven of your votes out and they all voted the right way. Forty-seven votes for Frank Hague, A. Harry Moore and the rest of the ticket. No bullet votes.

"Those are grand qualities in a man, especially one who wants to make a career in politics. Well, Jack, your work has been noticed. You're the new precinct captain."

Yes!

"Thank you, Mr. Murphy. You won't regret it."

"It's Al, Jack. And, I wasn't the only one who noticed. You've got friends at City Hall too."

Lynch asked, "Who might that be?"

"For starters, your brother and Commissioner Hague's nephew. And me. Mr. Hague wants to see you in his office tomorrow morning at ten thirty sharp. Since you're obviously not in trouble, I think he's going to offer you a job."

With that, Maureen Corcoran, Al's widowed daughter who was seated in a corner, looked up from her darning and stared at Jack. She smiled.

"I don't know what the job is but get back to me. I want to know the particulars."

"Yes, sir. Thank you, Al. Thanks for giving me the chance."

"It was nothing. Thank you for producing for me. Keep it up."

Jack got up ready to leave. Maureen asked, "Can you join us in a cup of tea, Mr. Lynch?"

Jack looked at Al who nodded. "I'd be delighted, Mrs. Corcoran."

"Gracie! Come to the kitchen and say 'hello' to Mr. Lynch."

A very cute girl of about seven appeared, a miniature copy of her mother.

"Well, it's easy to see where you got your good looks, Gracie," said Jack.

"From her grandfather, no question about that," said Al Murphy, not a bad looking man at that. Everyone laughed including Grace.

A jubilant Lynch was at Hague's office, right on time.

Terry Lynch hugged his brother. To Jack's surprise he hugged his brother back and meant it.

"Congratulations, brother of mine," said Terry.

"What is it?" asked Jack.

"You'll see," said Terry, opening the door.

Hague stood up and came to greet him. "Jack Lynch. How are you?"

I'm surprised he knows my first name.

"Fine. Commissioner."

"I think you'll feel even better in a couple of minutes. I like the work you did as block captain. All your voters doing the right thing. I understand you had to carry a couple of them on your back to the polls."

"Not really, Commissioner. I just gave them a helping hand."

"Good work, no matter how you did it. Okay. Let's get down to business. I know what you do for the Clan na Gael and all that secret stuff too."

Holy Christ! Some secret organization. Everybody knows about us except some of the blind, deaf and dumb.

"Well, sir, I can't speak to that. Even if I was involved, I understand those people take an oath not to discuss it."

Good, he knows how to keep his mouth shut, thought Hague.

"Sure. Sure. But do you think that a leader of a group like that would have good contacts in every city in Hudson County?"

"I think he would."

"Do you?"

"Yes."

"I thought you would. Now for a couple of technical questions. How many ounces are there in a pound?"

"Sixteen," said a completely puzzled Lynch.

"Good. Now, how much do you think a thumb weighs?"

Lynch didn't hesitate. "I think that depends on the greed of the grocer."

Lynch thought Hague might have smiled. A little. "You're my man, Jack Lynch. You are the new clerk in the office of the County Superintendent for Weights and Measures. How do you like that?"

Sweet Jesus. I can't believe it.

"I'm overwhelmed, Commissioner. I never expected anything like this. Thank you. You won't regret it."

"Of course I won't. The job just opened up yesterday. The old clerk got caught taking money from the storekeepers. Not for the organization—for himself. I won't tolerate that. The job comes with a car so you can get around the county. There's always an election coming up so don't neglect your precinct work but I want you to make friends—political friends—everywhere from West New York to East Newark. We're going to need them in the campaigns to come.

"You'll like the superintendent. He isn't going to bother you when you are doing organization work. I appointed him and he's agreed to you being his clerk. See your brother. He'll give you the particulars of the job. I expect results, Jack. Don't let that Irish stuff get in the way."

"No, sir." Lynch stood, shook hands with Hague, thanked him and turned to leave.

"By the way, Jack, the job pays $35 a week."

Fat Jack Lynch was very pleased. *A good solid, steady salary. Something to build a new life on.*

I wonder if I could take Maureen Corcoran to mass some Sunday. See what happens. Who knows? Maybe she's the one I'm looking for.

Terry Lynch filled his brother in on the job and gave him a sheet of paper with a list of his duties.

"Okay. Now you know about 'Rice Pudding Day', right?"

"I think so. That's when you have to give part of your salary back to the organization. How much?"

"Three percent of your annual salary. Be sure to put it away."

"Sort of like that new income tax Wilson put in."

"Not at all," said Terry, "Think of it as insurance. You know how people pay four bits a week to make sure they get buried? Well, you're going to pay a buck a week to make sure you don't get buried."

"Makes sense," said Fat Jack Lynch.

Home Rule is Rome Rule

The colonel in charge of Section IIIb, the intelligence arm of the German General Staff, spoke to the officer who gathered information on Great Britain.

"So what do you make of this Home Rule situation?"

The captain said, "Well, sir, you can always depend on Ireland making things difficult for Great Britain when she can. Asquith is determined to implement Home Rule this year and I think he will coerce those Protestants and loyalists in the North into accepting it."

"So the Protestants are balking."

"More than that, they are ready to fight. They are convinced that Home Rule means the vast Catholic majority in the whole island will overwhelm them. They will fight to maintain their dominant position. Their slogan is 'Home Rule is Rome Rule'."

"Really? How can we take advantage of this?"

Section IIIb was convinced Germany would be at war with Great Britain within a year if not sooner.

The captain had a ready answer. "Both sides, the nationalists—Catholics if you will, and the loyalists—mainly Protestants, have organized large paramilitary groups. Both are looking to buy rifles and ammunition. Neither knows how the British Army will react if ordered to enforce Home Rule."

"Let's accommodate them," said the colonel, smiling. "We have lots of weapons."

"Of course, there is an arms dealer in Hamburg who will give them a nice price and deliver the arms and ammunition to them."

"Do it," the colonel ordered.

The British Army took a hand in March, 1914, when the commanding officer of the British troops in Ireland backed by hundreds of his officers threatened to resign rather than take action against the Unionists in Ulster. This was the Mutiny at the Curragh.

The Liberal government backpedalled furiously saying it was all a "misunderstanding" and that the government would never use force to implement Home Rule in Ulster.

Not good enough for the Unionists; weeks later the Motor Corps of the Ulster Volunteers unloaded 25,000 modern rifles and three million rounds of ammunition in a secret, efficient operation distant from a ship in Belfast Lough. The weapons were German.

The Nationalists now knew they could not depend on the British Army. The more militant faction began to take control of the movement.

Using borrowed money, the Irish Volunteers bought 900 single shot old Mausers dating back to the Franco-Prussian War and 29,000 rounds of black powder ammunition from that same arms dealer in Hamburg. It was landed in a helter skelter, highly publicized operation near Dublin. The weapons were German.

A detachment of the King's Own Scottish Borderers was sent to intercept the shipment but failed to find the nationalists.

On the way back to Dublin they were heckled by a crowd at Bachelor's Walk, A shot was fired, followed by a volley. Three people were killed and thirty-eight wounded.

Ireland was on the brink of civil war.

Sir Roger Casement, who had helped arrange for the arms shipment, hurried to America to raise money for the Irish Volunteers. No fan of Home Rule, Sir Roger wanted an independent Ireland and had resigned from the British Consular Service a year earlier to devote all his talent to that cause.

Fat Jack Lynch met twice with Sir Roger. Once when he delivered Clan na Gael funds at a small group meeting and the next morning when he and Jerry O'Leary met with the aristocratic Irishman alone.

"Home Rule is dead," Sir Roger told them. "We are going to

have to get rid of England ourselves but I think we might be able to persuade a powerful ally to help us."

"Who might that be?" asked O'Leary, a New York leader of Clan na Gael.

"Germany. She's ready for war and it likely that one of her opponents will be Great Britain. You remember what they say, 'England's Adversity is Ireland's Opportunity.' But we need money. Lots of it. That's where the Irish in America come in. We depend on you."

"We'll do what we can," said Lynch. 'Do we still call you Sir Roger?"

"Certainly," said Sir Roger, puzzled by the question. "Later we may ask you to do more than just raise money."

"We'll be ready," said O'Leary. Lynch nodded in assent.

Sir Roger had one more meeting before he left America for Germany. He conferred in Washington with Ambassador Johann von Bernstorff and his military attaché, Colonel Franz von Papen.

Germany was ready for war too. The Army Bill passed the year before prepared for war in 1914. It raised the size of the "peacetime" army to almost 900,000 and provided for 17,000 more horses. Naval war plans were implemented and the Kiel Canal linking the North Sea with the Baltic was widened and deepened to accommodate the largest war vessels. Every necessity from bullion to fodder was stockpiled.

Dr. Walter Scheele's agricultural chemical factory in Hoboken was up and running. The German sleeper agent was ready. America was not.

Looking for a Miracle

Mickey McGurk, naturally neat, had dressed with care, as much care as he had shown with his uniform that morning when he was summoned to City Hall.

Now evening was coming on and he had to face another older man and he feared that it would not turn out as well. But it had to be done. Hannah was right; things couldn't go on like this. Months and months lost in each other but avoiding everything and everyone they loved.

Not easy to do, even in a big city. Lots of people knew something was going on. Some of the girls at Colgate who saw him frequently but were never introduced. The cop on a rainy beat ducking into an Italian restaurant on Brunswick Street who didn't believe for a minute that the blushing Hannah was Mickey's cousin yet was content at roll call to say, "I saw Mickey McGurk with a good looking blonde at that wop place last night."

Mickey's habit of continuously reading the street, and his good eyesight, held off embarrassment a number of times. Twice they did an about face and turned to the right at the next corner.

Enough. Time to come clean. Time to face her father. Time to roll the dice.

The walk from his furnished room on Booreum Avenue to the Pohlman Hall near her house wasn't long and McGurk intended to get there right on time. He wouldn't keep Mr. Ganz waiting and he certainly didn't want to be there early.

He had seen Otto Ganz there several times before and he had run into Sophie Ganz twice while she was shopping on Central Avenue. The encounters had been brief, pleasant and totally inconsequential. A remark or two on the weather, inquiries into health and happiness of Hannah and Billy, perhaps a memory of a moment at Lake Hopatcong and then a salute with the nightstick and goodbye. Goodbye and great relief.

He hadn't seen Billie who probably was busy after school playing ball or hanging over the Palisades throwing rocks down on kids from Hoboken who had yet to master the concept of gravity. Most intelligent kids avoided adults, let alone cops, who usually meant trouble.

The bartender barely had time to glance at the door as it opened and Otto Ganz was off his stool. He grabbed Mickey's elbow and wheeled him back out with a smile.

"Such a nice evening. Maybe we can go for a little walk and find a place with good beer and we can talk quietly there."

Oh, lord! The old man wants to avoid a row where people know him—and me. Where the hell can we go to do that?

They talked of the weather and sports and then Mr. Ganz turned left—at the hundred steps leading down to Hoboken. *Of course.*

They settled down in a booth back of the bar in a tavern Mickey had never been in.

Two big schooners of beer were brought to their table.

"*Prosit!*"

"*Sláinte!*" It was one of nine words in Gaelic Mickey knew.

"Interesting," said Ganz, "here we are in America and we toast each other in different languages. That wasn't English, was it?"

"No, sir. Gaelic."

"Call me Otto, Mickey."

McGurk hesitated. "I can't do that, sir," he said, shaking his head.

"This is bad. You don't want to be my friend?"

"No, sir," replied Mickey quickly. "I don't want to be your friend. I want to be your son-in-law."

"Ooof," groaned Ganz, taking a long pull on his beer. "So, my wife was right. I'm not surprised, she usually is. Sophie knew you and my Hannah have been meeting behind our backs.

Walking down the street, sitting in the park, having coffee. Someone always is watching. This is not a city you know; it's a collection of villages. You do something, someone else sees you doing it. We said nothing to Hannah. We don't trust you, but we trust our daughter. She was brought up right. She knows what is right and what is wrong. We thought this infer...infa..."

"Infatuation," said Mickey.

"Ja, such a word. So we thought this in-fat-u-a-tion would burn itself out. You come from such different cultures. We didn't think it would last. But now I realize we were wrong. You are not that Irish. Hannah, we learn, is not that German. You are Americans. I am an American citizen and I love this country even more than the Fatherland but I will never be the kind of American you are." Otto Ganz paused. "Or Hannah."

Ganz took another pull on his beer. So did Mickey.

"In the old country, I doubt that this situation could arise. And if it did, I would say, 'No!' and that would be that. Before I say anything more, Mr. McGurk, I want to ask you some questions. I think you will answer them honestly?"

"I will, sir."

"Is it necessary that you and Hannah must marry and marry soon?"

McGurk caught his meaning. "Absolutely not!" Then he started stammering. "No... never... nothing like that. Hannah wouldn't... I wouldn't..."

"You wouldn't, hah! You're a man. Given a chance, why wouldn't you act like a man?"

Mickey prudently let that question hang.

"So, this wedding, if there was such a wedding, would take place in a more normal way, ja?"

Mickey, whose heart was pounding, nodded yes and smiled. Otto Ganz did not smile.

"Is it not true," he asked, "that you Irish sometimes don't marry until you are fifty?"

Mickey's heart skipped. "Maybe in the old country, Mr. Ganz, but not here."

"No?" said Otto sounding disappointed. "How old are you?"

"Almost twenty-four, sir."

"And my Hannah is twenty-one. Both of you are very young. You have lots of time. Years.

"I know, in America, young people marry for love. It is different in Germany. Your parents search out the right person and if you don't hate her, you marry. Then you fall in love. And you never stop loving her or your children. Or your family. Everyone is happy, or as happy as life lets them be. So you say you love my daughter?"

"I do, sir, with all my heart and I know Hannah loves me too."

"Really? Ja, I'll grant that she probably thinks she does. But how do we know that it's not what you Americans call 'puppy love?' You really don't know each other. You have spent little time with us. Has Hannah even met your family?"

"No, sir."

"Of course not. Let me ask you some more questions. I know you are a Catholic, you know Hannah is a Lutheran. You don't see this as a problem?"

"Yes, sir, of course it is a problem but Hannah and I will solve it," said Mickey, without a lot of confidence.

"So you two young people, ignorant if not stupid, will solve a problem that has divided the whole of Europe for five hundred years. Thousands on both sides have died making their arguments and you two are going to solve this—this war?"

Mickey knew he was ignorant but now he felt stupid. "What do they say: 'Love conquers all,'" he said lamely.

Otto Ganz roared with laughter, hit the table with the palm of hand, drained his schooner, and looked up—red faced but smiling.

"You know, I like you, Mickey. Sophie even likes you a bit. Billy likes you a lot. And you say Hannah loves you. I'll find out about that when I get home. I think she will still be up."

Otto laughed again. "But let's say she does. Let's talk about the wedding. Will you get married in Bethany Lutheran Church? Hannah in a beautiful white dress. Me walking her down the aisle. Her family and friends on one side, yours on the other. A reception with lots of beer at Pohlman Hall. Is that what you see?"

Oh, lord, thought Mickey, envisioning empty pews on his side of the church.

"I don't think that would work, sir."

"No? Well, we're not Old Lutherans, you know, I suppose Hannah could have the same kind of wedding at your church."

The Jesuits had taught Mickey more than the rudiments of church doctrine. "Not exactly."

"How 'not exactly'?"

"We'd have to get married in the church rectory."

"Speak up, boy. Suddenly, you're muttering. That is not very manly."

"I said we'd have to get married in the rectory." Mickey said it loud enough that a couple in the booth opposite turned and looked at them.

"I know your priests live pretty well. But how could we cram a couple of hundred people into a rectory?"

Mickey blushed. "There would only be Hannah and me and two witnesses. But we could still have that reception at Pohlman Hall."

"Only two witnesses? Not even the parents? What about children? Let's be evenhanded. Would the first be Catholic and the second Lutheran and so on?"

Mickey sighed. "No, sir. Hannah would have to agree to bring up the kids Catholic. But she wouldn't have to convert. She could still go to her own church."

"Hannah could go to her own church. Without you. Without her children. How tolerant of the pope. Does Hannah know about these things?"

"I doubt it. We never discussed religion," said McGurk.

"No, you were too busy playing kissy-kissy behind the bushes at Mosquito Park."

Otto stood up, as did Mickey. "All right, you were man enough to face me, so I will give my answer."

Mickey braced himself.

"This is America. Things are different here although I think the things that matter never change. Nevertheless, I will not say 'no' to you marrying Hannah—not yet. I don't think I will have to say 'no' because I don't think Hannah will ever marry you. Also, there will be no formal engagement—no ring—not yet. There are some more conditions you must agree to but I will tell them to you on the way home. You agree so far, Mr. McGurk?"

An elated Mickey blurted out, "You bet! Yes, sir. Mr. Ganz."

I better not start calling him 'Papa' just yet.

They had been silent until they reached the hundred steps. There in the shadow of the giant Koven Stove Works, Otto Ganz pointed. "I work there, Mickey. For many years. I am a tool and die maker."

Mickey was impressed.

"You know in Germany the tool and die makers, the skilled men, the professionals are Protestant. Catholics are farmers, peasants, laborers."

"It's not that way here, sir."

"No? How many Irish tool and die makers do you know?"

Mickey knew none. "There are other ways to get ahead. In fact, I was just promoted to sergeant today, Mr. Ganz."

"Well, congratulations, Mickey. So, this is your lucky day, ja?"

"Let's hear the rest of it first before I shoot off the fireworks," said Mickey.

Otto Ganz laughed. "This is funny; I don't think you are going to mind this although I think it will doom you.

"I want you to get to know each other better. Much better. You will go places together. Out in the open where everybody will see you. You will eat supper sometimes with my family; Hannah will eat sometimes with yours. You will go to our church enough to understand how we worship. Hannah will do the same. You and she will go to family celebrations. Weddings, funerals, Christenings. You will go out together with your friends. Both sets.

"You and Hannah will not go to bed together. You will not! You understand?

"You will be a couple—but not an engaged couple. Your people may approve, they may not. My people may approve, they may not. Let's see how you and Hannah handle that. I warn you it will be a *kulturkampf*. But this time, I do not think you will win."

McGurk didn't have the faintest idea what the older man meant. But he'd find out. He thought he had heard the word before, maybe in a German class at St. Peter's.

"Do you accept my conditions, Mr. McGurk?"

"I do, sir." They shook hands. Ganz's hand was as hard as McGurk's.

They started up the steps. "You know, Mickey, it is easy to come down these steps to work but it is getting harder to climb them going home. Maybe I'm getting old."

* * *

On his next day off, Mickey went down to St. Peter's and sought out his old friend, Father McBride.

"Well, well, Mickey, you're looking good. I hear you're a sergeant now."

McGurk was not surprised. His stripes were only a couple of days old. *Of course, Father McBride would know. They keep tabs on what the Jesuits call "ours."*

"So what brings you here? Do you need to go to confession?"

Mickey laughed. "No, Father, I go to confession up at St. Anne's. I was passing by and I thought I'd stop in. But I do have a question though. What is *kulturkampf*? I don't even know if I am pronouncing it correctly."

"Close enough. Why the interest in German history?"

"Just curiosity, I guess."

"Sure," said the priest who certain it wasn't mere curiosity. "*Kulturkampf*. It was a clash between cultures. It meant a very bad time for Catholics in Germany thirty or thirty-five years ago. Otto von Bismarck, you've heard of him? Well, Bismarck thought that Catholic Church had too much influence in Prussia especially in education. So he made a deal with the Protestants and the secular anti-clericals and clamped down hard on the Catholics who were a bit more than a third of the population.

"They shut down schools, passed punitive legislation—not as bad as the Penal Laws in Ireland but bad enough—put about half the bishops in jail along with a lot of clergy and more than a few laymen. He threw the Dominicans and Franciscans out of the country. The Jesuits too—talk about a death wish.

"But the Germans were smarter than the Irish. They didn't revolt. Bismarck would have smashed them. They formed a political party and fought him at the polls. Elected a lot of members to the Imperial parliament.

"Then the secular wing overplayed its hand and began attacking the Protestant churches too. The old Iron Chancellor wouldn't stand for that. He was a pietist, you know. The coalition broke down and Bismarck made peace with the Catholic party. That was the end of *Kulturkampf*. You could say the Catholics won."

"What a pietist, Father?"

The priest looked at Mickey quizzically and then answered.

"The Lutheran Church in Germany split into groups after the state joined the Lutherans with the Reformed Church. One group, the Old Lutherans, refused to go along with the merger because they thought it watered down the doctrines preached by Martin Luther. The pietists cared less about doctrine. They cared more about reading the Bible, individual piety and they showed more flexibility in their dealings with other Protestant denominations.

"When they emigrated to this country the Old Lutherans joined the Missouri Synod Lutheran Church and the pietists became part of the Evangelical Lutheran Church."

"What are they up at Bethany Lutheran, Father?"

The priest now stared at McGurk. "Well, they're certainly not Missouri Synod. Why the sudden interest in Lutheran theology?"

Mickey McGurk told him. Told him all of it. Mickey left nothing out.

"Oh, boy," said Father Mc Bride, "you're in a real mess. I think her father is right. It'll never work. Walk away. Walk away before you really break her heart and yours."

"I can't, Father. I love her. We'll work this out."

"You will, will you? Well, let me tell you something, mister. The Counter-Reformation isn't over. The church is very strict when it comes to dealing with Protestant churches. Did you know you are forbidden to go into a Protestant church unless you are on duty as a policeman?

"Sure you can get away with going to a friend's funeral or slipping into the last pew during a wedding. But attend a Protestant service? No way. That would be scandalous.

"You'd have to be careful if you ever were tempted to do such a devilish thing. You certainly couldn't take communion or participate in any way. The only way you could get away with it would be to sit quietly like you were watching a play at the theatre. But of course, you wouldn't do such a thing."

Mickey understood. "What about Hannah coming to Mass?"

"She'd be most welcome. Of course, she couldn't go to Communion but then neither can half the congregation who didn't go to confession on Saturday and are dripping with mortal sin on Sunday."

"What about hanging out with her family and the rest of it?"

"No problem there, son. This is America. We all have to get along and the more we understand each other the better it will be for all of us. But, again, I counsel you. Give her up. The odds are this can't end well unless you end it now."

"I understand, Father, and I am going to think about what you've said. But I do love her. I want to ask you for a favor, Father. If this doesn't end, will you come to dinner the night I take her to my mother's house?"

"Not a chance, boyo. Not a chance. We're not all cut out for martyrdom."

Sarajevo

Gavrilo Princip pulled the trigger.

The young Bosnian Serb extremist shot and killed Archduke Franz Ferdinand and his consort on June 28, 1914. The archduke was the presumptive heir to the throne of Austro-Hungary.

Princip was one of six assassins armed and trained by the Serbian Military Intelligence and dispatched to Sarajevo. Serbia intended to carve out an independent state for the South Slavs in the Balkans from a tottering Austro-Hungary.

The assassinations electrified Europe but Austria waited more than three weeks before it moved against Serbia. The Dual Monarchy was determined to crush Serbia. Backed by Germany, it presented Serbia with an ultimatum that Austro-Hungary knew could not be accepted although Serbia came close to doing so.

No matter. On July 28, the Austro-Hungarian Empire declared war on Serbia.

The very next day Britain, which was the only big European nation without conscription, called for international mediation to stop the slide towards all-out war.

No one listened.

That same day Russia, the traditional protector of the Slavs, urged Germany to show restraint while partially mobilizing herself. Germany warned Russia against mobilization and began mobilizing too.

A day later Austrian warships shelled Belgrade, the capital of Serbia.

On July 31, Russia began fully mobilizing despite German demands that she stop.

Instead, the civilized nations of Europe went to their doom like lemmings following each other off a lethal cliff.

During that horrific first week of August: Germany declared

war on Russia; France and Belgium mobilized; Germany declared war on France and invaded Belgium; Great Britain declared war on Germany, a declaration also binding on Canada, Australia, New Zealand, India, and South Africa; Austro-Hungary declared war on Russia; the British Expeditionary Force, 120,000 strong landed in France and the British and French invaded the German colony of Togo in West Africa.

Though Italy was a signatory to the Triple Alliance with Germany and Austro-Hungary, she refused to march. Then less than a year later, lured by the promise of chunks of Austria after the victory, she joined the Allies.

On the other side of the world, Japan, allied to Great Britain since 1902, declared war on Germany and Austro-Hungary on August 25. Japan quickly rolled up Germany's leased territories in China and her island possessions in the Pacific. Japan didn't even have to mobilize. It was a walkover. Getting those islands away from her in the 1940s would cost many thousands of lives.

Woodrow Wilson was quick to proclaim our neutrality and American industry was even quicker to gear up to supply the war needs of Europe.

The British blockade began immediately. Germany's U-Boats put to sea.

Europe went to war singing, garlands on their cannons, each side sure of a triumphant victory by Christmas. By the end of August, it was truly a World War with fighting in Europe, Africa, Asia, the Pacific Islands and on the seven seas.

The bloody war would last more than four years. Seventeen million would die, twenty million would be wounded and the world they knew would be shattered. Everyone's world would be changed.

Gavrilo Princip was captured, tried and convicted of murder by Austro-Hungary but was spared execution because he was not quite twenty years old. He died in prison of tuberculosis seven months before World War I ended.

Flight of the Zeppelins

A beefy Zeppelin with a cauliflower ear was behind the wheel of the big Ford touring car with Sergeant Mickey McGurk riding shotgun. They were in uniform which was unusual for "Zepps."

"Where we headed, Sarge?"

"To City Hall. To pick up the Commissioner."

No further identification was necessary. No more questions were necessary either.

Commissioner Hague's handpicked Zeppelins were his eyes, ears and very strong right arms. The Zepps, as they were quickly nicknamed, got their orders directly from the director of public safety and reported solely to him.

They engendered hatred and fear in a lot of other policeman and with good reason. If a Zepp spotted a cop goofing off, cooping, slovenly in appearance or generally failing to live up to the new high standards set by the commissioner, said cop was on the carpet the next morning. More often than not, he was out the door by noon.

His place taken by a young tough totally committed to becoming a good cop with a willingness to obey orders and with unflinching allegiance to his new boss, Frank Hague.

Hague had already fired scores of policemen and more were leaving each week. Morale in the department was rising as the more obvious misfits were tossed out.

The Zepps were also envied by other policemen who wanted nothing more but to be asked to join their ranks. Lots of cops started to imitate the Zepps. The rate of cracking skulls went up.

The Zepps, most of whom were Irishmen from the Horseshoe, were a cocky bunch with a flair for dressing like their dandy of a boss. They wore straw boaters at a jaunty angle in warm weather and many of them sported derbies when it was cooler. Their work was done in plain clothes for the most part although most people had little trouble identifying them. They donned uniforms for special events such as raids.

Like tonight.

McGurk's car was trailed by two other touring cars holding a dozen uniformed Zepps. They parked in a line behind City Hall motors running, headlamps off. A dozen or so men absolutely silent, fingering their nightsticks.

Mickey climbed the stone stairs to the commissioner's office. Two other uniformed Zepps and the commissioner's secretary greeted him. The secretary slipped into the office.

The door was flung open and out strode Commissioner Frank Hague, director of public safety in Jersey City.

McGurk fell in alongside him. The stairs were wide enough to accommodate them and then some.

"Good evening, Commissioner."

"Good evening, Mickey. How's your mother?"

"She's fine, sir. Still as feisty as ever."

"Good. Tell her I was asking for her. You still going with that girl up in the Heights? What's her name—Hannah?"

"Yes. Kind of. We're still walking out."

"Walking out?" Hague half turned to the Zepp behind him and asked, "What century is this?" The Zepp answered without breaking a smile, "The twentieth, sir."

"Good. I thought the sergeant might be losing track. How you getting along with that father of hers? That Dutch tool and die maker."

"Very good."

"Have you got him in 'the organization' yet?"

"No, sir. I think he'll be for Otto Wittpenn until one of them dies."

"Not to worry. Lots of people vote for me after they're dead."

Hague said that with a straight face. The three Zepps never cracked a smile. Such facts are rarely laughed at.

They reached the automobiles. Hague and McGurk got in the

back seat. The two Zepps crammed in with the driver up front. The driver turned on his headlights. The other cars did so as well.

"Okay, sergeant. Here's what's happening. We are going to shut down the girlie show at the Empire.

"When we get there, have one of your men find a call box and order the precinct to send a paddy wagon and about a dozen extra men. They don't know about the raid. I didn't want some mug to tip off the manager.

"I don't want anybody in the audience arrested unless they give you trouble. Don't take any shit from them, though. Use your nightsticks and send them home. I don't want any of those guys arrested.

"Now I want all the girls crammed into the paddy wagon just as they are. They'll freeze their asses off but that will be a good lesson to them. I want the manager or whoever is in charge of the girlie show arrested, handcuffed and frog-marched out to the squad car. Mickey, did you get in touch with that reporter friend of yours on the Jersey Journal?"

"Yes, I did. I told him I didn't know what the story would be but I thought it would be a good one. He and his photographer are in a car behind ours. I told him to meet us here at City Hall."

"Good work. I want a picture of me in the middle of the stage when I shut that goddamn place down. I want a picture—a picture that can be printed—of the girls going into the paddy wagon and I want a picture of that pimp in handcuffs. You think they can do that?"

McGurk laughed. "I know that photographer. He'll get those shots if he has to hang upside down from the top of the curtain. He lives for that kind of stuff."

"Good. I'll talk to the girls at the precinct. They can find their own way home and they can damn well find their way to a ferryboat within seventy-two hours or I'll have them arrested. Then they can get on that ferry after they've been in jail for thirty days. Okay... okay. Off we go."

Hague asked the driver, "Do you know where the Empire?"

The Zepp, who had practically worn out a seat in the front row of the Empire Burlesque Theatre, hesitated. "I think so, sir.... It's around the corner from All Saints Church, isn't it?"

Hague, who was leading this raid to please the pastor of All Saints Church, said it was.

The commissioner called all burlesque shows "girlie" shows. The chorus girls did show a lot of flesh but not as much as the "coochie coochie" dancer who would bring the show to a climax, so to speak.

Hague intended to end prostitution in Jersey City and drive out what he called "dope fiends" while he was at it.

The commissioner wasn't too wrong in tagging the ladies of the burlesque shows as prostitutes since many—even most—of these "actresses" weren't above a little discreet freelancing. But they were hardly streetwalkers. That didn't matter to Hague. *A whore is a whore.*

The caravan pulled up a block short of the Empire. One Zepp walked quickly to the theatre and went inside, probably flashing his badge to get in free. His job was to signal the others when the chorus line was on stage.

Burlesque shows followed a set pattern: songs, followed by ribald comedians, acrobats, musicians and soloists. Only then did the chorus line kick its way on stage. The chorus sang and danced and, of course, was followed by the exotic, erotic dancer who would bring the all-male audience to a heightened state of attention. Some of the men had newspapers draped across their laps. They were called "newspapermen." Jackie Farrell called himself a "journalist."

The chorus line came on stage kicking high, showing all of their legs, their thighs and bare arms around each other's shoulders, half visible breasts jiggling, little bustles on their rears swaying provocatively; wide smiles pasted universally on their faces. Oblivious to an audience that was hooting and hollering.

The Zepp came out of the theatre and pumped his arm up and down. The caravan glided down the block and blocked the entrance to the theatre. The reporter and his photographer were out of their Model T almost as fast as the Zepps.

Hague remained in the automobile as McGurk briefed his Zepps with the reporter listening in. The photographer fiddled with his equipment.

The reporter tethered himself to McGurk. "How you doing, Jackie?"

"It looks like it is going to be a good night, Mick. What do you want from us?"

McGurk told him and Jackie Farrell, a young police reporter, nodded. He explained things to his grinning photographer as McGurk busied himself with the tactics of the raid.

When all was ready, McGurk saluted Hague who, emerging from the touring car, walked briskly through the lobby and down the center aisle trailed by four Zepps with nightsticks at port arms.

The ushers, who were there to keep the audience in line, suddenly vanished as if they were part of the magician's act. So did the candy butchers.

The girls kept singing and dancing but a murmur was rising from the audience as Hague climbed up the stairs to the right of the stage and strode to the center. He didn't look at the chorus girls. Two Zepps guarded the stairs. Two stood directly below Hague.

"I am the director of public safety of Jersey City."

Hague pointed back at the chorus girls without looking at them. "This is an immoral performance contrary to the laws and customs of Jersey City. What's more, there are juveniles here—boys—being corrupted by these...these strumpets!"

The women, who had stopped dancing, were now muttering in indignation. Hague ignored them. Zepps appeared in both wings.

"Therefore I am closing this theatre until further notice. This show is over. There will be no more girlie shows in Jersey City! Do you hear me, no more! Anyone who fails to obey my orders and those of my policemen will be charged with inciting a riot and sent to the state prison in Trenton for ten years."

The commissioner had no idea what the penalty was for "inciting a riot" but then neither did the audience which immediately fell silent. Policemen were at every exit and in the lobby now. The paddy wagon had arrived and was at the stage entrance behind the theatre.

"Now, I could have every one of you arrested and charged with aiding and abetting this disgraceful performance. But I am not going to do that. I am going to give you a chance to mend your ways. Get out of here. Go home to your wives and mothers. And you might do well to discuss this with your confessor come Saturday."

The audience bolted for the exits as if they were lifeboats.

"And remember! It was Frank Hague who gave you a second chance. I'm your friend, not your enemy."

As soon as the exotic dancer Sultana, a Syrian-American from New York, heard the commotion she slipped out of her working costume, which didn't take long, and into her street clothes, which took longer. She was seated with her costume on her lap and a needle in her hand when a Zepp threw open the door to her dressing room.

"Who are you?"

"I'm the seamstress. Who are you?"

"I'm a police officer. We just shut down this joint. You're out of a job, young lady. You better go home. You don't want to get mixed up in this."

"Oh, my! Heavens, no. Thank you officer. I'll leave at once."

The Zepp, not the brightest one on the squad, did not notice the heavy makeup on Sultana's face as she brushed past him. He was busy looking at her shapely figure.

This night was discussed in many a saloon but not in any kitchen. Wherever those men and boys were supposed to be, it was not at the Empire Theatre.

There had been several bursts of flash powder during Hague's declaration as the photographer made good on the deal. The commissioner was always aware of the photographer and he tried to give him something to work with. He never smiled.

The photographer headed for the paddy wagon as Hague strode slowly up the center aisle which emptied at once. Men still in the other aisles neither looked at him nor spoke to him. They maneuvered to keep their backs to him. He recognized a few of them anyway. Only then did he smile. *These chance sightings might be of some use come election time.*

Once outside, the patrons scattered in every direction. None lingered.

Meanwhile, a considerable crowd of neighbors had formed across the street, held back by cheerful policemen who bantered and joked with them.

When they saw Hague, the neighbors clapped and cheered. In response, he clasped his hands above his head like a triumphant boxer.

As McGurk held the car door open, the pastor of All Saints Church walked up his hand outstretched.

"Good work, Frank! Good work! You did God's work tonight. Yes, indeed."

Hague, who permitted the clergy more informality than most, was at his pious best.

"Thank you, Father. But you should take the credit. You told me about this horrible place."

"Ah, well. There's credit enough for both of us, Frank. You should be mayor. Mark Fagan is a nice enough fellow but he lacks the heart to do what should be done. Not you, Frank. You are the embodiment of the Church Militant."

Hague lifted his index finger to his lips. "Be careful, Father.

The Protestants might hear you. They vote too."

The priest and the commissioner shared a laugh. "No matter, Frank. You can count on my support."

"Father, I appreciate that almost as much as I appreciate your prayers." Neither laughed. "Now, if you will excuse me, I have to get to the precinct and see this through to the end."

"Of course, Frank. Once again, good work."

McGurk climbed into the auto after Hague.

"When the photographer is finished with that pimp take him to the back room of the Fourth Precinct. Don't kill him. Just give him a good beating and make sure he knows why he's getting it. Then take him to the ferry. Make sure he is conscious and can walk. Put him on the ferry. Tell him if he comes back to Jersey City, you will kill him. He'll believe you."

"Right, Commissioner."

Backstage, the Zepps were handling the ladies of the chorus gently and familiarly. Some, obviously, were on a first name basis.

"Nah, Lois. I don't think they're going to charge you, just take your picture and fingerprint you and then let you go."

"I've already been fingerprinted."

"They'll still let you go. But I wouldn't sign any long term lease on your flat. You're for the ferry. You are going to have to get out of town and stay out or else."

"Jesus, Jerry. How am I going to live? What will I do?"

"I don't know. Maybe you can get a job at Minsky's."

"Sure," said Lois, a worried frown cracking her thick makeup. "Can I get my coat? It's cold out."

"Nope. Sorry."

"You bastards."

The photographer shot away as the women were helped into the paddy wagon by the now somber cops. The women, huddled together for warmth, complained and cursed.

There was room for them and a ring of cops in front of the

desk sergeant. The women were still pressed together, not a coat among them.

Hague went up to the desk sergeant's raised platform towering over all. He made eye contact with the women of the chorus.

"I was elected to clean up Jersey City and clean it up I will.

"We don't want your kind here. We won't tolerate your kind here. I don't care what your problems are. They're not mine."

Hague glanced at the precinct clock. "You have exactly seventy-two hours—three days—to clear out of Jersey City. If you don't go, we'll find you. Believe me, we'll find you. You'll do thirty days for soliciting and then we'll put you on the ferry. We'll repeat the process as often as necessary."

"Jail food is better than no food," murmured one woman. "Says who?" hissed another.

"You're going to be photographed and fingerprinted so we can find you if we have to. And then you are going to get out of my city for good."

One young woman, tall, strawberry blonde with blue eyes, very beautiful and clearly Irish, boldly raised her hand. "Mr. Commissioner. I was born in Jersey City. This is my home. I was born in the 'Show."

Frank Hague stared at her for a few seconds. He didn't recognize her.

"Anybody else from Jersey City?" A few hands were raised. Sheepishly. Hague stared again for some for very long seconds.

"All right. Those of you, God help us, who were born in Jersey City, go home to your mothers if they will have you. But you're done with this business and I don't want hear a peep out of you for the rest of your lives."

Hague waved his hand and pointed to the precinct door and said: "As for the rest of you, when the cops are done with you...out! And don't come back."

With that, Frank Hague—looking neither right nor left—

walked out the precinct leaving in his wake some sobbing and much profanity.

The Irish girl said, "My poor mother's dead."

"Then you better find an aunt in a hurry or you're for New York."

"I already have an aunt, thank God."

The Big Ditch

The Panama Canal opened for ship traffic between the Atlantic and Pacific Oceans on August 15, 1914, but there was no great celebration when the workaday cement boat, Ancon, made its way across the fifty mile isthmus.

The grand plans to have an international fleet of warships sail from New York to San Francisco via the canal, slicing 8,000 miles from the voyage, and arriving in time for the Panama Pacific Exposition had to be scrapped. The warships were dispatched elsewhere. What would become World War I had erupted just days earlier in Europe.

President Woodrow Wilson stayed home in Washington, DC, and never did visit the Panama Canal.

The canal itself was one of the wonders of the modern world, built at a cost of what would now be billions of dollars and thousands of workers' lives. But the Americans had done it.

The dream of linking the oceans and avoiding the long and treacherous voyage around the tip of South America dated back to 1534 when the King of Spain ordered a search for a better route between Spain and Peru.

A railroad of sorts was built across the Isthmus of Panama in 1855 thanks to the California gold rush. That helped but not a lot. What was needed was a canal to handle oceangoing ships with cargos measuring thousands of tons or with passengers by the hundreds and thousands.

First came the French in 1881, under the command of Ferdinand de Lesseps, whose workers had dug the sea level Suez Canal joining the Mediterranean to the Red Sea.

But the jungles of Panama, then a province of Columbia, were quite different and more deadly than the sands of Egypt. The French effort ended in 1889 in bankruptcy amidst charges of chicanery and corruption but not before as many as 20,000 workers lost their lives mainly to mosquito borne diseases.

The Spanish-American War demonstrated the American imperial need for a canal and President Theodore Roosevelt meant to have one. Years of dickering and false starts ended in 1903 when the Columbian senate refused to ratify a canal treaty and Roosevelt was informed that Panamanian rebels were ready to revolt against Columbia.

Roosevelt acted. Columbian forces sent to subdue the rebels found their way blocked by American warships. The rebels proclaimed the Republic of Panama on November 3rd and the United State recognized the new state within hours and on November 6th, Panama's new ambassador to the United States signed a treaty giving America the right to build a canal and administer a Canal Zone five miles on each side of it.

Roosevelt's critics, especially the non-interventionists, exploded. One newspaper called it "an act of sordid conquest." Roosevelt was unfazed.

Two of Roosevelt's appointments were brilliant. The first, Colonel George Gorgas, was named chief sanitation officer and vanquished the mosquitoes which carried the deadly scourges of malaria and yellow fever. Despite these successful efforts, most of the 5,000 workers who subsequently died building the canal succumbed to disease. The second, Colonel George W. Goethals, was put in charge building the canal which used 1,000 foot long concrete locks to raise ships up and down 85 feet to a gigantic man-made lake. His workers had to move 200,000,000 cubic yards of dirt and debris to do it.

The cost was about $375,000,000, incredibly, almost six percent lower than the 1907 estimate.

Fortifications cost another $12,000,000 but created a military base that allowed the United States to dominate Central America. The last Marines left Nicaragua in 1933. Panama remained an American protectorate until 1939.

It was left to President Jimmy Carter to return the Canal Zone and the canal to Panama by signing a treaty in 1977 which gave Panama control on December 31, 1999. The transition was and remains trouble free.

The futile opposition to the giveback was fierce and centered on the cry, "We built it; it's ours."

Perhaps, one opponent was more accurate, "It's ours. We stole it fair and square."

Kulturkampf

Mickey McGurk had finished supper at his mother's house and was sitting at the kitchen table enjoying a cup of black, unsweetened tea while his mother cleared the table.

"Say, Ma. What are you doing next Sunday evening?"

Amelia McGurk wiped the oilcloth on the table with a wet dish rag. "I'll be doing what I always do on Sunday night. Nothing. Why?"

"Well, I'd like to come to supper and I want to bring a friend with me."

"Supper it is. You know you don't need an invitation to bring a buddy or two along with you. No trouble at all, I'll just throw some extra potatoes in the pot. Who ya bringing?"

A silent moment, then. "Oh, you don't know her. Just a friend of mine. I'd like you to meet her. That's all."

"Dear Jesus! That's all! Just like that! That's all?"

Mrs. McGurk had squeezed her dishrag so hard, water was dripping on the table's oilcloth. "What's her name? Do I know her family? Where did you meet her? How long have you been going out? How come you're just getting around to introducing her to me?"

McGurk put up both hands. "Whoa, Ma, whoa! This is no big deal. Just supper with a nice girl. I thought you two would hit it off. That's all."

I'll bet it's more than that. I have enough friends. "What's her name and no more shilly-shallying."

"Hannah Ganz and she's from the Heights. You don't know the family."

"Damn right! I don't know anyone named 'Ganz'. What manner of name is that?"

"German."

"Dear Mother of God! German! German! Six million Irish girls in the 'Show and you want to bring a German home to me?"

By this time, Mrs. McGurk had her hands on her hips. Not a good sign. The dishrag was lying limp on the oil cloth. Not moving.

"Ma, Hannah is an American, born right here in Jersey City."

"I don't care if she was born in the stable right next to the Baby Jesus. A German!"

"Ma, isn't your sister married to Fred Wild? Isn't he a Dutchman?"

"That's different. Fred Wild is a decent man. He has a good job, he's a good provider and he's a good Catholic. There's always an exception to the rule. Besides, I'm not talking about Fred Wild. I'm talking about Hannah what's-her-name. I suppose she goes to St. Nicholas with the rest of those heinies."

McGurk looked directly at his mother. "Actually... no."

Amelia McGurk frowned and thought. *She can't go to St. Anne's; the relatives would have told me what was going on. Where else? St. Paul of the Cross? St. John the Baptist? Where else? Dear God, no!* Amelia McGurk, terrified at the possibility, quickly changed the subject.

"No matter."

She looked around. "I'll have to give this place a good cleaning. You know those Germans. You can eat off their floors."

Mickey McGurk was relieved. He was ready to tell his mother that Hannah was Lutheran but he didn't want to—not yet. He'd want a cigarette and a blindfold first.

"Don't go to any trouble, Ma. Hannah's a good sport. I just want you to like her."

Like her? She'll be lucky if I don't dump a pot of boiling water over her square head.

Then Mrs. McGurk had an idea worthy of Machiavelli or a ward leader. "You know, we could make a bit of a party of it. I'll invite your sisters and we'll have cake after supper."

"Oh, no! Nobody but you, me and Hannah. I'll need your

word on that."

"All right. It was just an idea."

McGurk was fully aware that there was not an Irishwoman alive who thought any female—not a Ziegfeld girl—was fit to walk down the street holding hands with her brother. He'd not fall into that trap.

"Besides, it's not like we're engaged or anything. We're just friends."

Mrs. McGurk smiled. "Of course you are, son. Don't worry, I'll make her welcome."

"Thanks, Ma. Well, I got to be going."

"Are you off to see her then?"

"No, Ma. I got to work in the morning. I'm off to bed."

As long as you're in that bed alone. Amelia McGurk kissed her son's cheek.

Mickey McGurk thought, *Sunday was going to be a long, long day. Maybe I can borrow Jimmy's Model T. That would make things easier.*

* * *

He saw Jimmy Cribbins the next day. "Good morning, James! How are you on this fine, beautiful day?"

"James? Uh, oh, you want something, my friend."

Mickey laughed. "As a matter of fact, I do. I know you are working Sunday, so can I borrow that automobile of yours if your fireman buddy hasn't got dibs on it?"

"I'll have you know I own that automobile free and clear. I bought him out. So you need a car on Sunday? Just when I was thinking about getting in the auto renting business too."

Mickey frowned. Jimmy grinned. "Just kidding, pal of mine. Sure, you can borrow the old heap. What's up?"

"I'm going to dinner at Hannah's and then we're going to supper at my mother's."

"So you want the car to get out of town fast?"

"Aw, it won't be that bad. Ma's promised to make her welcome."

"Fill the gas tank before you get there."

Both men laughed. Mickey hadn't told Jimmy he was going to church with the Ganz family too. That was part of the old man's deal. Mickey didn't like it but there it was. Still, he didn't have to blab about it either.

* * *

Mickey pulled the Model T up to the curb in front of the Ganz home. Billy was sitting on the stoop waiting for him.

Mickey looked even better than the car which was gleaming in the morning sunshine.

"Can I sit up front with you, Mickey?"

"Your father sits up front. You go in the back with the ladies."

"Jeez, I always have to sit in the back."

"If your mother hears you say 'Jeez', you won't be able to sit anywhere."

Mickey rang the doorbell as Billy ran through the door. Mickey stood at the open door, literally hat in hand, until Otto Ganz came out.

"Sergeant McGurk! How good to see you. Come in, come in. Have you had breakfast?"

"Yes, sir."

"Good, so have we. I see you have an automobile. Is it yours?"

"No, sir. But I'm saving up for one," said Mickey who hadn't given a thought to buying a car.

"Good. I like thrift in a man. I cannot understand how these American boys work hard all week and then squander their pay on a Saturday night."

"Me either," said Mickey who had squandered with the best of them until he met Hannah. Now he actually did have a bit of money in the Provident Savings Bank.

"Mother! Mother, look who's here!" said Otto Ganz as if McGurk had just wandered by and decided to drop in.

Sophie Ganz was wiping her hands on her apron as she greeted Mickey.

"Mr. Mack Gook, how nice. I expected you for dinner, but you're early. We are just getting ready to go to church..."

"I thought I'd go with you, if that is all right."

Silence. Hannah, who was standing next to her mother, sucked in her breath and held it.

"Ja, of course. Everyone is welcome at Bethany Church. The pastor will enjoy meeting you," said Sophie Ganz who had a vision of an instant conversion until she remembered that Pastor Schoenfelder's sermons were—in a word—boring. Usually, she had no idea what the man was talking about. But fifteen or twenty minutes into his discourse, it was amusing to watch the wives jab nodding husbands with sharp elbows. Her own man got his share of jabs.

Still, he's bound to be impressed with the choir which was really good. When the choir sang "Ein Feste Burg ist Unser Gott" the stained glass windows rattled. The soloist was good too although she had to avoid the high notes she just couldn't reach.

Billy led the parade into church followed by his sister, mother, McGurk and his father. The church was about a fourth of the size of St. Anne's on the Boulevard. No statues. A cross, not a crucifix, on the flower-flanked altar. No kneelers.

Okay, thought Mickey, *we either sit or stand. One less thing to worry about.*

McGurk might have been interested in the particulars of the church but the congregation had but one particular interest—him.

They all knew each other and a few of the men recognized him out of uniform. He didn't look German or Scandinavian. He looked Irish. An Irish Lutheran? But one thing was quickly deduced, he—whoever he was—was there because of Hannah.

Several young men thought, *The Iceberg has struck again. Poor bastard!*

McGurk got through the ups and downs of the service just a nanosecond or so behind the Ganzs. He shared a hymnal with Otto whose voice was deep, loud and just a bit off-key. McGurk didn't know any of the hymns.

Oddly enough, he was one of the few in the congregation who understood and actually appreciated Pastor Schoenfelder's twenty-five minute sermon which explored con-substantiation. Of course, he didn't agree with it since Catholics believe in trans-substantiation. But he didn't intend to bring up that centuries-old debate with a living soul.

The service ended without McGurk committing any major gaff. There had been no communion service which was a great relief.

The congregation gathered for coffee and assorted goodies from a nearby German bakery.

The men tended to separate from the women but one middle-aged woman, unable to contain her curiosity, walked right up to him.

"Welcome to Bethany Church. I don't think I've ever seen you here before... Mister...Mister?"

"McGurk. Michael McGurk. No, I've never been to Bethany before. It was a lovely service."

"I do hope you'll join us regularly, Mr. McGurk. Where do you go to church now?"

"Oh, you know. Here and there."

With that, Sophie Ganz put herself directly in front of the woman almost blocking her view of the flustered Mr. McGurk.

"Mr. Mack Gook is a friend of our family, Gertrude. Und, as it happens, he is a Catholic. I believe he goes to St. Anne's on the Boulevard."

Sophie, frowning slightly, her eyes daring Gertrude to say just one word, just one word more, addressed Mickey without turning. "Isn't that right, Michael?"

"It is, Mrs. Ganz. It is."

Gertrude, smiling wanly, said, "Isn't that nice. Now you must excuse me, I have to say hello to Mrs. Hoffman over there. She's been sick, you know."

"Of course," said Sophie, "give her my regards."

Off Gertrude went to spread the word, a process that took far less time than Pastor Schoenfelder's sermon and which proved much more engaging.

Heads kept turning in their direction but no one who stopped to pass the time with the Ganz family mentioned the spreading scandal. But then someone must have whispered something to the pastor, who headed their way as the entire Ganz family, save Billy, stiffened.

"Ah, Mr. McGurk, I believe. Welcome to our church."

"Thank you, sir."

The pastor couldn't resist either. "Tell me, what did you think of my sermon on the Body and Blood of Christ?"

He expected McGurk to fumble, mumble and at best resort to a platitude or two. That's what his congregants usually did.

"Well, Pastor, I'm not trained theologically and I'm certainly not equipped to discuss that subject with a scholar such as yourself." The minister was not taken in by such a weak attempt at flattery. "But the Jesuits, who taught me, came down on the side of trans-substantiation."

The minister nodded his head. "Naturally. But as an intelligent man, doesn't it make more sense to believe that while the Body and Blood of the Savior is there, so too is the bread and wine? Side by side—as everyone can see."

If I was an intelligent man I wouldn't be standing here when I could be in a waterfront dive being thumped by a bartender.

"Certainly, it makes sense. Trans-substantiation defies reason. That's why we think it is so miraculous."

The pastor shook his head; he'd heard that old argument before. "Well, thank you for paying attention. I appreciate that. Please feel free to visit us again. You're welcome."

"Thank you, sir. Well, Pastor, as Thomas Aquinas said, 'Don't worry too much about theology. It'll all be made clear to you when you die.'"

The pastor shook his head again and made his goodbyes to the Ganz family. To Sophie he said softly, "*Keine Sorge, es ist vielleicht nicht ernst.*"

Mickey, who took two years of German at St. Peter's, understood him.

Sorry to disappoint you, Pastor. It is serious.

Dinner went well. Mrs. Ganz and Hannah prepared sauerbraten, spätzle and red cabbage all washed down with a schooner of good beer.

McGurk offered to help with the dishes but Mrs. Ganz, taken back a bit, said, "No, no. Hannah and I will do them. You go have a cigar with Mr. Ganz. On the stoop."

With Mickey safely out of hearing, Mrs. Ganz, who was washing, turned to Hannah who was drying.

"The nerve of that verdammt Gertrude Steinel! Who does she think she is? That loafer of a husband of hers drunk every Saturday night and she thinks she can laugh at my family! We'll see about that. And that goes for the rest of those plattdeutsch bitches too!"

"Mother!"

"Don't 'mother' me, Hannah. They better not laugh at me or mine!"

Hannah saw her moment. "You mean Michael McGurk too?"

"Ja! At least until you have the good sense to walk away from him. But until then, Michael Mack Gook may be a papist, but he's my verdammt papist!"

"Mother!"

There's still a lot of time to kill before supper at Chez McGurk, thought Mickey over his cigar with Otto Ganz.

"Are you all right?" asked the older man. "That was some going over you got in church. Even the pastor. Gott im Himmel!"

"That was no problem, Herr Ganz." Mickey had started to use the German honorific. "The people were nice, really. And your pastor was very considerate. Besides, I am different. It wouldn't be reasonable not to expect them to react to that. They'll get used to me."

"Oh, so you are going to go to Bethany like a good German?"

"Well, once in a while."

"Ja. That's all I asked. Just to get to know us." He sounded disappointed.

"I thought I'd take Hannah to a picture show. You know. 'The Perils of Pauline.' Maybe a photoplay."

Otto sighed. "A nice dark theatre, ja?"

"Maybe Billy would like to go with us. He could sit in the middle," said Mickey.

Otto looked at Mickey quizzically. "Why not? I have to keep my end of the bargain."

McGurk said, "I'll have plenty of time to get him home before supper at Ma's."

"Ja. When do Sophie and I get to meet that mother of yours?"

"Soon. You and Ma will get together soon." *Say when the polar icecaps melt.*

The picture show went well. Billy, plied with both popcorn and candy, was urged to sit up front where he could really see the action. Hannah and Mickey settled in the middle of the last row held hands, smooched, and, after a while Mickey's arm fell asleep across her shoulders.

Mickey was aware of tightness in his crotch. So was Hannah. Both were content. Sort of.

* * *

Mickey's mother lived on the second floor left of a six family house, still in the 'Show but on a much better street than he grew up on. She took in boarders who were instructed to stay away until at least ten o'clock that night or else.

Amelia answered Mickey's knock. She was dressed in her best dress. Mickey knew this since his mother had long since told him, "Remember. This is the dress I want to be buried in."

She wore her graying hair back in a bun and there was a brooch at the neck of her dress. Her hands were red from scrubbing.

"Come in! Come in! You are welcome in my home. Hannah, isn't it? I've heard so much about you!"

Mickey had told her virtually nothing but he suspected Irish relatives had been quizzing German neighbors up in the Heights.

"I'm glad that lout of mine was on time. Supper's just about ready. I hope you are hungry?"

Hannah, who was still recovering from dinner, said brightly, "Yes, I am, Mrs. McGurk."

"Good, good. Let's go right to the table."

Mickey helped Hannah to her seat.

His mother said, "You're having a good effect on him; he usually has the manners of a teamster."

Hannah blushed but smiled anyway.

Supper was the best Amelia could offer. Pot roast, brown gravy, mashed potatoes, canned peas and sliced store-bought white bread. All prepared on a cast iron, coal fired stove which heated a reservoir of water too.

"Would you like a glass of beer with supper, Hannah?"

Hannah and Mickey hadn't thought to discuss that. "Yes. A small glass would be nice. Thank you."

"I know you Germans like a glass of beer and, believe it or not, so do the Irish."

All hands laughed as Amelia pulled out a quart bottle of Trommer's out of the icebox. The bottle cap was off and an exjelly glass full of beer was in front of Hannah quite quickly. The glass didn't hold a head. Neither did Mickey's or Amelia's. All the glasses came from the same grocery shelf down the street.

Hannah tasted the food, made yummy sounds and said, "Everything is delicious, Mrs. McGurk. Really delicious. You shouldn't have gone to all that trouble."

"Ah! No trouble at all. We always eat like this on Sunday night, don't we, Michael?"

"We sure do, Ma," said Mickey remembering the usual fare of a ham sandwich and a glob of grocer's potato salad.

Supper went as well as dinner. As Amelia got up to clear the table, Hannah rose and said, "Let me help you with the dishes, Mrs. McGurk."

"Oh, no. You're a guest here. You don't do dishes."

"Please. I do dishes at home. I would feel terrible if I didn't help you. Please, let me help."

Mrs. McGurk knew that allowing Hannah to help would close the distance between them somewhat. She looked at Hannah's pretty, pleading face. She relented.

"All right, Hannah. We'll do the dishes and we'll have a nice talk without his nibs hanging on our every word. That's no fun."

To Mickey: "Go downstairs and smoke a cigarette or two."

"I don't smoke cigarettes."

"Then smoke a cigar. Or walk around the block. Or climb a tree. Out!"

Mrs. McGurk washed and Hannah dried. "Now then. I hear you work at Colgate's."

"I do."

"What's it like?" Mrs. McGurk didn't know anyone who worked there despite its constant odiferous presence in the neighborhood.

"Pretty much like a clerk's job anywhere I guess. But a funny thing happened on Monday."

"Really? What happened?"

"There was no work. I got there. The gate was locked. There was a hand printed sign on it that said 'No Work Today.' Nobody knew what was going on."

"What was going on?" asked Amelia, who already knew.

"Well, we went back to work on Tuesday and the guard told us what had happened. On Monday, before the factory opened, there was a line of men waiting. The guard told them we weren't hiring that day and they said they weren't looking for work. They said they were the health inspector, the plumbing inspector, the electrical inspector, the fire inspector and some other kinds of inspector that I don't remember. The guard let them in and a half an hour later the plant was shut down. I don't what happened then except that the plant superintendent, Mr. Swanson, met with somebody at City Hall and we went back to work the next day."

That would be Frank Hague, God love him.

"So was anything changed when you went back?" asked Amelia, who again already knew.

Hannah thought. "Yes. Now that I think of it, there was. There had always been a sign by the guard shack that said 'No Catholics Need Apply.' The sign was gone."

"So what do you think of that?" asked Amelia.

"I think it was about time."

You're not going to make it easy for me, are you, young lady?

Buy It Up or Blow It Up

Count Johann von Bernstorff, the Ambassador to the United States of America and Mexico, was on leave in Germany when the heir to the Austro-Hungarian crown was assassinated in Sarajevo.

He received his instructions and $150,000,000 in German Treasury notes from his foreign minister, Arthur Zimmermann.

"War with Great Britain may break out any day," said Zimmermann. "You are to sail from Holland but it is possible the British Navy may intercept your ship anyway. You know what to do if that happens?"

"Yes, Your Excellency. I am to make for the side opposite the boarding party and drop the weighted suitcase with the Treasury notes into the ocean."

"Correct. Try to make sure no one sees you do it. We can print more."

Zimmermann's instructions preventing the Treasury notes from falling into British hands were crystal clear but how they were to be used was more ambiguous. Deliberately so.

Von Bernstorff, ambassador since 1908, was trusted by his superiors. He was an able diplomat, a popular figure in Washington and a man with a nimble mind.

Germany expected Woodrow Wilson to declare and enforce America's neutrality.

"The man's a dunce when it comes to foreign affairs," said Zimmermann. "He may huff and puff but he will never go to war no matter what we do. Besides, the war may be over before Wilson finds out it was declared."

The ambassador smiled at the minister's little joke but he did not share his low opinion of the American president.

Von Bernstorff had met and had lunch with Wilson when he was president of Princeton University and the ambassador was receiving an honorary degree.

He found Wilson to be highly intelligent and obsessed with domestic affairs. He was stiff, not very gregarious. The ambassador was surprised when he was elected governor of New Jersey but not stunned when he became president of the United States, given the split among the Republicans. He hoped to take advantage of their brief acquaintance when he returned to Washington.

Zimmermann said his chief task would be to keep America neutral if she couldn't be persuaded to join the Central powers.

"After all," said Zimmermann, "America has already fought two wars against England. Why not a third?"

The ambassador, diplomatically silent, put no credence in that notion.

Germany was aware of America's industrial potential and it fully expected it to start producing massive amounts of war materials, especially munitions.

"Corner the market on munitions, if you can," said Zimmermann.

The ambassador couldn't resist. "What about the British Navy? Will our High Seas Fleet be able to prevent it from blockading our coasts?"

"Probably not," said Zimmermann. The Allied blockade would prevent Central Powers' ships from leaving America too.

"Then Great Britain, France and Russia will be able to buy and ship American munitions at will while any I buy will sit on a dock unable to get to Germany."

"I do not think that will happen, Herr Ambassador. But it is conceivable. If you cannot buy up those munitions, then blow them up."

"Sabotage?" asked von Bernstorff.

"Yes, if that is called for," said Zimmermann.

"How will we do that? There are only four of us in the Embassy and that chemical fellow in Hoboken."

"You will think of something. We send you help when we can," said Zimmermann, ending the interview.

The ambassador sailed for America two days before Great Britain declared war on Germany.

His voyage was uneventful and his commercial attaché had no difficulty converting the German Treasury notes into American currency, bonds and securities. At a bit of a discount, of course; America was a vigorously capitalist country. Everything, it seemed, was for sale.

More than ninety German ships already in or heading for American ports were interned there for the duration of the war. British and French warships prowled at the three mile limit keeping them bottled up.

One such arrived later than most. This German merchant ship had been supplying German commerce raiders at sea until engine trouble forced her to limp into Chesapeake Bay.

The Allied warships there were scrupulous about checking on any vessel leaving the Bay but they paid no attention to a scruffy tramp, flying the Dutch flag, coming in.

Sometime later, its captain, Frederick Hinsch, would present the ambassador with his greatest triumph frightening both him and millions of Americans.

Murder Most Foul

Frank Hague and Nat Kenny were still neighbors although neither lived in the slums of the Horseshoe any longer.

They lived in elegant brownstones off Hamilton Park. A quiet, safe neighborhood. A good place to raise children. Frank Hague Jr. was twelve now, and his adopted sister, Peggy, was younger.

On this night, the blocks surrounding the park were thick with taxis, horse drawn hacks and with automobiles looking for a place to park. The people came and entered Nat Kenny's brownstone. Two uniformed policemen were at the door to greet them and screen them as well. The people muttered responses. Somber, they were. No wonder.

They came for a wake. Kenny's elder son, Ted, was dead. Murdered.

The parlor and the dining room had been cleared of furniture. Ted Kenny's closed coffin was in the parlor against the three, tall, heavily curtained, front windows. A kneeler, flanked by candles was in front of the casket. Flowers filled the front part of the room. Mass cards were stacked high on a nearby table.

There were easy chairs in front for Nat Kenny and his wife. The rest of the room and the dining room were filled with wooden folding chairs. Except for a handful of men, it was women who sat on the hard chairs. Nat Kenny was not next to his grieving wife.

The door to the spacious kitchen was closed. Inside, the men smoked, drank, laughed softly and talked politics.

Kenny and Frank Hague were together, an empty circle around them insuring privacy.

"So, Nat, is our good mayor handling the arrangements?"

Jersey City Mayor Mark Fagan was an undertaker. "Good Lord, no. Fagan's a Republican, Frank."

"So I've heard."

Kenny chuckled. "No, McLaughlin's handling it."

Hague said, "Well, God knows, the Irish have undertakers to spare. We manage to keep all of them in business. Nat, I can't tell you how sorry I am for your troubles."

"Thank you, Frank. I know you are."

"I promise you this, Nat. We'll get the guy that did this to Teddy. Don't worry about that."

"Ah, Frank. It won't bring him back, will it? But maybe it will be a comfort to his mother. And to me too, I guess. I can't imagine why this happened. I didn't think Ted had any enemies."

"We all have enemies, Nat."

"You know McLaughlin didn't get Ted's body until yesterday. They had to do an autopsy. They said it was the law. Do you know what they found, Frank?"

"I do not," said Hague, who did.

"His ears were mangled. They said the killer stuck a chisel or a railroad spike into his ears, Frank. After he was dead."

"Jesus, Mary and Joseph," said Hague.

"That's not what killed him. Somebody stuck a knife or something into his temple and right into his brain. Who would do that? What kind of a man would do something like that?"

"I don't know, Nat."

"Sure, we've all seen a man beaten to death or even shot. But to stick a knife into his brain and then mutilate his ears, who does that?"

"We'll find out, Nat, we'll find out and then we'll find him," said the commissioner of public safety.

"Ah, Frank, I'm sick of it. I'm sick of talking about it. I rely on you to find Ted's killer."

"You certainly can rely on me, old friend." Hague meant it.

Nat Kenny had been looking to find someone to run for ward constable back in 1899 and had a conversation with an ambitious young man named Frank Hague.

"I want to run, Mr. Kenny, but I don't have a dime."

Kenny had stared at him for a minute, evaluating him. Then he reached for a cigar box under the bar. He counted out $75, more money that Hague had ever seen.

"Is this enough?"

"Yes, sir," said the soon to be constable who never forgot his benefactor.

Now, Hague looked around the room at the men at Ted's wake. "You know, Nat, the loss of Ted is going to hurt the organization in the Second Ward. I know you've been grooming him to take over someday."

"I was that, Frank." Kenny hesitated. "Frank, no one could have loved Ted more than I did. But that's his father talking. When it came to politics, the boy had shortcomings."

"Shortcomings?"

"Oh, yes. Shortcomings. Probably my fault. The way I brought him up. I wanted him to have it easier than you and I did. I spoiled that boy. He was arrogant, Teddy was. He thought he was better than anyone else. Our people hate that. You have to be one of them. It doesn't matter if you're rich, so long as you are one of them."

Hague, who was on his way to becoming rich, nodded approval.

"You know, Teddy was a bit of a bully in school. He stayed that way, God help him. He'd talk you to death if you were bigger than him but if he had you by twenty or thirty pounds the argument was apt to be short. It didn't help that he was good at everything he touched. A good student. A reverent altar boy. A fair hand with the girls. A great baseball player.

"Did you know he had a tryout with the Skeeters a few years ago? They offered him a contract. He turned them down. He told me he didn't want to spend all that time on the road every summer. To tell you the truth, I was disappointed. I could see myself in the stands cheering for my boy, fans slapping me on the back. It wouldn't have done any harm politically either.

"But for all that, Frank, I think a lot of our people saw through him. They knew he was a fake. He didn't care about them. He just cared about himself."

"Nat, Nat. You're being too hard on the boy."

"Oh, I wouldn't say any of this to anybody else, Frank, certainly not to his mother. The boy was a disappointment, Frank."

"I'm sorry for that, Nat, and I'm sorry for your troubles."

Hague nodded to a young man across the kitchen who returned a smile and a salute. "What about your other boy, Johnny?"

"Ah, now there's a comer, Frank. And I'll not be sorry to lean more on him than I have."

John V. Kenny was short and thin. He was called "John V." or "The Little Guy" to differentiate him from the dozen or so other John Kennys living in the 'Show.

His father waved him over. "Johnny, say hello to Frank Hague. You've met before, haven't you?"

"We certainly have," said Hague, shaking hands with the young man. "I've had my eye on him for a long time, Nat. I'm sorry for your troubles, Johnny."

"Thank you, Commissioner," said young Kenny, looking up at the taller Hague.

"I know you're doing good work in the Second, Johnny. What else are you up to?"

"I've got my own business now, Commissioner, washing and cleaning passenger cars for the railroads."

"That pays well, does it?"

"It does. And I have a half a dozen men working for me now and I've just hired a foreman to make sure the work goes well. That'll give me even more time to work for the organization."

"That sounds grand, Johnny. When this is all over, why don't you make an appointment with my secretary and come over to see me in City Hall. We can talk."

Nat beamed. The baton would be passed when his race was over.

Some days earlier McGurk had been summoned to his "uncle's" office. "Mickey, get down to Skeeter Park. Nat Kenny's kid has been killed. They just found his body there."

"Which kid?"

"Ted."

"How'd he die?"

"How the hell should I know? That's why I want you down there. I want to know everything that's going on. And I want to know the minute you know. Call me. Nat Kenny is important. Did you know Ted?"

"Sort of. He was a couple of years ahead of me at St. Mike's. Yeah, I knew him."

"Sounds like he wasn't a friend."

"He wasn't. I didn't like him."

"Why not?"

"I don't know. One time he was picking on one of my kid cousins and I told him to pick on someone his own size."

"What happened?"

"He laughed and backed down. I kind of lost track of him. Until today, that is."

"Birddog this, Mickey, it's important to me."

"Right, Commissioner."

The cops on the scene weren't thrilled to see a sergeant from the Zeppelin Squad walking towards them across the baseball diamond at Skeeter Park. But they already knew whose body they were standing around and knew it was just a matter of time until someone connected to the commissioner showed up.

In fact, they had avoided doing anything substantive until he—whoever he was—showed up.

"Good to see you, Sergeant," said Tony Aiello, one of the first Italian detectives on the Jersey City force.

"Hello, Tony—and it's Mickey. Are you in charge?"

"I was until you showed up, Sergeant...Mickey."

"You still are. I'm no detective. I'll be sort of a liaison officer. If you need something or somebody, I'll make sure you get it. As you can imagine, the commissioner is taking a personal interest in this case. Nat Kenny is an important man."

"I know. And his kid isn't just another corpse, right?"

"I can see why they made you a detective, Tony. What have you got?"

Tony grinned and then his face turned serious. "Not much, Mickey. He has a small hole on the side of his head. Probably shot with a .22. Maybe one of those single shot pistols everybody carries around. Although people usually shoot themselves in the foot with them, I never heard of one being used to murder somebody."

Aiello pointed across the field. "I don't know where he was shot, but he was dragged across the grass, across the diamond and dumped here. I don't know what to make of his ears."

Mickey bent to take a closer look. Ted Kenny's dead eyes stared up at nothing. The skin and tissue were badly torn on both ears but there was almost no blood.

"Wow. That's different."

"Yeah. I get all the easy ones. Somebody—probably the killer or killers—brought him here from wherever he was killed but why they did that I don't know. It wasn't as though they wanted to hide the body. The groundskeeper saw the stiff the minute he walked onto the field."

"So you're clueless?"

"Mickey, please."

Both laughed. "Tony, you said killers. Why not one killer?"

"Maybe it was one killer. But Teddy there was a pretty big boy. I figure he was at least a hundred seventy five pounds. That's a lot of dead weight to haul all over the place."

"I take it you didn't find a cartridge case."

"No. But you wouldn't with a single shot .22. It stays in the chamber."

"Two sets of footprints?"

"No set of footprints. Dragging the body through them wiped them out."

"So what's next, Tony?"

"Well, Teddy boy has a date with the morgue. They'll have to do an autopsy on him. We'll search around and try to find something that will help us and then it's beating on doors trying to piece the case together."

McGurk asked, "Are you sure it wasn't robbery?"

"His wallet was on him. There was $25 in fives and singles in it."

"Really?"

"Yeah. The kid on the beat who got here first is brand new. And besides, you never know when a Zeppelin might float by."

* * *

A couple of days passed with Tony talking to friends and relatives of Ted Kenny, trying to get a picture of the victim. Mickey was with him but usually kept quiet while the detective made his inquiries.

"We're not doing too well," said Tony. "Maybe the coroner will have something for us."

The coroner did. "I thought he was shot too when I first saw him. But he wasn't. There was no bullet in his brain. The killer shoved something long, thin and pointy through his temple and into his brain. Death was instantaneous. He didn't suffer for more than a second. He wasn't dead much more than twelve hours when I got my hands on him."

Tony said, "Long, thin, and pointy."

"Probably a good sized ice pick. That makes hole like a .22."

This was not good news. Lots of criminals favored ice picks as a weapon and that meant the Kenny case might be even more complicated than they thought.

Tony asked, "What about his ears? What caused that?"

"The scientific answer to that question is: you got me, pal. It was something metal, maybe an inch or so wide. A chisel. A railroad spike. Something like that."

"Oh great. All we got to do is find an ice pick and a railroad spike on somebody and we've got our man," said Tony. "Anything else?"

"Yes. Although, I'm not sure how this helps either. He had a couple of rough wood splinters in his right cheek and there was a lot of sawdust on the front of his jacket."

"Sawdust. Only in the front?"

"Yes. There was nothing in the back but dirt. Probably from where you found him."

Tony said, "Okay. Well, thanks, Doc."

"Good luck, gentlemen. I think you'll need it."

* * *

Mickey and Tony sat nursing cups of coffee in a little place on Montgomery Street.

"Mick. Are you sure the commissioner wouldn't like you to take over this case? I could go back to doing what I do best. Making beautiful Italian babies. I wouldn't be offended."

"Not a chance, Tony. In case you haven't noticed, none of your Irish colleagues are beating down the door trying to get in on this case."

"I noticed. All right. What have we got? Ted Kenny gets himself killed sometime Friday night somewhere. His killer sticks an ice pick in his brain and gouges out his ears with a railroad spike. Teddy gets splinters in his cheek and sawdust on the front of his jacket. Then he or they haul him away somehow and take his body to Skeeter Park and drag him across the infield. Teddy is dumped face up between home plate and first base with $25 in his wallet. That's what we got."

"Yeah," said Mickey, "the poor bastard didn't even get to first base."

Tony's head snapped towards Mickey. "What did you say?"

"Huh? I just said, he didn't get to first base."

"Hold that thought. Didn't that cousin of his tell us he was sweet on some girl over on Monmouth Street?"

"Yes."

"I wonder if his sweetie is an Italian? And if she is, does she have a brother? And could this brother be sending the world a message while he administers the proverbial ounce of prevention?"

"What do you mean, Tony?"

"He didn't get to first base with the sister and the brother will make sure he doesn't get another chance to try again."

"Oh, I get it."

"Let's go, Sergeant."

After a few more questions were asked of a few more women, Tony and Mickey were seated at the kitchen table at a flat on Monmouth Street with Josephine Morelli and her highly suspicious widowed mother.

"Now, Josephine. Did you know Teddy Kenny well?"

Josephine glanced quickly at her mother before she answered. "No. Not well. I saw him a few times here and there but we weren't romantic or anything."

Her mother rolled her eyes. Her lips couldn't be tightened further.

"I see," said Detective Aiello. "Did Teddy know your brothers too?"

"I don't understand. I don't have any brothers."

"Of course not. I meant family members. You know, like cousins or uncles. People like that. We're just trying to get a good idea of what Teddy was like."

"He was sweet. But no one in my family knew him."

Her mother glared at Josephine and, in broken English, said, "That's a right, Mr. Detective. I don't know that Ted. If I do, she don't know him either. Nice people no get themselves killed. He was not a nice man. No."

Dead end. Tony and Mickey sat down to think it out again.

"Okay. Let's deal with the sawdust.

"Where could he have picked up sawdust on the front of his jacket but not on the back?"

Mickey answered, "A sawmill obviously. A carpenter's shop. Lots of factories. Anywhere where they make furniture. Or caskets. Or pallets."

"How about saloons?" asked Tony Aiello.

"Saloons. Of course. I hope you'll still talk to me when you're chief of detectives."

"I wish. Lots of saloons still put sawdust down on the floors."

"Yes, but those floors are in pretty good shape," said Mickey. "They have some rummy clean and maybe polish them every so often. That wouldn't account for the rough wood splinters in his cheek."

"Right. What about in the cellars where they store the beer barrels? I've seen duckboards down there and they're pretty rough."

McGurk said, "All right. But that means they kill him there. Drag him across the duckboards to pick up the splinters, then haul him upstairs and then drag him face dawn through the sawdust and then take him to Skeeter Park somehow."

"You know what, Mickey? We're making these killers work too hard. They're going to go on strike. Let's take it a piece at a time. We'll start with the saloons."

"Nat Kenny's first."

There were forty saloons in the 'Show alone. They were on the fourth when a man pushed through swinging doors. He was balancing a big slab of ice wrapped in burlap on his right shoulder, steadying it with his right hand. In his left he held a pair of ice tongs.

"Hiya, Mickey. How's it going?"

"Better, Tommy. Much better now."

"Glad to hear it. See ya."

Aiello said nothing. He just stared at the iceman as he went around the bar to deliver his ice.

"Sweet Jesus. An ice man killed Ted Kenny," said Mickey McGurk.

"That's the man," said Tony Aiello. "Stuck an ice pick in him. Hauled him away in his ice wagon face down. Unloaded him. Took his ice tongs, jammed them in Teddy's ears and dragged him across the infield. Left him there, and galloped off into the sunset, his ice wagon bouncing behind him."

"But why?"

"Who knows?" said Tony. "Maybe his horse will tell us when we find him. Okay. Our job just got a lot easier. There can't be more than a half dozen ice companies Downtown. We'll find out who was working Friday and go from there."

There were nine ice companies but they got lucky on their first stop.

"Yeah. Billy Cunningham was working that Friday. His route goes right up Montgomery Street, past Skeeter Park, up the hill and ends with the saloons on Bergen Square."

Tony asked, "What does he do when he's done with his route?"

"He heads for the barn. He takes care of his horse, cleans the wagon, does a bit of paperwork and goes home."

"What did he do that Friday?"

"I don't know. He was late so I went home. That happens sometimes. The saloons take lots of ice on Friday night. You know, for Saturday. Saturday's their big night."

Mickey said, "Okay. Is Billy out on his route now?"

"No. He quit a couple of days ago. Said he was tired of cleaning the horse. Billy said he was leaving town. He was going to hop a freight and try his luck out West. Say, what's this all about?"

Tony said, "Nothing serious. We just want to talk to Billy. We think he might have seen something Friday night. That's all."

Mickey, Tony and two more detectives headed for Cunningham's neighborhood. When they had picked up what information that was easily available Tony and Mickey knocked on the door to the flat where Billy lived with his mother, another in the long line of widows in the 'Show.

"We're looking for Billy, Mrs. Cunningham."

"He ain't here. He's gone away. Why do you want to see him anyway?"

"Nothing important, Mrs. Cunningham. Do you know where he is?" asked Aiello.

"No. But he said he'd write when he gets there. I think he's going out West somewhere."

Mickey said, "Well, I wish him good luck. I hear there are lots of jobs in California. Is that where he's going?"

"I don't know. Someplace out West."

Aiello looked around. "It looks like you are going to need some luck yourself, Mrs. Cunningham. How are you going to get by while he's looking for work out there?"

"Oh, I do all right," she said "My daughters will help out." Pointing to a bundle of garments she said, "And I do piece work, you know."

Aiello had about a dozen relatives who did piece work and he knew it paid in pennies, not dollars.

He said, "All right. Sorry to bother you, Mrs. Cunningham. Tell Billy we said 'hello' when you hear from him. Goodbye, now."

"I will. Watch your step when you go out. There a brick loose on the stoop."

"We will, thank you."

Mickey and Tony regrouped. "So do you think our Billy is out

West with Buffalo Bill, Mickey?"

McGurk snorted. "He may be a killer but he is not going to leave his mother in a lurch like that. And she knows it."

McGurk imitated the widow. "'Watch out for the loose brick on the stoop.' That's not how a mother should react when the cops show up looking for her baby boy. He's around here someplace. Certainly not in the 'Show. Maybe not in Jersey City. But he's here somewhere close."

"You know, Mickey. You'd make a pretty good detective yourself if you Zepps weren't so good at clubbing people."

"Thanks."

* * *

Tony and Mickey were sharing a beer with one of the Cunninghams' all knowing neighbors in a room back of a saloon. That's where women and "families" had to go now that the city passed an ordinance forbidding women to drink at the bar in saloons. Frank Hague pushed for that ordinance to the vast satisfaction of the city's wives who wanted their husbands chaste if not sober.

"That's a lovely family. The Cunninghams. I knew Billy at St. Michael's," said Mickey McGurk, who hadn't heard of him until a few days before.

"Then you were in the same class as Ted Kenny too," said Mrs. McGrath.

Aiello bit his lip. She continued, "Billy and Ted were great friends. He was always talking about Teddy. In fact, they went to the ball game together not three weeks ago. I thought it was a great thing. Billy being nothing but an iceman and Ted being such an important man, what with his father and all. I know there's some who think Teddy is stuck up. But they'd change their tune if they knew about Ted and Billy. They would. What a terrible thing, him being killed. What kind of madman would do that? Have you caught him yet?"

"We're getting close Mrs. McGrath. Very close."

Mickey changed the subject. "Say, doesn't Mrs. Cunningham have some relatives living out of town?"

"She does. Her sister. She lives in Newark. In the Ironbound. They're very close."

"Of course, the sister."

Mickey snapped his fingers twice. "Missus... Missus..."

"Capparelli. She married some guinea out there. No offense."

"None taken," said Aiello.

"He's a very nice man," said Mrs. McGrath, trying to make amends. "Or so I am told. I never met him."

"That's right. Paul Capparelli," said Mickey.

"No. Peter Capparelli."

Within the hour Mickey was on his way to Hague's office.

The Learning Curve

Money wasn't the problem; finding competent people to blow up things was.

The military and naval attachés at the German Embassy in Washington had no experience with sabotage but orders were orders.

Berlin had ordered them first to recruit anarchists to do the work and then a month later demanded that the Canadian railways be crippled.

Things did not go well at first.

Asked one anarchist of another on the West Coast, "Did you read about that explosion in that railroad tunnel in Canada?"

"I did."

"What do you say we go to the Krauts and tell them we did it? It might mean a nice payday."

"Do you think they will believe us?"

"Why not? They can't get into Canada to investigate. Blowing things up. That's what they offered to pay us to do, isn't it?"

It was. The German counsel paid up.

Paul Koenig, chief detective for the Hamburg-American line, set up a sabotage net of sorts on the East Coast as ordered by the military attaché.

In 1900, a pair of Irish-Americans, members of Clan na Gael in Buffalo, tried to destroy Canada's Welland Canal which links Lake Erie to Lake Ontario. The damage they caused was slight but they got life in prison for their efforts.

The Germans thought they'd have a crack at it. A German soldier-of-fortune was given plans to the canal and dynamite by other Irish-Americans and off he went. The plot failed. The canal was well guarded.

There were some small successes. The Roebling wire and cable plant in Trenton was dynamited on New Year's Day, 1915.

An obvious industrial accident, said the press. A few other blasts were attributed to the same cause. Such fires, explosions and other mishaps were frequent in early twentieth century America. Corsair capitalism was hard on workers and equipment. Money that should have been spent on safety was not and went straight to the bottom line as profits.

Then Captain Franz von Rintelen, a naval intelligence officer, arrived in New York using a false Swiss passport. Passports were little used before the war but now, with British warships intercepting and inspecting neutral ones, it was prudent to carry one. In fact, the Imperial embassy in the United States was busy stealing, buying and forging American and neutral passports so at least some of the German reserve officers stranded here could get back to the Fatherland.

The captain's mission was to prevent American munitions from getting to the Allies. The well-financed von Rintelen, using the name Frederick Hansen, set up a business and took up residence at the high-toned New York Yacht Club.

His early efforts weren't very impressive either. He formed dummy companies and bought and destroyed gunpowder. That was futile. America's capacity to produce munitions seemed limitless. Mr. Hansen even tried to buy the du Pont powder factory. No deal.

Then Dr. Walter Scheele ferried over from Hoboken to meet with von Rintelen. They concluded that perhaps the ships carrying the munitions could be sabotaged. The chemist returned to his factory to perfect his incendiary bombs.

Berlin sent its ambassador the names of three Irishmen in America who could help with the sabotage efforts. The names were supplied by Sir Roger Casement who was in Germany trying to tie her closer to the cause of Irish liberation.

One of the names was Jeremiah O'Leary of New York City.

Westward, Ho

Terry Lynch's power rested on the fact that he was Frank Hague's gatekeeper. Even if Hague hadn't summoned you, Lynch could quickly get you in to see the commissioner, he could delay your entry or even deny you entry. Small time politicians were slow to cross Terry Lynch.

He liked that power. Today he'd see if it worked on Mickey McGurk, the commissioner's "nephew."

Looking up from his desk, he said, "What can I do for you, Sergeant?"

"I need to see the commissioner, Terry."

Lynch shook his head sadly. "I don't know, Mickey. He's got meetings until five o'clock. I could get you in first thing tomorrow morning at nine."

"No dice, Terry. I've got to see him now. This is big time stuff. I know he'll want to know what I'll tell him."

"What's that?"

"Nice try, Terry. If the commissioner wants you to know, I presume he'll tell you. Now, stop fooling around. Open the door."

Lynch rose and reached for the door. "You've got me all wrong, Mickey. I'm just doing my job."

"Right."

Lynch announced, "Sergeant McGurk on urgent business, Commissioner."

"Come in, Mickey, sit down. What's up?"

"We know who killed Ted Kenny, Commissioner. An iceman. Guy named Billy Cunningham."

"Billy Cunningham? I never heard of him. Do I know his family?"

"I don't think so. Lives alone with his mother. I don't know anything about his father. Pretty sure he's dead."

Hague asked, "Did he know Teddy?"

"Yes. They went to St. Mike's together. But we don't think they were friends. His name never came up in the investigation until we tumbled to the fact that an iceman did it. Then the trail led right to him."

"Why did he do it?"

"That we don't know."

"We'll talk about that later. Good work, Mickey. You and that wop detective did a great job. Where is that son of a bitch Cunningham? In jail?"

"No. In Newark. Hiding out with relatives."

"In Newark?" Hague got up and reached for his hat. "Let's go."

"Go where, Commissioner?"

"To Newark. I'm going to arrest that rat."

"You can't do that, Commissioner, we don't have jurisdiction in Newark. In fact, I'm not sure you have jurisdiction anywhere."

"What are you talking about?" asked Hague. "The victim is from Jersey City. Right? The killer is from Jersey City. Right? The murder was committed in Jersey City. Right? What the hell does Newark have to do with it? Let's go."

They went. Tony Aiello took the wheel. Another car with two Zepps trailed behind. Newark was seven miles west, a short ride.

On the way, Hague further quizzed Mickey and Tony about Cunningham, his family, the crime, about everything they knew. He wanted to be ready when he'd see Nat Kenny.

"Why did he do it, Detective?" Hague asked Aiello.

"I don't know, Commissioner. We don't know. It's real puzzle." But we'll find out. He'll tell us."

"Are you sure he did it?"

"Absolutely."

"That's good enough for me."

Tony thought, *It might not be good enough for a jury. We need a confession.* He was confident they would get one. He might need help from Detective O'Rourke whose muscle was matched by his icy disposition. Tony was sure O'Rourke liked to hurt people. Maybe he was compensating for his inevitable yet totally unsuitable nickname, "Mamie."

A carload of plainclothesmen was already there, watching the house. Their sergeant strolled up to Hague's car. He saluted. "Commissioner."

Tony asked, "Is Cunningham inside?"

"No. He's at work. The neighbors say he and his uncle-in-law will be home in a few minutes."

"Where's he work?"

"In a scrap yard in Kearny. The uncle got him the job. He loads scrap into gondola cars. The old man is the foreman. Decent family, I'm told."

"Do the Newark cops know we're here?" asked Mickey.

"No way, Lieutenant. We were told to lie low."

"You did good," said Hague.

"Thank you, sir."

About ten minutes later, two men came up the street. The older man was wearing bib overalls, a faded blue shirt, a stained tie and a battered fedora. The younger, smaller man was filthy and hatless.

Two plainclothesmen crossed the street and walked behind the pair, pistols drawn. Hague, Mickey, Tony and two more plainclothesmen headed directly for the men.

Tony, who had a folded white paper in his left hand, held it up and said, "Mr. Capparelli. I have a warrant for the arrest of William Cunningham. Stand aside, sir."

Capparelli did, unaware that the "warrant" was a menu from a Chinese restaurant. Billy Cunningham didn't move. He looked confused.

Hague said, "William Cunningham, I am arresting you for the murder of Edward Kenny. Why'd you do it, you little piece of shit?"

Cunningham said nothing.

Hague turned to Aiello and said, "Search him and then book him for murder."

Hague left immediately, returning to Jersey City to find Nat Kenny and tell him his promise was fulfilled.

Tony instructed Cunningham, "Put your hands up on the side of that house, lean back and spread your legs, boy."

Cunningham obeyed and said nothing.

Aiello's hands ran down the sides of Cunningham's legs and stopped at a long thin pocket where carpenters stash their folding rulers.

"Lookee, lookee," said Tony, displaying an ice pick with a bottle cork on its tip. "What have we got here, Mr. Cunningham?"

Cunningham looked at him like he was daft. "It's an ice pick. I always carry an ice pick."

"Is this the one you used to kill Ted Kenny?"

Billy flushed, looked down and said nothing.

In the touring car, Billy, now handcuffed, was wedged between Tony and Mickey in the backseat.

"Billy, we're going to talk when we get to the stationhouse," said Aiello, "so I want you to think about what happened that Friday night before we get there."

Mickey knew who the "good cop" would be during the interrogation. O'Rourke would be the "bad cop", a role he relished.

Silent Billy thought: *As if I've thought about anything else since then.*

There I was heading for the barn when he came out of Monmouth Street and yelled at me.

"Hey, sport," he said. "How about a piece of ice. It's a hot night and I've got a long walk ahead of me."

Like an idiot, I stopped. I should have ignored him and kept going. But I was really annoyed. That bastard still didn't know my name. It was like I didn't exist. It wasn't but three weeks before when I saw him at a Skeeters' game. Sat down next to him. "Hello, Ted," says I. He looks at me and says, "Do I know you?"

"Sure you do. I'm Billy Cunningham. We were at St. Mike's together."

He keeps looking at me. "Sorry. I don't remember you," he says and looks away.

I didn't say another word. I got up and walked out of the ball park, I was that embarrassed. I tried to forget about it until that night.

I remember he said, "I'll give you a dime for your trouble." That did it. I hopped into the wagon and he walked around to the back. I sliced off a nice thin piece and handed to him. He reached for it and said, "Thanks."

With my left hand I stuck the ice pick in his head. He dropped like a rock. I heard the dime hit the cobblestones. Or at least I think I did.

Why did I do that? I don't know. I hated him. He picked on me in school. He insulted me every time I saw him. I couldn't stand him.

No, that's not true. I wanted to be his friend. I wanted to be like him. I wanted everybody to like me. But I couldn't be like him. I was jealous. I don't know why.

I just stuck him. I never hurt anybody before. Oh, my God, what have I done?

Nobody was around, thank God. I thought about leaving him there in the street. Then I thought I had to hide him so I wouldn't be caught. So I dropped the tailgate and jumped off. I could barely pick him up. He was that heavy. It was hard but I managed to get him into the wagon and close the tailgate.

Where to go? Where to hide his body? Skeeter Park. That's where I saw him last. When he insulted me. I'd hide the great baseball player in the baseball park. Sure, they'd find him but not until I got away. I'd have to run. Get out of town.

I turned the wagon around and it was all I could do to stop from racing up Montgomery Street, as if my old nag could race anywhere. I stopped in front of the big tradesman entrance. It was easy to get into the park. Kids do it all the time. I took the bar off the double door and in a minute I was inside with the door closed. Nobody could see me now.

I didn't know where to hide him. It didn't matter, really, they'd find him as soon as he started to stink. Then I had a thought that me laugh. Imagine, I was laughing. Dear God.

I lowered the tailgate and dragged him half way out. I thought he would be stiff. He wasn't. I put him down on the grass. Lord, was he heavy. I wasn't sure I could drag him all the way to where I wanted to put him. Then I thought of the ice tongs. I put them in his ears and when I lifted up on the handle the tongs pushed in. Made a mess of his ears but I knew he couldn't feel it now .He still weighed a ton but I had the leverage I needed and I could drag him across the grass, across the infield until he was across the foul line between home plate and first base.

I remember thinking, "Okay, Mr. Big Shot, your whole life is a home run. Me, I never got to first base. Let's see how you like it."

"All right, Billy, we're here. We're going to book you. That means we'll take your picture and your fingerprints and after all that's done, we'll talk."

"Okay. Thank you," said Billy Cunningham. Aiello and McGurk just looked at each other.

Not long after that, Aiello said, "Are you comfortable, Billy? Feels a lot better with those handcuffs off, doesn't it. Would you like a cup of coffee or something?"

"Could I have a glass of water?"

"Absolutely. Right after we talk a bit. Now you know me and Sergeant McGurk. But you don't know Detective O'Rourke," said Tony, pointing to the hulking man standing against a wall with his arms folded, glaring at Cunningham. "And you don't want to know him better either. He's a very impatient man, he is. And you certainly want to 'trip the light fantastic' with Mamie O'Rourke."

Mickey and Tony laughed, O'Rourke just shook his head. Billy was confused. Like every kid who grew up in the 'Show, he knew the words to what they called "East Side, West Side" but he didn't understand what Tony was saying.

"Billy, trust me. You want to talk to me. I want to do what's best for you. But I'm not the most patient man either. You've got to tell me everything. You should get it off your chest. You'll feel better. Okay? Now, why did you murder Ted Kenny?"

Billy looked at Tony. Silent tears were running down the young man's face. "I didn't murder him."

"You didn't kill Teddy Kenny?"

"Oh, I killed him all right but I didn't murder him," said Billy Cunningham.

"What do you mean you didn't murder him?"

Billy looked at Aiello very intently, his lip quivering a bit. "Murder means you did it on purpose. It wasn't like that. I just killed him. It just happened."

Billy started sobbing.

"Mickey. Why don't you go get Billy that glass of water. Put some ice in it, will you?"

McGurk rolled his eyes and left the room.

"Take your time, Billy," said Aiello. "Don't drink too fast. You want more, we'll get you more."

Billy gulped the water down. "Thank you," he said.

"Okay, Billy, now tell me, why did you kill Teddy?"

Billy was silent until he saw Aiello glance at O'Rourke who stirred. You don't grow up in the 'Show without sensing when danger was near.

"I'm not sure," said Billy quickly. "I liked him but I hated him. He bullied me as a kid. He insulted me. But I wanted to be like him. I don't know. He was everything I wasn't. It wasn't fair. I don't know. It just happened. I'm sorry it happened. I don't know why I did it. Really."

"Okay, Billy, maybe we'll get back to that later. Here's what I want you to do now. I'm going to get you a paper and a pencil. I want you to write down everything that happened that Friday night. Everything. Don't leave anything out. I'll know it if you do.

Then we'll have to start all over again but it won't be me in the room. It'll be Detective O'Rourke and he's no friend of yours. Don't let that happen, Billy. Write it all down. Don't leave anything out. Okay, Billy?"

Billy picked up the pencil. "How do I start?"

Aiello said, "Start with where you were, what time it was and what you were doing when you first saw Teddy Kenny that Friday night. Then take it a step at a time. Write down everything that happened. One thing after another. Okay?"

"Yes," said Billy Cunningham who started writing, his tongue between his teeth.

It took him more than an hour.

"Okay. I'm done," said Billy, who was visibly relieved.

"Now sign it, Billy."

"What do you mean, sign it? I never really learned that fancy writing stuff. The nuns tried but it didn't work. All I can do is print."

"Printing your name is fine, Billy," said Aiello.

Mickey got Billy a cup of black coffee and then he and Tony took the confession to another room and read it carefully. O'Rourke stood, propped against the wall, arms still folded, willing Billy to make a break for it or something. Billy sipped his hot coffee.

"Well, what do you think, Mickey?"

"Well, it's not 'War and Peace'. Billy's a poor speller. His grammar is unique. But all in all I think it's a good confession. It's a straight forward story of his killing Ted Kenny. It'll stand up."

"Yeah. But it's still light on motive. Think we should go back and try to get more out of him?"

"I don't think there's more to get. I don't think he's sure in his own mind why he did it. Hatred, jealousy, revenge. It's all there. It's just fuzzy. I think it would be a waste of time."

Billy had finished his coffee before they returned.

"Okay, Billy. You did a good job. We're going to clean you up now, feed you a meal and let you bed down."

"What happens next?" asked Billy.

"I'm not sure. You'll stay in jail but you're really in the hands of the lawyers from now on."

"I'm not really worried about myself," Cunningham said. "I did it. I got to pay for it. I know that. But what is going to happen to my mother? She doesn't know what I did. I just told her I had to leave town."

"I don't know, Billy. She said your sisters would take care of her."

"They can't take care of themselves," said Billy.

"I'm sorry, Billy. I can't help you there," said Aiello.

Billy shook his head. "You know, you were right. I do feel better now that I told somebody what I done. But I want to go to confession. Real confession. You know, with a priest."

Mickey said, "I'll see if I can get Father McBride from St. Peter's over to see you."

"Why him?" asked Aiello.

Mickey smiled. "He's pretty easy when it comes to handing out a penance."

"Unlike us," said a disappointed O'Rourke, his arms still folded.

Too Proud to Fight

Her speed was supposed to save her.

When the RMS Lusitania was launched she had a top speed of more than twenty-five knots and was unquestionably one of Cunard's great liners.

For her first trip across the Atlantic after the outbreak of war, Lusitania was painted a drab gray making her less visible to the German High Seas Fleet or any commerce raiders prowling about. She sped to New York without incident.

Soon it was determined that German surface ships posed little threat to her so she was restored to her pre-war grandeur. Submarines were a different, if little understood, threat.

Germany had twenty-nine U-boats at the start of the war, not all oceangoing. They sank five British cruisers in the first ten days of the war. An obvious threat with no obvious solution except speed.

If you could outrun a U-boat at high speed, its captain could not position his boat properly and draw a bead on you.

Passenger traffic on the Atlantic was understandably diminished but shipping lines could still make a profit especially if costs were cut.

Lusitania burned 910 tons of coal a day. Shutting down one of her boilers cut fuel and crew costs. She still could make twenty-one knots, faster than any other liner still in service.

On February 4, 1915, Germany declared all the seas around Great Britain a war zone. Her U-boat captains were free to sink any Allied ship. That was not unrestricted submarine warfare. Neutral ships would be unharmed.

An ominous advertisement placed by the German Embassy on April 22 appeared in American newspapers next to Cunard's Lusitania advertisement. It warned that travelers entering that war zone did so at their own risk.

RMS Lusitania, on her 202nd transatlantic voyage, sailed from New York and was making less speed than her reduced top speed on May 7, 1915, when she was hit by a single torpedo on her starboard side. She was eleven miles off the Old Head of Kinsale and Ireland was visible on the port horizon.

RMS Lusitania quickly sank taking 1,198 souls with her, 128 of them American.

America was outraged. Britain expected her to declare war against Germany.

It didn't happen.

Three days later, President Wilson gave a speech to naturalized American citizens in Constitution Hall in Philadelphia and, in an obvious if unstated reference to the Lusitania, said:

"The example of America must be a special example. The example of America must be the example not merely of peace because it will not fight, but of peace because peace is the healing and elevating influence of the world and strife is not. There is such a thing as a man being too proud to fight. There is such a thing as a nation being so right that it does not need to convince others by force that it is right."

The British press, not realizing that most Americans did not want to go to war, scolded Wilson, "Too proud or too scared?" they screamed. Dud shells on the Western Front were dubbed "Wilsons."

Wilson sent two strong notes to Germany deploring submarine warfare.

Foreign Minister Arthur Zimmermann said to an aide, "Words. Words. I told you that fool would never march against us."

Of course, more than torpedoes could sink a ship at sea. There was fire.

Peace Breaks Out

Mickey McGurk tried to be casual. "So what did you think of Hannah, Ma?"

"I thought this wasn't serious," said Amelia McGurk, who knew better.

"Come on, Ma. It's a simple question. What did you think of Hannah?"

"I liked her, God help me. What's not to like? She was sweet, she was respectful and she was helpful, unlike those lazy sisters of yours who fight about who is going to help while I finish doing the dishes. And I've seen some that were worse looking too. What she sees in you is a mystery for the ages."

"Thanks, Ma."

"She's not a Catholic. I know that, no thanks to you, but I don't think she hates us like a lot of Protestants. All in all, I'd mark her down as a good girl that I'd be happy to see you with, except...."

"Except what, Ma?"

"Except that you have lit the fuse to a barrel of dynamite. You idiot."

Now it was Hannah's turn. Sophie Ganz tried to be casual. "How did you like Mrs. Mack Gook, Hannah?"

"Mother! I've told you a thousand times Michael's name is McGurk!"

"Ja, Mack Gook. So?"

"Mrs. McGurk couldn't have been kinder. She was sweet. She was hospitable. She made me feel comfortable even though I was scared to death. She's smart and she's tough and that's the way she raised her son. She's a widow, you know. She had to raise a houseful of kids on her own. The McGurks are poorer than we are. Poorer than most people we know. I liked her. I respect her. Her cooking isn't that great, though. I think Michael liked yours better."

"Of course. Did the question of religion come up?"

"I'm not sure. I told her about the 'No Catholics Need Apply' sign coming down at Colgate's and she asked me how I felt about that."

"What did you say?"

"I told her the truth. I said it was about time. She nodded her head like I had just given her the right answer."

"Ja, well, it probably was the right answer. This is America, not the old country. Nothing else?"

"No it was a very pleasant evening."

I'm afraid you are in for some very unpleasant evenings, my lovely daughter.

There were more cultural obstacles to overcome. There was an outing to Scheutzen Park where Michael impressed Otto Ganz and his fellow burghers with his marksmanship.

"Well, I was only a Sharpshooter," said Mickey, "not an Expert. But we routinely fired from the six hundred yard line—prone. I was pretty good at that."

"How many meters is that?" asked an onlooker in German.

"More than five hundred meters. Much more," answered Otto Ganz, ever the tool and die maker.

Most of the middle age men nearby had served as conscripts in the German Army and were proud of it.

"No! More than five hundred meters! We weren't that good at two hundred!" That was a typical comment.

"Are all American soldiers that good at shooting?"

"I'm not sure about soldiers. The Marines are. They pay us extra if we are good shots."

"What's a Marine?"

A former sailor answered, "Naval Infantry, I think."

"So, Mr. McGurk. From how far away do the not-so-good shots fire?"

"Six hundred yards. Just like the rest of us."

The one-time conscripts looked at each other, puzzled. Half didn't think McGurk was telling the truth. Unhappily, the other half was sure he was.

The affair at Scheutzen Park was a love fest compared to High Mass at St. Anne's on the Boulevard.

Mickey and Hannah were surrounded by his cousins before, during and after Mass. Fortunately, Hannah didn't suffer from claustrophobia.

Hannah was thoroughly confused by the Mass with all that up, down, kneeling, bell ringing and nobody singing except the choir and the priest. And they were singing in Latin, of which she knew not a word. Neither did most of the Catholics.

Most people were fingering Rosary beads. Pastor Schoenfelder had told her Catholics, unlike Lutherans, worshipped the Virgin Mary too. It certainly looked like they did, despite what Mickey told her.

There were lots of statues. Hannah could figure out which ones were of Jesus. And she was sure of one or two depicting Mary but that was it.

Mass wasn't an ordeal but it was disconcerting. Things got worse afterwards.

The Irish had relationships which were baffling to her. One woman married to one of Mickey's first cousins once removed walked up to Mickey and Hannah.

"Hello, Aunt Agnes," said Mickey. "How are you? I haven't seen you since I left for the Marines."

"I'm fine dear. You look well." She turned to a tall beautiful, strawberry blonde.

"I'm not sure you've ever meet my daughter, Peggy."

The mystery cousin was well into her twenties. Mickey looked puzzled while Peggy looked blank.

She looks familiar somehow but I'm sure I never met her. I didn't even know Aunt Agnes had a daughter.

"No, we never met but I'm glad to meet you now, cuz," said

Mickey as he kissed her on the cheek and introduced her and her mother to Hannah.

Peggy McCann knew exactly who Mickey was. The man looked much like the boy. She couldn't tell whether he had recognized Marge the Barge or not but she was grateful and relieved.

Suddenly they were surrounded by other cousins, girl cousins, eager to get at Hannah.

Hannah kept telling herself to keep calm. *The questions! The looks! The phony smiles! One or two were pleasant enough, like Peggy; maybe they felt sorry for her.*

But the rest! They were—what was it the Irish called such women? Harpies—that's it. They're harpies!

But then came the wedding. Another cousin was married at St. Anne's. Mickey and Hannah went to the ceremony which seemed to Hannah to be more—well, normal—than Mass.

The reception was in a big hall in the back of a saloon on Palisade Avenue, owned by another older cousin of Mickey's. There wasn't much food. Just ham sandwiches, in waxed paper, piled up on big trays. Hard boiled eggs and plates full of sliced cheese.

There was lots of beer though—and hard liquor too.

There was an old man playing a fiddle and a much younger man on the accordion.

The dancing started sedately enough. Lots of the women danced with each other while the men worked up the courage—liquid courage—to ask for a dance.

As the afternoon and evening wore on the dancing got more interesting. The Irish danced in a line, men and women facing each other. To and fro and then linking arms and twirling around. Faster and faster. Hooting and hollering, when the dance ended, the men rushing off to drink some more.

Hannah danced with Mickey. The steps weren't hard to follow. She danced with two of his male cousins and then came a slow dance—what they called a lament. Mickey's cousin, the tall and beautiful Peggy McCann, who had been decent to her at Mass, walked up and said, "Come on, Hannah. Let's show these lugs how to dance."

And they did. At the end of the dance Hannah knew she had at least one friend in McGurk's family. *Thank God!*

The piles of ham sandwiches hadn't diminished much by the end of the evening but the kegs and bottles had taken a beating. A number of men had already passed out and were slumped in their chairs or supporting their heads with a table.

By then, Hannah had won over most of the McGurk cousins — male and female — except for a couple of "harpies" who would resent her until Judgment Day, if not longer.

Mickey, himself, was a bit tipsy. Hannah had never seen him like this. But he wasn't belligerent. He was loving, a bit too loving. At least in public.

Happily, it wasn't a very long walk to Hannah's house. But she had to push him away twice.

"Enough, Michael! We're not even engaged, you know."

"That's not my fault."

"I don't care whose fault it is. Enough. I'm going inside now. I love you, Michael, but enough. Go home. Take a cold shower. Good night, my love."

"Good night, sweetheart."

Mickey McGurk did not go and take a cold shower. He went to the nearest saloon and got drunk. He found himself, the next morning, reeking with booze, fully clothed, sprawled on top his bed covers. The door to his furnished rooms was wide open.

Oh Lord, he thought, *I better get married soon.*

Hannah was sitting at the vanity in her bedroom combing her blonde hair which fell down to her shoulders. She stared at herself and tried to make a candid appraisal. Clear blue eyes, a neat nose and mouth, ears that didn't stick out, a firm chin, no freckles, a slender but good strong body, and nicely shaped legs. *I would say I am more than pretty. I know I'm smart. I even have a job.*

Black Tom: Terror on the Hudson

A prize for any man.

Hannah sighed. *But the only man I want is the one that no one wants me to have.*

She brushed harder. *Well, we'll see about that. Michael McGurk is the man I want and I will do what I have to make sure I get him.* A sudden sense of relief washed over Hannah Ganz like balm. *That's it. Done.*

Not much later, Mickey was enjoying a cigar with his favorite Jesuit. "Hannah is willing to marry in the church and bring up the children Catholic."

"Good, then there is no impediment to the marriage. Your parish priest will be happy to marry you in his rectory."

"Can't we get married here at St. Peter's, Father?"

The priest thought, reviewing the entire situation. "It'd be a bit unusual, but I suppose it could be done."

"Would you marry us, Father?"

"I guess so. But first I'd want to talk to Hannah. Make sure there's no coercion going on here. I know what your mother's like."

"Butter wouldn't melt in my mother's mouth when she finds out we're getting married at St. Peter's."

"Really?"

"Now, let me ask you another question, Father. A hypothetical question."

Here it comes, thought Father McBride.

"Let's take it as a given that we're married by you. Suppose then, that we go through another ceremony—a more formal one—in her church. What happens then?"

"Well, I seriously doubt that her minister would perform such a ceremony. But if he did, you would be giving scandal and committing a grievous sin. A grievous sin."

"Would such a sin be unforgiveable?"

The priest knew exactly what was happening. *But then...*"You were taught, Mickey, that no sin is unforgiveable except, perhaps, despair."

"Well then, Father," said Michael McGurk, "we certainly don't want to get involved with despair, do we?"

"Of course not, Michael. I'm glad that this discussion was purely hypothetical and you have no intention of committing such a sin."

"Of course not, Father."

Next, Hannah Ganz had a long, awkward conversation with her mother who, by its conclusion, understood that marriage was inevitable. She consoled herself with the fact that her daughter was still a virgin. At least that had been avoided. Unlike the daughters of some of her friends who marched down the aisle looking like hot air balloons.

Daughter and mother stood before Pastor Schoenfelder in the church office.

"Do you have to get married?"

"No!" answered Hannah, somewhat indignantly.

"I didn't think so. You've always been a good girl. You have an excellent reputation.

"You know, I don't approve of these mixed marriages. Marriage is hard enough without that burden. But, I know you have been—what did your father call it—'walking out' with this Irishman for a long time. So I have to presume you know what you are doing."

Sophie was emphatically nodding her head. That wasn't lost on the minister.

"Now we can plan this wedding. But before we go any further, let me caution you. Do not tell me anything I don't want to hear."

Pastor Schoenfelder was no fool. He pointed a shaking forefinger at them. "Do...you...understand...me?"

Both women nodded 'yes', Sophie Ganz giving thanks to God in the process.

"Now let me look at my calendar. When do you want to get

married?"

Predictably, the few short months after that dragged on until Hannah, in her best dress garnished with a corsage and Mickey with a flower in the buttonhole of his best suit, were standing before Father McBride at St. Peter's.

The witnesses were Jimmy Cribbins and Amelia McGurk, of all people.

Amelia had accosted Jimmy when he came to pick her up. "You know, it's all your fault, Jimmy! None of this would be happening except for you. You dirty thing."

"What?" asked a flabbergasted Jimmy Cribbins. "What do you mean? I didn't do anything, Mrs. McGurk."

"Oh, no? Then who was it that took my Michael off to Lake Hope-pat's-hat-on to meet a bunch of Dutchmen? Lucky for you they're in love or I'd give you what for."

"Jeez," Jimmy said.

The wedding was short—almost sterile—except for Father McBride's warm off-the-cuff remarks.

Mickey kissed his bride. Then, Amelia pushed him out of the way, grabbed, and kissed Hannah McGurk. "You're my daughter now. I'll love you to the day I die. And if any of my other daughters give you any trouble, I'll break their heads."

Tears came to Hannah who realized she loved her mother-in-law too. Jimmy was glad Amelia wasn't breaking his head.

That night, in her home, Mickey said to Hannah, "We're man and wife now, my Hannah."

Hannah caressed his cheek. "I know, my love. But we've waited so long. Could we wait until after the wedding in my church next Saturday?"

Mickey held her at arm's length.

"Right. Cold showers, three times a day until Saturday." They both laughed. He kissed her and then left.

Sophie, smiling broadly, watched Hannah walk into the kitchen. "So that Irisher has left you already?"

"Just until Saturday."

"Good. That gives me some time to tell you some things you should know."

"Mother!"

* * *

The wedding at Bethany Lutheran Church was as lovely as it was traditional. The bride's side of the church was packed, the groom's side holding many fewer but a good turnout considering.

Amelia McGurk, her daughters, their husbands, uncles, aunts and cousins sat in the first few rows. Tony Aiello, friends, Zeppelins, cops, their wives and girl friends were in the rest of the pews.

Each side stared at the other as if they were on a badly lighted street. Everyone smiled and nodded as you do to something potentially dangerous in the hope that it wouldn't pounce on you.

Most of those on Mickey's side were resolved to get to confession as soon as possible.

Not Hans Mannstein who was the only "Dutchman" on the Zeppelin Squad. He regularly went to Bethany Church and had kept Mickey's secret from the squad for a very long time.

Naturally, he told the Catholic Zepps to follow his lead in church. He had resolved to stand when he should sit and sit when he should stand, thinking that would result in some hilarity.

His wife dissuaded him saying that if he tried to ruin the wedding she would plunge a three inch long hatpin into his thigh the second he made the attempt.

"And you better hope I don't hit something else by mistake," she added.

Hans was particularly careful to stand and sit slowly enough for the Catholics to follow.

Hannah was beautiful in white, her face a bit pale, but beautiful.

Sadie Ganz and Amelia McGurk were dressed handsomely and nodded regally to each other like queens at a royal wedding. They resolved to become good friends. Wise if they were to share grandchildren.

Hannah's father, the groom, the best man and the ushers were well turned out in rented gray morning clothes. The maid of honor and the bridesmaids were dressed in identical, flattering green gowns.

Billie Ganz was Mickey's best man and Peggy McCann, who had become a close friend, was Hannah's maid of honor.

But the star of the show, undoubtedly, was Hannah, from the moment she walked down the aisle with her beaming father until she kissed her husband who led her back down the aisle beaming just as brightly. Hannah smiled broadly too, her complexion restored.

Every unmarried woman in the church—even widows— sighed.

But Tony Aiello had eyes only for the maid of honor, Peggy McCann, and pestered his friend until he introduced him to his statuesque cousin.

The Ganz family had booked the main floor of Pohlman Hall for the reception. The handful of members who didn't know Otto Ganz or didn't like him would quietly drink their beer on the upper floor. Most members had been invited to the reception.

Amelia McGurk had warned all of her family, many of Mickey's friends and some of the Zepps that, "If you embarrass me in front of those Protestants, I'll personally butcher you." That word spread to the rest.

They were also informed, "You will drink nothing but beer and damn little of that and you will dance like gentlemen and not like the savages you are. There'll be no second warning and no mercy."

She was believed and her edicts were reinforced by every woman of her acquaintance.

"There's scandal enough without you lot adding to it," was the conclusion accepted by all.

That the beer at Pohlman Hall was good helped. Of course there were a few who wanted to have something stronger— Amelia or no Amelia—and they snuck up to the bar and asked, "Can I have a touch of the Irish?"

"No, I'm sorry; we don't have any call for Irish whiskey. But how about schnapps or Jägermeister?"

"Yay-gurrr-what?"

"Jägermeister. I can't guarantee you'll like it. Some do, some don't."

They didn't and sorrowfully, but bravely, went back to sipping their beer, their women watching them like Temperance ladies.

The Irish enjoyed the music provided by the usual German band. Soon they were singing "Ja, Ja. Ja" and swaying their beer mugs to the music.

An Irishman went up and said something to the bandmaster who replied with a negative shake of the head.

"Not to worry," said he and in a clear, strong, tenor began to sing "The Irish Rover."

By the time the second chorus came along, the Germans were pounding the tables in harmony with the Irish.

"No, no, never... no-no, never... no more,

"Will I play the Wild ...Rover,

"No, no, never...no more."

Again and again.

None of the Irishmen and few of the Germans had ever heard the word "gemeinschaft" but it was rising up to their hips by the time the reception ended.

"Those Irishers, they're not such bad fellows."

"You got to hand it to those Dutchmen, they can hold their beer all right."

It wasn't an unbreakable bond, but it was something more than mere tolerance.

Of course, Tony Aiello danced every dance with the lovely and amused Peggy McCann. The fact that she was two inches or so taller than him in her heels didn't bother either of them.

Hannah and Mickey had long since vanished from the reception. Jimmy drove off with them, tin cans rattling behind his Model T.

They were off to Hoboken and the Lackawanna Railroad Terminal to catch the night train to Buffalo and then by auto to a week at Niagara Falls. If they were like most newlyweds, they'd be lucky to get a glimpse of the Falls from anywhere but their hotel room.

The young couple was thoroughly exhausted by the time they got to their hotel.

Hannah went into the bathroom to change. Mickey stripped down to his shorts and climbed into the double bed.

By the time Hannah returned in a revealing negligee, feeling terrified but strangely excited, Mickey was fast asleep.

Hannah gratefully slipped in beside him, careful not to wake him and, in an instant, was asleep herself.

The sun was inching its way into the room when Hannah slowly awoke.

Mickey was curled up against her, his left hand reaching around and cupping her lightly covered left breast. She didn't know where his right hand was.

He was hard against her. She could feel him, every inch of him. She didn't move. He did.

He pushed against her. His hand gently squeezed her breast.

Mickey was breathing harder. So was she. A bit. She didn't know why, but she pushed back a little against him.

Mickey reached over and took her right shoulder and turned

her towards him.

Now her breathing came more quickly. They sat up. In an instant, the negligee was up, over and out and his shorts were gone.

They lay face to face, their arms around each other, her breasts against his chest, their legs intertwined. Kissing.

Then she was on her back, Mickey up against her right side, his hand moving between her legs. Kissing. Tongues seeking each other out.

Am I supposed to be doing this? thought Hannah briefly, very briefly. Mickey was kissing her face, her hair, her neck, and then her breasts. His hand and fingers moving all the while.

Hannah could barely breathe. But she did. She kissed him. Then she held him in her hand and gently moved him back and forth. Mickey choked out, "Dear God, that's good!"

All the while, they were murmuring endearments to each other. Sweet nothings.

Mickey was on top of her, all but panting. "Hannah, my love, I know you're a virgin. This could hurt. I'll don't mean to hurt you. If it hurts, I'll stop."

"Shh! Shh! My love, just love me, love me."

Mickey arched his back and hesitated. "Help me, Hannah."

She did. She grasped him firmly and slowly guided him into her body.

There was a bit of resistance; she expected that, and then a bit of pain; she expected that, too. There'd be blood as well but she didn't care. Mickey and she were one.

Mickey felt the resistance, a bit of a wince and then an incredible grasping softness.

Different. Different from anything he had experienced before. But then no one had ever loved him before. He began to move. After a few strokes, Hannah did too. Her push meeting his stroke.

They kissed. And kissed. Then Hannah felt something.

Something building. She moved faster. So did he.

Then, for both, something, an all-consuming moment, a feeling like no other. They came together. Came as one. Were one.

They clung together sweaty and gasping. Still kissing between gasps.

Minutes later, Hannah looked at her husband and asked, "Can we do that again, dearest one?"

Mickey smiled at her and said, "Give me a few minutes, my love. Give me a few minutes."

And so went the week. Intimacy. Fulfillment. Pleasure. Hesitancy. More trust. No. Let's try it. Wonderful. More intimacy. More fulfillment. More pleasure.

Hannah: "Where did you learn about…these things?"

Mickey: "You know. In one of those French books. The French know all about… these things." His first lie as a husband.

The room service waiters had bets on when they would emerge. The grizzled old waiter who bet on the third day won.

They came out, blinking in the sunshine, on their way to the Falls. They went home four days later after three more glorious nights.

Theology had not been discussed.

The Irish Washerwoman

The seven o'clock Low Mass was being said in the majestic St. Patrick's Cathedral.

Two members of the New York Bomb Squad, disguised as washerwomen in skirts and kerchiefs, fiddled with their mops and buckets against a far wall.

"You know, Vinnie, you are just about the ugliest woman I ever saw," said one to his taller colleague.

"That may be, Brian, but if we put a little rouge on you and maybe a touch of lipstick, there's many a lad on the squad that would try to steal a kiss."

"And there's many a lad that would be shot dead on the spot," said Brian.

"Aha! So you would play hard to get?"

Other men, in plain clothes, from Acting Captain Thomas Tunney's Bomb Squad were scattered through the congregation paying more attention to what was going on around them than what was happening on the altar. Another set of "washerwomen" toiled on the other side of the cathedral.

One of Tunney's men, an Italian, had infiltrated an anarchist cell and learned that another attempt would be made to bomb the landmark cathedral. He knew when but he didn't know who would plant the bomb or where it would be placed in the cavernous church.

Some movement caught Brian's eye. A man lit the fuse on a bomb and then moved away from it.

Pointing, Brian said, "There he is, Vinnie. You get him, I'll get the bomb."

Hiking up his skirts, Brian sprinted for the bomb under a pew. He managed to pull the still sputtering fuse from the bomb. Brian's hands were shaking.

Vinnie and other cops had grabbed the bomber, an Italian

anarchist, and dragged him outside to a waiting Captain Tunney.

The priest, his back to the congregation, had not even noticed the commotion.

Brian emerged with the bomb wrapped in his kerchief.

Tunney said, "Good work, Kelly." He paused and then added, "Jesus. That was too goddamned close."

"Tell me about it, Captain," said Brian Kelly, his hands still shaking.

The thirty-four man unit had been christened the Bomb Squad in 1914 after war broke out in Europe. It had been the Italian Squad before then and had much success fighting organized crime among the new immigrants. Tunney had succeeded the legendary Lieutenant Joe Petrosino who was assassinated in Sicily in 1909. More than 200,000 New Yorkers attended Petrosino's funeral when his body was returned to the United States.

The job of the squad was not to disarm bombs but to figure out who was going to throw them and arrest them, preferably before the act.

Acting Captain Tunney and his men had much work ahead of them.

A Lesson in Fractions

"I want to go to that little Italian restaurant we went to when we first started going out," said Hannah McGurk to her husband, Mickey.

"Cavaletti's?"

"That's the one."

"I didn't think you liked Italian food all that much."

"Good memories make the food taste better," said Hannah with a warm smile.

So there they were sitting at a small table for two with a candle in a wicker-bound wine bottle giving off just enough light to read the menu.

They ordered. Mickey said, "You're right. This does bring back old memories. Good memories. Do you remember going up and down the street, jumping into hallways when somebody came by?"

Hannah and Mickey laughed. "Do I remember? I thought we'd be doing that until we were old and crippled. I thought we'd never get married."

Mickey reached across and took her hand. "But we did, my love, we did."

The pasta arrived. Mickey was wolfing it down while Hannah pushed it around her plate, eating a couple of strands now and then. She left her glass of Chianti untouched.

They went through the small talk of the day until the table was cleared and coffee arrived.

"I don't feel like having any wine tonight. You drink it," Hannah said, offering the glass to Mickey.

"What's up, Hannah? You're not yourself tonight. What's wrong, honey."

"Nothing's wrong, Mickey. I just have something to tell you."

"So tell me, honey, cops don't like mysteries."

Hannah looked straight at her husband. "I'm pregnant, Michael McGurk. We're going to have a baby."

McGurk's mouth dropped open. "Are you sure, sweetheart?"

"Of course, I'm sure. One. I've missed two periods. Two. Dr. Marrone told me so this afternoon."

Mickey McGurk leaped up, knocking over his chair. He wrapped his arms around the still-seated Hannah, kissing her head, her cheek, her neck and finally, her mouth.

His loud "Thank you! Thank you!" rocked the room.

"Mickey, stop. You're embarrassing me," hissed Hannah, eyes cast down on the rocking table.

Mickey jumped up, causing Hannah's wine to slosh over onto the table cloth. He faced the mostly Italian clientele which was now staring at them.

"We're pregnant. We're going to have a baby," he bellowed. He sat down to nodding heads, applause and cries of "Bravo" and "Bene."

Hannah, yet to look up, said, "Next time—if there is a next time—I'll tell you in a library."

The patron arrived with three small glasses. He placed one in front of both Hannah and Mickey and held up the third.

"To the baby, *Sergente*. A long, healthy life. *Salute!*"

Everyone in the place, including Hannah and Mickey, grabbed a glass, yelled "Salute" and took a sip of whatever they had.

Mickey couldn't stop talking and asking questions in the restaurant, on the way home and in their bedroom.

"Mickey, I'm sorry. I don't know the answers. It's my first child. I'll talk to my mother, she's had two children. You talk to your mother, she's had even more."

"I'm not talking to my mother. You talk to my mother."

"All right, but I want you there."

"I'll be there but when you start talking about that, I'm going downstairs to have a cigar."

Hannah laughed. "It's true. I've heard it all my life but it's true. You great big men are nothing but great big babies."

"Guilty as charged, your honor," said Michael McGurk, as he again covered his wife with kisses.

Amelia McGurk loved her daughter-in-law and even liked having her to supper. Mrs. McGurk, as has been noted, was not an enthusiastic cook.

She asked Mickey, "Is this another one of those occasions where the lodgers have to leave town?"

"I guess so, Ma."

Amelia McGurk, indeed, guessed, came to a conclusion and couldn't have been happier. She cooked everything she knew Hannah liked and laid in a couple of big bottles of celebratory beer.

Hannah waited until the table was cleared and the tea had been poured.

"Mom," she said (Mama was reserved for own mother). "I have something to tell you."

"Do you, dear? Now I wonder what that could be?"

Hannah smiled brightly. Mickey held his breath. "I'm pregnant. Mickey and I are going to have a baby."

Amelia moved to embrace Hannah. "God love us all. That's grand, Hannah. Grand." Amelia ignored her son. "When is the baby due, Hannah?"

"I'm not sure. I have to go back to Dr. Marrone tomorrow for another exam. We'll probably know then."

"Dr. Mahoney? I don't know any Dr. Mahoney."

Mickey answered, "It's Dr. Marrone, Ma. M-a-r-r-o-n-e. He's got a big house and an office on the boulevard, not far from us."

His mother continued to stare at him. "He's Italian, Ma. But he's a really good doctor."

"Do the McCanns know him?"

"He's their doctor too, Ma," said Mickey.

"All right then," said his mother, accepting the family seal of endorsement.

Hannah couldn't help herself. "So, Mom. You know your grandchild will be half German. Is this the first time something like this has happened in your family?"

Amelia laughed and waved her hand at her daughter-in-law. "Not at all, sweetie, not at all."

Amelia, whose maiden name was Cassidy, continued. "My father told me he had a German grandmother. Had the same first name as you—Hannah. Her last name was Schultz or Schwartz or something like that. She was born in the city way back when but her folks were from the other side. At least, that's what my father said."

Hannah was truly surprised. Mickey was pole axed.

"That makes her Mickey's great-great-grandmother," said Hannah with delight.

"I suppose so," said Amelia McGurk, who hadn't given the relationship a thought until now.

"Ma, why didn't you tell me this before?"

Now Amelia was perplexed. "Why would I bother? It was my father's business, not mine. And certainly not yours. It was a long time ago," Amelia said, dismissing the subject.

I can't wait to tell my mother, thought Hannah. *My Mickey is 1/16th German.*

I can't wait until my sisters find out, thought Mickey. *Their husbands will be demanding knockwurst and sauerkraut for supper.*

Hannah and Mickey laughed about it all the way home. So did her mother the next day. But her laugh was triumphant.

"I knew it. I knew it. All along. Michael was too nice, too decent a boy. He's not a drunk. He'd never hit you. He's careful with his money. I knew it. He had to be German. It didn't matter that his name was Mack Gook. He had to be German."

"Mama, Mickey had sixteen great-great grandparents. Only one of them was German."

"It's enough," said her mother, dismissing the subject.

Hannah's father was more thoughtful. "You know, I always

thought that boy was too disciplined to be a real Irishman. This is good. Very good."

By the time services rolled around at Bethany Lutheran that next Sunday, Michael's ancestry had swollen to "almost half German."

"Catholic, mind you," said Sophie. "But German." Her audience was appreciative.

Mickey's sisters were not. "What do you mean, one of Grandpa's grandmothers was German? What is that—1/80th or something? Too little to matter. I'm not even going to tell my husband. You know how he is about those krauts." The husband found out and took to calling her "Helga" when he was annoyed.

Hannah had an easy pregnancy. Didn't put on more weight than Dr. Marrone wanted. She didn't drink any alcohol. She didn't make a big thing about it. Just kept staying she wasn't "in the mood."

"You know we should start thinking about names now. I don't want to wait until the baby is born," said Hannah. "Godparents too."

"Okay, sweetheart. What do you want to call the baby if it's a boy?"

"Michael."

"No. I don't want any kid of mine growing up and answering to 'Junior.' I'm flattered but no thanks."

"All right then. How about Otto, after my father?"

"Otto. Otto McGurk. Are you kidding?"

"I am not. Otto is a nice name. And the boy will be more German than Irish anyway."

"What are you talking about, woman? Make sense."

"Didn't they teach you arithmetic at that fancy school of yours? Because of me, the baby will be half German and because of you he will be another 1/16th German. That adds up to 9/16ths German and only 7/16ths Irish. Argue with that Mr. Smarty-pants."

"My son will only be 1/32nd German because of his great-great-great grandmother, Miss You-Should-Have-Paid-More-Attention in Class. The difference is too small to pay any mind to."

"Not to me or my family."

"Listen, love. Do you think anybody is going to think a boy named McGurk is German?"

"No," Hannah said.

Mickey said, "Now, I admit, a girl is different. If we have a daughter, darling, we can call her 'Sophia Amelia' or 'Amelia Sophia.' I'd be happy either way and I think both grandmothers would be happy too."

"Done," said Hannah. "Now back to the boy."

"Did anyone ever tell you, you're like a dog with a bone," said Mickey.

"Ha! A 15/16th Irishman calling me stubborn."

"Fair enough. Okay, back to the boy. What do you want to call a boy?"

"I already gave you two names. Your turn."

"Okay. How about 'Francis' for my dead father?"

"Yes," said Hannah. "I like that. We'll call him 'Frankie.'"

Mickey was elated.

He said, "Let's give him 'Otto' for a middle name. The Irish will think the 'O' stands for O'Connor or something and the Germans will know better."

"Oh. Mickey that's wonderful," said Hannah who, in turn, covered her husband with kisses.

* * *

Sophie Ganz was satisfied. "If it is a girl, we'll marry her off to a nice German boy and that will be the end of that Irish nonsense," she said, no more concerned with genetic fractions than Michael's mother. "If it is a boy, we'll call him 'Little Otto'. The Irishers can call him what they want. I suppose the godparents have to be Catholic?"

"I'm afraid so, Mama. I gave my word," said Hannah.

Her mother sighed and said no more.

Mickey's mother was satisfied.

"If it's a girl, why don't you make it Sophia Amelia? Her mother's a decent sort and God knows she has to be disappointed to have you for a son-in-law."

"Ma. I love Mrs. Ganz and she loves me."

"Does she now? Will wonders never cease? I'm happy you'll name a boy after your father. He didn't live longer enough to leave much of a memory let alone anything else. This will help. As for 'Otto', why not? Who pays attention to middle names? What's your middle name?"

"John."

"Does your wife ever use it?"

"No."

"Well, there you are. Otto it is, poor little creature. Who's going to be godparents?"

"Hannah wants Peggy McCann for godmother. They've become great friends."

"Good choice. Peggy's a lovely girl and she'd raise that baby properly if the two of you were killed in a train wreck or something."

"Nice thought, Ma."

"Well, you're going to be a father, idiot. You have to start being practical. I'm glad it's not going to be one of your sisters. No matter which one you picked, the others would hate you. This way, they'll just be annoyed—as usual. Who's the godfather going to be?"

"I'm going to ask Frank Hague, Ma."

Amelia stared at her son for a second. "Aren't you the sly one? He's going to think you named it after him."

"No, he's not. I'll tell him the truth. But it wouldn't hurt a boy to have one of the most powerful men in Jersey City as his godfather. As you say, I'm just being practical. Suppose Hannah and I get killed in a train wreck?"

"Bite your tongue, idiot."

* * *

Mickey was nervous about approaching his boss with such a request. The Irish thought being asked to be a godparent was a great honor. The Irish took it seriously. Not as seriously as the Italians, of course. Becoming a godparent among them bound you and your family to the child and its family for the next three or four generations at least.

Mickey asked. Frank Hague looked at him and said flatly, "Mickey, I've turned down dozens of requests to be a godfather. It's too dangerous. If you say 'yes' to one and 'no' to another, you've made enemies for life. I can't afford that. Neither can the organization."

"I understand, sir," Mickey said, sighing.

"But since you're 'family' I'm going to do it. I'm honored that you asked."

"Thank you, Uncle Frank. Thank you."

"Who's the godmother going to be?"

"My cousin, Peggy McCann."

"I don't think I've met her. But I like the McCanns. Good organization men. You can depend on them. Grandpa McCann runs a clean place too, I'm told."

"He does that."

"Have you thought about names, Mickey?"

"We have. If it's a girl it will be Sophia Amelia after our mothers and if it's a boy it'll be 'Francis' after my dead father." Mickey did not mention a middle name.

"I remember your father, he was a decent man. Died too young. Goddamn railroads. I'll bet it'll be a boy. We'll call him

'Little Frank'."

No one had called Frank Hague "Francis" since he first clenched a fist.

* * *

Hannah's time approached rapidly. "Where are you going to have the baby, *liebchen?*" asked Sophie Ganz.

"Dr. Marrone is on the staff of Christ Hospital. He wants me to have it there."

Christ Hospital was nearby on Palisade Avenue and had been founded by well-off Episcopalians reluctant to trust the care at the Catholic hospitals in Jersey City, a sentiment Sophie understood.

"That's good. I had you and Billy at home but I think a hospital is better."

"That's what Dr. Marrone thinks too."

So it was that the baptism for Francis Otto McGurk was held in St. Anne's Church on the Boulevard less than two weeks after his birth at Christ Hospital. The baby weighed in at seven pounds, eight ounces and was a voracious eater. Hannah, who was breastfeeding him, was happy but close to exhaustion.

"When will this son of yours sleep through the night?" demanded Hannah.

"Oh, I don't think that happens until they're a year or two old." Hannah threw a pillow at the giggling Mickey.

The big, gothic church on the corner of Hudson Boulevard and Congress was packed.

Several upfront pews were full of McGurks, Burkes, Mannions, Beglins, O'Connors, Rinaldis, Morgans, McGlinches and McCanns. They shared them with the Ganz Family, some of their relatives, the Slagers and the Mannsteins. Tony Aiello, more cops and friends of Hannah and Mickey McGurk made a nice contribution to the crowd.

The rest of the cavernous church was filled with politicians, ward-heelers, jobholders, hangers-on and the just plain curious.

They were there to see, and hopefully to be seen by, the star of their show, Commissioner Frank Hague, director of public safety and soon to be the uncontested political boss of Jersey City.

When Hague was introduced to the godmother, Peggy McCann, he asked, "Have we met? Your face seems familiar."

"No, sir," Peggy lied, thinking back to that night at the station house. "I'm sure I'd remember."

Screened by the crowd and thus unseen was the Rev. Dr. Schoenfelder, pastor of Bethany Lutheran Church. He was wearing a tie, not his clerical collar.

He had assured Hannah when she had asked, "It doesn't matter whether I baptize the child or if the pope does it or a Hottentot witch doctor does it, the baptism is valid as long as it is done properly."

The Reverend Schoenfelder was there to make sure it was done properly. It was.

Frank Hague, as usual, had given the altar boys a silver dollar each, which insured piety, and the priest who performed the baptism was eager to show his appreciation of Hague's efforts to "clean up" the city. The baby cried on cue when water was splashed on his head.

Mickey McGurk and Otto Ganz were really worried that this vast throng would show up at Pohlman Hall for the reception. The bar bill could bankrupt a small country.

Frank Hague put an end to that when he apologized to the grandmothers at the top of the stone steps in front of the church.

"I am so sorry, Mrs. Ganz, Mrs. McGurk. I'm afraid I can't go to the reception. I have a very important meeting at City Hall in a few minutes. I can't avoid it. Please give Hannah my best regards and tell her she has the grandest baby in the world."

With that, he vanished into his car and most of the crowd vanished with him to parts unknown.

It was too early in the day for serious drinking but the remnant at the club did the best they could. There was no music, but singing broke out anyway, the Germans and the Irish joining in with each other humming and la-la-ing when words failed.

All had a good time.

Near the reception's end, Paddy McAlinden, Mickey's old mentor when he first became a policeman, cornered Heinrich Bauer. Bauer was the club's secretary and general factotum.

"Heinie, I'd like to join the club," said McAlinden.

"Paddy, you know you're welcome here anytime. Why, I've had a beer with you at the bar lots of times."

"You have, indeed. But that's the point. When I come here, I come as a cop. What I want is to be able to bring my wife and kids here on a Sunday afternoon and enjoy your beer garden. Come on, Heinie. You've had a mob of Irishmen here a couple of times now. We're pretty well behaved."

"Ja, better than we expected."

"Well then. When little McGurk grows up, are you going to let him join?"

"Of course, his mother's German."

"Well, if you're going to take a McGurk, why not a McAlinden?"

"I'll talk to the board."

Bauer never got back to him. McAlinden continued to drop in, especially when the night was bitter. McAlinden took no offense. Bauer couldn't get into the Ancient Order of Hibernians either.

Fire at Sea

Captain von Rintelen thought that the incendiary device was ingenious.

Dr. Walter Scheele had invented it in the laboratory of his chemical plant in Hoboken. It was not much bigger than a good-sized cigar, made of lead and divided into two parts by a copper disc.

Cheap chemicals were poured into each end that was then sealed with wax.

The chemicals ate away at the disc and when they met the explosive reaction shot fierce flames out of both ends. The width of the disc determined how long it would be before that fiery reaction.

"Where will you manufacture these...these..."

"Cigar bombs," said Scheele. "I don't have the facilities to make the lead tubes. They have to be manufactured elsewhere. When they are ready to be used, the discs can be inserted and the chemicals and wax added."

"Is the timing precise?" asked von Rintelen.

"Within fifteen minutes or so," said Scheele.

"Excellent."

Von Rintelen knew the tubes could be made by the skilled machinists aboard the SS Frederick der Grosse now tied up and interned at a Brooklyn pier. The tubes could then be stored at a centralized location until needed.

"All right, my dear Doctor, we have the weapon we need. Now I will get the men I need to use them."

Von Rintelen and Paul Koenig met the next day with one of the men Sir Roger Casement had singled out to the Germans, Jeremiah O'Leary, a leader of the Clan na Gael in New York.

"What we want you to do, Mr. O'Leary, is have some of your men—longshoremen—stuff these small cigar bombs in flammable cargo aboard British ships. The idea is for them to catch fire at sea and, with luck, sink. Can do you do this, sir?"

"I can and will, Mr. Hansen," said Jerry O'Leary. "I know Ireland and Germany are partners now. Our common enemy is England."

"That she is, Mr. O'Leary. What about on the other side of the river? Lots of English ships sail out of Hoboken and other places in New Jersey."

"Do not concern yourself, Mr. Hansen. I have just the man for that."

Fat Jack Lynch was very pleased indeed. "Thank God. I told you those fucking Orangemen would kill Home Rule. We're going to have to kick the Brits out ourselves. This will be a good start. Let them lose this fucking war with Germany and the next thing you know, Ireland will be free. I'll get the men we need, Jerry. Good men. Men able to keep their mouths shut. Of course, it might take a couple of dollars to sweeten the deal."

"No problem, Jack. You'll work with Paul Koenig of the Hamburg America Line. Do you know him?"

"I don't, but I'll bet you'll introduce us." The Irishmen shared a laugh.

Fire at sea is particularly dreaded by seamen and has been since ancient times. Use too much water to put out the fire and that would sink the ship. Use too little and the ship burns and sinks. Seamen hate fire.

Soon British ships were sinking in the Western Ocean, not victims of German torpedoes but rather of fires that mysteriously broke out in their cargo. Their crews drowned or were plucked from the sea by other more fortunate ships. Some crews doggedly put out the fires and their ships limped into port with cargoes usually ruined.

None of these ships sailed from Black Tom in Jersey City where the Lehigh Valley Railroad was shifting coal trains to another waterfront terminal in favor of more profitable freight—munitions.

It's Only a Mass

Sergeant Mickey McGurk was sitting in his tiny office on a Friday morning typing a report with two fingers.

His friend and onetime partner, Detective Tony Aiello, stuck his head in the open door and said, "Got a minute, pal?"

Mickey looked up, smiled and said, "For you, Tony, anything. Take a pew. What's up?"

"Thanks," said Tony as he sat in one of the two mismatched chairs in front of McGurk's desk.

"I just wanted you to know I'm going to be up in your neighborhood for a while, at least until I figure out what mutt is burglarizing those stores on Palisade Avenue."

McGurk said, "I heard about that. Three of them, wasn't it?"

"At last count. Same *m.o.* —break a pane of glass in the back door and reach in and unlock the door. I don't think I'll be hunting a criminal mastermind, though. He doesn't know enough to cover his hand with a towel or something. We found blood on two of the doors."

"Well, it shouldn't take you long to crack the case, Tony. Just shake down anyone you see with a bandaged hand."

"Good idea. Say, since I'm going to be nosing around up there on Sunday anyway, what say I go to church with you and Hannah."

"Hannah's going to Bethany to show off the baby but you're welcome to join me at St. Anne's. What happened, Our Lady of Victories burnt down and I didn't hear about it?"

Tony laughed. "No, it's still standing. Truth is I want to go to St. Anne's for a reason."

"Could that reason be one of my cousins, say the tall one, the strawberry blonde, with blue eyes?"

"You have other cousins? Yeah, I'm been thinking about Peggy a lot lately."

"I hope those thoughts have been absolutely pure. I remember you boasting about your skill in producing Italian babies."

Tony laughed. "Mostly pure. I'd just like to get to know her better. She and I had a real good time at your wedding and it was fun at the Christening too but I'd really like to see her more than every year or so. She's not going with anyone, is she?"

"No. Despite being in what I think is called 'show business', Peggy has never shown any interest in any man that I know of."

Peggy McCann had appeared in one episode of "The Perils of Pauline" and had bit parts in two photoplays filmed at the Pathé Studios on the Paterson Plank Road. That's all the 'show business' Mickey knew about.

"I know. I saw that 'Perils of Pauline' six times. Lord, she is beautiful," said an obviously smitten Tony Aiello.

"Smart, and independent too. Hannah loves her dearly and so do I. I would not want to see her heart broken or even see her annoyed," said Mickey.

Tony put both hands to his chest. "Honest to God, Mickey, I just want to take her to Mass and maybe out for a bite to eat to see if anything clicks. If it doesn't, I swear the only time she'll ever see me again is when you have your kids baptized."

Mickey took a long look at his friend. "Okay. Show up at my house in time for the nine o'clock Mass. That's the one the McCanns go to. She'll be with her mother and father."

"Mickey," asked Tony, "do you think she'll go out with me?"

"As you detectives say, I haven't got a clue."

After Mass, Mickey called out, "Aunt Agnes. How are you?" The McCanns turned toward him, Peggy's eyes locking with Tony's briefly.

"Why Mickey McGurk," Aunt Agnes said. "It's so good to see you. Don't you usually go to the eleven o'clock?"

"Usually. But Tony Aiello and me are working on a case so I thought we'd get any early start. You remember Tony, don't you,

Aunt Agnes?"

"I do indeed. At your wedding. I really enjoyed watching you and my daughter dancing, Mr. Aiello."

"Not half as much as I did, Mrs. McCann." Peggy realized she was pleased with Tony's reply. Her father seemed less impressed.

Aunt Agnes said, "I'm sorry you boys have to work or I would invite you both back to our place for breakfast."

Tony gave Mickey a furtive, plaintive look. McGurk said, "Do me a favor, Aunt Agnes, take Tony here and feed him. That will give me some time to help Hannah with the baby before we start with the gumshoe thing."

"Certainly," said Aunt Agnes, "you'd be most welcome, Mr. Aiello."

"Thank you, Mrs. McCann," said Tony, grinning. Peggy smiled and Papa Jim's face was blank.

Tony Aiello had never been more charming or gracious. He praised Mrs. McCann's cooking, told jokes that Papa Jim laughed at, made small talk that amused Peggy who wondered what was coming next.

Tony rose. "Well, Mrs. McCann, Mr. McCann, thank you for the wonderful breakfast and the hospitality but I've got to get to work."

"You're welcome anytime, Tony," said Mrs. McCann, putting her seal of approval on him. "Peggy, why don't you see Tony out."

"Sure, Momma," said Peggy. Tony was relieved since he had not figured out how to get her alone.

They lingered on the stoop. "I had a wonderful time, Peggy. Your mother and father are great. Say, I may be working on that burglary case for some time; do you think I might escort you to Mass next Sunday? I mean if your folks don't object. I could take you all out for breakfast. It would be fun."

Peggy was trying to decide whether this should end now.

What if this guy is serious? I like him. A lot. But he really doesn't

*know me. This could end very badly. I should make an excuse and say
'no'. But I don't want to. I want to see him again. Why do I feel like
this? Men have no place in my life. Or didn't. But it's only a Mass. I've
never gone to Mass with a boy—a man. Why not? There's really
nothing at stake. Is there?*

* * *

Mickey was still pecking away at the same report on Monday
when he looked up and there was Peggy McCann.

"Peggy. What a surprise. I didn't think you even knew where
I worked. Sit down, cuz."

Peggy sat down on the other mismatched chair. "Thanks. One
of your friendly Zepps, a very friendly Zepp, guided me to your
office."

"Well, I'm glad to see you. Hannah was just saying it was time
we had you to dinner again. Your godson is getting big and sassy
like someone else I know…You didn't just drop by, did you?
What can I do for you, cuz?"

Peggy said nothing and waited until she was sure that
Mickey's attention was fixed on her.

"You probably know that your friend, Tony, wants to go to
Mass with me next Sunday and then take the whole family out to
breakfast."

"I do. You should have a good time. He's a terrific guy. I hope
you two hit it off."

"That's what I'm afraid of," said Peggy.

"Why? If you are oil and water, you say 'goodbye' and tell
him your Sundays are tied up for the next twelve years or so.
That would be the end of it. Nothing to worry about. It happens
all the time."

"I know that, Mickey. But the problem is that maybe I don't
want to brush him off—not right away and maybe never if we
get serious."

"Well, that is good news. I can't wait to tell Hannah. I know he is ga-ga over you, so I don't see any problem? Your folks aren't going to balk because he's Italian, are they?"

"I doubt it. That's not my problem and I think you know it."

Peggy looked down at her lap for a few seconds. When she looked up, she looked directly into Mickey McGurk's eyes. "Do you know who I am?"

Oh shit, he thought, *I knew this would happen.*

"Sure, you are my cousin, Peggy McCann, my son's godmother."

She kept looking into his eyes. "Let me try again. Do you remember who I was?"

Mickey didn't blink. "Why don't you tell me who you think you were?"

Tears started to form in Peggy's eyes. "I think you know. I think you've known since Momma Agnes introduced us. I am Margaret O'Brian. Marge the Barge, punchboard of the 'Show and you know it."

Mickey was quiet for a few seconds; he wanted to make sure he said this right.

"No. You're not Marge the Barge. I knew Marge the Barge. I even took advantage of her, God forgive me. I felt sorry for her. I knew she had no future in the 'Show and nothing to look forward to but pain and misery.

"No. You're not Marge. That poor creature could not have grown up to be the beautiful, talented and intelligent woman who is my cousin, Peggy McCann."

Peggy was crying openly now and Mickey reached across the desk and took her hands in his.

"Marge is gone, buried long ago in the muck of the 'Show. Let her be, Peggy. Forget her. You've got a long and, I hope, wonderful life ahead of you. I know who you are—Peggy McCann."

"Oh, Mickey. I love you," said Peggy.

"And I love you, cuz. My wife loves you even more," said Mickey.

Peggy hesitated and then asked, "Does Tony know?"

"Of course not and, even if he did, it wouldn't matter to him or he's not half the man I think he is," said McGurk.

"Does he know I'm in 'show business'?"

"You bet. I think he's responsible for half the gross receipts of that 'Perils of Pauline' chapter. He thinks you're a better actress than Pearl White."

Peggy laughed. "I didn't have a line in that thing."

"I don't think he noticed."

Peggy got ready to leave, much relieved. "So do you think he'll ask me out again?"

"As the detectives say, case closed."

Tony was at St. Anne's at eight thirty, a half-hour early. He was starting to get nervous when he finally saw Peggy strolling down the Boulevard from Irving Street—alone.

"My parents send their apologies. They had to go to the seven. My cousin Rita is sick and they had to go to Bayonne to visit her. But I still can go to breakfast with you if you want."

Breakfast was marvelous and the food wasn't bad either.

"So what time will your parents get home?" Tony asked.

"Probably around suppertime," said Peggy.

Tony brightened and then frowned. He realized this might be a critical moment. "Do you have other plans or could you go to a photoplay and dinner with me before I take you home?"

Peggy made him sweat a bit. Then she smiled and said, "No, I don't have any plans, Tony. That sounds like a very nice day. I'd be very pleased to go with you."

The day was more than nice.

They shook hands when Tony saw her to her door. He held her hand a bit longer than he should have. She didn't pull away.

This has been the best day of my life, thought Tony as he walked off. A date had been made for next Sunday at the twelve o'clock

Mass. They would spend the whole day together.

Momma Agnes was brewing tea when Peggy walked into the kitchen. Poppa Jim was sitting at the table reading the Sunday paper.

"Well, how did it go?" asked Agnes.

"Wonderful, wonderful, Momma," said Peggy as she twirled around the kitchen table. Poppa Jim looked up from his paper.

"He's smart, he's funny, and he's a real gentleman," said Peggy.

"And he's handsome," said Agnes.

"That too," laughed her adopted daughter who went off to her room singing.

"Well, what you think of that?" Agnes asked her husband.

"What do I think of what?" responded Jim.

"Her and Tony, imbecile."

"Good lord, woman. What are you talking about? They've only be together a couple of times. It was just a Mass," said Poppa Jim, terrified at the thought of losing his daughter.

"Right," said his wife.

Peggy popped her head out of the bedroom, "By the way, he's taking me to Mass next Sunday. The twelve o'clock. Is it all right if I bring him home for supper, Momma?"

"Of course, sweetheart. He is a nice young man and I like him and so does Poppa Jim." Poppa Jim made a noise that sounded like "Harumph."

After a couple of more Sundays, it was obvious that Tony was sincere and that her daughter was falling in love. Agnes asked her husband again, "Well, what do you think?"

"He's shorter than her," said Jim.

"That's just her heels. He might even be a tad taller than her in his stocking feet."

"I'd just as soon they keep their shoes on, thank you very much," said Poppa Jim. "Well, in case you haven't noticed, he's an Italian." Jim pronounced it the Irish way, "Eye-talian."

"Really? And what is Lutz Rinaldi? You know, the guy who married your cousin, Mary. Aren't you godfather to their daughter?"

"That's different," said Jim, who played pinochle with Rinaldi once a week. "Lutz is… Lutz is an artist." Rinaldi made stained glass windows in a garage on Zabriskie Street.

"Tony is all right. I sort of like him. But he is just a cop."

"A detective," answered his wife. "And I suppose there aren't any Irish cops?"

"I give up," said Jim.

* * *

The courtship of Peggy and Tony was proceeding rapidly and Peggy was determined there would be no secrets between them. There was one secret she had never told anyone except a priest.

Tony gave her the opening. "Say, I noticed that once in a while you say 'Momma Agnes' or 'Poppa Jim'. What gives?"

Peggy sighed and said, "Momma Agnes is my mother's sister. She and Poppa Jim took me in as a teenager after my parents died. I love them dearly and as far as I am concerned they are my parents."

"Well that makes sense," said Tony. "You poor kid, you must have had a bad time of it. How did your parents die?"

"My mother died on Snake Hill, a hopeless alcoholic."

Tony shook his head. "The curse of the Irish. And your father?"

Peggy took a breath. "My father died when I pushed him off a roof."

Tony was incredulous. "Excuse me?"

"I said my father died when I pushed him off a roof. After he raped me."

Peggy was pale and her hands were shaking. She thought she knew how Tony would react but how could she be certain? Tears began to form.

She told Tony the whole story from Marge the Barge to her father and how she killed him. She was weeping and was looking down at her lap when she finished.

Tony took her hands in his and said, "Peggy, look at me."

She did and saw nothing but love and compassion there.

"You poor baby," he said. "That's all over now." Tony kissed her gently.

Peggy wept as she clung to him. Tony patted her back and kissed her cheek. Finally the tears stopped flowing.

Tony said, "That miserable son-of-a-bitch. I hope he's burning in hell."

"Don't say that, Tony. The part of me that doesn't hate him, loves him. He was my father."

Tony said, "All right then, a thousand years in purgatory."

"Five hundred," said Peggy.

"Seven-fifty," said Tony.

"Done," said Peggy.

They both laughed and then they kissed again.

I can laugh about it, thought Peggy, *I love this man. I do.*

Once again Agnes asked Jim, "Well, what do you think?"

This time the answer was different. "I like him. I think he is a terrific guy. He treats my daughter like the queen she is. He even seems to enjoy us. Lutz tells me he's a good pinochle player too."

"Lutz Rinaldi?"

"Yeah. Lutz is a cousin or something to Tony's father. I have to say, Tony is a good looking guy, for a guinea."

"We don't use that word in this house," said his wife.

"Sorry. Well, anyway, if things go the way I think they are going, I'm going to have me some beautiful grandchildren."

One more set of parents to go.

An Explosive Team

The SMS Dresden was finished.

The light cruiser's engines were clapped out, her twelve boilers fouled, her coal bunkers nearly empty, and the Royal Navy was relentlessly searching for her.

Anchored in the lee of a small island, she was in Chilean waters. Her captain decided the only way to save his ship and her crew was to notify the Chilean authorities and accept internment for the rest of the war. He dispatched a boat to the mainland to do just that.

This would end the remarkable voyage of the Dresden that began when she was unable to get back to Germany after the outbreak of war.

She sank four British merchantmen in the Atlantic before she joined a German squadron in the Pacific. She emerged from the Battle of Coronel without as much as a scratch to her paint. Back to the Atlantic for the disastrous Battle of the Falkland Islands, she was the only German vessel to escape the lethal salvos of the British.

Off to the Pacific again and the final humiliation of internment.

Her end was worse.

The British trapped her where she was anchored. The captain of the Dresden signaled the two British warships that his vessel was no longer a combatant.

Both British vessels opened fire. The Germans managed to get off three rounds before her guns were silenced. The British cannonade continued until a white flag was displayed on Dresden's conning tower.

The Germans scuttled the ship, an explosive charge in her forward magazine blowing off her bow, sinking her in thirty-eight fathoms of water.

Eight men died and twenty-nine were wounded in this one-sided engagement but most of her three hundred and sixty man crew managed to get to the mainland and were interned in Chile.

One such was Lothar Witzke, a handsome, well-built, twenty-something, naval cadet. He managed to flee internment and made his way to San Francisco where he was now standing in front of the German consul-general.

Another man, older, tall and with his arms folded, was leaning against a wall parallel to the consul-general's desk.

"I must congratulate you on your escape, Cadet Witzke," said the consul-general. "That showed determination, innovation and skill. Obviously, we cannot return you to Germany and the Navy but we do have work for you that will help the Fatherland."

"That is my desire, Herr Consul-General."

"We must do all we can to impede the flow of war materials to the Allies and sometimes it is necessary to take drastic—even violent—action to do that. Do you have any experience with explosives, Cadet Witzke?"

"Yes sir. I was assigned to the gunnery department of the Dresden and it was my unhappy duty to set the charges in the forward magazine which scuttled the ship. I know quite a bit about fuses, gun powder, shells and the like, sir."

"I see," said the consul-general. "I am going to assign you to work for my best man, Herr Kurt Jahnke. Your targets will be munitions in the United States consigned the Allies."

"But isn't America neutral, Herr Consul-General?" asked Witzke.

"She is; we aren't." The consul-general gestured to the man by the wall. "Herr Jahnke?" The man on the wall moved and Witzke turned toward him.

Jahnke said, "Tell me why you really wanted to escape from Chile."

Witzke blushed as Jahnke stared at the cadet. "Well, sir, I wasn't going to win an Iron Cross sitting on my ass in Valparaiso, was I?"

"Ha! The Iron Cross," said Jahnke, holding up two fingers. "Stick with me, youngster, and you will get two of them."

Witzke did.

A Warm Sicilian Welcome

"How come you no go to Mass anymore?" asked Tony Aiello's mother.

"What do you mean, Mama? I go to Mass every Sunday, you know that."

"How come you no go to Mass with the family then? Huh? You miss two months in a row. I count. Eight Sundays."

"I went to Mass, Mama. I've been really busy. I told you about that big burglary case up in Hudson City." Actually that case was solved rather rapidly when a beat cop noticed a man with two bandaged hands and told Tony about him.

"So I went to church up where my old partner lives. We've been working very closely on that case, you know."

"I know. I know a lot more than you think I do. Listen, Mr. Big Shot Detective, you think I don't know what's going on in my own family? What do you I think I am, stupid—like you? I know everything."

I was afraid of that. I'm not ready for that. I'm about to be dropped into the shit.

"You think I don't know you've been going to St. Anne's on the Boulevard? Do you think I don't know who you are going to Mass with? Is that what you think, *mio sole idiota?*"

"Now, Mama."

"Don't you *Mama* me. Did you really think Lutz Rinaldi, your father's cousin, wouldn't tell him you were sneaking around with that Irish girl who's his wife's cousin?"

Jesus. Is everybody in this town related to everybody else?

"We weren't 'sneaking around', Mama."

"No? Then how come I have never heard you mention her name?"

"Her name is Peggy McCann and I never mentioned her because there's nothing going on. We're just friends."

Carmela Aiello looked at her son and wiped her hands on her apron. She threw her hands up in supplication.

"*Gesu Cristo!* So when am I going to meet this—this friend? At the Christening?"

"Mama! Take it easy. I swear nothing is going on. You don't need to meet her now. Maybe I'll bring her home someday. When I get to know her better. If I get to know her better."

"Lutz says she is a movie star?"

"Well, she was in a couple of movies. She was hardly a star, Mama."

"You should be going out with nice Italian girls who couldn't find their way into a movie theater unless their brothers took them. I want to meet her now. Your father never met a movie star. I'm sure he would enjoy flirting with her, the old goat. Bring her home after Mass next Sunday. She can help me make dinner."

"Mama, I'm not sure she'd come. We don't know each other that well. She might not want to come."

"Good. Then you won't have to waste your time going to Mass with her anymore."

"Okay, I'll ask her. But, Mama, you're right, she's Irish. I doubt that she can help you cook Sicilian."

"Don't worry, I won't embarrass you. I'll boil some potatoes for her."

"Mama. Be nice, please. Not this Sunday though. The Sunday next. That gives her some time to think it over."

"Forget her. You think it over, *stupido.*"

His boss said Tony could have the next Sunday off. "Sure. You've being working like a dog. You've earned it." Mickey had already called Tony's boss. Mickey knew full well why Tony wanted that Sunday off.

"In fact, take the next couple or three Sundays off. Anything comes up, I can always change my mind and the watch list."

"Thanks, boss."

Peggy was excited about Sundays with Tony and her mother

knew it.

"I'm glad to see you so enthusiastic about your religious duties, Peggy."

"Oh, Momma. I know it's only been two months. Do you think there's anything there? Am I dreaming?"

Agnes said, "When I see him look at you, I start thinking about a mother-of-the-bride dress."

Now Peggy laughed. "You always looked lovely in blue. You know all the cousins are teasing me about him already. That's a good sign, isn't it?"

"That's no surprise. The family knows it is time for you to get married and give up that 'show business' nonsense."

"Oh, Momma, he's so handsome. So gentle."

"Of course he is. I'm sure he got those broken knuckles trying to pull daisies out of the ground," said Agnes.

"Oh, Momma. Should I even be talking about such things? I can't help it. He's so different from all the other boys I ever knew. He listens to me like he's interested in what I'm saying. He's a perfect gentleman. He's poetic. He's romantic. He's just wonderful. And he's not married."

Agnes and Peggy laughed and hugged each other.

Peggy was proud, holding on to Tony's arm, walking towards the church steps that Sunday. She was hoping some of the other girls were envious. *That's always pleasant.*

The women were smiling and funny, all of them talking to Peggy but watching Tony out of the corner of their eyes. Appraising. Appraising.

For the most part they liked what they saw. He was handsome, pretty tall, well-dressed and he didn't treat Peggy like she was a soda bottle he was taking back to the store.

A couple of them had always been jealous of Peggy's good looks. Their thoughts were practical.

Let her marry that guinea. Then maybe half the men in the parish will stop mooning about making goo-goo eyes at her.

Their men formed a half-circle around Tony and talked about sports, the weather, the war. They had already accepted him. A detective. A square shooter, well-spoken, for a wop. Lutz Rinaldi was a good sort. So was Tony Aiello.

It took a full twenty minutes before Peggy and Tony could get into the church. Mass had already started. They slipped into a pew in the back. An old biddy grudgingly moved towards the center, giving them a dirty look, as she shuffled along the pew like it was the death plank on a pirate ship.

Peggy didn't care. It had been a lovely morning and Tony was taking her out to eat.

After Mass they stood around talking to friends and relatives for another ten minutes or so. Then they took the Boulevard jitney to the last stop and walked a couple of blocks to the Canton Tea Garden on Bergen Avenue.

"I know it's a little early for dinner. I hope you like Chinese food," said Tony to Peggy who was prepared to eat anything Tony paid for.

"I love it."

Later after what Peggy thought was a sparkling conversation with more wit than substance, Tony became quiet, toying with his fried rice.

Finally, he said, "You know, I like to go to restaurants once in a while but when I think of Sundays, I always think of the whole family sitting down to a home cooked meal."

Thank you, Lord. Here it comes. Be careful. Don't blurt out 'Yes' with your mouth full of egg foo yung.

"Say, I've got an idea. Next Sunday, what do you say we go to my house for a dinner after Mass?"

Peggy looked at him solemnly. "Your house? You mean meet your family and all?"

"Well, sure. My family will be there, of course. You'll like them. Especially my sisters. But we're really going for the food. My mother is a great cook."

"I'm sure she is," said Peggy, who had burned the last piece of toast she made. "But... what I mean... I'm not sure what I mean... but won't your family read more into it? My coming to dinner, I mean."

"Nah," Tony lied. "Those days are gone. This is America. They know we are just friends. Good friends."

Tony took Peggy's hand in his. "They don't have to know that I want us to be more than good friends someday."

Peggy melted. She composed herself. "Well, when you put it like that. Okay. Sure. Why not?"

Tony clapped his hands together.

The next Sunday rolled around quickly and Tony, in a car he borrowed from a friend, drove Peggy Downtown to Vroom Street. Tony lived with his family on the second floor of a well-kept four family brick building. Peggy thought it looked very respectable. Peggy knew many Italians were poor and lived in the slums some of the Irish had fled. She had been ready for anything. This was a nice surprise.

Peggy's first thought on walking into the Aiello flat was: *Whatever that is, it smells delicious.*

Tony's younger sisters, Theresa and Doreen, ran to her. "Welcome, Miss McCann. Welcome to our home," said Theresa, the older one.

"It's Peggy, please. I take it you are Theresa. That means you are Doreen."

Both girls hugged her at the same time. Italians hug everybody. Even if you're just there to read the gas meter. It doesn't mean anything.

"Oh, Peggy, please sit next to me at dinner."

"No. She should sit next to me. I'm older."

"I asked first."

"How about I sit in the middle?"

The sisters nodded their agreement as their mother arrived wiping her hands on her apron.

Madonna! She's as tall as a tree. My poor little boy.

Carmela Aiello was about five two in her lace up black shoes with the wide heels. Her hair—black with a few strands of gray—was pulled back into a bun. She had no discernible waist. She was still wearing her go-to-church maroon dress but her apron, big as a butcher's, covered most of it. Her eyes were brown, her skin a rich olive. Her face seemed more masculine than feminine. She wore no makeup.

"Mama, may I introduce you to my friend, Peggy McCann?"

"Ah, your friend. How nice. You are welcome in my house, Miss McCann."

She kept wiping her hands on her apron.

Uh oh. No hug. She says I'm welcome but her eyes are hard—very hard.

Finally they shook hands. Carmela Aiello's hand was as hard as her eyes. "Thank you, Mrs. Aiello. I'm so glad to be here. Tony can't stop talking about you and your family."

"Really? Me, I can't get two words out of him, but then I'm just his mother. It's nice to know he's paying attention to somebody."

Peggy had her Irish temper firmly under control. *I don't care what the old battleaxe says, she is not getting a rise out of me.*

"I hope I'm not intruding, Mrs. Aiello."

Carmela waved her hands. "Oh, no. Tony brings lotsa girls home for dinner."

Peggy looked at Tony who quickly asked, "Mama, refresh my memory. What girls did I bring home?"

"Me? I can't remember them all. Carlotta. Marcella. Rose. Beatrice." Her voice trailed off.

"Oh, you mean my cousins? The ones you asked me to pick up for Christmas and Easter dinner." Carmella remained silent.

Aha! So I'm the only girl he's ever brought home.

"Tony tells me I'm in for a treat. He says you are going to show me how you cook a real Italian meal."

"I don't cook Italian."

Peggy panicked and immediately looked at Tony for help. He mouthed the word "Sicilian." Peggy put her hand to her forehead.

"Of course. How stupid of me. You are Sicilian, not Italian. Forgive me."

"No matter," said Mrs. Aiello who believed the Irish couldn't tell a chicken from a turkey either.

She turned to Theresa. "*Cara figlia*, take our honored guest into the parlor." Theresa, Doreen and Tony were incredulous.

"The parlor, Mama?"

"Of course, only our best is good enough for Miss McCann."

The last honored guest to be ensconced in the parlor was Grandpa Luigi and he was in his coffin.

Carmela was proud of her parlor. The sofa with its hard cushions, the two upright chairs, the pillows, the hassock, the tables, the lamps with doilies under them, the vase with dried flowers, the reproduction of the Sacred Heart, the photographs on the walls, mostly of relatives who were long gone. The furniture was all solid hardwood. An axe would bounce off and might be blunted in the attempt. Naturally, no one was permitted in there without specific invitation. It was a well dusted monument to the good life in America.

"No junk," she would say to herself. "I don't got junk in my parlor."

Tony excused himself as soon as Peggy and the girls were seated. He headed for the kitchen. "Mama. You said you wouldn't embarrass me. You put her in the parlor. You wouldn't put your worst enemy in there."

"Yes, I would."

Her husband rose. "I better go in the parlor before that girl thinks no one in this family has any manners."

Antonio said, "Ah, Miss McCann, I am Antonio Aiello, Tony's father."

He was two or three inches shorter than Tony with the same well-groomed wavy brown hair. His nose was broad but not broken. A thin moustache lined his upper lip. Antonio was muscular and looked powerful. He was wearing a three-piece brown suit and across his vest was a gold chain. A gold watch was probably in one vest pocket and a small, unusable, gold plated knife in the other.

Antonio took Peggy's hand and kissed it. "Ah, nothing brightens a house like a beautiful woman. I must congratulate my son."

Peggy was flustered. "Er, how do you do? Er, thank you. Nice meeting you."

Now that was a gracious reply, you dummy. Well, at least I can see where Tony gets his charm. But if I was Mrs. Aiello, I'd keep this one on a short leash. Until he's at least eighty.

Tony was adamant. "Mama, you go into that parlor and bring Peggy back into the kitchen where she belongs."

"Into my kitchen?"

"Yes. Don't disgrace me, Mama."

She stood at the entrance of the parlor again wiping her hands on her apron. "I see you have met 'il Principe.'"

"I'm sorry?"

"My husband. That's what I call him sometimes. You know, like 'sweetheart.'"

"Oh, of course, I must say Senor Aiello is as charming as his son."

Mrs. Aiello laughed. Or she may have snorted. "I'm sure. Usually, I'm too busy to notice. Well, Miss McCann, you're not going to see how I cook a Sicilian meal sitting in the parlor. If you don't mind, please come into the kitchen."

"Yes," said her husband, "come into the kitchen. It's much — how do you say it — cozier."

Peggy was happy to be released from exile and back into Tony's presence. They were all seated at the big table with its nicks, cuts and chipped legs. The unpainted top had been scrubbed white with use and love.

Peggy was standing at Carmela's elbow watching her cook. Watching but not understanding. Carmela was in constant motion. Occasionally, she said something under her breath but nothing that Peggy could hear.

Carmela asked, "So do you live with your family?"

"Yes, Mrs. Aiello. But as soon as I get steady work, I hope to get a place of my own. I don't want to take advantage of my family's generosity forever."

What's the matter with the Irish? Do they hate their families?

Theresa sighed. "I wish I could live on my own."

Her mother was quick. "You'll move out of here when your husband says so."

"But, Mama, what if I don't get married?"

"Good. Then you can take care of your father and me." Theresa sighed more loudly.

"Doreen, hand me that spoon." Carmela pointed. When Peggy looked towards the spoon, Carmela dropped a big pinch of sugar into the gravy with her other hand.

Why should I share my secrets with her?

Antonio said, "Miss McCann. We understand you are a movie star. You certainly look like one."

Tony smiled. His mother, her back to the table, rolled her eyes and shook her head.

"Please. All of you. Please call me Peggy."

Doreen said, "Back to being a movie star, Peggy."

"Doreen, I'm not a movie star. I never was. True, I had bit parts in a couple of movies and it was fun working with Pauline White. But it isn't a real job. I doubt that I've made much more than a hundred dollars when you add it all up."

"A hundred dollars is a lot of money," said Carmela.

"Not when you spread it over a couple of years, it's not."

'True," said Theresa.

"Bah, that just proves the movie bosses are fools. They have you and they pick hags for their movies," said Antonio, pointedly looking at his son who had a sudden need to look at the ceiling.

The meal was delicious, Carmela accepting compliments from all like bread soaking up gravy.

Peggy had learned nothing about Sicilian cooking except to appreciate it when you eat it.

Carmela's verdict: *She'd probably burn toast.*

Tony, taking Peggy home, was gushing. "I told you. My family loved you. I never saw them take to anyone like they took to you."

"Even your mother?"

Tony hesitated. "Well, my mother isn't from the same village in Sicily as my father. He says they are a hard, suspicious lot but they warm up once they get to know you."

Well, that shouldn't take more than fifty or sixty years. Dear God, what am I getting into? Should I shut this down now while I still can?

Envy is Deadly

Captain Franz von Rintelen was all but snubbed in certain circles in both Berlin and at the German Embassy in Washington. His "von" was of recent origin and he was thought to be a parvenu, what Americans called a "social climber." The military attaché, Franz von Papen, found him particularly distasteful. The feeling was mutual; von Rintelen thought of the military attaché as a "bungler" who had made a hash out of the earlier sabotage efforts.

But it was, ironically, his social striving that brought von Rintelen even more audacious success when it came to sabotage at sea.

A well connected woman of his acquaintance wrote the Russian military attaché in Paris and recommended one of von Rintelen's shell companies as an excellent import firm. The attaché, a wine connoisseur, consigned a shipment of wine to E.V. Gibbons, Inc. The wine was easily sold and turned a profit. Then the Germans suggested to the attaché that they could handle Russian exports from the United States just as efficiently.

The Russians bit. Von Rintelen borrowed $3,000,000 from a New York bank on the strength of his Russian contracts, bought supplies for the Russians, loaded them on ships, got paid, damaged or sank the ships and then repaid the loans before anyone got suspicious.

Irish longshoremen put two of Dr. Scheele's cigar bombs in the SS Phoebus' three holds before she set sail for Archangel. Fire at sea crippled her and destroyed her cargo. She was towed into Liverpool by a British warship.

Ship after ship went down or their cargoes were ruined in successful attempts to quench the fires. The distraught Russians never suspected von Rintelen.

Even two barges of Russian-bought munitions caught fire and

sank while being towed from the busy railroad terminal at Black Tom to a waiting ship anchored at Gravesend. Apparently von Rintelen's Irish friends had contacts at Black Tom too.

The SS Kirk Oswald was on her way to Archangel with a cargo of sugar when she was diverted to Marseilles. The cigar bombs didn't have time to ignite and the French discovered them when the cargo was unloaded. The cigar bombs were easily disarmed.

The French promptly sent some to Captain Tunney and his Bomb Squad. Tunney was already having Paul Koenig of the Hamburg-American line followed because "that son-of-a-bitch spends all together too much time on the docks checking on ships that will never sail."

Tunney now had a good idea who was planting those bombs. So did the British who began tightly guarding ships while they were being loaded.

Success can engender even more envy. The consistent complaints of the military attaché about von Rintelen prompted Berlin to recall him.

In August, 1915, von Rintelen, using his fake Swiss passport, sailed for the Netherlands aboard the SS Noordam from Hoboken. When she docked in Southampton, the British arrested him.

It was if they knew exactly who von Rintelen was and exactly when and where he would arrive.

The German embassy picked a new sabotage chief for the Eastern United States. That was Paul Hilken, an official of the North German Lloyd steamship line. He would work closely with Frederick Hinsch, the larger than life merchant marine captain, to the point where they divided a target list between them

Hinsch wanted the Lehigh Valley Railroad munitions terminal at Black Tom put on his list. He and von Rintelen had walked around the Black Tom terminal unchallenged by the handful of bored guards the British had hired. More than three quarters of the munitions bound for the Allies from New York Harbor passed through Black Tom.

Captain Hinsch would not forget Black Tom.

We Must Act Quickly

Tony's godmother was from the same village in Sicily as Carmela. Close as sisters, neither had a brother. The next day they sat at a table in the kitchen in a flat above an Italian grocery store on Brunswick Street drinking black coffee. They spoke in a Sicilian dialect that was virtually incomprehensible to anyone born much further than twenty miles from their village.

"I have a serious problem, *comare*. Very serious," said Carmela.

"If you need money, we can…"

"No, not money. I said it was a serious problem. Not money." Carmela's husband had a good job. He was a master bricklayer. Of course, it was slow in the winter but Carmela put money away and both Tony and Theresa chipped in for room and board. It was expected.

"Then what?" asked Julia Monetti.

"It's my son—your godson—Anthony." She had wanted to baptize her son Antonio, but was persuaded that Anthony was more American.

"Tony? Oh my God, what's the problem, Carmela?"

Carmela sat, blew air through her lips and bit them. "This is hard for me," she said. "But I am afraid my boy, my precious Anthony, is going to be lost to me."

She paused, as if to give her next words more weight. "He is going to Mass at St. Anne's on the Boulevard with a girl." Another pause. "An Irish girl."

Julia Monetti clamped her hand to her mouth.

"He says she's just a friend. I don't believe that."

"Neither do I. No man has female friends—unless they are related," said Julia. "They are looking for just one thing, the pigs. But if they get it they usually walk away and sniff after the next one."

"Not my Tony. Not with this one. I've met her. She's been in my house. Ate with my family."

"Dear God, it's gone that far?"

"Yes."

"What does she look like?"

"Tall as a telephone pole but with a better figure. Not bad looking if you overlook that pasty Irish skin with all those spots on it."

"Freckles?"

"Yes, that's what they are called. I don't see how anyone could find them attractive."

"You're not a man, Carmela. Can she cook?"

"I think there would be a better chance of her burning the house down than her putting a meal on the table. She seemed hopeless to me."

"Did Antonio marry you for your cooking?"

They both laughed and Carmela's chin jutted out a bit.

"Of course not. But he found out I can satisfy him both in bed and at the table. Did I tell you this Irish girl was a movie actress? Not a star. But on the screen nonetheless."

"Not bad looking, huh? No wonder she's turned Tony's head."

"Tony's? She turned Antonio's too and she'll turn Vito's if you are stupid enough to let him anywhere near her."

"Don't worry about that," said Julia, smugly. "When he's done with twelve hours at the store and then laying with me for an hour, he's too tired to light a cigar."

They both laughed again. "Okay, *comare*. Let's be serious. I may be wrong, but I've always thought you wanted my Tony to marry your Angelina. Do you still feel that way?"

Julia looked straight at Carmela. "Yes. I do. I always thought it would be wonderful to share grandchildren with you. But it looks like that is not going to happen." She was crestfallen.

"Why not?" asked Carmela. Julia's face turned curious.

Carmela asked, "Is this how Sicilian women act? Shed a tear

and forget about it? Or do we sit down and plot?"

Julia's reply was strong and instantaneous. "We plot, *comare*. We plot." Two Sicilian women could easily concoct a feasible plot. Three probably could bring down a government.

"Good. Now what do we do?"

Julia spoke first. "My daughter is a virgin. We get Tony to seduce her. Then he'll have to marry her. Our husbands would see to that."

Carmela thought for a few seconds. "Good idea. Very Sicilian. But it won't work."

"Why not?"

"Tony won't do it on his own. He's very careful around Italian girls, let alone Sicilians. He knows the consequences."

Julia asked, "So what then?"

Carmela took both Julia's hands in hers. "Angelina must seduce Tony."

Julia pulled her hands away, shocked. "Do you know what you are saying? My daughter's not a tramp. She's a virgin. She would never do that."

"We have a better chance with her than Tony," said Carmela, "Just how badly do you want to see them marry?"

"I really want that but not at the cost of ruining her life."

"What do you mean?" asked Carmela.

"Suppose she is successful and Tony wakes up in the morning and is regretful about what happened. He knows what comes next. Supposing he packs a bag, catches a train and goes out West and becomes a cowboy or something."

Carmela choked down the impulse to laugh. "I see your point, *comare*. But couldn't the bloody sheets be put away and then, when a real wedding does take place, hung out the window for all to see? Who is going to get close enough to tell the age of the bloodstains?"

"Hmmm," said Julia.

Carmela wanted to cement the deal. "It's always prudent to

235

have another plan in case one fails. I swear, if my Tony sleeps with her and doesn't marry her, I will make it my life's work to see that Angelina is married off properly. She won't suffer in any event. It's a risk, but not a big one. The rewards will be great. Grandchildren."

Julia took both of Carmela's hands in hers. "You swear?"

"I do."

"Then, done. Now let's talk about how we set this up. We have to get them alone. In a place where nature can do its work. Not easy."

Both women thought as they drank another demitasse of black coffee. That's what they called it. They would think "Espresso" was an Italian train.

Julia folded her hands in front of her and shook them like some sort of victorious athlete. "I've got it. They can make love right here. Alone. In this flat. On her bed."

Carmela was skeptical, very skeptical. "How could that ever happen, *comare*?"

"It's really simple. Angelina works in an embroidery factory on Leonard Street."

"Where's that?"

"Not far from—what do they call it now—Union City. Will you let me finish?"

"I'm sorry. Go ahead."

"Every night she takes the Number 18 bus down Summit Avenue, past the Five Corners and down Newark Avenue to Brunswick Street. It's very convenient. But not on Friday night. She works late on Friday. They have a half-day on Saturday. My husband doesn't want her taking the bus at nine o'clock at night. Too many drunks from that big laundry around the corner. So he takes the automobile and drives her home himself."

"So?"

"So my husband is not going to be there next Friday to drive her home. He has a brother who runs a farm in Mendham. We go there for a week each summer. We help out on the farm. We have lots of fun. That young man who works for Vito will run the store. He's a nice boy, the brother of a godchild. He probably won't steal too much.

"Anyway. My husband will drive us up to Mendham after church on Sunday and we won't be back until the next Sunday. Angelina will be here alone. All week. She'll need a ride next Friday night. I'll ask my godson to make sure she gets home safely. After that, it will be up to Angelina."

Carmela was frank in her admiration. "Julia. If you were a man you'd be the mayor or a really important gangster. That's brilliant. But a problem remains. As you say, your daughter is a virgin. Naïve. Not wise in the ways of women. A woman of the world would have no trouble carrying out our plan. That Irisher, for example. But your darling Angelina?"

"Do not concern yourself, *comare*. I have until Sunday to teach my daughter what she needs to know and to get her firm commitment to do it."

"But will she do it?"

Julia said, "She is Sicilian."

Carmela asked, "Do you think she really would want to marry my Tony?"

"Of course. He is handsome, strong. He has a good job. He is a pleasant man even if he is a policeman. My husband says he has a good future. He is a good catch. I'd marry him myself if I was single. Of course my husband will be disappointed. He wants the store to stay in the family. Maybe, Tony would take it over when it's time?"

"I wouldn't get my hopes up. But we must act quickly," said Carmela.

* * *

Angelina was seated next to Tony on the front seat when he

pulled up in front of the darkened store on Brunswick Street.

"Thanks for the ride, Tony. I appreciate it."

"You're welcome, cuz. Do you want me to walk you upstairs to your door?"

"If you don't mind. There's something I need to talk to you about if you have a few minutes."

"Sure."

He followed her up the stairs admiring what he saw. Angelina was nineteen with dark eyes and raven black hair and as for her body, well, as a neighborhood boy once forlornly said, "She's like a basket of ripe melons, you don't know which one to squeeze first."

She had to unlock two locks. Tony noticed that the door to the Monetti flat was solid oak, not easily breeched.

Her old man probably keeps money up here until he can get to a bank. I hear he's loaded.

Angelina was wearing a straight skirt and a silk shirtwaist. She looked very pretty.

"Why don't you sit down, Tony, and I'll make us a pot of black coffee."

"Sounds good." They were seated at the kitchen table.

Angelina, as her mother had suggested, asked, "Would you like to have some anisette in your coffee?"

"I would but I think I'll skip it."

"You sure?"

"Yes. Now tell me, Angelina, what did you have to talk to me about?"

She fluffed her hair and looked at him with the hint of a smile. "Do you love me, Tony?"

Tony was silent a few seconds too long. "Of course, I do, Angelina, you're my cousin."

Angelina laughed. "I don't mean like that, Tony. We're not really relatives, you know. Have you ever thought about loving me like a man loves a woman?"

"No," Tony lied.

"So you don't want to marry me, Tony."

Uh, oh! What the hell is going on here?

"I'm probably the only single man in a five block area who doesn't want to marry you, Angelina. I love you, but no, I don't want to marry you. You're my cousin and that's that."

Angelina smiled broadly. "Well, I don't want to marry you either, Tony."

"Angelina. What is this all about? Why are we even talking like this?"

Angelina looked straight at him. "My mother wants you to marry me but she is afraid some Irish girl is going to get you first."

So Carmela Aiello's fine hand is in this somehow.

"So what I was supposed to do was get you up here, ply you with anisette, kiss you, rub you where my hand has never been, take you to my bedroom and seduce you. Then you would have to marry me."

Tony was shocked but somehow the idea was not repellent. "But you don't want to do that?"

"Not if I don't have to. You'd make a great husband, Tony. But this is America. I am never going to marry a man who doesn't love me. And I have enough cousins, thank you. The truth is I love another."

Tony was relieved. "Can you tell me who?"

"I can but you mustn't tell anyone. It would get back to my father. His name is Vinnie Malfetti. He works in my father's store."

"So how did this secret romance start?"

"When the weather is really bad. When it snows, or rains very hard. My father sends Vinnie in the car to pick me up from work and take me home."

"And are you sure he loves you and not the store? You don't have any brothers."

Angelina laughed. "I think he loves us both but I don't mind sharing him."

She stood up. So did Tony. Angelina walked around the table until she was directly in front of him. "I told my mother I would do this, so I will. I know you haven't had any anisette, Tony, but do you want to kiss me—like a man?"

Tony stood stock still. She was trembling slightly. He reached over and held both arms tight to her side. "Yes, I do," he said. He leaned over and kissed her on the cheek.

"Goodnight, cuz. See you around."

"Oh, Tony," Angelina said, throwing her arms around his neck and kissing him on his cheek. "Thank you, cuz."

"Right. But don't come crying to me when that boy friend of yours turns out to be a bindle stiff. What are you going to tell that conniving mother of yours?"

"The truth. You wouldn't even kiss me. I'm going to tell her I think you like boys better than girls."

"Sweet Jesus."

Carmela and Julia were back sharing a pot of black coffee.

"I'm sorry, Carmela. But your son just wouldn't cooperate. He kept telling Carmela she was his 'cousin'."

"Ha, if cousins refused to do it with their cousins there'd be a lot fewer funny looking kids back in Sicily," said Carmela.

"Angelina also said she was afraid he might like boys better than girls."

"Do you think we could get her to mention that to the Irish girl?" Both women laughed out loud and sipped their black coffee.

"No, if Tony would turn down a beauty like Angelina than it's more serious than maybe even he realizes. I must come up with a better plan."

"Who, this time?" asked Julia.

"Me," Carmela said. "If I cannot get Tony to love another, then I must get the Irish girl to love me."

"Explain that to me," said Julia who, while she loved Carmela as a sister, did not think her particularly lovable.

"Remember the old saying, 'A son is a son till he takes him a wife; a daughter's a daughter the whole of your life'?"

Julia said, "I do and how true it is. I can think of dozens of mothers who lament that their sons have gravitated to their wives' families and they see them as infrequently as priests who don't want money."

Carmela said, "That's a problem with the Irish girl. She has a mother, really her aunt but her mother nonetheless. She'll be drawn to her. It's only natural, I don't resent that.

"But I will be her children's grandmother too. And those children will be named Aiello. They will be Sicilian whether she likes it or not.

"The trick is to try to make her want to be with me. That way I'll see her, Tony and the children for dinner every Sunday afternoon. Maybe she'll even want to live close to me. My husband's talking about buying the building we live in. Maybe, they'll live across the hall from me. Then, in the future, my girls and their families can live downstairs."

Julia sucked in her breath at the audacity—and seeming impossibility—of such a scheme. But she knew this. Carmela was no dreamer. She was as practical as a rolling pin.

"How will you do this?"

"It will take time but not too much time. All young girls want to be loved. I will love her. Do you know how hard it is to dislike someone who loves you?"

"I don't know, children do it all the time," said Julia.

"But not for long. Love and hate change places like partners at a dance. It is indifference that dooms you. I am not indifferent to the Irish girl. It may be that my son loves her, so why shouldn't I?"

"I'd love to be there to see it happen," said Julia.

"You be there doing the same thing when your Angelina picks

out a man to be your son-in-law. Meanwhile, I'll make sure you're invited to the children's birthday dinners. As Tony's godmother."

"You make it sound like it has already happened."

"It has."

* * *

Carmela quickly approached Tony. "You know, son, I really like Peggy. Maybe I was too nervous to show it."

You, nervous?

"She might have gotten the wrong impression. Invite her back for Sunday dinner. Only this time, maybe, she would go to the early Mass with us at Our Lady of Victories. That way she could meet some of my friends. Then we could start the gravy together."

"For real? You would let her watch you make your gravy?"

"No. I would help her to make my gravy. She's got to learn sometime if you are serious with her. You can't eat burnt toast the rest of your life."

Tony thought for a minute.

My mother has given up after that Angelina fiasco. What is she up to now?

Another thought intruded. *Yes. You know, I think I am serious. Very serious. But Peggy didn't sound very enthusiastic when I dropped her off. Maybe, this will help.*

"I'll ask her, Mama. But you're right. She might have gotten the wrong impression last time."

"She'll come if she thinks you're worth it. But even if she doesn't, I don't want you to give up on her. You hear me? I really like Peggy, Tony."

Sweet Jesus.

Tony repeated his mother's words—except the part about the burned toast—to Peggy. "See, I told you. She really does like you, Peggy."

"What about the part about being 'serious', Tony?" She looked directly into those brown eyes. "Is this serious?"

He held her stare. Neither blinked. "Yes, it is. I am very serious, Peggy." She smiled as did he.

"Then, okay, I will come to Mass with your family, meet your mother's friends, and help her in the kitchen."

"Does this mean I get to kiss more than your hand now?"

Peggy threw her arms around his neck. "Yes, my darling." The height difference had almost disappeared. Peggy was wearing shoes with heels an inch shorter and Tony's shoes had new heels almost a half inch higher.

And kiss they did. Peggy softened and Tony hardened. The first part of their courtship was over.

On the way to Mass the next Sunday, Peggy said to Tony, "You know, some of the Irish wives I know are already making pasta."

"Really?"

"Yes. They mix ketchup with hot water to make gravy." Tony didn't believe her.

Carmela Aiello was witty and vivacious. Her eyes sparkled like brown jewels. She introduced Peggy to her friends and relatives after Mass as if she was a long lost daughter.

The friends and relatives responded in kind. Not that Peggy could understand a fifth of what was being said. Most of the women burst into Sicilian when they got excited. But Peggy knew. They accepted her because Carmela accepted her. That was enough.

Once they were in the flat, Carmela said, "We'll go into the bedroom, Peggy and change into house dresses. We don't want to mess up our good clothes."

On the bed was a brand new house dress. It was Peggy's size and pretty too, as far as a housedress went.

Is this the same woman I met just two weeks ago?

When they emerged, Tony said, "Peggy, you look lovely."

"Oh, Tony, it's just a housedress."

"Peg, you'd look lovely in rags. Or in nothing."

Peggy, the veteran of burlesque, stage and screen, blushed. Carmela smiled.

"Now, Peggy, let's make our sauce."

Peggy paid strict attention. At a certain point, Carmela said, "Peggy, now listen to me. This is important." She gestured at the pot. "Right now. You must put a big pinch of sugar in. It cuts the bitterness."

Peggy understood.

Paper, Paper Everywhere

A pair of Federal agents was tailing the editor of a German language newspaper in July 15, 1915, when he emerged from a meeting at the Hamburg Amerika line in Manhattan with Dr. Heinrich Albert, the German commercial attaché and sabotage paymaster.

The agents split up when the Germans did. Dr. Albert, carrying a large portfolio, caught an elevated train, sat down and promptly fell asleep.

He bolted upright when the train reached his station and he rushed out the car's doors—without his portfolio.

The alert agent grabbed it and went out another door as a frantic Albert came back to retrieve it.

Up the briefcase went until William McAdoo, Secretary of the Treasury, realizing the importance of its contents, took it to his father-in-law, President Woodrow Wilson who merely instructed him to bring it to the Secretary of State.

Inside were papers detailing various German schemes that were being bankrolled by the Embassy and aimed at denying munitions to the Allies. Colonel von Papen was spending as much as $2,000,000 a week to disrupt Allied munitions shipments.

The Secretary of State had a problem, though. He could not admit that Federal agents had stolen the private papers of an accredited diplomat so he did the next best thing; they were leaked to a New York newspaper.

The newspaper articles were sensational but, in the end, their only effect was to saddle Dr. Albert with the title of "Minister Without Portfolio" to the great amusement of Washington's social set.

Wilson still refused to allow anything to budge him from his position of neutrality.

Then there was Dr. Constantin Dumba, the appropriately named Austro-Hungarian ambassador to the United States who gave a packet of material to a sympathetic newspaperman to take to Vienna.

An unsympathetic waiter overheard the conversation. "I tell you I think the stuff in that package is important," said the Bohemian waiter. "They were talking about sabotage all night. I understand German. I know what they were saying." The waiter was talking to a Federal agent who was very interested.

The newspaperman was arrested by the British when his ship docked in Falmouth.

Dumba's papers contained one with a plan for inciting strikes at munitions plants and otherwise derailing deliveries to the Allies. Bethlehem Steel plants were a particular target. A memo noted that Colonel Franz von Papen heartily endorsed the plan. There were also some nasty references to both Wilson and the United States.

This was too much for Wilson, neutrality notwithstanding, who demanded Dr. Dumba's recall.

Surveillance was intensified on von Papen and the naval attaché.

Meanwhile, President Wilson continued to look the other way as mysterious explosions boomed across the United States.

Another would be German saboteur, arrested in Weehawken, identified von Papen as the man who supervised his efforts to use miniature bombs to disable Allied ship rudders.

Now this was too much, even for Wilson.

Von Papen and the naval attaché were declared persona non grata and dispatched back to Germany.

The German ambassador hurried to assure Wilson that he had no idea what his subordinates were doing since he dealt only with diplomacy. "Whatever they did, they did on their own responsibility," he said.

President Wilson chose to believe the popular Count von

Bernstorff.

The British guaranteed von Papen safe conduct according to existing diplomatic protocols. Such safe conduct did not apply to his luggage or his papers apparently. These were searched by the British and included128 check stubs detailing payments to his agents.

Once in Germany, von Papen met with Sir Roger Casement. Their efforts to recruit Irish prisoners-of-war to fight against England failed. For good reason.

"What do you think, Barney, should we go over to the Huns?"

"We'd be fools. We took the King's Shilling. If we change sides and the Brits win the war, they'll hang us as traitors."

"Good thinking, Barney."

Black Tom

No one was quite certain how Black Tom got its name.

Some said it was because of an old black man named Tom who lived in a shack on the island and made his living fishing in the river.

Others denied that but had no plausible alternative to offer.

In any event, it got its name long before the railroads came and hardly anyone alive remembered when the railroads didn't dominate Jersey City's waterfront.

Hoboken had great liners that docked at its piers, not so Jersey City which dealt in ferry boats, tugboats, barges, lighters and the occasional ocean-going freighter.

Traffic back and forth across the North River—as the Hudson was sometimes called west of Manhattan—was constant, especially during the daylight hours. Some cargo was offloaded onto lighters and taken to waiting ships anchored at Gravesend. Ferries ran as long as passenger trains pulled into the terminals.

Black Tom Island, at first, was charted as part of the State of New York. It was a geographic anomaly that Bedloe's Island, with its Statue of Liberty, Ellis Island, with its great Immigration Hall and Black Tom Island, with—or without—its shack, were part of New York despite the fact that they were much closer to Jersey City than Manhattan.

That changed, at least for Black Tom Island.

The railroad came to Black Tom in 1883. The National Docks Railroad connected the National Storage Company Docks there with the Pennsylvania Railroad tracks elsewhere on the waterfront. Ownership changed hands a couple of times until the Lehigh Valley Railroad gained complete control in 1900.

The Lehigh Valley Railroad moved its endless stream of coal cars filled with anthracite and boxcars packed with other cargo down its own railroad tracks in Pennsylvania to that 150 feet wide causeway linking Black Tom to mainland Jersey City. As time passed, Black Tom literally grew as more fill was hauled in to swell its girth.

Black Tom, no longer an island, became part of Jersey City. How and when that happened is lost in the legal mists along with the origin of its name but most first year law school students would bet there was some tax advantage attached to the move.

If Miss Liberty could look over her right shoulder, she would see something that looked like a rocky door knob attached to Jersey City. That was Black Tom.

With the coming of the Great War, Black Tom bound cargo switched from mostly coal to munitions and other cargo bound for the Allies.

A mile long wharf had six piers and could handle tugboats, barges, lighters and ships. Six huge warehouses of the National Dock and Storage Company filled up with war material. Switch engines hauled boxcars back and forth. Trucks and even horse drawn carts made their way up and down the causeway dodging the trains. All kinds of activity were intense at Black Tom during the daylight hours from Monday through Saturday. Then the whistles blew. Nothing moved on Black Tom from dusk on Saturday until dawn on Monday.

Then Black Tom was, as the railroad men called it, a dead yard.

Black Tom got its water, electricity, telegraph and telephone service from Jersey City. The city's fire department protected it. But not the police. Black Tom was private property and beyond the domain of the local police unless they were called in.

Never mind. The Lehigh Valley Railroad had its own police force, the same one that couldn't stop street urchins from pilfering tons of its coal as its trains rolled through Jersey City.

So every day hundreds of thousands—perhaps millions—of pounds of shells, ammunition, black powder, TNT, dynamite, and other explosive materials were sidetracked onto Black Tom ready to take the next leg of the journey across the Atlantic Ocean.

These munitions and goods were bought, paid for and shipped by agents of Great Britain, France and Russia. Such were the fruits of neutrality. Good jobs and high profits created here; quality goods exported there.

To be fair, America would have sold the same munitions to Germany and the Central Powers if they could pay for it and, more importantly, if a way could be divined to evade the British blockade. British cruisers rode on the three mile line outside every major American port. Get past them and there was still a blockade of German ports to be faced. But that was their problem, not that of neutral America.

No one expected trouble. This was America, not Europe.

The munitions were supposed to be in and out of Black Tom within twenty-four hours. None was to be stored there overnight. That was the rule. Usually, that schedule could be followed but then there was that thirty-six hour stretch over the weekend when Black Tom was a dead yard.

No one was at Black Tom then except for some watchmen and a few, no more than eight, lackadaisical guards hired by the British to keep an eye on things. No one else was there except anyone who took a notion to wander about.

Crewmen from the idle lighters and tugs would pass through on their way to Johnson or Communipaw Avenues to get drink or a bottle of whiskey. The guards saw some but not others. Anyone could drift in from the land side. You might see him on the causeway, you might not. But why bother, anyhow? There wasn't much to steal here. So shadows came and went unnoticed.

Security was worse on the river side. Anyone could pull up to a pier in a small boat unnoticed even if it was in a relatively noisy motor boat. Moonlight isn't all that revealing in a place where there were no street lights.

Black Tom was, obviously, defenseless. But did it need to be defended? America was neutral.

The big problems the watchmen and guards had were entertaining themselves and fending off the swarms of mosquitoes against which there was no sure defense. Whiskey fueled the former, smudge pots the latter. One worked, the other didn't.

Sergeant Mickey McGurk brought Black Tom to the attention of Commissioner Frank Hague, director of public safety of Jersey City and his "uncle" by marriage.

"Black Tom? I've heard of it, but I've never been there," said Hague. There were no registered voters on Black Tom. "The railroad owns it, right?"

"Yeah. The Lehigh Valley. Have for a long time. Fifteen years or so."

Hague asked, "So what are they shipping out of there? Coal?"

"Not any more. Munitions. Every kind of explosive imaginable."

"So? There's a war going on and, thank God, that means everybody's working."

"Commissioner. I'm talking about thousands of tons of explosives sitting there. Just sitting there, sometimes for days at a time."

Frank Hague's forehead furled. "But it's safe. Right?"

McGurk shrugged. "Maybe. Maybe not. It's supposed to be in and out in twenty-four hours. That's not always happening. Not on a Sunday, not ever. The stuff just sits there."

Frank Hague calculated what advantage might be had out of this situation.

"Good lord, Mickey! If some of that stuff ever went up by accident, we could have real trouble on our hands. I imagine that the railroad or the British or somebody is making certain that accidents like that don't happen."

"Maybe so, but not that me or my partner could see. We walked right in there at night. Looked all over the place. Walked all over. We didn't see anyone except a couple guys standing around a smudge pot who waved to us as we walked out."

"So what did you do?"

"Waved back. I figured I'd tell you and see what you want to do—if anything."

Hague bit his lip and nodded his appreciation. "Mick, you mentioned a rule. Who makes the rules for this kind of thing?"

"The Feds. It's an interstate shipment. That's strictly Federal."

"So if I wanted shut down Black Tom, could I pull a Colgate on them and send my inspectors in?"

"You could try, Commissioner. But you know the railroads. A half-hour later their lawyers would have you so buried in writs you'd have to breathe through a straw."

"How about the state?"

"I don't see how."

"Could I get through to the government in Washington? You know, talk to the people in charge."

"Sure. And you'd be in Holy Name Cemetery ten years before they did anything."

Hague was puzzled. "So there is nothing I can do? I don't believe that."

"Maybe Congress would listen to you. You must have some clout there?"

"Some... A little...Not much," Hague said.

Hague hadn't shown much interest as yet in Congressional elections. Senators had been appointed by state legislatures but a new constitutional amendment meant that they would be elected by a direct vote now. That might give him some leverage. House members were elected every two years and were a skittish bunch. Hague wasn't optimistic.

"Tell you what, Sergeant. Let's you and me go down to Washington and talk to those congressmen and senators from New Jersey and maybe even a couple from across the river. We demand that they stop moving munitions through Jersey City.

You get as much information as you can about what's going on at Black Tom. You brief me before we go and sit next to me in case I forget anything. You know, whisper in my ear. Let's see if we can't rattle a few cages."

"Right, Commissioner. But you know, you may be wasting your time. You got to believe that the railroads have bought up those congressmen by the dozen. They're not going to say 'boo' unless they get the okay from Pennsylvania."

"I know that. What do you think I am, an idiot? What I want to do is get it on the record. The Jersey Journal will write up a story on it and it'll show me looking out for Jersey City. That'll play well come election day. Won't it? Besides. Who do you know in Jersey City that likes the railroads? Not the people that work for them. Not anybody who's had somebody killed or hurt working for them. Not the people that live near the tracks. Not anybody that has to pay sky high prices to ship something from here to Podunk. Who likes the railroads? Nobody, that's who."

"Don't like them myself," said McGurk.

"Of course you don't. They killed your father, didn't they? Gave you mother a couple of bucks and said 'sorry for your trouble.' I hate them. The greedy bastards."

McGurk gathered up as much information as possible about munitions at Black Tom. He spent hours at City Hall reading from his typed notes to his "uncle" who occasionally interrupted with a question. It was obvious; the commissioner was memorizing the material. Hague did not ask McGurk for his notes.

The Hudson and Manhattan Railroad ran above ground from Jersey City to Newark. Frank Hague, Mickey McGurk and their valises took the train at Grove Street and ultimately connected with a Washington bound passenger train at Penn Station in Newark.

Settling themselves in comfortable coach seats, Hague said, "I may hate the greedy bastards, Mickey, but this is the only way to travel. Look, you could even keep the windows open now that they're burning anthracite. That soft coal would choke you to death and turn you blacker than that minister over at Incarnation."

Mickey smiled. The Episcopal Church of the Incarnation was a Negro parish notorious for admitting only the light skinned to its tony ranks. Its minister was only a shade or two darker than either Hague or McGurk.

"That's not hard," he said.

Hague watched an automobile bump along on the road parallel to the tracks. "Those automobiles will never replace trains. I don't care what those nutcases predict."

McGurk had never been to Washington and he was not sure Hague had either. He knew that Hague had been refused entrance to the Democratic National Convention in Baltimore a few years earlier, a slight he had never forgotten and for which some New Jersey politicians had already paid dearly. *Maybe, he went sightseeing in nearby Washington. No. Not very likely. He'd head home to plot revenge.*

Hague's secretary, Fat Jack Lynch's kid brother, had arranged for Hague to visit five congressmen, including one from Manhattan, and New Jersey's two senators over a three day period. It had taken three weeks to set up the schedule. He didn't tell Hague that two of the congressmen's aides had in essence said, "The representative's time is very valuable. Who is this person?" Hague wouldn't have thought it funny.

Lynch's persistence finally got results and the appointments were made. None was for longer than thirty minutes.

Hague himself made a phone call from a pay phone in the terminal. He emerged and said, "You're on your own tonight, Mickey. I am having dinner with Joe Tumulty. His car is picking me up at the hotel."

McGurk knew who Tumulty was although he had never met or spoken to him.

"Is he going to arrange for you to see the president?"

"Are you kidding? I've crossed that miserable son-of-a-bitch more times than I can count. He wouldn't spit at me if he thought I was dying of thirst."

"Are you going to fight him if he runs again in November?"

"No way. I've had enough trouble with him. I just don't want him annoying me next year. That's why I'm meeting with Joe. To see if we can have a truce. I'll support him and he doesn't go out of his way to hurt me. I think that's the best deal I can get."

The restaurant was not one Tumulty frequented. It was in far off Georgetown and it was unlikely he would run into anyone who knew both Hague and him.

"You're looking well, Commissioner. Apparently being director of public safety agrees with you."

"You bet it does, Joe. I like it almost as much as I'll like being mayor."

Tumulty smiled and nodded. "Always to the point, Commissioner, always to the point."

"You know me, Joe. But if you want to talk about something else until after we eat, that's jake with me too."

"No, no, Mr. Hague. I've got to tell you it is refreshing to talk to you after dealing with those blowhard weasels down here day after day. They want you to think they are selfless servants of the people when you know they would steal a hot stove if they could find a pair of asbestos gloves."

Hague laughed though he never entertained the idea that a man should grow poor in public service.

"But first let's talk about the president getting re-elected before we talk about me."

"A lovely thought," said Tumulty.

"I'll back him to the hilt."

"Thank you. I appreciate that."

"But will he appreciate that?" Tumulty was silent. Hague sighed.

"You know, Commissioner, getting re-elected isn't going to be as easy as slipping in last time. I doubt that the Republicans will have to contend with Teddy again. It will be a unified party against us in November."

"Who will the Republicans nominate?" asked Hague who probably knew the names of no more than three contenders.

"I think it will be Hughes."

"Hughes?"

"Charles Evans Hughes. The Supreme Court Justice. He used to be governor of New York."

"Oh, that Hughes." Hague had actually heard of him and ventured an opinion. "He'll be tough to beat in the East."

"He'll be very tough to beat in the East and, unfortunately, in lots of other places too. It will be a close election. Wilson will win if all goes well," said Tumulty.

"What could go wrong?"

"A number of things but the war and Mexico are the worst. The country doesn't want to go to war and both sides know it. They are pushing us to the limit. The Germans with their submarines and the British with their blockade. We'd actually be justified to declare war against either side."

"Really?"

"No. Not really. The public is leaning towards the Allies. There are not enough Germans and Irishmen to counter that."

"There are in Jersey City."

"Perhaps. But it is a big country, Commissioner. President Wilson is actually a full blown pacifist when it comes to Europe."

"Yeah. But he doesn't mind putting the boot to Mexico when it suits him."

Tumulty was defensive. "There have been provocations. Severe provocations. And that outlaw, Pancho Villa. No one knows what that lunatic is going to do next. Meanwhile, Europe is being bled white. Millions of their best young men dead. Casualties that make our Civil War bloodletting look like

Saturday night dustups. Europe wants us in this war. If for no other reason than perhaps our power would be enough to end it. Britain desperately wants us on their side. Sympathy for the Allies has grown since the German army behaved so badly in Belgium and France."

"Do you believe all that stuff, Joe?"

"Of course not. But some of it is true. Lots of our fellow countrymen believe all of it. Woodrow Wilson will be nominated again and he will run on the slogan 'He Kept Us Out of War.' So from the convention until November we will have to walk a tightrope with the winds of war buffeting us from both sides."

"Can we do it?"

"Yes. I think so. As long as nothing happens that demands a declaration of war. Besides, we're not ready. Every day of peace helps us build up our army and navy. The army can barely handle the situation in Mexico let alone anything else."

"Teddy Roosevelt has been making a lot of noise about 'preparedness.'"

"Yes he has, indeed. But then, our friend Teddy always carries a big stick but he rarely speaks softly."

Hague was not familiar with the quotation but he chuckled anyway. He had a talent for that.

Tumulty asked, "Now, what about this Black Thumb thing?"

"Black Tom. It's the usual railroad nonsense. Cutting corners. Ignoring safety rules. Lots of munitions go through Black Tom every day. As long as they keep going through, there's probably nothing to worry about. But I don't like them sitting there overnight. That could be dangerous, although it's probably safer than it looks. Still, accidents happen and I certainly don't want to see a boxcar of dynamite go up."

Tumulty said, "Nor do I. But it is the railroad's problem. I can't believe they are indifferent to having their property destroyed in an explosion like that. What about saboteurs?"

"Saboteurs? In Jersey City? I don't think so," said Hague. "I know my Zepps have picked up rumors that longshoremen are planting firebombs on British ships. But if there is trouble, it happens at sea."

Tumulty was noncommittal. "Yes. We've heard those rumors too. Well, perhaps that famous Zeppelin Squad of yours can keep an eye on things at Black Tom. Help prevent accidents, maybe."

"They can't get in, Joe. It's private property. The railroads."

"Of course. They have their own police forces, don't they? What railroad owns Black Tom?"

"Lehigh Valley."

"Well, we can have someone put a word in the ear of the Lehigh Valley Railroad's police chief. That might help," said Tumulty.

"Maybe. I hope so."

"Meanwhile, Commissioner, good luck in your dealings with Congress. You know the railroads have many friends there. Don't expect too much."

"I certainly won't. But thanks for your concern. You can count on my support at the convention and in November."

"Good."

Hague said, "Tell the president I'm with him."

"Of course. But the president will know that in any event. He'll see the results."

Hague said, "I'd really welcome his support next year. But I realize he may be too busy here in Washington to come to Jersey City."

"I'm glad you understand, Commissioner. The whole world is vying for the president's time. And attention. I doubt there is any chance he will involve himself in local politics next year."

Hague understood and was satisfied. Woodrow Wilson would be neutral in Jersey City as well as in Europe.

Good enough.

One congressman, from central New Jersey, kept Hague and Mickey waiting in his outer office for forty-five minutes. Hague fumed but said nothing. Representatives were up for re-election every two years. Hague would make his feelings known then.

Another noted. "Haig? That's a Scottish name isn't it, Commissioner?"

"Not the way I spell it, it isn't," said Hague without even a suggestion of a smile.

Hague patiently and, Mickey thought, competently laid out the dangers of using Black Tom as a major assembly point for exporting munitions.

The congressman was polite, showed sympathy, oozed sincerity and committed himself to nothing. That was so with all of his colleagues that they visited.

Hague was steadfast but bored. He wanted to head back to Jersey City yet he had to go through the motions. The Jersey Journal, much gratified to have a local story dispatched by Associated Press from the nation's capital, gave his trip front page treatment.

Hague, the reformer, looked good. That was what mattered.

However, Hague was not the only one to read the Jersey Journal's stories with interest.

There were some—unknown to each other—who read and took a step away from speculation and moved a step closer to action.

Weeks later Hague's secretary read from a letter sent by one of New Jersey's congressmen which stated that it was the "sense of Congress that Jersey City is an appropriate port for the shipping of munitions overseas." Nothing would be done.

Hague added the congressman's name to a growing list of those who would lament slighting Frank Hague.

Woodrow the Weak

"I despise Wilson."

That's how Teddy Roosevelt summed up his feelings about President Woodrow Wilson, the man who had bested him in the three-way race for president in 1912.

His antipathy really wasn't based on Wilson's approach to domestic problems. Both were leaders of the progressive wing of their party; the principal difference being that Roosevelt would have used the Federal government to implement needed social change while Wilson, fearing big government, favored a more decentralized path.

No, the visceral dislike was rooted in their polar opposite personalities and, more importantly, their approach to foreign affairs.

When Roosevelt was president, a Greek-American businessman, Ion Perdicaris, was kidnapped and held for ransom in Morocco by Ahmed ibn-Muhammed Raisuli.

The next day Roosevelt ordered a naval squadron to Morocco. Waiting a month to give the warships time to get there, a blunt message then was sent to the Sultan of Morocco.

"Perdicaris alive or Raisuli dead." Perdicaris was released two days later and the squadron sailed for home.

The RMS Lusitania was torpedoed and sunk by a German U-Boat on May 7, 1915, killing 1,195 people including 128 Americans.

Three days later, Wilson gave his "Too Proud to Fight Speech" preferring to chastise the Germans with a series of diplomatic notes.

Roosevelt was choleric. He thought that the United States had little choice but to declare war on Germany and fight on the side of Great Britain.

In a letter written to a friend he said, "If Lincoln had acted after the firing of Sumter in the way that Wilson did about the sinking of Lusitania, in one month the North would have been saying they were glad he kept them out of the war and that they were too proud to fight and that at all hazards fratricidal war must be averted."

Roosevelt knew American public opinion was against entering the war. He also knew the American army was unprepared for this kind of war. Barely a hundred thousand strong it was 1/20th the size of the German army and was poorly equipped. The highly politicized part time National Guard was in much worse shape.

Roosevelt, who had led the "Rough Riders" in their famous charge up San Juan Hill, favored universal military training.

Thus was born the "Preparedness Movement." If Wilson wouldn't act to strengthen America's army, some famous, influential private citizens would. Roosevelt threw his support to General Leonard Wood, the former Army chief of staff, who wanted to build up a strong army and navy for defensive purposes.

A pair of former Secretaries of War also backed Wood's concept of requiring 600,000 men who turned eighteen each year to undergo six months of military training and then be assigned to reserve units, not the National Guard.

Wilson abhorred the concept and it drew fierce opposition from women's groups, churches, pacifists and others who feared a big military. It went nowhere.

The Preparedness people, who were certain war was inevitable and strongly leaned towards joining Britain, turned to the Plattsburg Movement. More than 20,000 young college graduates learned the rudiments of military service at summer camps there during 1915 and 1916.

Plattsburg was not a people's movement. These young men were members of America's social and financial elite. No attempt was made to recruit from the middle or working classes.

At first, Wilson's Democrats opposed the Preparedness Movement seeing it as a political threat but bloody battles in Europe and pressure at home soon had the administration co-opting some of the preparedness demands. Bills introduced into Congress in 1916 would greatly expand the army and navy but would do so over a four year period. Conscription was not considered.

These efforts did not alarm the Germans who, convinced Wilson would not intervene anyway, thought they would win the war long before 1920 when America might be ready.

Meanwhile Wilson doggedly tried to end an endless war by proposing negotiations with himself as a mediator.

One bizarre proposal demanded negotiations and warned that if one side agreed and the other didn't, America would declare war on the recalcitrant party. Neither side believed that.

Roosevelt criticized Wilson's policies as "timid" and "spiritless." He wrote books attacking Wilson, Germany and pacifism but most Americans still opposed entering the war.

Said Wilson on his demand for neutrality, "There is something better to do than fight; there is a distinction waiting for this country that no nation has ever got. That is the distinction of absolute self-control and self-mastery."

As harsh as her father was on Wilson, Alice Roosevelt was worse. She called Wilson a "slimy hypocrite."

The Bomb Squad

Commissioner Frank Hague, Jersey City's director of public safety, was one of the most "neutral" men in the nation. He didn't give a damn about any of the warring parties.

His interests, when most expansive, didn't go beyond the three mile limit in the east and pretty much stopped at the Delaware River in the west. Most of the time, his geographic boundaries were the Hudson and Hackensack Rivers.

Hague was engaged in wars of his own. Since taking over as director of public safety in 1913, he had purged and reformed the police and fire departments, and just about eliminated prostitution in a port city, an unheard of phenomenon but one much applauded by the clergy and women of Jersey City.

Hague's concurrent campaign against what he dubbed "dope fiends" was succeeding as well.

Drug addiction had long been identified with older, middle class women trying to cope with female maladies and had been ignored by everyone except, perhaps, their relieved husbands.

But in recent years things had changed. The "sporting crowd," including actors and actresses, prostitutes, pimps, thieves, gamblers, entertainers and homosexuals, were taking drugs for pleasure.

One could get opium, morphine, cocaine or heroin in restaurants, laundries, saloons, whorehouses, dance halls, pool rooms, gambling dens, theatres and, even, cigar shops.

But then Hague got the word from the Zeppelins that many boys were being exposed to drugs. The lower classes were imitating their grown up idols.

"That's it," ordered Hague, "get rid of them. Run them out of town. The Chinks can go back to selling chop suey and washing clothes. The rest of them go to hell. Make sure they know they are not to come back."

The Zepps, backed by the rest of the police force, already had the "sporting crowd" on the run as it was, so this was just one more reason to dump them on the ferry boats.

So un-prescribed narcotics, for the most part, vanished from Jersey City. More applause from the clergy along with some muttering from a sub-group of husbands who took their wives doctor-shopping. Hague earned more praise as a reformer.

His "organization" grew more powerful in both the city and the county and many in Trenton were taking notice as well. Hague might appear dour but he was a happy man. Come May, 1917, and he would be mayor of Jersey City. Nothing must be allowed to interfere with that.

There were troubles in the neighborhood as well. In 1914, New York City transformed its "Italian Squad" which had considerable success suppressing the "Black Hand" and its extortion racket into the "Bomb Squad" led by Acting Captain Thomas J. Tunney. The Bomb Squad was not a bomb disposal unit. Rather its thirty-four men kept an eye on misbehaving Italians, anarchists, and would-be saboteurs of all stripes. Most worked undercover.

The squad proved its worth a year later when anarchists were caught in the act of trying to blow up St. Patrick's Cathedral in Manhattan. It was an undercover Bomb Squad man who pulled the fuse from the bomb before it could explode.

Frank Hague was appalled. He had actually been in that church himself. "Those dirty sons-of-bitches! St. Patrick's Cathedral! Can you imagine, St. Patrick's Cathedral," he said to Sergeant Mickey McGurk of the Zeppelin Squad.

"What the hell are anarchists? All I know about them is they're always throwing bombs at something or somebody. You went to St. Peter's. You must have learned something there."

"Anarchists don't believe in government of any kind."

Hague grappled with such an alien concept. "How do they think anything gets done? How do they expect to get elected?"

"They don't believe in elections either. They believe we should all just live as one happy family, sharing everything... sort of. They're not very organized themselves, thank God, or they would be much more dangerous. Of course, there is the IWW."

Hague looked blank.

"The International Workers of the World...The Wobblies."

"Oh, the Wobblies. Are they anarchists? I met some of them during that Paterson Silk Strike a couple of years back. They sent some of their kids to relatives in Jersey City. To keep them safe. They seemed like decent people to me. I even met one of their leaders. A girl. Elizabeth Flynn, I think."

Mickey nodded. "Elizabeth Gurley Flynn. 'The Rebel Girl.' Yeah, she's one of their leaders all right. Not all of them are anarchists. Some of them are, though, and I don't think any of them are afraid of a stick of dynamite."

Now after his fruitless visit to Washington and with Black Tom on his mind, Hague sent for Mickey McGurk.

"Hmmm," said Hague. "That Tunney, on the Bomb Squad in the city, he must be an okay guy. I want you to meet with him. I want you to work together. Next thing you know those dirty anarchist bastards will be blowing up St. Michael's Downtown."

Not while my mother goes to Mass there they won't. They wouldn't dare, thought McGurk.

Mickey liked the idea. He already knew a couple of men on the New York Police Bomb Squad whose work brought them across the river once in a while. But then he saw a problem.

"Commissioner, that's a great idea. But, you know, those New York cops are very rank conscious. I don't blame them. It's really hard to make captain there." Hague snapped him a look, searching for a hint of criticism. None there.

Mickey continued, "Captain Tunney isn't likely to have much time for the likes of me. I'm only a sergeant. Sergeants do what you tell them to do; you don't talk strategy with them. You would do better, sir, to send a captain."

Hague thought for a moment. "Most of the captains I trust are dumb as a post. How about a lieutenant? Would he deal with a lieutenant?"

Then Mickey thought for a moment. "A lieutenant? I think so. Sure. He deals with lieutenants as close subordinates every day. He'd see a lieutenant in Jersey City as someone he could call on if he had to. That would work." That would mean better contacts for Sergeant McGurk too since the best man for the job obviously was the lieutenant who headed up the Zepps.

"Okay, then. You're an 'acting lieutenant' as of tomorrow. Get a hold of Tunney as quick as you can and tell him you have my full backing."

McGurk was incredulous. "What?"

"I said, get a hold of…"

"No, no! Did you say I was going to be a lieutenant?"

Hague shook his head and sighed. "Sometimes, I really wonder if you are any brighter than those captains of mine."

"No, no. I understand. Lieutenant McGurk is to make a deal with Captain Tunney, right… Uncle Frank?"

"Don't 'Uncle Frank' me, lieutenant, this is strictly business." Hague almost smiled.

Some hours later, Mickey McGurk presented his wife, Hannah, with a bouquet of roses. Hannah, brushing his cigar smoke away from her face, smiled and said, "How lovely. It isn't every day I get flowers. What did you do wrong, you bad boy?"

"Absolutely nothing. I'll have you know I got promoted to lieutenant today."

"Wonderful," said Hannah who, holding the bouquet, hugged and kissed him. "Does this mean you get a pay raise too?"

"You bet!" *I hope.*

"Even better," said Hannah, placing the bouquet on the table and giving him more than a gentle hug and a peck on the lips.

"Hot, damn!" said Mickey.

"Watch your language, Lieutenant," said Hannah, leading him by the hand to the bedroom, leaving the flowers to wilt on the kitchen table.

* * *

Captain Thomas J. Tunney was a tall, burly, handsome, well-spoken Irishman. He shook hands with Mickey McGurk and after the introductions looked at him and said, "You're a bit young for a lieutenant, aren't you, son?"

"I am that, sir. I've only been on the force a few years. I was a beat cop before I assigned to the Zeppelin Squad, sir."

"Yeah. I've heard of them and I've heard of your boss, what's his name?"

"Frank Hague, sir."

"Yes. I hear he's cleaned up your police force and I know he's palmed off every whore, pimp and drug addict he had on us. We really didn't need any more, thank you. You can tell him that for me," said Captain Tunney, who had no use for such vermin except as informants. And good informants some of them were.

"I will, sir."

"So, what more can the City of New York do for you and your boss, Mr. Hague?"

"Well, Captain Tunney, Commissioner Hague is an admirer of yours and your squad. He was especially impressed with the work you did at St. Patrick's."

"That was a near thing. We waited too long. A minute or two more and my career would have gone up with the cathedral. If you wanted to talk to me, you would have had to take the train to East Nowhere, Nebraska. I'd be the school crossing guard there. A near thing. I still get the shivers thinking about it."

"But the bums failed, sir. They failed."

"Yes, thank God."

"Well, when you think about it," said McGurk, "New York

here and New Jersey there are just one big port. People cross the river like it was a creek. In Manhattan at ten o'clock, Jersey City at eleven, half way to Brooklyn by noon. The political barriers—state and city—are much more obvious than the physical ones. I can't come here officially, you can't go there officially. But the rogues go where they will. That doesn't make sense, does it?"

"What's your point, Lieutenant?" said Captain Tunney, looking at his timepiece.

"Just this, sir. If our squads work together we can get more done than if we work alone. We could share information. Share contacts. Informants. Back each other up. Make sure we don't foul up operations out of rank ignorance. That sort of thing, sir. There doesn't have to be any kind of formal agreement. Nothing the press could make hash out of. Just an understanding, sir. Between you and me."

"Just between you and me, huh, young man? Well, I've got a boss to answer to and I'd have to run this past him before I could agree to anything? Don't you have to do that, too?"

"No, sir. Commissioner Hague said to tell you, I have his full backing."

"Yes... well. No offense, but the Jersey City Police Department is a nickel and dime outfit compared to us."

"We know that, sir. And if you'll forgive me, sir, we hope to learn a lot from you and your men."

Captain Tunney rolled his eyes upward. "God protect me from slick talking Micks."

Mickey laughed. "Are there any other kind, sir?"

"Okay. I'm not saying this is going to happen but let's say it might," said Captain Tunney who intended to get much more information out of McGurk than he gave back. "You've got a movie studio over there?"

"Yeah, Pathé Studios. At Congress Street and the Paterson Plank Road."

"Wherever. Do you have any contacts with the actors and

actresses there? Lots of them move back and forth across the river. All of them gossip. Some of them pick up useful information," said Tunney.

"Yeah, some," said Mickey, thinking of his cousin, Peggy McCann, who had been in an "Exploits of Elaine" episode with Pearl White and had bit parts in two photoplays.

"Get more. Do you have any contacts with the krauts in Hoboken? Besides cops, I mean."

"Yeah. Some." Thinking of his father-in-law and his German drinking cronies.

"Get more. We're picking up rumors that the Dutchmen are putting time bombs on British ships."

"What kind of rumors?"

"Rumors."

"How are they doing that? The Brits wouldn't let a German near their ships. They guard them, you know."

"No kidding? Are you aware, my lad, that the Irish don't much care for the English? The Germans can hire Micks to do their dirty work for the price of a pig's knuckle. If they won't do it for free, that is."

"So what do we care if the Irish plant German bombs on British ships?" asked McGurk.

"Because, Lieutenant, America is neutral and we want to stay neutral. It's hard to claim you're neutral when your people are setting ships on fire."

"Yes, sir. That makes sense. We've got excellent contacts among the Irish longshoremen."

"You ought to. Half your population works on the docks somewhere, don't they?"

"Just about, sir. Just about."

"You got anything worth blowing up over there?" Tunney asked.

"Black Tom," McGurk answered and then told Tunney about the munitions pouring through there.

"Jesus. I'd watch out for anarchists, saboteurs. Scum like that," said Tunney. "You know we nailed a saboteur in your neck of the woods not long ago. Over in Weehawken. The guy had small bombs not much bigger than a pencil that he was going to attach to the rudders of Allied ships and disable them at sea. The motion of the rudder would actually trigger the explosive. Ingenious. The Feds arrested him but we were there to watch.

"Say, another thing. There's a guy named Paul Koenig. Works for Hamburg Amerika Line? We know he's involved somehow. We thought we had him nailed on another case but a slick lawyer got him off.

"If he shows up, I'd look for trouble. He's a tough guy to keep tabs on, shakes off tails like they were flies. Wait a minute. I'll get you a photograph and a negative of him. Just might come in handy."

* * *

Later, Mickey, who told Hannah everything, told her about his upcoming meeting with his cousin, Peggy McCann. "I know Peggy's a good friend of yours. Do you want to come along? I'll treat you both to supper."

Hannah, who told no one else about Mickey's work, thought about it. "No, I don't think so. I don't think Peggy would like to have me there when you try to persuade her to become a spy."

"I'm not asking her to be a spy!"

"No? What do you call it then?"

"She'll be my confidante," answered Mickey avoiding the word "informant" which was a curse word to the Irish.

"Confidante? Oh my, that's certainly more elegant than spy."

Peggy and Mickey met in a little luncheonette just over the border in Union City where they were very unlikely to meet anyone they knew. McGurk explained what he wanted.

"Mickey, why should I rat on my friends just because they

favor one side or the other in this stupid war?"

"You're not ratting. You'd be helping to protect America."

"Is this where I stand up, salute, and sing 'It's a Grand Old Flag?'"

Mickey laughed and looked fondly at his prettiest cousin. "The idea is to keep America out of this stupid war. What we want to do is make sure nobody does anything here that forces us to pick one side or the other. We want to stay neutral, no matter what."

Peggy McCann, as smart as her cousin, replied. "That makes sense. Okay, I'm in, Mr. Zeppelin. Let me nose around Pathé and see what I come up with. But I can't promise you anything."

"Great," said her cousin.

Hans Mannstein was an easier sell. Mickey and he had grown closer since the wedding. Mickey considered "Hans" almost as good a friend as Jimmy Cribbins or Tony Aiello. Almost.

"Hans, you, me and, maybe, Tony, are going to be working closely from now on. The commissioner is worried that anarchists or agitators of some kind are going to be tempted to make trouble in Jersey City because of the war. The commissioner wants us to scout out problems before they arise."

"What kind of agitators?"

"Who knows? Irish, German, British, Wobblies, Hungarians, Russians, every kind of bohunk, Marxists, wops. You know."

"Oh! That narrows it down nicely. No problem. You think it'll take all three of us?"

"The only smartass kraut on the squad and I get him."

Hans said, "I've been hanging around the Irish too long."

McGurk said, "I want you to work closely with the New York Bomb Squad people. I think they have cops full time in Hoboken. Develop your own German sources too."

"You mean besides the thousand Dutchmen I already know?"

"Right," said McGurk. "Do you speak German?"

"As good as most people born in this country. I miss a word

or two when the old-timers are talking fast but not a lot."

"Can you read and write it?"

"No way. I play strictly by ear."

McGurk said, "Well, the one-eyed man in the kingdom of the blind…"

"Yeah, yeah."

Captain Hinsch and Mr. Graentnor

Captain Frederick Hinsch may have been interned for the duration in Baltimore but he certainly wasn't brooding about it. He was a favorite in the beer gardens, the stubes and the German restaurants in the city.

Everyone knew him. The big, beer bellied, merchant skipper who could be depended on to share a schooner of beer, to sing the chorus of an old favorite or to dance with the widows and old maids. Hinsch's laughter could shake a room. He was every inch the old sea dog ready to have a bit of fun while he was ashore.

Baltimore's German-American community, sympathetic to his plight, was happy to have him in its midst.

But Captain Hinsch would disappear for long periods of time, sometimes months, but then he would be back, beer stein in hand, as if he never had left.

"Where do you go, Captain, when you leave Baltimore?" asked one burgher on his return.

"Everywhere," he answered. "I have friends everywhere."

"And a girl in every port, eh, Captain?"

"That too, my friend. That too."

Captain Hinsch never went to New York City but Mr. Francis Graentnor did. They were the same man.

He was still big but not as conspicuous. Subdued, soft-spoken, as befitted a man who did not want to draw attention to himself, Mr. Graentnor usually was there to meet Paul Koenig, his subordinate in the sabotage ring he headed. While highly suspicious of Koenig, the Bomb Squad did not know Mr. Graentnor existed.

His meeting over, his orders given, Mr. Graentnor was leaving on a long trip indeed. He needed someone to go with him, someone no one knew, who could help him with the two heavy suitcases which contained more than clothing. Someone he could trust.

Mr. Graentnor considered himself a superb judge of character. Decades at sea demanded that.

He looked around the waiting room at Penn Station and focused on a young man sitting with a small battered suitcase between his legs. He sat down next to him and, taking out a charged pipe, asked, "Do you have a light, my friend?"

"Sure."

Puffing on the short-stemmed pipe, Mr. Graentnor looked up at the big clock that could be seen from everywhere in the enormous waiting room and asked, "So when does your train leave?"

"Not for three hours," said the young man.

"Ah. That gives us time to talk." Then sticking his big hand out, "I'm Francis Graentnor."

"Michael Kristoff. You sound German."

"Ja. I am. You?"

"Nah. Slovak. Been here since I was a kid though."

"Where are you headed, Mr. Kristoff?"

"To Ohio. I'm going to going to visit my sister."

"That's nice. Is she expecting you?"

Kristoff laughed. "No. I'll just show up. That way she can't tell me not to come."

Graentnor laughed, but not as heartily as usual. "You have a good sense of humor," he said. "Well, we have some time to kill. Tell me, what do you think of this war?"

"It's a mess," said Kristoff. Then looking at Graentnor, he said, "But I don't mind telling you I hope Germany wins. I've cousins in the Austro-Hungarian army and we don't know if they are alive or dead. The fucking British won't let the mail through."

"Ja, that's sad. Well, it's going to be hard for Germany to win what with your greedy corporations selling all those munitions to the Allies," said Graentnor. "What do you do, Mr. Kristoff?"

"Not much. I was working at an oil company in Bayonne but

that's over. Before that, I was in the Army. Coast artillery at Fort Hancock."

Graentnor visibly brightened.

"How about you, Mr. Graentnor, what do you do?"

Graentnor held Kristoff's eyes and said softly, "I try to stop those munitions from getting to the Allies. Would you like to work for me? I'll pay you $20 a week and take care of all your expenses. We'll be traveling a lot but I see you are already packed. What do you say?"

Kristoff thought, *I've got nothing to lose. I'll cash in my ticket to Ohio.*

"All right, Mr. Graentnor. It's deal. Where are we headed?"

Graentnor clapped a hand on Kristoff's shoulder. "Who knows; I have friends everywhere."

Abie the Jew

Frank Hague sat, chair tilted back, fingers tented, ankles crossed, the heel of one of his highly polished shoes resting on his big desk.

Few people were ever permitted to see him in such a relaxed pose. Mickey McGurk was one.

"So, what can I do for you, Mickey?"

"I'd like Tony Aiello assigned permanently to my team."

"Team, is it? You're building a nice little empire there what with you and that Dutchman..."

"Hans Mannstein."

"Yes. Your buddy, Hans. Why do you want Aiello?"

"First off, we work well together. Second, he's a good detective. Third, we don't have anybody who's in tight with the Italians. Lots of them are radicals like anarchists and Marxists. There's more and more of them. Everywhere. Used to be you'd find Italians in the 5th Ward. Now they're everywhere."

Hague was silent for a few seconds. He said, "They're starting to vote too. Not like us. They're not as interested on politics, but it's a start. This guinea detective of yours, is he an organization man?"

"Not yet. Like you say, they're not that interested in politics. But he will be. He's smart and he's ambitious. He'll be quick to figure out which side his bread is buttered on."

"Good. He's yours. You know, he'll be the first Italian on the Zeppelins," said Hague.

"He'll like that."

"Maybe. But I don't think the Irish will."

"Too bad," said Lieutenant McGurk.

"Okay. So have you been keeping an eye on Black Tom like I asked you to?"

"I have, Commissioner."

"So what do you think?"

"It scares the bejesus out of me," said McGurk.

"Me too. Goddamn railroads. All they think of is making a buck. To hell with everything and everybody else."

Hague straightened up. "So do you think it's as dangerous as I told those stupid congressmen it was?"

"Worse. You'd think they were still shipping coal out of there instead of every kind of bomb, shell, explosive and munitions known to man. The watchmen are asleep most of the night. The guards the Brits hired are no better. They spend more time ferrying booze back from the Whitehouse Tavern than they do patrolling the place. It's pathetic."

"An accident waiting to happen, huh?" asked Hague.

"Waiting to happen? Really? They've had a half dozen fires there in the last month alone."

"Fires? Who told you that?" Hague asked. "The fire department? I haven't heard anything like that."

"They don't call the fire department. They put them out themselves. Small fires, they say. 'Nothing to worry about', one of the guards told me."

"What causes the fires?" asked Hague.

"Who knows? Certainly not the guard I talked to."

"Good lord. Have you talked to the railroad's chief of police? What's his name?"

McGurk said, "Leyden. Cornelius Leyden. Yes, I talked to him—for all the good it did me. He told me everything is under control. They don't have any problems they can't handle and they certainly don't need any help from the Jersey City police."

"I'll bet," said Hague.

"The Lehigh Valley Railroad doesn't like you very much, Commissioner."

"Life offers few consolations but that is one of mine. So what can we do about it?"

McGurk said, "I don't know. You can make sure the fire

department is ready to roll if anything gets out of hand there. Other than that, I don't know what you can do."

"Well, thank God, I'm already on record saying the place is dangerous. If Congress won't act, if the state won't act, if the railroad won't act, there's nothing I can do about it. It's private property and you don't win in court against the railroad."

"No you don't," said McGurk.

"But I swear to you, if one of those boxcars catches fire and blows up, I'll arrest everybody in sight," Hague said.

"On what charge?"

"Don't worry about that. I'll think of something. One more thing before you go. How are you getting along with that Captain Tunney guy over in the city?"

"Famously. I don't deal with him much, not directly. But his people and mine are trading information all the time."

McGurk said, "The longer the war goes on, the more we have to worry about different outfits trying to drag us in on their side. It's not that there is much of a threat here. The railroads control most of our waterfront. The idea is that we don't want any trouble spilling over from Hoboken, Manhattan or Brooklyn. Tunney knows for sure that somebody is putting time bombs on British ships that set them on fire at sea."

"How'd he find that out?"

McGurk said, "By accident. A British ship was headed for Russia when it was diverted. Submarines probably. Anyway, it docks in France and they find the time bombs when they unload the cargo. They were supposed to blow up three or four days later."

"So why should we worry about that?"

"Tunney thinks the bombs were made either in Hoboken or on one of the German ships interned along the river."

"We don't have any German ships interned here, do we?"

"Nope, but we have lots of Irish dock workers ready to hurt the English any way they can. There's no barbed wire fence between us and Hoboken either."

Hague said, "That's not a bad idea. There should be. Bombs or no bombs."

* * *

Not long afterwards, Mickey sat Tony down to discuss his new assignment. "You're assigned to my team fulltime, Tony, any problems with that?"

"Are you kidding? It couldn't be better. First, I get on the cops. Then I make detective. Now I'm a Zeppelin led by the illustrious Lieutenant McGurk, famed throughout the Western World for his steel-trap mind."

Mickey laughed. "Yeah. We also needed a first class bullshit artist and who better than you?"

"Who indeed? Seriously, Mickey. Thank you. It means a lot to me and it will mean a lot to the future Mrs. Aiello."

Peggy. Terrific.

"Does that poor creature know what fate awaits her?"

"Soon. We're pretty far along."

"Great, Tony, I'd love to have you for a cousin-in-law."

"Hell, even my mother wants me to marry her. I'm doomed. Again, thanks, Mickey."

Tony reached out and shook Mickey's hand. Hard. "You'll never regret this."

"I know I won't. But don't thank me. Thank Frank Hague. He's the one that approved your transfer."

Tony nodded. "Fair enough. Tell your uncle he's got my vote, my family's vote and all the Italian votes I can round up for him in the 5th Ward."

"Right. That's the kind of 'thanks' he understands, Tony. Okay, now let's talk about the job. You know we're sort of a miniature version of New York's bomb squad. We keep an eye on anybody whose enthusiasm for the war in Europe might spill over and cause us trouble here. As you know, sometimes we get other assignments but that's our primary duty."

"Yeah. There's a lot of scuttlebutt about what you two are doing and I figured you were some sort of spies and not just for the commissioner," said Tony.

Mickey knew the Zeppelins had a reputation for turning in cops who didn't meet Frank Hague's standards and it didn't bother him. The police force was infinitely better now than when he was a rookie on the beat.

McGurk said, "I keep an eye on the Irish. Hans Mannstein watches the Germans, especially in Hoboken, and I want you to monitor the Italians and the crazies."

"What, you expect some shoemaker to sink a ship with his hammer and nails?"

"Very funny. You know, I already regret putting you on the team." They both laughed. "Captain Tunney, over in New York, says lots of Italians are anarchists and would just as soon throw a bomb as make a speech. Is that true?"

"I don't know. There are a few guys around who don't go to church and like to shoot off their mouths. Nobody pays attention to them. It's hard to believe they're dangerous."

McGurk said, "Find out for sure."

"How?"

"Don't nose around yourself too much. Get other people to do it. If you're too obvious, it won't take the bad guys too long for find out what you're up to and then you're finished."

"Well, we don't want that, do we? What should I do? Recruit some informants?"

"Tony, the Irish don't like the word 'informant'. Too much bad history associated with it. I like the word 'confidante'."

"Okay. No informants. Lots of confidantes. But why would anybody sign on as a confidante?"

"Try patriotism first. That'll work most of the time. For others, we'll have some walk around money. And the clincher is that the organization is in a position to do favors for people if we ask. And no questions will be asked."

"Frank Hague again."

"You got it," said McGurk.

"There is one thing, Mickey. I'm supposed to go out to Kearny today and interview the guys Billy Cunningham worked with. The prosecutors want to strengthen their case. Maybe he said something to somebody at work. All they got is that confession. They want to cover all the bases. Anyway, they're hoping Billy will plead 'guilty' and it doesn't go to trial. Second degree murder. No premeditation. No electric chair."

McGurk said, "I hope that works out. I like Billy better than I liked Teddy. Off to Kearny you go. Write up your report and then get back to me."

"Okay, boss."

* * *

The scrap yard was vast. Railroad tracks snaked in and out. Gondola cars stood next to large piles of scrap metal. Cargo ships were tied up to a wharf with dockside cranes loading scrap metal into their holds. Switch engines puffed about moving gondola cars.

Tony Aiello headed for a hut about half the size of a small kitchen with a peaked roof and a single shaded window.

Peter Capparelli was there, seated at a battered desk. A girlie calendar hung on the wall. There was a filing cabinet but no other chair. Apparently visitors weren't supposed to linger.

"Mister Capparelli, we meet again," said Detective Tony Aiello.

Capparelli stood. "You're that copper from Jersey City."

"I am. But I'm not here to give you any *agita*, Mr. Capparelli. We know you didn't have any idea what Billy did. Nor did your wife, from what I understand."

"No. We were told Billy wanted to strike out on his own and he needed a place to stay and a job until he could. He's family so we took him in."

Aiello said, "I can understand that. Did he ever talk to you about any problems in Jersey City?"

"No. Never. He didn't talk much, at least not to me. I went with him to and from work on the trolley. I didn't see him much at work. And he didn't spend much time with us at home either. Except for eating supper, he pretty much stayed in his room. With the door closed. I got to tell you, Mr. Policeman. I may be married to one, but I don't understand the Irish. Their families are strange. Not like ours."

Tony thought, *No, not like ours who would hide a murderer until he died of old age.*

Capparelli said, "If you want, I can take you to the guy he worked with. My best worker. He talks a lot but he works hard. Maybe he can help you."

"Good. What's his name?"

"Abie the Jew." Tony didn't blink.

The pair walked a couple of hundred yards to a gondola car where a short, extremely muscular man in his late twenties, stripped to the waist, was standing atop a pile of scrap metal.

"Abie," Capparelli shouted. "This is the cop that came for Billy Cunningham. Come on down and talk to him." Then Capparelli walked back to his hut.

Abie wiped his hands on an old rag.

"Pleased to meet you, Mister, Mister..." Aiello probed.

"Just call me Abie the Jew. Everybody does."

"Why do they call you that?"

"Who knows? Maybe so they don't mistake me for Abie the Gentile or maybe Abie the Czar's brother-in-law. It's funny. In this country, they call you names but they don't kill you. That's better. Not good, but better. Maybe someday we'll make it good."

"Who's we, Abie?"

Abie the Jew took off his wire-rimmed spectacles and polished them with the filthy rag and held them up to the sun.

God knows how he can see through them.

Placing the glasses crookedly on his nose, Abie answered. "You and me, Mr. Policeman. Us and all the other workers of America. Maybe someday we'll make it good. But I'm not sure you can count policemen as workers. What do you say?"

"Call me Tony. Look, we'll talk politics in a minute. I got to ask you this. Did Billy Cunningham ever talk to you about anything that happened in Jersey City?"

Abie the Jew looked at Detective Tony Aiello and asked, "Why should I tell you anything Billy did or did not say to me? Billy was a worker. Not a good one, but a worker. Policemen. I've never had anything but trouble from policemen."

"Come on, Abie. I'm not a Cossack."

"True. The cops here only beat you, they don't kill you. That's better too. Look. I'll tell you the truth. The boychick never told me anything that would interest you or me for that matter."

"Thank you, Abie."

"You believe me?"

"Sure. If you were lying, you would have been much more inventive."

Abie the Jew said, "I like you. What is it...Tony? Even if you are a policeman. Can we talk politics now?"

"You bet. What do you think of the war in Europe, Abie?"

"I hate it, Tony. Thousands, maybe millions of workers on both sides killing each other while the fat cats get rich selling them the bullets. It's an atrocity. That's the political answer, Mr. Policeman. If you've got a minute, I'll tell you why I really hate this war."

"Take your time. I'd really like to hear about it," said Tony.

"So there I was, big shot me. My family is from a little shtetel, miles from anywhere in the Ukraine. But me, the big shot, do I stay in the shtetel and live a quiet life and get to go to a quiet grave? I do not. I go to the university in Kiev. Do you know how hard it is for a Jew to get into the university in the Ukraine? Or anywhere in Russia? Do you know what he has to put up with once he gets there?

"No? Well, it doesn't matter. I did it. I put up with it. I was going to be an advocate. What you call a lawyer. I finished my studies. I did well. I was going to spend my life doing good in Kiev, the capital of the Ukraine. I had all the answers to the world's problems. All you had to do was ask me.

"But first I had to go back to the shtetel and marry. My parents had arranged a marriage for me. That was the way things were there. Naturally, I was curious about my bride-to-be. I needed a wife. I was tired of cooking and cleaning for myself. Besides, you know, there was that other thing. Anyway, I'm introduced to her, my Rachel.

"Tony, she was beautiful. She was gorgeous. An angel. Hair as black as onyx, skin as white as alabaster, feet as tiny as a Chinese maiden's and her body—modestly covered, mind you—but radiating the promise of unspeakable delights. And me. I'm struck dumb. Mr. Talks-a-mile-a-minute is stammering and sputtering. Thank God, the bargain had been struck or I think she would gotten up and run out the door. But she didn't. She's as sweet as she is beautiful. Me. I can't wait for the wedding.

"And then, do you know what happened, Tony? Some idiot Serb shoots some imbecile of an Austrian archduke and the next thing you know, every army in Europe is mobilizing.

"Does the Czar make me an officer and call me to Moscow to advise him? He does not. But I'm wise to what's going to happen next. I'm going to get conscripted. I'll be taken into the Czar's army where conscripts can be forced to serve for up to twenty years. And if the Germans don't kill me, I'll have my Yid ass kicked three times a day by some peasant sergeant.

"I had to get out of the Ukraine. Out of Russia. I had to leave my beautiful Rachel behind. We kissed for the first and last time and I walked out the door with a pack on my back and her dowry in a money belt around my waist. I swore I'd come back for her. I must have cried all the way to St. Petersburg.

"Believe it or not, I signed on as a stoker in a Danish ship sailing for Copenhagen the very day I got into St. Petersburg. It almost killed me. Shoveling coal into that furnace. I was an intellectual, not a worker. Well, I was a worker by the time we got to Denmark. I jumped ship and signed on a British tramp heading for Southampton. Jumped ship again. Then I got onto an American ship going to New York. This time I paid. Steerage.

"So there I was in America. Friendless, but thanks to God and my darling Rachel, not penniless. That was a long time ago. I wrote to her. Lord, did I write. But I never got a letter back. I don't bother to write any more. I don't know if she is living or if she is dead.

"So that, my new friend, is why I hate this war. My reasons are both personal and political."

Tony pointed to the scrap heap. "Why didn't you set up shop here in America as a lawyer, Abie?"

"I couldn't even if I tried. My diplomas, my degrees. Those precious papers. I didn't put them in my sack. I was stupid. I just wanted to get out of Russia. I thought the war would be over by Christmas."

"Everybody did," said Tony. "So you have good reasons not to want to see the United States drawn into the fighting."

"Of course I do. I am not crazy. I know now this country is our last chance. We can make this a good country, maybe a great country. Getting killed isn't going to help anybody do that."

Tony asked, "Will you go back to Russia after the war, Abie?"

"No. I'll stay here. This is my country now. I will send for Rachel if, please God, she is still alive."

"You didn't spend that dowry, did you, Abie?"

Abie smiled. "Would you?"

Tony said, "Okay, so you're an American now. But I don't

think you're a Republican or a Democrat, my friend. What are you, Abie? An anarchist? A socialist? What?"

"Somewhere between this and that depending on the time of day and whether I've just had a good meal."

Aiello said, "That means the people who don't want America in the war don't have anything to fear from people like you?"

"People like me? No. But others, oi."

"What do you mean 'others', Abe? Who are the 'others'?"

Abie asked, "You ever hear of Luigi Galleani?"

"No. Why?"

"Well, probably some people you know—some Italians, some anarchists— do. He preaches what he calls 'Propaganda of the Deed'."

"I don't know what that means."

"That means he and his followers, the Galleanists, are willing to use violence to get what they want. The collapse of governments. They think the slaughter from the war will make the workers rise up and overthrow the governments. They are very dangerous men. They would love to see America in the war. They don't care on what side, either. It would just speed up the revolution."

"How do you know all this, Abie?"

"What? Do you think I hang around Kearny for the intellectual simulation? It's easy to get to New York. That's where I find lots of people like me. And them. They talk. I listen."

"I don't care if they talk until they're blue," said Aiello. "What I'm worried about is what will happen if they act. Especially if they act here, in New Jersey, in Jersey City."

Abie said, "Me too. But think about it. What's to bomb in Jersey City? Choo-choo trains?" Tony didn't answer. "Still, I worry too, Mr. Policeman."

"Call me Tony. Look, Abie. As I said, I don't care about their politics. Only if they are going to do something concrete. Something dangerous. Here. Would you be willing to keep an eye out for that for me? Could we meet every so often and talk about it? Could we do that?"

"So you want me to spy for the police, eh, Tony?"

"Abie, don't say that. You won't be spying. You'll be helping to keep your new country out of that insane European war."

Abie was amazed. "What a country! I talk to a policeman and fifteen minutes later, it's 'Abie the Patriot'."

Abie paused to think. "Why not? Why not Abie the Patriot? But I'm only going to tell you what I think you should know, Mr. Policeman. Don't look for me to give you the names of my comrades without cause."

"Fair enough."

"Besides I like the idea of being a spy. It's more romantic than breaking my back in a scrap yard. Who knows? Maybe I'll meet a beautiful Jewish lady spy."

"I don't think we have any of those yet, Abie."

The conversation over, Abie the Jew went straight to the little shack to talk to his anarchist comrade, Peter Capparelli.

"The policeman wants me to spy on us anarchists, Peter."

"Dear Jesus. What did you tell him?"

"I told him 'yes' of course. I'll get more from him than I'll give him."

"It sounds like a crackpot idea. What can you get from him?" asked Capparelli.

"You might be surprised what we could learn just from the questions he asks me. And, me, all I'll tell him is what he already knows or should know."

* * *

Tony checked in with Lieutenant McGurk the next morning. "Ready for work, boss."

"Good, Tony."

"By the way, I think I've got a confidante who's close to the anarchists in Manhattan."

Mickey was impressed. "How in the hell did you do that in less than twenty-four hours?"

"Talent...Intelligence...Dumb luck. You pick."

"Don't make me," said Mickey McGurk.

Easter Monday

"Uh, oh. Blinker is going to want to see this now," said the cryptographer in Room 40 handing off an intercepted German Naval message. He did.

Sir Roger Casement, who had been in Germany since war broke out, finally got the Germans to secretly send a shipload of arms to Ireland. He would go there separately by U-boat.

The German ship, disguised as the Norwegian merchantman Aud-Norge, carried 20,000 rifles, ten machine guns and enough ammunition to fuel the long planned Irish uprising against their English rulers.

But, thanks to Captain Reginald "Blinker" Hall, that smudge on the horizon on Good Friday was the HMS Bluebell and the weapons never got to Ireland. Blinker had known what to do.

Sir Roger's U-boat landed him on a beach in County Kerry that same day but he was feeling ill and he tarried nearby long enough for the British to capture him. The British whisked him off to the Tower of London where a hangman's noose as a traitor awaited him.

The Irish Volunteers and the Irish Citizens' Army rose up on Easter Monday occupying several important centers in Dublin and proclaiming the birth of the Republic of Ireland.

Fighting was brisk but sporadic until substantial British reinforcements with artillery landed two days later. Then the force of British arms pushed to Irish back into the General Post Office where they fought for days before their unconditional surrender.

General John Maxwell, a seasoned officer whose campaigns dated back to the Sudan, arrived two days before the surrender to take charge.

His decisions were draconic. He had more than 3,200 Irishmen and women arrested.

Of these, 183 faced secret, drumhead, "field" courts-martial which hurriedly condemned almost half to face the firing squad including all seven who had signed the document proclaiming the Irish Republic.

James Connolly, head of the socialist Irish Citizens' Army and military commander at the General Post Office, had been wounded in the ankle and couldn't walk.

He was taken by military ambulance to Kilmainham Gaol and helped onto a stretcher.

Four grim stretcher-bearers picked up Connolly and moved towards the prison's courtyard. Connolly had served seven years in the British Army himself and knew these soldiers had an unenviable assignment.

"Careful, boys," he said. "Don't drop me. I wouldn't want to get hurt."

Their muffled laughter didn't reach the stern officers awaiting Connolly. His hands tied behind his back, he was gently seated in a chair to face the muzzles of the British firing party.

No one could tell if, at the last moment, his lips quivered. His huge moustache covered his mouth. Connolly's stretcher-bearers wouldn't have thought it possible.

The execution of the Easter Monday leaders electrified Ireland and, indeed, the world. Dublin's population, at first, vilified the rebels but after the executions they were politically canonized.

One mourner, far away in New York City, was Jim Larkin, Connolly's great friend and predecessor as head of the Irish General Transport Workers Union.

Larkin now was plotting with the International Workers of the World—the Wobblies. A big strike was coming up. Big Jim had already had a demonstration of how Dr. Scheele's cigar bombs worked.

Fat Jack Lynch

The first "confidante" Lieutenant Mickey McGurk brought on board was Fat Jack Lynch, a man he known since he was a boy in the 'Show.

His first meeting with Fat Jack had been revealing. They had met at a saloon in Greenville where no one knew either of them.

Fat Jack had opened the conversation. "It's always good to see you, Mickey. I know you're a lieutenant on the Zeppelins now and I'm proud of you for that. I also know you're heading up some sort of Bomb Squad. Or at least that's what my kid brother tells me. What I don't know is why you want to talk to me?"

Fat Jack stretched out his arms. "And why here, in the middle of Greenville?"

"Because, Jack," Mickey said, "Lots of people—like your brother Terry—have big mouths and this is a private conversation."

"A private conversation? About what? I'm just a clerk with the county. Don't you know how many ounces are in a pound? I don't work on the docks anymore. I lead a quiet life. I'm walking out with a sweet lady now. I do a bit of work for your uncle. What do the Zepps want with me? I'm really puzzled, Mickey."

Mickey McGurk laughed out loud and shook his head. "Jack, you are a piece of work. I wouldn't be much of a cop if I didn't know that you were one of the leaders of the Clan na Gael hereabouts."

"The what?"

"Jack, don't play me for a fool. I know you made two trips to Ireland before war broke out."

"Just visiting the folks at home."

"Your folks are from Galway, Jack, not Dublin. And it's hard to understand how you could afford those trips on what little money you used to make on the docks. I also know you practically live in Manhattan what with meeting every class of Mick imaginable. Lace curtain Irish mostly, not another longshoreman among them. Could it be because whatever room you're in, Jack, you're the smartest one there?"

"You've been listening to the wrong people, Mickey. But if even half of what you're saying is true, do you think such a person would tell a copper how many of his comrades ate bologna sandwiches for lunch let alone anything of importance?"

"Jack, I don't care what the Clan na Gael or any other group of harps does in Ireland or New York City or practically anyplace else. I don't even care what they do politically in Jersey City. In fact, good luck to them, Jack, I don't like the Brits much myself."

"Then why are we palavering here in Greenville?"

"Let me start off, Jack, by asking your opinion of this war?"

"I want the English to lose."

"Of course, but does that mean you want America to jump in on Germany's side?" asked McGurk.

"No, that's impossible anyway. Before our people came here during The Famine, Mickey, practically everybody in America was English or at least British. They're still here. If we go to war, it'll be on the side of the Brits. The Germans and the Irish here don't count for zip; they'll roll right over us."

"So you don't want America in this war?"

Fat Jack Lynch said, "I most assuredly do not."

"Neither do we. By we, I mean Frank Hague, the Democrats and Woodrow Wilson. We want to make sure that nobody pulls or pushes us into war," said McGurk.

Lynch said, "I wouldn't worry about Wilson, if I was you. He's got his hands full with Mexico. The only time he pays attention to Europe is when a German submarine sinks a British ship with Americans on board. Then he rants and raves for a bit and goes back to worrying about Mexico."

"Maybe. Does he have to worry about the Irish?"

"Not really. Oh, we'll howl and scream and cause him grief.

But we're not going to do anything to hurt America. This is our country. We're a funny lot, the Irish. Most of our families have been in this country for generations, but to hear us talk you'd think we left the old place the day before yesterday. Yet we're Americans. As American as George Washington. Look what happened in the Civil War? We flocked to the colors although damn few of us cared anything about freeing the slaves."

"I know."

"Sure you do, Mickey, didn't both your grandfathers wear Union blue?"

"How do you know that, Jack?"

Lynch smiled. "I wouldn't be much of a Hibernian leader, would I, if I didn't know something about the coppers who are watching us out of the corner of their eye? You know, Mickey, I should be recruiting you. Your dad's father, John McGurk, was a first sergeant and then a lieutenant in the 164th New York. That was a Fenian outfit, my lad. Nobody would get that rank unless he was a bright green Fenian. What do you say, Mickey, can I sign you up?"

"I think I'll pass, Jack. But you've made your point. Now, back to the war. The Irish are sure busy for people who intend to sit out this war."

"Well, we don't intend to sit out anything," said Lynch.

"Can you tell me what you're going to do, Jack?"

"I can tell you this. We're going to raise money here and we'll ship it back to Ireland, in bales."

"What will the money be used for, Jack?"

"The same old thing. Plotting rebellion, rising up, getting beaten down and then going back to plotting."

"A bit futile isn't it, Jack?"

"Not at all. That's how we stay a nation, Mickey. Ireland may not be an independent state yet, but it's certainly a nation. We rise up and fight in every generation. Well, in most of them anyway."

"Is that all those big shots in New York want you to do, Jack, is to raise money?"

"Yes. For now."

"What do you mean, for now?"

Lynch said, "Who knows? Maybe, someday I'll make another trip to Ireland with more than money in my hand. You know what they say, Mickey, 'England's adversity is Ireland's opportunity'."

"Who said that?"

"Aw, who the hell knows? You think I went to St. Peter's like you?"

"Can you tell me anything about the boys in New York?" asked McGurk, hoping to pick up a couple of tidbits for Captain Tunney.

"You wouldn't be a pal of a Captain Tunney over there, would you?"

"I've heard of him," said McGurk. Lynch was obviously still the smartest person in the room.

"Well, I can talk about a couple of them. Everybody knows what they're doing. They make no secret of it. But maybe you never heard of them."

"Do you know Jim Larkin?" asked Lynch. "Big Irishman with a bomb-thrower's moustache. He was in the middle of all the labor troubles in the old country. He organized the Irish Transport Workers' Union in Dublin and took everybody out on a general strike. But the big money boys and the English hated him. He had to beat it out of town. He's here now and if there is a strike, look for him in the middle of it making a speech. A grand talker, Jim is. The Wobblies like him."

"That's the International Workers of the World. They're anarchists, right?" asked Mickey.

"There are those that say that. Jim's a republican too. He helped found the Irish Citizens' Army before he left."

"The what?"

"Socialists. Sort of a militia. They're there to protect strikers from the police or the English. And then there's Sir Roger Casement. I met him too. They sent him over to raise money. No 'lace curtain Irish' there, Mickey. He looks like, talks like, walks like and dresses like an English aristocrat. But he's Irish. He's always been a nationalist but it took the Boer War to turn him into a republican."

McGurk, a Democrat, had no trouble telling republicans from Republicans.

"How'd he get the title?"

"Queen Victoria's mistake. Got it for something or other that he did in the Free Congo or Peru, I think. I don't think the Clan na Gael completely trusted him at first. But he proved himself."

"Why? Did it bother them that he is a Protestant?"

"God, no. Look at the list of Irish leaders down through the years. Wolf Tone, Napper Tandy, Edward Fitzgerald, Robert Emmet, William Smith O'Brien, Charles Stewart Parnell. They were all Protestant. Of course they had one advantage we didn't have."

"What was that, Jack?"

"They could read and write."

Both men were silent for a few seconds. "So you're not going to talk about anybody else you met in New York?"

"No, I'm not, Mickey. In fact, I think I'm done talking to you now as well."

"Whoa! Wait a minute, Jack. I'm not asking you to tell me anything that affects Ireland. That's between you and the King of England. All that I am interested in is if some idiots are planning something here that could draw America into a war we don't want. If something like that should come up, would you give me a general heads up? No names or anything. Just enough information that I might be able to stop it before it happens."

"I don't know. I might. But I'd get to make the call. Understand this, Mickey. I'm no informer. If anybody calls me that, including you, I'll kill him."

"Of course, you're not, Jack," said McGurk. "No question about that." He was grateful that he had insisted on using the word "confidante" however he didn't dare to mention that to Fat Jack Lynch.

Jack and he met from time to time talking, mostly, about old times in the 'Show.

Mickey was aware of the tin cans with the slots on top for donations that appeared on every bar in the 'Show and a lot of other places in Jersey City too. There was no message on the cans but everyone knew where the money was going.

Mickey had a chance to sort of play double agent after he learned that the British had finally solved the mystery of a series of dangerous fires at sea. They met again at the saloon in Greenville.

"It must be serious, Mickey, if we're meeting in secret again. I hate to disappoint you but I have absolutely nothing for you. Nothing's going on. Truly."

"Ah, Jack, what a cynical man you are. How do know that I didn't just want to tell you how much I appreciate your kid brother guarding my uncle's privacy. I just love cooling my heels until he decides to let me in."

"He can be an asshole, can't he?"

"You said it, Jack, not me. No, I just wanted to get your reaction to a story I heard the other day. From some friends I have in the city.

Tunney, thought Lynch.

"It seems that a whole string of British ships have caught on fire at sea since the war began. Some of them even sank. The Brits, it seems, didn't have this problem before the war and, it also seems, there are no problems with ships sailing from ports elsewhere in America. Only in New York."

"Do tell."

"Yes. Well, the story goes on. One British ship, sailing from

Brooklyn, was bound for Murmansk. In Russia. That is a long, long trip. Dangerous one too. Anyway, this ship is diverted to Marseilles in France. That's about half-way to Murmansk, I think. They unloaded the ship and what do you think they found?"

"I have no idea," said Jack smoothly. The Irish had been lying under oath for a thousand years and were good at it.

"Time bombs of a sort. They looked like a big metal cigars. Wax on both ends. Chemicals on both sides eating away at a metal disc in the middle. When the chemicals met, whoosh! Flames shot out and next thing you know you had a nasty fire on your hands. What do you think of that, Jack?"

"Ingenious. I wonder who's making them?"

"The Brits think they're either made in a factory in Hoboken or on one of the German ships tied up in the harbor. But they can't prove it and we don't want them to prove it. You know what else, Jack? The Brits think some of those bombs are planted by Irish longshoremen."

"No! Say it's not true."

"Who knows, Jack? I just thought you'd be interested in the story. By the way, I hear the British have hired a bunch of guards to watch their cargo when it's being loaded."

"Well, that should cut down on their problems, Mickey."

"Frankly, I don't care, Jack, I just thought you'd like to know."

"Thanks, Mickey." Lynch had learned what happened in Marseilles months before McGurk did. The Brits had beefed up their guards dockside. The stevedore companies were being very picky in hiring longshoremen too. They didn't want to jeopardize their contracts. The Irish would have to find other uses for the cigar bombs they still had in their pockets.

Months later, Fat Jack Lynch asked for a meeting. It was just after the British executed fifteen leaders of the Easter Monday Rising in Dublin. This time at an old haunt in the 'Show.

"This is a heads up, Mickey and I don't care who knows it. My people are furious about what's going on in Dublin. We fight them fair and square and they beat us. All right. It happens. Then they court martial and shoot our leaders? James Connolly was badly wounded in the rising. You know those dirty bastards had to prop him up in a chair so they could shoot him?

"Meanwhile, they're going through Ireland like one of those new vacuum cleaners sucking up every republican they can find. Thousands of them. Off to prison in England. They are going to hang Sir Roger Casement too.

"So my hotheads want to strike back. Do something. Do anything. It's hard to reason with them they're that angry," said Lynch. "What do you want to do? I ask. Go to Ireland and join the Volunteers? The Volunteers are all in jail. The entire republican leadership is either in jail or in their graves. Of course, I say, You always can go to up to the prison and knock on the door. And yell 'Let me in. Let me in. I'm a republican too.' They look at me stupidly, which is no surprise. They know the Germans tried to help the Volunteers even if it was for their own reasons and not ours. So they're ready to help the Germans. I don't know how, but if I was guarding those British ships I'd put the cargo through a sieve."

"Do you have anything specific, Jack, anything here in Jersey City or even Hoboken?"

"No, I don't. Not at all. And don't ask me for names, I won't give them to you. Just watch out, Mickey, watch out."

The next day Lieutenant McGurk briefed the director of public safety on what Lynch had told him.

"Do you know what a pain in the ass those Fenians are?" asked Commissioner Frank Hague. "Not one of those goddamn idiots would go back to live in Ireland if you gave him a thousand dollars, a house and a ton of potatoes. It's all nonsense. My father wouldn't have gone back if you paid to put him on a ship and sent him there first class."

"I'm sure you're right, Uncle Frank, but that's not how they see it. They're Americans but they want to free Ireland."

"So they're going to free Ireland by setting fire to British ships and drowning some poor bastards who are just trying to make a living?"

"I'm not sure they're going to do that, Commissioner. In fact, I'm not sure what they are going to do or not do."

"Mickey, why can't they just get drunk on St. Patrick's Day and leave it at that? All right, you worry about them. I've got my own worries."

"Can I help, Uncle Frank?"

"You bet you will. You and all the Zepps, the cops, the firemen, the whole organization. Woodrow Wilson is going to be re-nominated for president in a couple of weeks and we got to get ready for the campaign. His campaign starts on Labor Day, you know."

"Who's going to be the Republican candidate?"

"Who knows? I hope it won't be Hughes. He'd be very tough in the East. Tough in New Jersey especially. With luck that goddamn cowboy will run again on the Bull Moose ticket. If Roosevelt splits the Republican vote again, Wilson wins in a walk."

It wasn't to be that easy.

The House on West 15th Street

"So, what did you find?"

"Nothing."

"No suitcases? No dynamite?"

"Absolutely nothing. I think that guy they grabbed up North was full of shit. I don't care what he said. The lady who rents the house—a German lady—was as nice as could be and took me right to a storage room. There was lots of junk there but no suitcases.

"She said there had been a couple of suitcases there but someone picked them up almost a year ago."

"And?"

"And, when I asked, she shook her head and said she didn't know what was in them."

"Did you search the rest of the house?"

"I didn't have a search warrant."

"Okay. Tell me what you did see. What about the house? Tell me about the house."

The Federal agent thought for a moment and then said, "Typical brownstone, three stories, entrance off a stoop, an entrance to the basement under the stoop. Parlor, dining room, kitchen and toilet on the first floor. Probably bedrooms upstairs. I didn't go up there. Didn't get into the rest of the basement either. Just the storage room.

"The lady's name was Martha Held. I think she was an opera singer in the old country. She was big enough. There were pictures of her when she was young hanging on the walls.

"She keeps two servants. A colored girl named Rose who answered the door and a bohunk woman who I don't think speaks any English.

"I hung around for a couple of nights like you said. Lots of men and women coming and going. Lots of music and singing.

Frankly, I think Mrs. Held is running a high class whorehouse for those German sea captains interned here."

His superior sighed. "So, a complete waste of time?"

"Yep."

"Well, write up a report. You think I should tell Tunney about what's going on at West 15th Street?"

"Don't waste your breath. He's not into whores. He's got enough on his plate just trying to keep track of that Koenig guy."

When someone was caught plotting to blow something up, it was treated as a law enforcement problem.

Law enforcement in America had always been the concern of big city cops and small town sheriffs. The Federal government steered clear of it except for the Secret Service tracking down counterfeiters after paper money became common.

President Theodore Roosevelt got the Feds into the business in 1908 when he created a special force of agents within the Justice Department called the Bureau of Investigation. They investigated antitrust crimes, labor strife, banking crimes, railroad fraud and, after 1910, prostitution that crossed state lines. But offenders were usually prosecuted in local courts.

In 1915, as part of his efforts to maintain strict neutrality, President Woodrow Wilson directed his son-in-law, William McAdoo, Secretary of the Treasury, to have the Secret Service investigate possible espionage. Spying was not all that was going on. People were blowing things up or were trying to. Federal agents made a number of arrests. But the defendants were tried in state or local courts. Some of the culprits had been convicted and were sitting in prison.

President Wilson was focused elsewhere.

Peggy McCann

Peggy McCann was sitting in a small room with about ten other girls at Pathé Studios in Jersey City. It was a casting call for another of Pearl White's serials.

Peggy had been in one already and had bit parts in a couple of photoplays too. She was hoping to get cast in this one. She didn't have steady work and she needed the money. She was sure Tony Aiello would formally ask her to marry him soon and a girl needed money for that.

She introduced himself to the girl on her right. "Hello. I'm Peggy McCann. I hope they need more than one of us."

"Me too. I'm Mena Edwards. It's the first time I've been here."

"You look familiar," said Peggy to the lovely young woman.

"Everyone says that. You've probably seen me in the advertisements for Eastman Kodak."

"Of course, you're the Eastman-Kodak girl. Well, I'm very pleased to meet you."

"Likewise. But they only pay when they take my picture. I could use the money."

"Me too. I haven't had steady work since Alphonse the Magnificent."

"What a name," said Mena Edwards, "That sounds like a story to kill time with. Let's hear it, Peggy."

"Okay," said Peggy, "Alphonse the Magnificent is a magician. Talk about runts. A little Italian, he's about five feet five with his hands over his head.

"Funny enough though. It was his wife who hired me. I was listed with one of those fly-by-night theatrical agents in Manhattan and I got a call for a magician's assistant. I knew what that meant, a big smile and an itty bitty costume.

"She—Andrea is her name—was Alphonse's assistant until she got pregnant and after a while she couldn't pull it off any more. They tried some kid—a niece, I think—for a while but as Andrea said, 'She made him look like a clown, not a magician.' So I end up auditioning for her. She was due to have the baby any minute.

"'Let me see your legs, she says,' so I hiked up my skirt, way up. I thought the agent would fall out of his chair he leaned that far forward. 'Good,' she says, 'very good. The audience will be busy looking at your legs; they won't see how clumsy my husband is.'

"I got the job. Two shows on Saturday. One in the afternoon, one in the evening. Four dollars in cash after the second show.

"The first show was a riot. I made a mistake and it made the act. Naturally, I haven't got the staging down yet so I move one way and he moves another. Bang. There we are. Him with his head buried between my breasts. I give the audience a shocked look. The place goes wild. Cheers, laughter, whistles, applause.

"He hears the racket and he's smart enough not to move. We stand absolutely still for the better part of a minute. We part. I smile and curtsey. He holds his crotch, makes a face and bows. The place goes wild again. We exit to terrific applause.

"His wife is waiting in the wings, her arms folded above her big belly. Her husband starts, 'Honey, it was an accident.' 'Be quiet,' she says and looks at me. 'You heard the crowd. That worked,' she says. 'It stays in the act.'

"Me, I'm not so happy, so I say, 'Now wait a minute...' but she interrupts me. 'Do you want the job or don't you?' I needed the job so I said, 'Okay. That stays in the act but how about an extra dollar, you know, for my trouble?' Again she says, 'Do you want the job?' You know the Calabrese. Hard. What the hell, I say, 'Yes. I do.'

"She gives her husband a look like he's already in his coffin and says, 'Good. He won't give you any trouble. I guarantee it.'

"So there I am, twice every Saturday, with that little wop's big nose deep in my chest. Still, it's a living. Sort of. Anyway, Andrea has her bambino and six weeks or so later she's back and I'm out. She looks pretty good, a little thick around the middle but not bad.

"She thanked me, gave me a couple of extra dollars and told me, 'The tit thing stays. The baby helped.' Then she pushes them up with both hands. 'See,' she says. Alphonse the Magnificent just stood there grinning."

"That's a terrific story, Peggy." She looked carefully at the tall, very pretty Irish girl. "Say, I have an idea."

Peggy listened.

Mickey McGurk had asked his cousin, Peggy McCann, to keep tabs on the actors, actresses and production people at Pathé Studios.

Peggy was to listen for gossip, and there was always gossip, at the Pathé Studios at the Paterson Plank Road and Congress Street or anyplace else actresses and actors were to be found.

Of course, there were a lot fewer of them nowadays since Commissioner Frank Hague had run many of them out of town as "morally objectionable." Those remaining gossiped incessantly. They heard things that no one else did.

Peggy went to see Mickey the next day. "How you doing, cuz?" he asked.

"Okay, I guess. Hiding my bills, enjoying myself with my beau, Tony Aiello, and sneaking around playing spy for you."

"Confidante, not spy, Peg."

"Right. I was at a casting call at Pathé and I might be on to something that really would interest you."

"Let's hear it."

"It's a place on West 15th Street in Manhattan. A brownstone full of good looking girls and a hell of a lot of Germans. Important Germans."

"I'm interested. Very interested."

"Well, I was talking to this girl at Pathé, a New Yorker named

Mena Edwards. You know who she is?"

"No. I don't think I've heard of her."

"Sure you do. Mena is the 'Eastman Girl.' She's in all those advertisements for their cameras. She lives in Manhattan. She likes to party and she likes to talk."

"Okay, sure. I've seen the ads. She's a pretty girl. Very photogenic," said Mickey.

"Well, we were looking to get a part in one of Pearl White's things but we both struck out. They wouldn't touch Mena because she's still under contract with Eastman Kodak and apparently I'm too tall now. Pearl's leading man took a look at me and said, 'They'll think I'm standing in a hole.' They would.

"So we were commiserating with each other in the back of Grandpa McCann's saloon. Mena pops up and says we shouldn't be so glum. She knows where there's going to be a great party that night and we should get dolled up and go together."

"West 15th Street?"

"Yep. 123 West 15th Street to be exact."

Mickey wrote down the address.

"Anyway, Tony's working and I'm thinking this is just some more show business stuff and he won't object to that. He thinks actors and show people are all fairies.

"I met Mena at her hotel and off we went. The house was your typical three floor brownstone. It's owned by some middle-aged German opera singer who, I might add, can still belt out those old arias when she wants to. The party was in full swing. Lots of booze. Beer. Champagne. Fabulous food laid out on three or four big tables. Somebody was playing the piano. Everybody was singing in German. No show business types. Just Germans."

"Do you understand German, Peggy?"

"No. Just a few words like everybody in the Heights. But Mena says she can speak some and I think she understands more than she lets on.

"So. Mena tells me some of those guys are German sea captains. She said two or three others were German diplomats from Washington. She didn't know who the rest of them were but they were sure German."

"Were there any Americans there?"

"Maybe. There was one guy I think they called 'Christy' but he didn't mix with the girls.

"Mena and I tore into that food, I'll tell you that. It was great. The beer too. I noticed men going in and out of one of the rooms and closing the door behind them. You know me, I'm nosy. I walked up and opened it, pretending I did it by mistake. They all turned and looked at me.

"'Whoops,' I said, 'Looking for the powder room. Sorry gents.' I think they were looking at maps.

"I stayed for a couple of hours. Said goodbye to Mena and headed home. What do you think?"

"Peg, I think you've hit pay dirt. When are you going back?"

"Do you want me to go back?"

"Absolutely. Listen, Peggy, I think you know Tony, Hans Mannstein and me have split up our work with the confidantes. The Irish are mine; Tony has the Italians and radicals and Hans deals with the Germans. I want you to work with Hans. You know him, don't you?"

"I've seen him at wakes and weddings. But wait a minute, cuz, why can't I work with Tony? We're together all the time anyway and that way he won't get nervous about what I'm doing. I don't want to scare him off."

"I'm afraid that's a bad idea, cuz. Tony is too close to you. So am I. Besides, Hans speaks German. I'll set up a meeting with him. Good luck."

"Wait. Wait. You clear this with Tony first. Okay?'

"No problem," said Mickey McGurk and it wasn't.

* * *

"Peggy, good to see you again," Hans Mannstein said as he stood to shake her hand. They were in a Chinese restaurant.

"You too, Hans."

Peggy was taller than Hans but when she sat and their eyes were just about level with each other. Peggy McCann had long legs.

They exchanged some small talk and ordered food and Chinese tea.

"Peggy, I know you have already talked to Mickey about what you are going to do for us. But it's important—vital—that you don't discuss what you do with anyone other than me. Can I have your word on that?"

"Oui, mon capitain."

"So it's going to be like that, huh?"

"Well, you deal with Micks, you deal with smart...alecks." Peggy laughed and waved her hands around. "I'm sorry but of this feels like one of the awful photoplays they make at Pathé."

"Well, I'm not a spymaster, Peggy. I'm just a cop who wants to stop trouble before it starts and I hope you'll help me.

"Good. Now all we want you to do is tell us what you see and hear there. If you notice anything unusual, we want to know about it. Let us do the detective work. We need you to be our eyes and ears. We'll sort it out. If you get your hands on anything that's written, bring it to us. Okay?"

"Hans, let me ask you. Why do the Jersey City cops care what a bunch of Dutchmen are doing in New York City?"

"Problem is, Peggy, there are hundreds of German seamen from interned German ships all over the waterfront here in Jersey. We want to know what they're up to and we think the guys at West 15th Street are their leaders."

Peggy persisted. "How much trouble could a bunch of dumb sailors cause that couldn't be handled by a couple cops with billy clubs?"

Hans hesitated, puffed his cheeks out, exhaled and said,

"Maybe enough to drag this country into their goddamn war."

"Jesus. You're serious. I had no idea. I really am sorry. I'll behave. I promise. How often do you want me to go there?"

"Once a week, if you can swing it. When's the big party night?"

"Saturday, Mena says."

"Be careful how you talk to Mena Edwards, Peggy. We don't know anything about her except that she's the 'Eastman Girl.' And that doesn't automatically make her 'Citizen of the Year'."

"Okay, I'll be careful."

Hans said, "Let's say we meet back here for supper every Monday night at six. Okay? You can bring Tony if you want but he pays for his own supper."

"I just might do that. Okay. But suppose I don't have anything to tell you?"

"Come anyway, you'd be surprised what a cop can learn by asking questions."

"Good enough. One more thing, Hans, but I'm having a hard time finding and keeping full time work. Now you want me to work on Saturdays. Is it possible that I might have, you know, a small salary to cover my expenses and all? I might have to go there on Sunday too. Meet with Mena during the week. Carfare. All that, you know."

Hans knew Lieutenant McGurk had what he called "walk around money" that could be used.

"I see. How much do you think you need?"

"How about five dollars a week?"

"Jeez. How about four dollars? And that's more than many a man makes in a day."

"Ah," said Peggy McCann sweetly, "but wouldn't it be worth it to keep America out of the war?"

Hans shook his head and chuckled. "I guess it would at that. Five it is. Okay. I'll see you next Monday. You'll get your gratuity then."

"Gratuity, is it?" Peggy McCann was never averse to getting a tip.

She saw Tony the next evening. "You sure you're okay with me going to parties over in Manhattan?"

Tony said, "You're not going to parties. You're spying on a pack of square heads. Besides, from what you told me, they're usually too much in the bag to give anybody trouble. Right?"

"That's right," Peggy lied.

"If they get fresh," Tony said, "you just back off. That's all. We'll put a wig on Hans Mannstein and send him over there."

"They never get that drunk, Tony."

"Whatever. But don't get so carried away with this spying thing that you forget to plan for the wedding."

"What wedding?"

Tony smiled at her. "Our wedding, my love."

"Our wedding? I don't remember you asking me to marry you and I certainly don't remember saying 'yes'."

Peggy stood up, hands on her hips, waiting.

Tony sighed and got down on one knee. Taking her hand, he said, "Peggy, my darling, I love you. I have never loved anyone else and if you don't marry me, I'll die a lonely old man. And think of our children, if you don't marry me, they won't even be born. Peggy McCann, or whatever your name is, will you marry me? Please?"

Peggy giggled and yanked him to his feet. "Of course I will. I love you too, Tony, and I want to spend the rest of my life with you."

They kissed, passionately, interrupted only by the need to breathe.

Tony spoke. "This is really going to please my mother. If you need help, believe me, she'll help you plan."

"What's to plan? We announce the banns, get married at St. Anne's and have the reception in the back of Grandpa's saloon. All we have to do is set a date."

Tony shook his head. "You do realize you are marrying a Sicilian, don't you?"

A Colossal Distraction

President Woodrow Wilson was re-nominated by the Democratic Party on a platform he wrote himself. But the platform committee added the words, "He kept us out of war." Wilson objected but the platform committee insisted.

There it was, the motto for his re-election. But the world just wouldn't cooperate.

The Brits were no help. Not only had they savagely put down the Easter Monday rebellion in Dublin but now it looked like they were going to hang the Irish revolutionary Sir Roger Casement for high treason. Irish Americans were very angry.

Worse, the British Navy now stopped ships carrying tobacco to neutral ports on the grounds that smokes might make their way into the hands of German soldiers thus raising morale. The American South, Wilson's electoral heartland, was infuriated.

Of course, the Germans and their submarines did nothing to improve Wilson's disposition.

In March, they sank the English cross channel steamer, Sussex, with a heavy loss of life including some Americans. Wilson made his usual diplomatic demand. This time the Germans backed off unrestricted submarine warfare for the time being.

A month later, the German Imperial Navy High Seas Fleet fought the Royal Navy to a draw in the Battle of Jutland. No one expected that. But the High Seas Fleet steamed back to port and never challenged the British again.

Wilson managed to give the impression that he and the nation were still neutral.

Meanwhile, he moved to build up the Army, the National Guard and the Navy, a process that would take four years. Wilson's Republican critics dismissed his efforts as too little, too late. The Preparedness Movement, which favored intervening on the side of Great Britain, was highly critical of the president.

Wilson had walked that neutrality tightrope for going on two years now. It demanded much time and attention. And then there was Mexico.

If Mexico was overshadowed by the Colossus of the North, the president of the United States considered the country to his south to be a colossal distraction.

The personification of that distraction came in the form of a full-bodied, illiterate, but highly charismatic guerilla leader named Pancho Villa.

Pancho Villa was as vindictive as Woodrow Wilson, or Frank Hague for that matter.

Wilson had permitted Mexican government troops to travel across American territory on the El Paso and Southwest Railroad to give Villa and his Division del Norte a good thrashing at a battle back in Mexico. But most of Villa's force got away.

Pancho Villa was not a good sport. In the pre-dawn darkness of April 9, he and five hundred or so of his men attacked Columbus, NM, a watering stop on the El Paso and Southwest. The hungry, ill clad men looted the small business district before they burned it and they had a lot of fun shooting up and terrorizing the town of four hundred. Eight civilians were killed.

But things did not turn out well for Villa. He expected little resistance. Two of his officers had scouted the town and reported it was defended by only thirty soldiers. The rest of the 13th Cavalry was presumably out there somewhere on the sixty-five mile stretch of border it patrolled.

Not so. More than three hundred and twenty-five troopers were in town or at their tent camp nearby.

The troopers fought the raiders with everything they had. Cooks and stable hands weighed in with an axe and a baseball bat among other things.

More effective were two temperamental French machine guns that created a crossfire in the middle of town. They fired 20,000 rounds between stoppages.

Villa's force was decimated. Sixty-seven of his horsemen died on the spot and thirteen more died of their wounds. Five were captured and hanged. The 13th Cavalry lost ten men.

The 13th chased Villa back into Mexico.

Wilson's attention was forced south. General John J. "Black Jack" Pershing and 7,000 troops soon were deep into Mexico searching, unsuccessfully, for the bandit leader.

In his train was a squadron of Flying Jenny airplanes and eleven trucks hauling supplies, the first time either was used by the US Army in combat.

They still would be there, well past the election and into the New Year.

Wilson did not consider invading Mexico an act of war. He had done it before. It was more like catching a bad boy and taking him to the woodshed. But it was a distraction from the important things Wilson wanted to do.

Through it all, Wilson balanced himself on his neutrality tightrope once again and shakily moved forward towards the election in November.

Report from the Front

Frank Hague moved through his city like the tribal chieftain he was. Seeing and being seen. Shoring up the weak. Drawing confidence from the strong. Analyzing, always analyzing.

His organization needed lots of work. He ruthlessly rated it as pretty good, but was it good enough?

Hague had to grant favors, hand out jobs, spot and reward the up and coming. Make new alliances. Ease has-beens out without making enemies of them. Such was the daily work of an ambitious politician in a time and place when a handshake meant everything and principles counted for little.

Frank Hague was in his element but time was running out. He had little time to get ready for the dress rehearsal, namely the election of the president of the United States in November, 1916.

The real election, the only one he truly cared about, would be in May, 1917, when Jersey City would elect five men to the city commission and those men would choose a mayor from their own number. That mayor would be Frank Hague or he and his organization would have failed. Commissioner Frank Hague, the city's director of public safety, had been working towards that goal for fifteen years. He did not intend to fail.

When his organization reached that needed degree of efficiency, Hague would be able to get elected himself, would be able to get others of his party elected and, uniquely, he would be able to deliver the vote of Jersey City and surrounding Hudson County to any candidate he chose. Then, whatever he demanded would be his.

That would be real power. Unassailable power. He knew no one who had ever had that kind of power in New Jersey politics. Hague got almost as much pleasure in anticipating it than he would get in wielding it.

The problem was in helping Woodrow Wilson get re-elected.

Wilson was a man Hague detested and who detested him in turn. Wilson was re-nominated by the Democratic Party in June. Of course, he would not formally accept the nomination until Labor Day and the official campaign wouldn't start until then. The Republicans, as Joe Tumulty predicted, nominated Supreme Court Justice Charles Evans Hughes, the former governor of New York. Theodore Roosevelt's Bull Moose ticket in 1912 had split the Republican vote which resulted in Wilson's election. This time Roosevelt refused the Progressive Party's nomination and thus it was a two man fight. A tough fight for Wilson to win. Roosevelt vowed to campaign against Wilson.

Now, it wouldn't bother Hague if Wilson lost. It would please him. But what Hague couldn't risk was Wilson winning without Hague's unstinting support.

That vindictive son-of-a-bitch would go out of his way to campaign against me in May. Might even show up himself. He's done it before and he beat the hell out of me. No, if anybody wants to know, I'm a Wilson man through and through. All I want him to do is leave me alone.

Wilson was nominated on the platform, "He Kept Us out of War." Now if he could just fulfill that promise until Election Day.

Lieutenant Mickey McGurk's little bomb squad wasn't being overwhelmed with useful information.

Said Fat Jack Lynch, "I tell you, Mickey, my people want to hurt the English in any way they can. Those executions. They can't stop talking about them. The one thing I can't get out of my mind is those bastards carrying James Connolly out on a stretcher and then tying him to a chair so they could shoot him. And then they lock up every republican from eight years old to eighty. The entire leadership is in jail."

"So the republican movement is dead, Jack, at least in Ireland?" asked McGurk.

"No, that's not true. The leadership may be locked up but the people are thoroughly aroused now. Did you know that when the British first paraded their prisoners through the streets of Dublin the people—the Irish people— spit at the republican soldiers. The separation women were ready to tear them apart."

"Separation women?"

"Women whose husbands or sons are at the front with the British Army. The government pays them a separation allowance. It keeps them from starving.

"Then came the executions. The people of Dublin were appalled. Sure, they thought the leaders would be jailed, but not shot. They turned against the British overnight. But whether they're for the revolution or not doesn't matter. It's hopeless, for the moment. My hotheads know that but they won't listen to reason. They still want to go to war. They're daft, Mickey, daft. But I don't think they're up to much, at least not around here."

McGurk said, "But maybe I wouldn't want to sail in a British ship, huh, Jack?"

"I wouldn't advise that under any circumstances, Mickey."

"Say, Jack, how's the fundraising going now that the Rising has been put down?"

"Now, that's the oddest thing, Mickey, the money is flowing in faster than ever. We don't know what to do with it. So we're putting it away, someplace safe. Until the next time."

"There's always a 'next time' with the Irish, isn't there, Jack?"

"Indeed. It looks like they are going to hang Sir Roger Casement too. That'll set them off again, it will. I think I told you I met him when he was in New York a couple of years ago?"

"You did."

"But I don't think I told you what I saw at that meeting."

"No, I think that's one of the many things you neglected to tell me," said Mickey.

"Yeah. Well, he was here raising money and I was delegated to bring a bundle of it to him at the Waldorf-Astoria. So I put on my good Sunday suit and headed for the ferry. Now even when I look my best, I don't look like I belong at the Waldorf. The doorman looks at me like I've got something nasty on the sole of my shoe.

"'I'm just a delivery boy,' says I. 'I've got something important for one of your guests.' He marches me over to the front desk and stands there until a bellboy leads me away to the room where Sir Roger is meeting with some important people. Irish people. Some guy in evening clothes answers my knock and invites me in when I tell him I'm John Lynch from the Clan na Gael in Jersey City."

"John?"

"Yeah... well it was the Waldorf. Anyway, there's six of them in the room. All in evening dress. And they're the oddest looking group of guys I've ever seen. One of them, I swear, had that stuff on his eyelashes, you know, like actresses use?"

"Mascara?"

"That's it. They were all looking at me in a weird way. I was uncomfortable. It was like they were sizing up a girl. Sir Roger popped up, shook my hand and welcomed me. I gave him the bundle of big bills and he said, 'Gentlemen, let's show our appreciation for the Clan na Gael.'

"They all applauded and Sir Roger looked at me and asked, 'Can you join us, Mr. Lynch?' I'd sooner join a pack of Chinamen smoking opium, so I got out of there in a hurry. Mickey, they were all Irish. It's hard to understand that Irishmen would be that way."

"I don't know, Jack, what about Oscar Wilde?"

"Oscar Wilde? Who the hell is he? Sounds German to me," said Lynch.

"No, he's an Irishman, Jack, and one we can be proud of."

* * *

Tony Aiello met his confidante, Abie the Jew, in a drug store in Kearny. Abie got there first and was drinking hot tea from an ice cream soda glass. The glass was in its usual metal holder. "Tea tastes better from a glass," Abie said. Then nodding to a used tea bag, he said, "Of course, that's not much of a samovar."

"How you doing, Abie?"

"Can't complain."

"Good. What's up?" asked Tony.

"Not much, I think. But there was one thing that might interest you. You know, the cloak makers are on strike in Manhattan?"

"Yeah, I read about that big rally with all the bands."

"More than 40,000 people. Ninety bands. A big nothing."

"What do you mean, Abie?"

"A lot of noise. That's all. They're going to crawl back to work on their hands and knees. They won big in 1910 but the bosses are going to give them bupkis this time.

"Now the 3rd Avenue Railway is out on strike too but they are going to win. The IWW—you know, the Wobblies—and that whole crowd are helping and if they have to break some heads there's no ideological problem. But the cloak makers are Jews and they think they can talk the bosses into being nice. If it works, they should talk to those sharks eating everybody down at the Shore. About the same chance of success. Imbeciles. I was at a big meeting when 'Big Jim' Larkin, that Irish Wobbly guy, told them flat out. 'If you had the IWW to lead you, you would win. But you don't.'

"One of our more stupid anarchists asks Larkin, 'How can you be a Catholic and a revolutionary at the same time?' Larkin laughs and says, 'I stand by the Cross and I stand by Karl Marx.' Confused the hell out of everybody."

"I'll bet," said Tony. "I don't understand the Irish half the time either and I work with them every day."

Abie said, "That's not what I wanted to tell you. A big mob of people, mostly anarchists, lots of them Italian, got really frustrated so they marched over and wrecked that newspaper—

Il Progresso Italo-American—because the editor wouldn't print a demand for the release of some Italian guy, Carlo Tresca, facing the rope in Minnesota.

"One of the people the cops arrested was an Italian kid from Hoboken, Gaetano Giccoma. He's twenty-six, and he lives at 919 Willow Avenue. Why I wanted you to know this is…this is the first time I've heard of an anarchist from New Jersey involved in anything violent. Maybe, he won't be the last. That might mean trouble here. I don't want America in this war, Tony."

Tony wrote down the name of the arrested man.

"Thanks, Abie. Now is there anything I can do for you?"

"You mean, besides paying for my tea? Maybe, that hotshot commissioner of yours could get my Rachel out of Russia before it's too late?"

"He would if he could, Abie."

Abie sucked his teeth. "He could do that and I would hold my nose and vote for him. Twice. At every election."

Hans Mannstein reported that Captain Tunney's three cops working fulltime in Hoboken were still looking for Paul Koenig but hadn't spotted him. The seamen interned there were bored but not causing any trouble.

It was Peggy McCann's brief report that electrified Mickey McGurk.

"Mena Edwards wants me to go to supper Friday night with her and a couple of older Germans. One of them is that Paul Koenig you're always talking about."

McGurk briefed her: "Pay attention to every word this Koenig guy says. It might be important. I don't know who that sea captain from Baltimore is but listen to him too. Above all, don't be nervous."

"Are you kidding? My wedding's less than a month away and I'm off to supper in New York with a couple of Krauts. Why should I be nervous?" asked Peggy.

Dinner was at the Hofbrau House at Broadway and 26th Street

in Manhattan. The women met their escorts there. Mena presented Peggy to Paul Koenig of the Hamburg-Amerika Line and he in turn introduced Captain Frederick Hinsch of the Eastern Forwarding Company.

Captain Hinsch, a heavy, middle-aged man, looked like a sea captain disguised as a successful businessman.

Koenig was somewhat younger, not as heavy, with thinning hair and a moustache. His clothing was a bit frumpy.

The food was good, Captain Hinsch's sea stories were entertaining and Koenig flirted with both women. The captain did not.

Peggy, between bites, paid attention to every word that was said.

Hinsch asked Koenig, "I know Christy is already here; when are our other friends coming?"

Koenig said, "Jahnke and Witzke? Not until just before the big party. They have some business to finish on the West Coast first."

"What party is that? Are we invited?" asked Mena.

Captain Hinsch whose English was heavily accented, "I'm afraid not, my dear. All men, I am afraid. Very boring. Just business."

After coffee, Captain Hinsch stood and said, "Ladies, I am afraid, that no matter how delightful it has been, we must call it a night. I have to get back to Baltimore tomorrow and I think Paul has to go to work early. Ja?"

"I do, sir."

"You will see that the ladies get back to their hotel, Paul?"

Peggy said, "I have an early engagement too. The Tubes are not far away. If you could drop me off there?"

"Of course," said Koenig. "Now remember ladies, there is a war on. Don't repeat anything you heard here tonight?"

Peggy laughed. "Of course not; who would I tell?"

All three members of the bomb squad showed much interest in what Peggy reported.

McGurk asked, "What I want to know is why a merchant

marine captain from Baltimore was meeting with that so-called detective?"

"I really don't know," said Peggy. "But I definitely got the impression that Captain Hinsch was Koenig's boss. He all but kissed his you-know-what."

"Tell me again about the friends who are coming to a big party. Did you get their names?"

"I know Hinsch said 'Christy' is already here. I think Koenig said 'Yankee' and 'Whiskey' were coming but he could have said 'Yankee Whiskey'. Sorry. I'm just not sure." Mickey made notes.

"Have you ever met or heard of this Christy before?"

"I'm not sure. I might have heard the name the first time I went to West 15th Street."

"When is the party?" Mickey asked.

"I don't know. All the Captain said was women weren't invited."

"What kind of party do you throw without women?" asked Hans.

"A dull one," said Tony.

McGurk asked, "What was it that Koenig didn't want you to repeat, Peggy? How can Hinsch be Koenig's boss?" She had no answers for him.

Mickey concluded, "We don't have enough information. Peggy, you are going to have to go back to West 15th Street tomorrow night and try to find out more about this party. Meanwhile, I'll pass on what we have to Captain Tunney."

As Tony was saying goodnight to Peggy, he asked, "So, how did the evening end?"

Peggy O'Brian thought briefly and said, "At the door of the Hofbrau house without even a handshake."

Tony said, "Good. You're almost a married woman, you know." Then he kissed her.

Mickey McGurk got Captain Tunney on the phone, something he didn't often do because it was a long distance call between states with different telephone companies and, thus, expensive.

Tunney said, "We know Koenig of course. He's slippery as an eel. Everywhere he shouldn't be. Tough to follow. He likes to turn a corner and when my man rushes to follow him, the son-of-a-bitch jumps out of a doorway and says 'Boo!' A real pain in the ass.

"We know Koenig is up to no good, we just don't know what it is. I don't think it's throwing parties for stranded seamen. But this other guy, Hinsch, we never heard of him before."

Mickey said, "He's from Baltimore. He's with some outfit called the Eastern Forwarding Company."

"Nope. Never heard of him. You know it's possible they were doing honest business with each other. But I doubt it."

Mickey did not tell Tunney about Peggy going back to West 15th Street. He had never mentioned that address. He didn't want Tunney to know that the rinky-dink Jersey City police force was operating in Manhattan.

The Grand Tour Ends

Michael Kristoff knew not to ask his boss any unnecessary questions—he didn't like it. If Mr. Francis Graentnor wanted him to know something, he'd tell him otherwise Kristoff would have to find out for himself.

When Graentnor hired him, he told Kristoff they would work to interrupt the flow of munitions from the United States to the Allies but he didn't say how he intended to do it.

Even to a person like Kristoff, who might be a bit slow, the method became obvious after a few weeks on the road. Mr. Graentnor was dealing with a German sabotage ring that began in the East and spread through the industrial Midwest.

Not that he was doing the dirty work himself. There were no explosives in Mr. Graentnor's big, heavy suitcase—the one with no clothes in it. There was money, a lot of it, and blueprints, schematics and two ledgers.

Kristoff thought about running off with the locked suitcase and the money. But he didn't. Kristoff was afraid of Graentnor and thought that the big German would somehow hunt him down and kill him.

Kristoff read the newspapers. So did Mr. Graentnor and usually within days of leaving a city there would be a report of an "industrial accident" somewhere near that city. Graentnor would say, "Ha! Das ist sehr gut." The meaning was unmistakable.

Initially Christy—Graentnor always called him that—was ordered to handle routine chores like buying railroad tickets, doing the laundry or keeping an eye on the big suitcase when the maid cleaned the room.

Gradually their relationship warmed and Graentnor began to trust Christy to deliver packets of money to nameless men or to accompany him to meetings which were always held in German.

Christy only understood a few words at first but he was picking up more of the language a bit at a time.

Mr. Graentnor was a good companion, a great storyteller. Now they were back in New York after months on the road. Christy had a money belt full of cash. He had little opportunity to spend his $20 a week salary.

Graentnor handed him a piece of paper with a hotel address on it. "Go see this man. He will give you an envelope with a lot of money in it. It is yours. You have proven your loyalty and your ability to follow orders." Christy beamed. He wasn't used to praise.

"We are planning a big mission and you, Christy, will be an important part of it.

"After you get your money, go back across the river and find a room. Tomorrow, go to the Eagle Oil Company next to Black Tom in Jersey City. You know where that is?"

"Yes."

"The foreman's name is Eugen Hoffstadt. He will give you a job. Consider any salary you get as a bonus.

"Your real work is to scout out Black Tom. Snoop around, make friends with the guards, learn their schedules, figure out the routine of the place and do so quickly. We will move within weeks. Someone will get in touch with you.

"Now if you should get caught and are arrested, they will question you. Stick as closely to the truth as possible without disclosing anything important. You can tell them I hired you and we traveled all over. Tell them you think I deal in used motors but you're not sure. Tell them you were curious about Black Tom and wondered whether you could get a job there.

"Do you have any questions?"

"No, sir."

"Sehr gut."

Christy was excited. He had never been a part of anything big.

123 West 15th Street

"Who is that gorgeous piece of ass? The tall one over there," asked Kapitan Josef Posner, pointing his cigar directly at Peggy McCann.

"Oh, her. I don't know her name but don't waste your time, Kapitan. You'll get nowhere. She looks glorious but she's just here for the food. Once, I tried to hug her from behind and, I swear, I think her elbow touched my spine. She's a cold fish."

"That may be," said Posner, taking a puff on his cigar, "but I want to get laid."

Peggy was dressed in a loose blue skirt and a stylish white shirtwaist. She had left her hat with the maid. She looked very fetching.

The first time she came here with Mena, she figured out that after two hours or so the Dutchmen decided the girls were there for more than just decoration. It was worse than being in the 8th Grade.

Peggy O'Brian knew how the game was played with the men at 123 West 15th Street. She knew what the men wanted—and what they often got—but she had no intention of obliging them. Still she had to flirt enough to keep them interested or, she was sure, she wouldn't be welcome. That would be "goodbye" to those five needed dollars and a terrific meal here every week. She wouldn't risk that. It was constant work fending off the German men while getting them to talk to her. She often used the oldest excuse in the book besides a headache.

Peggy liked teasing men. She particularly enjoyed their frustration after what they expected never arrived. She loved the control. Men didn't awe her. They were pigs.

You can't trust them, she'd tell herself. *They'll use you and throw you away. Better you use them and throw them away. Of course, Tony is different. Very different.* She loved him.

Since the start of the war in 1914, this typical brownstone many blocks inland from Manhattan's two rivers was what would now be called a "safe house." Top ranking German diplomats from Washington, military and naval attachés, merchant sea captains, spies and saboteurs, all made use of it. Countless plots were hatched here. Some successes were celebrated here.

The timed cigar bombs, invented in Doctor Walter Scheele's Hoboken plant and manufactured aboard the SS Friedrich der Grosse at a Brooklyn pier, were stored here along with the chemicals that armed them. From this house the fire bombs went into the hands of willing longshoremen and others.

But tonight Peggy was here to fill in the conversational holes that came with dinner with Paul Koenig and that sea captain. She would do her best. Peggy knew she better get going while everyone was relatively sober. *How to start?*

She wandered over to what she now thought of as the "map room."

The door was open and sure enough some men were hunched over the big table. They didn't take notice of her and she easily looked over the shoulder of a very short man. They were looking at one of those funny looking maps with all the little numbers on the blue water. She read the map's legend, "North River." It meant nothing to Peggy.

"It seems you are very interested in what is going on here, Fräulein."

Peggy turned and saw a man at least three inches taller than she. He was handsome, forty-ish, trim, sporting a van dyke beard, and he was smoking an aromatic cigar. He looked like a high ranking officer. A sea captain.

"Not really," said Peggy, "just curious."

"You are Irish, no?"

"I am," said Peggy who looked as fresh as a morning in the Irish countryside.

"Then we are allies. We Germans want to see the Irish free of those English chains. We will help you. We are on the same side."

"How marvelous." *And what's in it for you, Fritz?*

"Ja, we help each other. We all should do what we can. Don't think we seamen are sitting around the harbor doing nothing to help win the war. We may be stuck here but we still send English ships to the bottom."

"How do you do that?" asked Peggy.

The captain, who had more than a bit to drink, backed off some, but not enough. "Well, we make things. On one ship we have machinery that makes a little cylinder that can make a big fire. Would you like to see one?"

"I would. It sounds more fascinating than an old map, Captain." She flashed him a bright smile.

"Come, we store them on the top floor." They climbed two flights of stairs.

Peggy opened the door to a room and hardly had time to recognize it as a bedroom before the door closed and she was shoved face down onto the bed.

A strong right hand kept her flat while the left put the cigar into an ashtray on the night table.

She felt both hands pull up her skirt and yank her silk underwear down over her buttocks. Peggy realized she was moments away from being raped.

She was desperate. "No, Captain, not like this! Let me turn over. It will be more fun for you. And me."

"Ja?" She felt the pressure on her back ease.

Peggy turned. She saw the captain kneeling over her, his erection sticking out of his open fly like a 6.5 inch gun protruding from a turret.

With her left hand she grabbed it and pulled toward her, with her right she clutched the cigar and jammed it onto his penis, immediately causing it to become the new center of pain in the known universe.

The captain screamed and catapulted backwards over the low

bedstead. He completed his back flip but if his balance was lost in his agony, his momentum was not. He hit his head on the wall behind cracking the plaster and rendering him mercifully unconscious.

Peggy jumped out of bed, put the cigar back in the ash tray, pulled up her underwear and, taking the key out of the keyhole, locked the door behind her.

The key was shoved into a potted plant before a Teutonic voice asked, "Well, Fräulein, where did Kapitan Posner go?"

"I believe the good captain is upstairs resting."

The German leered at her. "Of course he is."

Peggy retrieved her hat and left immediately. Her parents were asleep when she got home. She didn't wake them. She went to the kitchen sink and washed her hands for five minutes, scrubbing her left one with rough brown soap.

She finally fell asleep and drifted off into a nightmare. The captain was kneeling over her leering. In her dream she smiled and grabbed his erection, plunging the cigar onto his penis. The ashes from the cold, dead cigar fell onto her hand. She awoke sweating and terrified. She could feel her heart beating wildly. She slid out of bed, padded the few feet to the kitchen and washed her hands again.

She met Mickey, Hans and Tony for breakfast at Mickey's flat.

"I'm sorry," said Peggy. "I didn't learn much. I did see one of those maps with the little numbers."

"A nautical chart," said Mickey.

"And I think the name of it was the 'North River' but I don't know where that is," said Peggy.

The men looked at each other. The North River is another name for the Hudson between New Jersey and New York. The river on the other side of Manhattan is called the East River.

"Do you think that was the Hudson?" asked Hans.

"Probably," said Mickey. "We'll have to get us a chart and see if we can figure out what they were looking at."

Peggy, looking serious said, "Also one of the ship captains told me they were making something on a boat that could cause big fires and were stored upstairs in the house. That's all he said. I didn't see anything. I think his name is Posner."

"Good work, Peggy," said Mickey. "Now we know where they keep those cigar bombs. Did you hear anything more about 'Christy' or 'Yankee' or 'Whiskey'?"

"I did not."

Mickey thought of his old bunkmate, Kurt Jahnke.

"Is it possible 'Whiskey' and 'Yankee' are garbled German names?"

Peggy thought for a moment. "Sure. It's possible. But I can't be certain. Sorry."

"You've got nothing to be sorry about, Peggy. You did good. You're not Mata Hari," said Mickey.

Yeah. They're going to shoot Mata Hari, thought Peggy. *Thank God I don't have to shoot myself.*

"Okay. We still need more information," said Mickey. "We'll study a chart of the river and maybe, Peggy, you can ask this Captain Posner some questions."

Are you kidding? If that son of a bitch can sit up and take toast, he'll strangle me. I don't know what I am going to do.

Peggy's face was ashen, something no one noticed but Tony. They went to a late Mass and sat down for lunch at a little Greek restaurant they liked.

Tony took Peggy's hand. "You're not yourself today, sweetheart. What's bothering you?"

"I don't know, Tony. Probably, just that the wedding is sneaking up on us. I guess I'm a bit nervous."

"Sorry, love, I don't buy that. My mother says you're the happiest bride-to-be that she's ever seen. It's that place in the city, isn't it?"

"What do you mean, Tony?"

"I don't know. Something happened there. Something that

really upset you."

Peggy panicked. "No, Tony, honest to God nothing happened."

"Yes, it did. Something you don't want to talk about. You didn't get raped, did you?"

"No! I swear to God, no!"

Tony squeezed her hands. "Sweetheart, I believe you, but something happened. All right, let me put it this way, if I was there with you last night would I have walked away smiling at the end of the evening?"

If you had been there, one big Kraut would be dead.

Tears were forming in Peggy's eyes. "No, Tony."

"Okay," said Tony. "No more questions. You'll tell me when you're ready. But hear this. You are not going back to that place. Never."

Peggy felt enormous relief but she said, "Tony, Mickey says it's very important I go back. Remember, Hans said that I might learn something that would keep us out of the war."

"I don't give a shit what Hans or Mickey says. You're not going back and that's final. Do you understand?"

Peggy McCann, strong of will, strong of body, fiercely independent, frightened of no one, looked at her fiancé, the man she loved, and said, "Yes, Tony."

"Don't worry, I'll tell Mickey myself. Now we're getting married on July 29 so you, your mother and my mother should just concentrate on doing all those nutty things women do and enjoy yourselves."

* * *

Tony's meeting with Mickey wasn't very pleasant.

"What do you mean, Peggy's not going back to West 15th Street?" Mickey demanded.

"It is very simple," said Tony. "Something bad happened to

her the other night. She won't tell me what but she's not going back to that square head whorehouse no matter what."

"Tony, be reasonable. We might be on the brink of finding out something important."

"Reasonable, my ass. Listen to yourself, Mickey. What is she going to find out from a bunch of drunken Dutch sailors? Something that's going to change the fate of the nation? Hah! The thought of anyone of them touching her hand, let alone anything else, is enough makes me want to shoot up the place after I break a few heads."

"Tony, honest to God, I know how you feel. But who am I going to send there, my mother?"

Tony looked at Mickey and said softly, "How about your wife? She speaks German."

Mickey balled his fists but said nothing.

What the hell is wrong with me, thought Mickey, *am I ready to pimp my friend's fiancée, my own cousin, so I can make a couple of points with Captain Tunney?*

"You're right, Tony. Absolutely right. Enough is enough. Those Krauts in Manhattan can go to hell. They're not our concern. Peggy has enough problems just getting ready for your wedding which, my friend, I am looking forward to almost as much as you."

"Thank you, Mickey. I knew you'd do the right thing," said Tony. "So what happens now? I don't even want her pumping Mena Edwards for information. I want a clean break."

"Don't worry, Peggy's finished as a confidante," said Mickey McGurk. "I'll think of something else."

Mickey talked it over the next day with Hans who said, "I don't blame Tony. I wouldn't let my wife anywhere near that place. So what are we going to do?"

"What say you check the Zepps and see if anyone has a brother or an uncle or something that works at Black Tom. Maybe he'd keep his eyes open for us for a couple of bucks a week."

Hans shook his head. "Oh, yeah. That'll work."

"You got better idea, pal?"

"Sure, move Black Tom to Bayonne."

Reconnaissance

Five men met in a locked room at 123 West 15th Street in Manhattan.

They were in a half circle, intently studying a large scale nautical chart of the Hudson River. They were: Paul Koenig, head of the German sabotage efforts in the Northeast; Kapitan Josef Posner, master of the SS Westphalia interned in Hoboken; Kurt Jahnke and Lothar Witzke, journeyman saboteurs fresh from the West Coast; and Michael Kristoff, a naturalized American from Hungary assigned to Koenig for this mission.

Jahnke took control. They were discussing tactics now and he was the master tactician. They spoke in English since Kristoff knew little German.

"So this is the target. Black Tom. In Jersey City," said Jahnke.

I have an old Marine buddy who lives there. Mike McGurk. I wonder what he's doing now?

"When do we have to strike?" he asked.

"Tomorrow night," said Koenig. "The rail yard will be empty but there will be plenty of explosives in boxcars and on lighters. After midnight would be best. We don't want any people killed."

Jahnke asked Christy, "How well guarded is Black Tom?"

"It's wide open. There is no fence. It's not lighted. The watchmen and guards don't pay any attention to people coming and going. I know. I have wandered in and out of there dozens of times and no one ever did more than say 'hello' to me."

"There seems to be only one road but lots of railroad tracks leading to Black Tom," said Jahnke.

"That's right," said Kristoff, "but you can walk in and out on the tracks if you want to avoid something on the road. I've done it."

"How do you know so much about Black Tom, my friend?" asked Jahnke.

"I work close by at Eagle Oil. I was instructed to thoroughly scout out Black Tom. Nobody ever notices me."

"Do you think if we were to go to Black Tom this morning, we could walk around without drawing attention to ourselves?" asked Jahnke.

"Definitely," said Kristoff who was as confident as he looked.

Koenig asked, "Wouldn't that be dangerous?"

Witzke answered, "Not as dangerous as not knowing where we are going or where we will place our bombs to greatest effect. We must accomplish the mission but we would like to get out of there alive too."

Jahnke said, "We had no difficulty penetrating the shipyard at Mare Island but we approached it from the water side. Would we find any trouble if we landed on Black Tom from the river?"

"None," said Kristoff. "I doubt you would be noticed. The watchmen don't move around much and lots of the lighters tow small boats so their crews can get ashore when they are anchored."

Jahnke lighted a cigar, took a deep puff and said, "So maybe we just walk in, plant our bombs, wave to the guards and walk out, eh? You make it sound very easy."

"It is," said Kristoff. "The Americans are neutral. They don't expect any trouble and the railroads don't spend any more money on security than they have to."

Jahnke was skeptical. "We'll see. Speaking of bombs, tell us about them, Kapitan Posner."

"Ja, Herr Jahnke. You know about the cigar bombs we make. We will prepare two batches for you. One batch will be set to go off at about midnight and are colored red and the other will be timed for about two o'clock in the morning and are colored green."

"Are they reliable?" asked Witzke.

"Well, they won't explode. They just spit fire from both ends. That can be dangerous of course. We've tested them and they usually go off within fifteen minutes of the time we expect."

"Usually?" asked Jahnke, who had no experience with them.

"Human error," said Posner.

"That's not so comforting," said Jahnke, "but you have to expect some danger in a war."

"What do we do if one goes off prematurely?" asked Witzke.

"Get rid of it. Kick dirt on it. Drop it in the river. But I wouldn't worry too much about that. They're quite reliable."

"Very well," said Jahnke, turning his attention back to the chart.

What is this small inlet north of Black Tom?" he asked.

That's the Gap. The Lehigh Valley Railroad keeps tugboats there," said Kristoff.

"Could a small row boat be tied up there without raising concern?"

"Yes."

Kapitan Posner asked, "Why a row boat? Why not a small motorboat?"

Witzke answered, "Motor boats make noise and far too often the engine doesn't start or breaks down when you most need it."

Jahnke pointed at the chart to a spot just south of Black Tom.

"That's the Jersey Central Terminal," said Kristoff.

"Same question. Can we moor there without raising suspicions?"

"Yes."

"Very good. We have to pay attention to the tides and the current which could be quite swift. We will use that terminal though. Witzke and I will approach Black Tom by rowboat riding with the current and we will leave the same way while you, Herr Kristoff, will come in by land."

"Will that work, Cadet Witzke?" asked Jahnke who deferred to his junior partner on some things nautical.

"Let's see." He asked Kapitan Posner, "Did you bring the tides tables for the Battery?"

"I did. Here you are."

"Excellent," said Witzke who was a good navigator. Witzke studied the table or a minute or two.

"We're in luck. Low water is at around 2230. That means the current will be running south from the Gap to Black Tom at around two and a half knots until 2330. Then it will flow at from two to one knot until 0030 and about one knot for an hour after that. That should give us plenty of time both at Black Tom and more than enough to row south to the Jersey Central terminal before the bombs go off."

"Very good," said Jahnke. "I don't want to be at Black Tom more than a half hour or so. That's why we must look at it, the Gap, and the railroad terminal today. Our visits to Black Tom will tell us if approaching by water is a good idea."

"Visits?" asked Koenig.

"Yes. We will scout it out this morning by land and then again tonight in the dark. Things look different in the dark. Meanwhile, Kapitan, can you get a small rowboat to the Gap today?"

"Yes, Herr Jahnke, I have the perfect boat. We use it to maneuver around the hull when we are painting. It is very stable, seaworthy and easy to handle."

"We have to know exactly where it is moored."

"You will."

"We will also need a boat tonight at about 2330—a motorboat—to reconnoiter the way from the Gap to Black Tom and then to the Jersey Central. The crew must be absolutely reliable and closemouthed."

"You have just described my boatswain, a chief petty officer in the Naval Reserve. He will be your crew."

"I'll work up a dead reckoning plot for us to use," said Witzke. "Can you have your boatswain bring a flashlight with a red filter and a small compass?"

"I can," said Posner.

"Good. We'll meet your boatswain at your ship at 2330."

"He'll be ready."

Jahnke asked, "You have an automobile, Christy?"

"No," said Kristoff.

"Not to worry," said Koenig. "I have a good auto. I'm certain I wasn't followed here but I will leave on foot so if there are any watching policemen they will leave with me. The car is yours. Can you drive, Herr Kristoff?"

"Yes. I am a very good driver."

Jahnke puffed again on his cigar. "Very well. Let's go see Black Tom."

They took the ferry and Kristoff drove to the Gap which Jahnke and Witzke inspected closely.

Jahnke said to Kristoff, "Tomorrow night you will drop us off here and then drive on to the White House Tavern you spoke of. You wait to 2330 or so and then make your way onto Black Tom. Is that clear?"

"Perfectly." Then the three of them drove to the White House Tavern.

Kristoff said, "We can leave the car here and walk in."

"The automobile won't draw any attention?" asked Jahnke.

"No. There will be autos, trucks and wagons in and out of here all day and all night," said Kristoff.

It was mid-morning and Black Tom was noisy with purposeful activity. They strolled through the yard and down the causeway. No one even said "hello". They looked like three seamen off the lighters. Jahnke had said, "We'll split up and meet back at the tavern. We each have a particular mission. Pick out your targets. Two red for midnight, two green for 0200. Go."

Jahnke paid particular attention to the warehouses, Witzke inspected the lighters, and Kristoff wandered around the standing freight cars parallel to the long wharf. They spent another half-hour walking about to get a feel for the whole place.

From the tavern, they drove to the Jersey Central terminal and selected a space where they would tie up the rowboat and come ashore.

Jahnke pointed and addressed Kristoff, "You bring the auto and park over there. Wait for us. If you don't show up, we'll wait an hour and then if you're still not here we'll make our way back to Manhattan somehow."

"I understand," said Kristoff.

All three men went back to 123 West 15th Street.

Jahnke and Kristoff took naps while Witzke happily worked with his charts and tools producing the dead reckoning plot from Hoboken to the Gap to Black Tom to the Jersey Central, a distance of not much more than four nautical miles.

Soon it was pitch black.

The boatswain looked every inch the chief petty officer as he was introduced to his passengers. "Chief," said Kapitan Posner. "It is better that you don't know the names of these men." He pointed to Jahnke, "This is your commanding officer." The chief clicked his heels. The finger went to Witzke, "This is your navigator." Again the heels clicked. "And this gentleman is going as an observer." The chief looked at Kristoff, nodded and skipped the heel click.

Posner said to the chief, "You will obey any orders you are given tonight as if I have given them to you. Verstehen Sie?"

"Jawohl, Herr Kapitan," said the chief. All the men, except the boatswain, shook hands and Kapitan Posner left.

"All right, chief, make steam for four knots," said Witzke.

The trip from Hoboken down river was a lot more exciting than their daytime sightseeing trip especially to Kristoff who was quite frightened by the dark water and the darker shore and feared that he would drown before the night was over.

Witzke steered, frequently checking his compass, and navigated by following the black buoys in the channel, and then sheared off to starboard at the Gap. They spotted the small rowboat tied to a ring on a pier with enough slack to accommodate the tides. Jahnke looked around intently as did Witzke.

"Good," he said, "Let's move on." The chief opened the throttle of the small steam launch. Then Witzke took them between Ellis Island and the shore and did the same thing at Bedloe's Island where the light of the torch of the Statue of Liberty pierced the darkness. They were at Black Tom. It was easy to see the shapes of the lighters and barges at the six piers jutting out from the wharf. Jahnke spotted a big ring at the end of the wharf where they could tie up unseen.

Black Tom was indeed black. Not a light to be seen except for a shack just beyond the causeway.

"We go ashore," said Jahnke. "You too, Christy, even though you'll be coming in from the land side. It always looks different in the dark."

"What if we're caught?" asked Kristoff.

"Then the operation is off," said Jahnke as he and his partners went ashore and prowled around for forty five minutes without incident. They returned to the boat where the silent boatswain sat.

"Good," said Jahnke. "Back to your ship, Chief." Steam was ready.

The steam launch puff-puffed its way back until they were a quarter-mile or so from the berth in Hoboken. Then the chief suddenly threw the gear in neutral and eased up on the throttle.

"What's wrong?" asked Witzke in German.

"We are building up too much pressure," said the chief. "It could be dangerous."

The boat drifted slowly back downstream as the chief fiddled with the steam engine. Finally, he gave a valve a whack with a wrench and nodded his head in satisfaction.

"That should do it," he said. He put it in gear and opened the throttle. The vessel moved ahead, quickly making up the distance it had lost.

The chief was embarrassed. "I'm sorry. This boat is usually more reliable."

"Do not fret, chief. All is well," said Jahnke who looked at Witzke who could just about see him in the moonlight.

"Ja," said Witzke. "I voted for the rowboat too."

The three men returned to the safe house. A small party was going on. Jahnke and Witzke ignored it, climbed the stairs to their room and went to sleep almost at once.

Kristoff joined the party. Drank too much but said nothing he shouldn't have and then went to bed to toss and turn for the rest of the night.

Dawn of July 29, 1916, was exceptionally beautiful. None of the three saw it.

And the Band Played On

You could see the Hudson River from the front door of Ned McCann's saloon but not Black Tom, miles to the south, bustling with energy and work on this last day of the week, Saturday, July 29, 1916.

Three bartenders were hanging white paper bunting and white paper bells in the cavernous back room of the saloon. Ned McCann knew it was going to be more than just a wedding reception for his "adopted" grand-daughter, Peggy.

It was going to be a pre-campaign rally for the Hague organization in the Heights. The "dress rehearsal", the Presidential election, was three months away.

The wedding was one thing, Poppa Jim and he could afford that. But a blowout for the organization would half bankrupt him.

Two hundred invitations had been sent out but Ned, a shrewd businessman, figured that twice as many—maybe three times as many—would show up before the night was over. All of them thirsty.

Food wouldn't be a problem. Ned would put out his usual "free lunch" only more of it. He wasn't surprised when automobiles began to pull up and unload mountains of food. Italian food, German food, even a great tub of fried rice delivered by a Chinaman who bowed a lot but spoke no English. Ned would need more than one food table. Keeping it warm was his only concern.

It was the drink that worried Ned. He called his bartenders together.

"Okay, here's how we handle it. Draught beer, wine, birch beer, that's all free until we run out. But if they want anything else—whiskey, brandy, gin, highballs, fancy bottled beer—anything else, they pay full price. And if we run out of the free stuff—which I doubt—tap a new keg and charge for the beer too. Otherwise they'll stay here until the twelve o'clock Mass tomorrow and drain me dry."

"What about water, boss?"

"Who the hell drinks water? Get a move on. They'll be drifting in here around five thirty or six."

Ned, pushing eighty with a full head of white hair and a physique that shrugged off the omnipresent pains of old age, said, "I got to get home and get changed."

The Nuptial Mass at St. Anne's was at four o'clock. But the bride might be a bit late.

Six Zeppelins in their dress uniforms complete with white gloves served as ushers, Hans Mannstein among them.

Peggy's guests were seated on the left side of the church; Tony's on the right. The families and closest friends were led to the first few pews on each side.

The church was packed. The guests spent more time looking at each other than they did kneeling in prayer.

Tony and his best man, Mickey McGurk, waited on one side of the altar.

Down the aisle came the bridesmaids, Theresa and Doreen Aiello, followed by the matron-of-honor, Hannah McGurk, and then a remarkably beautiful and radiant Peggy on the arm of her Poppa Jim.

The bride met her man at the altar. The couple knelt on a prie-dieu in front of Father Kelly and his altar boys.

The priest turned his back on them and began the centuries old Nuptial Mass that would join them as husband and wife.

Father Kelly made the Sign of the Cross and said, "*In nomine Patris et Filii et Spiritus Sancti.*"

Most of the congregation had their Rosaries in hand. They were ignorant of Latin.

Vows exchanged and the Mass ended, the now-married happy couple walked back down the aisle to a triumphant pulsation of organ music and down the church steps under a growing shower of rice.

The bridal party headed off in a horse drawn carriage to a nearby photographer's studio. Mickey McGurk had lingered just long enough to give the altar boys silver dollars. The uniformed Zepps headed for his flat to change into plain clothes for the reception.

Ned McCann barely made it back to the saloon before the first guests drifted in. As predicted, they were thirsty. It was a bright, warm summer day.

Slowly the tables and the bar filled up.

The head table, set for eight, stood empty awaiting the wedding party.

That set off speculation. There were six in the wedding party and Father Kelly. Who would be the eighth person at the head table?

The wedding party along with Father Kelly arrived to great applause.

Ten minutes later Frank Hague walked in, to greater applause, and sat down next to Father Kelly in the middle of the head table. Peggy McCann Aiello was on his right.

The buzz of the crowd was growing louder. Frank Hague stood up. His ward leaders and their minions immediately began to quiet the crowd. "Shhh! Shhh! Let the man speak."

"I think some of you already know me," said Hague to dutiful laughter. "I am Frank Hague. I thank you for electing me to the City Commission. Who knows, next year you might give me a new job?" Enthusiastic clapping and cheering.

Hague continued. "But this is no day to talk politics. It's a day to congratulate Mr. and Mrs. Aiello on their marriage."

More applause cheers and whistles. "Now I'll ask Father Kelly to give us his blessing and say grace."

After the short prayer, Hague immediately began working the room. His secretary by his side, the leaders of the 11th and 12th

Wards flanking him and taking notes.

Lots of guests calculated whether they had enough time to get food before the mayor reached their table as he was moving in his usual counter-clockwise fashion.

The people in the food line pretty much stuck to their own ethnic cuisine—plus the fried rice since most of them had been to a Chinese restaurant. An adventurous few from each group tried something different.

"That's looks good. What is it?"

"They think the heinies call it sauerbraten."

The roll call of explanation and identification continued:

"Ravioli."

"Spaetzle."

"Manicotti."

"Wiener schnitzel."

"Boiled cabbage," which drew the response, *"Che Dio ci aiuti!"*

"What did she say?"

"God help us."

The wine and beer flowed freely and the children had a great time running through the tables while slurping down birch beer. Among them was Grace Corcoran.

Fat Jack Lynch had been at Al Murphy's flat talking politics when he asked Maureen Corcoran, "Has Gracie ever been to a wedding?"

"I don't think so. Why?"

"A couple of friends of mine are getting married on Saturday and I'm invited. It might be fun for Gracie if you went with me to the wedding."

Maureen Corcoran, widowed for five years and tired of it, looked at Jack Lynch, overweight, red-faced, eager, and the decently paid weights and measures clerk. She said, "You know, Jack, I think Gracie would like that and so would I."

When enough beer and wine was consumed the singing began. First an Irishman with a fine tenor voice stood up.

"There's a tear in your eye and I'm wondering why,
For it never should be there at all.
With such power in your smile, sure a stone you'd beguile,
So there's never a teardrop should fall,
When your sweet lilting laughter's like some fairy song
And your eyes twinkle bright as can be,
You should laugh all the while and all other times smile,
And now smile a smile for me."

The crowd roared out the chorus, a wave of sound almost strong enough to shatter the mirror behind the bar.

"When Irish eyes are smiling, sure 'tis like a morn in spring.
In the lilt of Irish laughter, you can hear the angels sing,
When Irish hearts are happy, all the world seems bright and gay,
And when Irish eyes are smiling, shur-r-r-e they st-e-e-e al your heart away."

The clapping, cheers, whistling and stomping continuing for almost a half-minute.

The crowd was in a good mood when Carmela Aiello poked her elbow in her husband's ribs and said, "Be a man. Get up. You know what to sing. Who the hell do they think they are?"

Antonio Aiello, as handsome as his son, stood up and the Italians shhhed the crowd.

His voice was not as clear as the Irishman's but it would do.

"C' 'na luna mezz'u mare
Mamma mia m'a maritare
Figlia mia a cu te dare
Mamma mia pensace tu
Se te piglio lu pesciaiole
Isse vai issa vene

Sempe iu pesce mane tene."

Here Antonio grabbed his crotch and the Italians howled.

"Se ce 'ncappa la fantasia
Te pesculia figghiuzza mia
La lariula pesce fritt'e baccala
Uei cumpa no calamari c'eggi'accatta…"

Everyone who had been clapping along with the Italians applauded although they had no idea what the lyrics meant.

Peggy turned to Tony and asked, "What's was the song about?"

"Well, it's in the Neapolitan dialect and lots of the words have double meanings and it's very funny. A daughter is telling her mother she wants to get married and the mother tells her she should marry a fisherman. She says a fisherman always has a fish in his hand."

"Is that when your father grabbed his you know what?"

"Yes."

Peggy giggled.

"And maybe the fisherman would give the fish to her daughter. And so on."

Peggy flirted with her husband. "Well, I hope your fish measures up."

"You'll see," said Tony, kissing her hand.

Otto, who had more beer than Sophie liked, said to her, "We should join in the fun. Let's sing 'Du, du liegst mir im Herzen'."

"No. No, I don't want to."

"Come on, Mama," said Otto pulling her to her feet, "pretend you're in the choir."

His bass voice rang out, "Du, du liegst mir im Herzen…"

Sophie's higher, better voice blended with his.

"du, du liegst mir im Sinn.

du, du machst mir viel Schmerzen.

weilt nicht wie gut ich dir bin.

Ja... ja... ja... weiltnich wie gut ich dir bin."

Mickey and Hannah sang along with the other German speakers. The rest of people chimed in with the "du, du" and "ja, ja" filling the rest of the lyrics with "la, la, la."

The Germans, the Irish, the Italians and the odd WASP or bohunk in the crowd had forgotten who was fighting who in that war so very far away.

Another cop at Hans Mannstein's table asked for a translation. "Well, it goes like this–you are in my heart, you are in my mind, you make me feel pain and you don't how good I am for you."

"My sentiments exactly," said the other cop to his wife who punched him in the arm.

Ned McCann checked with his head bartender. "How we doing?"

"We're doing fine. Beer and wine's holding up."

The bartender pointed to the packed bar. He said, "We're taking in almost as much as we would on a regular Saturday night."

"God is good," said Ned McCann.

There were almost as many women as men at the bar despite the presence of what seemed to be half the police force. The women were enjoying themselves and there were no floozies about to distract their men.

This was, as all weddings are, a chance for single men and women to socialize and maybe flirt with one another in a safe setting while their elders were intent on something other than watching them. The parents didn't have to worry. There was no place for them to sneak off to. Weddings begat weddings but not immediately.

The band had arrived by seven o'clock and set up in a corner. The dance floor was a fair size considering the numbers in attendance. It was a big room. Pathé Studios next door often rented it and used it as a set for their photoplays.

The band, a local favorite, alternated between old, slow favorites and modern faster numbers, the latter giving the old folks a chance to tsk-tsk at the younger generation.

At first the women danced with each other but gradually men asked women to dance. Italian men asked Peggy to dance and pinned currency to her dress.

"Hey! Is that wop trying to feel up my cousin?"

"Relax. He's just giving her money. It's their custom."

"Well, I don't like it."

"Okay. Then don't give her any money."

Wedding presents were piling up in the locked storage room where Ned kept his liquor. Doreen carried a white, silk-covered purse as Peggy and Tony visited each table of Italians. Doreen slipped the wedding envelopes into it. The newlyweds easily would be able to furnish their flat with this money.

Fat Jack Lynch said to Grace Corcoran, "C'mon, Gracie, let's dance." But the little girl replied, "I'm sorry, Mr. Lynch, I don't know how to dance."

"Aw, don't worry about that, I know enough for both of us," he said. Jack took her hand and headed for the dance floor. "Okay, stand on my shoes."

"But I'll hurt your feet."

"No you won't. Just relax and let me do the work. Okay?"

"Okay."

Lynch, who was a surprisingly agile dancer as are many heavy people, glided away, his feet easily bearing Grace's weight. The little girl called out to her mother. "Momma! Momma! Look at me! I'm dancing." Maureen looked at her daughter and Jack Lynch and liked what she saw.

They returned to the table after the dance, Gracie eager to get away and tell her friends what happened. "Thanks, Jack," said Maureen. "That was nice."

"She's a sweet child, I adore her. But you know what I would really like? I'd like to dance with her beautiful mother."

"Who could resist that, Mr. Lynch," she said, rising.

It was an old, slow favorite and Jack held Maureen at a proper distance from himself. There was a tap on his shoulder and he turned to see Frank Hague.

"I'm glad I caught you, Jack. I didn't want to leave without talking to you."

Jack and Maureen stopped dancing. So did a circle of couples around them, intent on listening to what might be an interesting conversation.

Maureen stood there holding Fat Jack's arm.

"Yeah. I wanted to tell you you're the new Assistant Superintendent of Weights and Measures. Your boss is retiring. Congratulations."

And here I thought he had retired years ago. "Thank you, Commissioner. Thank you very much. It's an honor. You won't regret it."

Hague turned to Maureen. "I believe you are Al Murphy's daughter."

Lynch answered, "She is indeed, sir. This is Mrs. Maureen Corcoran and my fiancée as soon as I get up the nerve to ask her."

Hague looked at Maureen. She smiled wanly and said, "Well, we'll have to see about that." But she squeezed Fat Jack's arm.

"Well, I'm off," said Hague.

Lynch put his arm around Maureen and started dancing. Maureen spoke quietly so no one else could hear. "That was the goddamnedest proposal a girl ever got."

Fat Jack pressed on. "But will you say 'yes'?"

"Of course, you boob," said Maureen, pulling Jack closer to her.

A ward-heeler sidled up to Al Murphy who was watching the couple with a smile on his face.

"Well, it looks like Fat Jack's getting up in the world, eh, Al?"

"We don't call him that anymore."

"No? Well, what do we call him?"

"Jack, John, Mr. Lynch or, sir to you, bub."

Ned McCann took his final tally. He had a few gallons of wine left, some dregs in a beer keg and a cash drawer stuffed with currency and coins.

* * *

The crowd started to thin out leaving only the hard core drinkers and couples enjoying a night out.

Hannah said to Mickey McGurk, "We ought to be getting home, dear. We have to pick up Francis early in the morning."

Their son, too young to stay up this late at a wedding, was staying overnight at a relative's home.

"You bet. But first I want a last dance with the most beautiful girl in the place."

Hannah teased him. "Sorry. Peggy left long ago."

"Ha!" said Mickey whirling her onto the dance floor. It had been a grand day. He danced with his wife and sighed contentedly as the band played on.

In the Dark of Night

The Saturday night party at 123 West 15th Street was still going strong but Mena Edwards the Kodak Girl was not there.

She had been frightened by what she had overheard the week before when two men were whispering about the "Jersey Terminal." One of them was Paul Koenig. She was spending the weekend in the Atlantic Highlands with a friend.

Paul Koenig wasn't at the party either. He was upstairs, in a bedroom, nervously smoking and trying to read a newspaper. He would wait up until the saboteurs got back—if they got back.

Captain Frederick Hinsch was back in Baltimore helping to load the merchant submarine Deutschland for its return trip to Germany. He had commanded the tug which greeted her on her arrival into Chesapeake Bay and towed her into Baltimore.

The night was black. A billion or so stars above shone brightly but gave off no light. The moon hadn't risen yet.

The small rowboat glided swiftly in the current, Jahnke at the oars maneuvering only to keep on course. Witzke had the red filtered flashlight which he used to check of the number of the buoys as they passed. It could be used without hobbling their night vision. His principal guide, though, was the lighted torch of the Statue of Liberty just off Black Tom.

The rowboat was securely tied to the ring, and the men split up to plant their bombs. They saw and heard no guards.

Witzke kept the flashlight but didn't need it. Everything was in silhouette. He walked along the wharf and picked out his target, a lighter which was sitting fairly low in the water.

Already loaded, he thought.

He waited and looked around for a few seconds before he stepped from the pier onto the vessel. *I was right*, he thought as he slipped into the hold and shoved his fire bombs into its lethal cargo.

Jahnke soundlessly walked until the row of warehouses appeared to his left. He tried a door. It opened. He couldn't tell what was stored there but he put two bombs, one red and one green, amidst what he thought to be cloth. He did the same at the next warehouse.

Kristoff came the longest way but had it the easiest. He just followed the railroad tracks to his target, the boxcars. He saw men inside the lighted guard shack which had two screened, open windows. Smudge pots smoked away outside trying unsuccessfully to drive off the voracious mosquitoes. There was also an open fire burning a few feet from them, sparks flying high into the sky before they died.

That's dangerous. They ought to be more careful, thought Kristoff who smiled at his own wit. Then he planted his cigar bombs.

The two men in the rowboat slipped away and headed south with the current. The other man started the long walk to the White Horse tavern, careful to stay in the shadows.

Black Tom slumbered in its last hours.

A Dead Yard

That same afternoon of July 29, 1916, was also very pleasant at Black Tom. It was warm, not hot, and a nice breeze was blowing off the river.

The men working the switch engines, the boxcars, the piers, the warehouses, the delivery trucks and the barges toiled in pleasant anticipation of Saturday night, just a few hours off, when many — if not most of them — would have a few drinks with friends to help them forget the week of hard labor behind them.

Then would come Sunday, the day of rest. Most of them would spend it with their families. Some, of course, would drink too much and Sunday would not be so pleasant for them or their families. It was the way of the working world in those days.

No munitions were to be left on Black Tom overnight, let alone over a Sunday. No one paid attention to that. The war brought more work than could be pushed out in a day. Sometimes the loaded boxcars would sit there for days or even a week.

This night more than 2,000,000 pounds of ordinance would be sitting in about 200 boxcars, more than a dozen warehouses and in a flotilla of barges and lighters at Black Tom. At the North Pier, parallel to the tracks, ten barges and lighters were moored. When fully loaded, the watercraft would be towed out to anchored freighters and off loaded. But not on Sunday.

Johnson lighter Number Seventeen, stuffed with munitions, had tied up at two thirty pm at the express order of the Lehigh Valley Railroad. No sense wasting money on a $25 towing fee. Monday would be soon enough.

The locomotives and switch engines, one by one, chugged back to the mainland. The delivery trucks, motorized and horse-drawn, were gone too.

Men waved goodbye to each other as they ambled off.

Gradually, as the afternoon wore on, fewer and fewer men were working until by five o'clock Black Tom was deserted except for the guards, watchmen, a straggler or two and the few crewmen aboard the lighters and barges.

Black Tom was, as the railroad men put it, a dead yard.

There were still hours of daylight to go at Black Tom on this long summer day.

The watchmen and guards faced a thirteen-hour shift. Tedious, boring, but mercifully free of any serious supervision.

Some would sleep now and again, one or two might walk about while others tended the smudge pots which were meant to ward off the armadas of mosquitoes which would fly in from the nearby wetlands with the setting of the sun. The smudge pots were as ineffective as the poorly paid guardians of Black Tom.

Whiskey would help to pass the dreary night. One of their number would be dispatched to get a couple of half-pints from a nearby saloon. No one would get dead drunk. Just sip enough to keep a pleasant buzz.

Black Tom was unlighted except for the guard shack and a lantern or two aboard the barges. The watchmen and guards used carbide lamps, kerosene lanterns and the occasional flashlight. Mainly, they didn't bother to move about too much after dark. Once in a while was sufficient. They stuck close to the guard shack. It was a rare night when anything of interest occurred. This was not to be such a night.

No fence separated Black Tom from the mainland.

Around midnight, a watchman thought he saw two men in a rowboat probably heading for Bedloe's Island a few hundred yards away. He didn't pay them much mind. He wouldn't have confronted them even if he saw them landing on Black Tom. What was there to steal?

Only minutes later, he spotted a small fire in some cardboard under a freight car.

"Now how in the hell did that start?" He looked around and

saw sparks shooting into the air from a trash fire near the guard shack. The wind was coming from the right direction.

There were red pails of water or sand scattered throughout Black Tom. The watchman snuffed out the fire with sand. Fire needs oxygen, heat and fuel to live and grow. Deprive it of one of these and it dies. But leave it unmolested and fire will double in size every five minutes.

I ought to tell the boss about this. He looked at the shack. He saw no one moving around. If the straw boss wasn't easy to find, he'd sure to be hard to find.

The hell with it. Lazy bastard. I need a drink. No one will miss me. Just one drink though. I'll tell him when I get back. The watchman didn't look inside the boxcar.

He cleared the yard and, in the light of the first streetlamp, he saw another man about a hundred yards ahead of him. *Probably going to the saloon just like him.* The watchman soon lost track of the man in the dark between lamps and he concentrated instead on getting that much welcome drink.

The clock atop The Jersey Journal, a long way from Black Tom on top of the Palisades, reached midnight. It was July 30, 1916.

The Jersey City slept. So did New York City.

Other little unseen fires at Black Tom were crackling, glowing and growing in size. An appetite insatiable. No one noticed.

At twelve minutes after midnight, a different watchman saw another fire on Pier 7 in the center of a string of freight cars near the shore end of the pier. The watchman saw a piece of waste burning under the boxcar door. The fire was menacing, flames licking at the door and floor of the boxcar. Wisps of smoke were seeping out of its wooden pores.

Oh, shit. This is bad. Real bad. He ran for a telephone and called for yard engines to pull out the ammo laden freight cars.

Many of the railroad men, the single ones, lived in cheap boarding houses within walking distance of the yard. Telephone calls roused them. The White House Tavern on Communipaw

Avenue was called too.

No one called the Jersey City Fire Department. The people of Black Tom could handle another little fire themselves.

Yard engines soon had steam up and started to pull cars down the tracks away from the growing fire.

It was too late. The fire had eaten through the floor and walls of one of the boxcars and was devouring the wooden crates protecting the munitions. Rounds began to cook off. Shrapnel filled the air. No one was fighting the fire.

Another fire could be seen on the deck of Johnson Number 17, on the North Pier not far from the railroad tracks. This lighter had a derrick on deck and its hold measured eighty feet by thirty feet. The hold was filled with a most deadly cargo. Its skipper was challenging the fire himself with a water bucket, recharged by dipping it into the river. No one helped him.

The master of a Lehigh Valley Railroad tug dispatched from The Gap, just north of Black Tom, could see the fire on the pier but not on the lighter. He steamed to Pier 7 and pulled a different lighter out into the river.

At forty minutes after midnight an American District Telegraph fire alarm attached to a sprinkler system in one of the warehouses automatically sounded. Two of the warehouses packed with munitions and other war material was on fire. The sprinkler system would not save them.

The Jersey City Fire Departments dispatched three engines and a ladder truck to the scene. The firemen could not board Lighter Number 17, the deck was too hot. But they started to fight the fire from the pier. They also attacked the blazing warehouses.

The watchmen and guards abandoned Black Tom as soon as the firemen arrived. They ran for their lives.

Every firefighter sizes up the scene as he arrives. His officers are paid to do that but everyone does it. At Black Tom, the firefighters' appraisal of the situation was uniquely the same. *Oh, shit.*

Men and equipment were moving steadily towards Black Tom as shrapnel peppered the Statue of Liberty and the Main Hall on Ellis Island, both easily within range of exploding shell and shot.

Minutes earlier, the night superintendent at Ellis Island had called a superior in Manhattan for advice.

"It's like a goddamn battlefield. Shells bursting. Fire everywhere. The building has been hits several times already. Nobody's been hurt yet. But I think it's going to get worse."

"Get them off the island. Take them to The Battery. We'll sort it out in the morning," said his chief.

So it was that five hundred or so frightened immigrants, some fleeing the war in Europe, found themselves on the ferry boat "Ellis Island" headed across the Hudson River. Among them were some poor souls who were being turned away from the Golden Door because they had been branded "mental defectives."

Of these, a group gathered on the stern of the double-ended ferry boat. They clapped, cheered and oohed and ahhed. They were certain what was happening at Black Tom was a fireworks display staged for their amusement.

Those who cared for Miss Liberty on Bedloe Island were taken off too. New York City police boats took the men, twelve women and thirteen children to Governor's Island. Miss Liberty's lamp remained lighted even as random shrapnel pierced her skin.

As the perfidious and pitiful watchmen ran, others hurried to help. Firemen—the second and third alarms had already sounded—policemen, locomotive engineers, brakemen, teamsters, reporters, the crews of tug boats, fireboats and Coast Guard cutters, all headed straight for Black Tom as the shells exploded overhead. Ambulances began to arrive too.

It is doubtful that any of these men were as fearless as they were brave although some of the younger ones hoped the night would bring a memorable adventure. It did. They came because it was what working class Americans did when there was trouble. They brought their equipment and their skills. They were redoubtable, mostly respectable, men. Family men.

None of them would have walked across the street to save the railroad's stockholders from bankruptcy. But they put their lives on the line because of their self-respect, affection for their peers who they wouldn't let down, and an inchoate sense of community. Mainly they did it because it was their job.

"Be careful!" their worried wives urged.

"I will, my love, I will. You know me. 'Caution' is my middle name."

Their wives knew and choked down the lie. Heaven itself was soon under a bombardment of prayer.

Of course, not all men had the same motives. One tug boat operator in Brooklyn looked across the water and saw the opportunity of a lifetime. It was the 4,800 ton freighter, the Tijoca Rio, loaded with building materials and tied up near Black Tom. He headed straight for it and pulled it out.

The tugboat captain was to get $9,000 in salvage money. Each of his crew got $1,500, more than a year's wages. While they were enriching themselves, albeit at great risk, other tugboats, New York City fireboats and Coast Guard cutters were dragging flaming barges out into the stream and pouring water into them to put out the fires and cool their lethal cargo.

The clock atop The Jersey Journal read 1:05 am when the first explosion—the smallest—claimed Black Tom's first victim.

Cornelius Leyden, chief of the Lehigh Valley Railroad Police, was there. He was standing next to the yardmaster by the river when a boxcar blew up. The yardmaster was knocked down by the blast. He cleared his head and rose, bruised and bloodied, but not seriously injured. The yardmaster looked around, confused. Leyden was not there. He was gone. Leyden's body would wash ashore a month later.

The skipper of another lighter was blown into the water. He swam to Bedloe's Island. Resting a while, he watched the spectacular fireworks and then swam back and boarded his lighter. He ended up in the hospital but he survived.

The explosion rocked the Downtown Jersey City wards. There had been an almost continuous rumbling for almost an hour from shells bursting but most people still awake thought it thunder. Those who looked out a window were puzzled to see a clear sky.

Alarm bells rang out in more firehouses as the 4th and 5th alarms were tapped out. Telephones jingled all over Jersey City.

Mickey McGurk answered his. "This is Frank Hague," the voice said needlessly.

"Yes, Commissioner."

"There's a big fire down at Black Tom and a freight car just blew up. The fire chief called and he's not sure his people can control it. The whole place may go up."

"Sweet Jesus."

"I warned those stupid bastards in Washington. You were there. The railroads aren't just a pain in the ass anymore. They're a fucking disaster. I'll send a car to get you. Get down there and find out what's going on."

"Should I meet you there?" asked McGurk.

"No, I'm headed for the 2nd Precinct. Use a call box to keep in touch with me. Harry Moore and John Milton are going to meet me there. I'm going to nail the sons of bitches responsible for this. You can't blow up my city and get away with it."

"Right, Commissioner." Hague had already hung up.

Hannah, wide awake and at his side, asked, "What's wrong?"

Mickey told her. She grabbed his shoulders. "You don't have to go down there, do you? It's your day off."

"Nobody is going to be off today, sweetheart. A car is coming for me."

A stern Hannah said, "Be careful! Don't be a hero. I need you.

Francis needs you."

"Don't worry, honey. I'm not a fireman. I'll stay in the rear with the gear."

"Of course, you will." She was a policeman's wife and she knew it was a lie.

Hans was there. Tony was not. Tony and Peggy were on the first and the last night of their honeymoon in Manhattan.

The scene was absolute black chaos but the policemen could see some order emerging. Switch engines were dragging off boxcars. Rescue craft were pulling out barges. Fire engines, yoked to hydrants, were pumping water to charge the firefighters' hoses. The injured were being treated and some hauled off in ambulances, some horse drawn.

But the fire was still winning. Now several huge warehouses were aflame defying the firemen who fought it while their comrades poured water on the neighboring exposures. The heat was almost unbearable. Almost.

It was 2:08 am when there was a more massive explosion as a freight car full of black powder went up, taking neighboring boxcars with it.

Most of the men working at Black Tom were flattened by the pressure wave which moved faster than the speed of sound. Scores were hurt, some seriously. A twenty-eight year old policeman, hit by flying debris, was not expected to live.

Mickey and Hans were blown into the water and, gagging, pulled themselves up a ladder attached to a pier.

"Jesus Christ," said Mickey.

Hans said, "I've got to learn how to swim."

They stood there, filthy river water streaming off them. Their clothes would dry on their backs. Their shoes would stay squishy.

Many plate glass windows in the financial district just across the river shattered. The district was virtually deserted on an early Sunday morning so injuries were minimal. Fire and burglar alarms sounded all over lower Manhattan and Jersey City.

The city that never sleeps awakened—panic stricken. People poured into the streets. Thousands of onlookers thronged to the river's shore. Manhattan's streets were clogged with autos, taxis and even horse drawn hacks.

The telephone lines between Jersey City and New York City severed. Police and fire officials in Manhattan and Brooklyn knew only what they could see across the river or the bay. Meanwhile, their people were scrambling to answer burglar alarms, finding only shattered glass littering the sidewalks when they arrived.

Shrapnel hit the Jersey Journal's clock at 2:12 am and stopped its hands.

The fire was not finished. Sixteen minutes later it finally ignited the cargo in Johnson Lighter Number 17's hold.

In the hold were 100,000 pounds of TNT; 3,125 cases of ammunition and explosive projectiles; and 417 cases of detonating fuses. This was the lighter that was docked at Black Tom to save a $25 towing fee. Lighter Number 17 was 325 feet from the pier when it blew up. Its courageous skipper vanished with his vessel. The river bed which had been seven feet from the surface a week before now had a crater twenty-one feet deep below where the lighter had been.

The pressure wave of the blast leveled the warehouses still standing, touched off scores of burning boxcars, destroyed barges and small craft at the six piers it pulverized, knocked down anyone standing at Black Tom injuring many as it moved out in a deadly, costly circle. Jersey City and Manhattan were hard hit.

Across the river, plate glass in thousands more windows and doors shattered. Much of the glass south of 33rd Street was gone. But some was spared as the pressure wave followed its own peculiar paths through the city steered by the skyscrapers. In midtown, a stained glass window in St, Patrick's Cathedral was blown out. Some windows broke twenty-five miles away. People in Maryland were startled awake by what they thought was an earthquake.

More people were hurt as the shock wave moved away from Black Tom and worse panic spread with the blast.

The pressure wave was capricious. Pure, unfeeling caprice. It was particularly cruel on Central Avenue in The Heights not far from the McGurks. A ten-day-old baby, in bed with his mother, was thrown to the floor and killed. The mother was not injured save for a lifetime of grief.

Peggy and Tony Aiello were shaken awake in their Manhattan hotel room bed. "Jesus, that sounded close," said Tony.

"What do you think happened, Tony?"

"Probably a gas main blew up. Happens all the time."

The lighter and eighty-seven freight cars of dynamite and its ilk had exploded. Where the boxcars once were was now a deep water-filled pond several hundred feet long.

Those little, unmolested fires, touched off by cylinders not much bigger than cigars, had done their worst. The rest was anticlimax. Fires still burned in the debris and firemen fought them. Boats still poured water onto the smoldering wreckage of what had once been piers and lighters. More than a hundred men still were being treated for their injuries. Rounds still occasionally cooked off and lit up the sky. Millions still were terrified. So it went through the night and for some time after the sun rose.

America would not know it for years, but it had just suffered the worst terrorist attack in its history until 9/11, 2001. Black Tom was no more. It was a dead yard.

Forever.

A Frightening Success

The mood at the breakfast table was jubilant.

Kurt Jahnke and Lothar Witzke had managed to grab a couple of hours sleep and now were having coffee and buttered rye bread with Paul Koenig at 123 West 15th Street.

Their bags were packed and in a few minutes Koenig would drive them to Grand Central Station where they would board the early train to Chicago. Another train and then another would ultimately take them to San Francisco more than a week later. Koenig had booked compartments on Pullman cars and as Jahnke said, the food in the dining cars was "not bad." A decent way to travel.

"It's hard to believe," said Jahnke. "Those little fire bombs caused all that destruction. I wish we had them on the West Coast."

"That's an idea," said Koenig.

"All that broken glass," said Witzke. "We were lucky to get back without a flat tire. That was a great triumph too, my friend." They all laughed.

"You should have seen it here," said Koenig. "This party was still going strong when the first explosion hit. No one knew what had happened. Then someone came in screaming 'the Jersey terminal is on fire.' The place emptied and stayed empty. I was in the parlor trying to read when that huge explosion rocked the house and shattered all the back windows. It's going to be impossible to get a glazier in New York tomorrow. But we can have some seamen board up the windows until we can get one."

"Such troubles," said a very unsympathetic Jahnke. Another laugh.

Koenig said, "We'll really have trouble when the Americans find out who destroyed the Jersey terminal."

"How will they find out, Herr Koenig? We were careful to

leave no trace and we will be gone in a few hours," said Jahnke.

"You will be gone," said Koenig, "but Kristoff will not. Where is he now?"

Witzke said, "He didn't want to come back here so we dropped him off at a saloon near a place they call Bayonne before we headed for the ferry. That was before the big explosions."

"Well, pray to God the Americans don't find him and that he has the sense to keep his mouth shut," said Koenig. "I did promise him more 'work' if this mission was successful. He may show up here looking for another job."

"Cheer up, Herr Koenig. This was the most successful sabotage effort ever and when we get back to Germany I think it means 'Iron Crosses' all around," said Witzke, who was to get two of them.

"If we get back to Germany," said Koenig.

* * *

The meeting Ambassador von Bernstorff had with his military attaché in Washington was less cordial.

"You people amaze me," said the ambassador. "First you can't find anyone who can handle a bomb without blowing off their arms and now you destroy half of New York."

"It was just a railroad terminal and some broken glass, Excellency."

Von Bernstorff stared at his attaché. "God knows how many people are dead, hundreds more injured, many millions of dollars in property damage. This is not just 'broken glass', this is a casus belli, you fool. Here I am working to keep America 'neutral' and you people deliver her on a plate to the Allies."

The military attaché said, "Excellency, our General Staff says that even if the United States does declare war, her army and navy won't be ready to fight for years."

"Is this the same General Staff that predicted we would win

the war in forty days by pushing through Belgium and flanking the French? That was two years ago. Make ready to burn all our secret documents."

"Yes, Excellency. But maybe the Americans won't find out we did it."

"Don't be stupid," said the German ambassador to the United States and Mexico.

Arrest the Arrogant Bastards

The six o'clock Mass at the mission church of Our Lady of the Rosary over on 6th Street was packed. Not everyone there was Catholic. All were grateful. Grateful that they were alive. Grateful that there weren't more people dead. It seemed a miracle to everyone that there weren't more. Not that anyone knew exactly how many people had died. But they knew the number was small.

Mickey and Hans were still at Black Tom. Tony had just arrived back from his truncated honeymoon.

"I'm going to have to check in with the Commissioner," McGurk said. "He's not going to be happy."

Tony said, "I think I'll stay here with Hans and keep asking questions. You know, talk to everybody we can get our mitts on. See if we can't get to the bottom of this."

"You taking good notes?" Mickey asked.

Tony said, "Hans has already filled half of a new notebook. I'm just getting started but as near as I can tell, we don't know much more now than when you started."

McGurk said, "You're right. But then this is so big. I never tried to investigate anything this big."

"No one has," said Tony, who had a lot more experience as a detective than Mickey McGurk. "You know both of you actually stink, don't you?"

"Really?" said Hans.

There was a call box linked to the 2nd Precinct just outside what was left of Black Tom.

Mickey McGurk was checking in with Commissioner Frank Hague every half-hour. "How's it going, Mickey?"

"Better, Uncle Frank. But it's still unbelievably bad. There's nothing left. They'll never use Black Tom again."

"How many dead?"

McGurk said, "Nobody knows. But I don't think there will be too many. Hardly anyone was here before the cavalry arrived and then, except for that cop, most of us got off light. Maybe a hundred or so got banged up a bit. God knows how many would be dead if Black Tom had gone up twelve hours earlier. What's the situation in the rest of the city?"

Hague said, "A lot of glass broken. A lot of alarms going off. Some people hurt, but none seriously. Although I heard that a baby was killed up in the Heights."

"In the Heights? Where? How?"

Hague said, "Don't know. Call the 6th Precinct. You know everybody up there."

"Right."

Hague said, "Okay. Me, Harry and John Milton are heading for City Hall now. We've got a batch of arrest warrants to draw up."

"Who you arresting, Commissioner?"

"Every one of those arrogant bastards that run that place."

"What's the charge?"

"Manslaughter, for openers," Hague said.

"Manslaughter, wow."

Hague said, "John Milton says there's dozens of charges we can throw at them. Assault, destruction of public property. Malfeasance, misfeasance and no goddamn feasance at all."

"The railroad will send a special train full of lawyers to Jersey City, Uncle Frank."

"Yes, they will but who gives a shit? I'll be there when the coppers fingerprint and mug those bastards. Even if they never spend more than a few hours in jail, I'll have the satisfaction of watching them humiliated like the two-bit bums they are. They'll have records and we'll keep those records until they are dead and buried. Maybe longer. Lieutenant, find out what happened. Get me evidence. Evidence of negligence. Milton says we have to prove them negligent. Get me the evidence. Do it."

"Yes, sir." Hague hung up. Mickey walked back to his team.

"Okay guys. Snap to it. We've got to get evidence that the railroad, the storage company and the lighter people have been negligent and their negligence caused this catastrophe."

"That shouldn't be hard," said Tony. "What's our next assignment, proving the sky is blue?"

Warrants charging manslaughter were issued for the arrest of Albert M. Dickman, superintendent and agent for Lehigh Valley Railroad at Black Tom, Alexander Davidson, superintendent of National Dock and Storage Company and Theodore B. Johnson, head of Johnson Lighterage and Towing Co. They weren't hard to find. All three were at Black Tom.

Their arrests startled them. As they were being marched to the paddy wagon, handcuffed, Dickman asked a uniformed policeman, "Officer, is this really necessary? We're respectable people. We'll accompany you to the station house without incident, I assure you."

The cop looked at him, snorted, and said, "I don't know about that, Mac. It's just routine. It's the way we handle all you dangerous criminals." The cop laughed. His charges did not.

Frank Hague was waiting at the station house. Milton had advised him not to speak to any of the men arrested. "You say, 'Good morning' and their lawyers will turn that into malicious false arrest," Milton had said.

Hague did not speak but he thoroughly enjoyed their predicted humiliation. One, after being fingerprinted, had asked a policeman if he could clean his ink-stained fingers. "Sure," the cop said, "When you get home."

Hague had whispered to his secretary, "Get me that cop's name. I like his style."

The trio was put in a holding cell with the flotsam and jetsam of the previous night's drinking. The smell of vomit, urine and excrement was rank. The newcomers had no handkerchiefs to put their noses. They had been taken away lest they commit suicide by knotting them together and doing themselves in serially.

Within minutes, their cellmates knew who they were and why they had been arrested. One inmate screamed for the turnkey.

"Jerry, you know me," he said. "I've spent a lot of time behind bars. I don't complain. But don't make me stay in a cell with these bags of shit."

"I see your point," said Jerry. "Anybody else want to get away from these so-called gentlemen?" They all did, at least all that were conscious.

Jerry the Turnkey cheerfully led the unkempt procession down the corridor to another empty holding cell. It had been slow the night before. Especially after the first explosion.

A delighted Frank Hague took the precinct captain aside. "Turn them loose. Turn them all loose. I don't care if they're accused of screwing donkeys. Turn them loose."

"If you say so, Commissioner."

"I say so."

It may have been early on a Sunday morning, but the corporate lawyers were there within an hour of their clients' arrest. For some reason, the system moved exceptionally slow even for a Sunday, but there was still some daylight left when the three executives were released on $5,000 bond apiece to await the action of the Grand Jury.

Hague also ordered the arrest of Eben B. Thomas, president of the Lehigh Valley Railroad and, for good measure, William G. Besler, president of the Central Railroad of New Jersey. Some of the Central's tracks had been used to shuttle freight cars full of munitions to nearby Black Tom. Neither man was within easy reach of the Jersey City police. When they did turn themselves in, each was surrounded by an impenetrable thicket of highly paid attorneys. Their humiliation was minimal. Hague didn't bother to go watch. He knew there would be little satisfaction and absolutely no fun. Their platoon of lawyers would see to that.

* * *

Mickey gathered his men by a fire department water can. He talked as they drank. "Okay, I have to get over to City Hall and report to the commissioner. What have you got?"

"Let me sum it up, boss," said Tony. "There was a fire at Black Tom and then the place blew up. A couple of people—maybe more—died. A cop was hurt bad. Lots of people—including a bunch of firemen—got hurt. It was the biggest fireworks display the harbor has ever seen. Tons of plate glass shattered in Manhattan and in Jersey City and the blast could be heard all the way to God knows where. That's it."

"Dear Jesus. Thanks a lot. Hours of questioning people and this is all you have? We're all going to be pounding beats tomorrow morning. Tony, how did the fire start?"

Aiello said, "I don't know. The fire guys can't agree. One battalion chief insists the fire started in a warehouse. A captain said it was a fire in a boxcar. Another is holding out for the lighter that blew up. Several think it was sparks from those smudge pots."

"Fires can't start in three or four places at the same time, can they?" asked McGurk.

"Nah. Everybody agreed to say it started in one place and the breeze carried sparks to the rest. They just can't agree on the one spot."

McGurk asked, "What about the watchmen? What did they see? What did they do?"

"Who knows," said Tony. "They vanished before when firemen arrived."

"Well, let's find them and talk to them. Hans, that's your job right now. Tony, you keep asking questions."

"See if you can grab a bite to eat too. I saw a Salvation Army wagon just outside of Black Tom. I'll try to get back by one o'clock."

McGurk said, "Okay, I see Jackie Farrell over there writing something down. I'll see if he learned more than you dumbasses."

"How you doing, Jackie?"

"Not bad, not good," said the young reporter. "This is the biggest story I ever worked on and The Jersey Journal doesn't publish until Monday afternoon."

"So?"

"The New York and Newark papers will have printed everything but the label on the yardmaster's underwear by then. It's a bitch."

McGurk said, "Too bad, pal. You got anything I can use? You know for the 'absolutely thorough investigation' that you'll be writing about."

Farrell laughed. "I'll show you mine, if you show me yours."

"Fair enough." McGurk told Farrell what he knew except that the watchmen had run off. Farrell already knew that.

Then it was Farrell's turn. "Sorry but I don't have much to add to what you got," he said. "Well, as my old city editor used to say, 'If you don't have the facts, make sure you drench your copy in color.' Color we got. But I got to find a second day lead. Can I quote you on that 'absolutely thorough' investigation?"

"It would be better if you quoted the commissioner."

"Sure. No problem."

McGurk said, "Say, Jackie. Why don't you go see him at City Hall? He's drawing up warrants for the arrest of a batch of railroad bigwigs. They're being charged with manslaughter. Is that of any interest to you?"

Farrell took a long look at McGurk to see if he was kidding. He wasn't. McGurk was innocent of the demands of daily journalism. "Yes, Mickey. I think it is. You have made my day. I owe you one, pal."

McGurk said, "Can I hitch a ride with you? I have to see the commissioner myself."

"A ride? You can have my firstborn, if you want. C'mon, let's go."

Terry Lynch was in his glory controlling access to the busy commissioner. Farrell got an "I don't know when the commissioner will be able to see you. Probably not today."

"I'll stick around anyway," said Farrell, wise to Lynch's ways.

McGurk got the door opened for him. "Mickey. You look like hell. What happened to your clothes? Sit down, boy, sit down."

"Thanks, Commissioner. I got blown into the river but I'm all right."

"Good. Okay, let's hear what's going on."

McGurk made his report. Hague was disappointed at its lack of detail. "That's it, Mickey?"

"Sorry, Commissioner. So far it's been all action at Black Tom. We know what went on after the fire department got the alarm. But before that, it's a blank except for what the switch engine guys could see when they got there. We'll get more. My guys are on it. But that's all I have now."

"Arson. How about arson? Could someone have set the fire?" asked Hague.

McGurk looked puzzled. "No. There's no suggestion of arson that I heard, Commissioner. This goddamn thing was an accident. An accident caused by negligence. We've already got a big file on the sloppiness at Black Tom. You've got a copy."

"I do indeed," said Hague who hadn't read it. "Okay. Those arrest warrants are being served. Some of them have already seen the inside of a jail. They didn't like it.

"That was the easy part. Now I got to make a statement to the press. They're all over me. Newspapers I never heard of. Milton volunteered to help but the way John writes it's no wonder the Assembly falls asleep when his bills come to the floor. I sent him off to the hospital to look after that cop's family. The docs think he is going to die."

"God, that's awful," said Mickey.

Hague looked expectantly at Mickey McGurk, the recipient of an incomplete but excellent Jesuit education.

Oh, no! "I've got an idea, Uncle Frank. Jackie Farrell from the Journal is outside waiting to see you. I'll ask him to help you with that statement. I think he'll be happy to help."

Hague said, "Farrell. I know his family. Decent enough kid— for a reporter. Okay. Have Terry send him in."

McGurk knew Farrell would make the commissioner sound and look good. He did. Frank Hague was pleased, very pleased.

Later he thought it might be a good idea to make use of reporters such as Farrell. People who could write. They didn't have to be on the city's payroll. They could be on "retainer" like attorneys. Why, their editors didn't need to know about the arrangements either. He'd call on them when needed. So it was to be.

* * *

Mickey McGurk slipped away from City Hall and headed for his mother's.

"It's about time you got here. My kitchen window's shattered and my best tea pot jumped off the shelf and killed itself. I was thrown from my bed, I was, but, by the mercy of God, I have nothing to show for it but a bum knee."

Michael put his arms around his mother. Amelia, who was not prone to great displays of affection, allowed him to do it.

"Are you sure you're not hurt, Ma?"

"I thought we was all being murdered. I thought there was British battleships in the river blowing us all apart."

Mickey chuckled. "British battleships? Why would you think that, Ma?"

"Well," she asked, "who else would be killing the likes of us?"

"Nobody's killing nobody, Ma. It was an accident. Somebody just got careless. A big, bad, noisy, scary accident."

"Bullshit," said Mrs. McGurk. "There was never no accident like that. You mark my words, Michael McGurk. Somebody did it. On purpose."

"If you say so, Ma. If you say so."

Mickey McGurk held his mother close and stroked her hair. She didn't back away.

* * *

Peggy, and Hans' wife, Hilda, were already in the McGurk flat with Hannah, pooling their worries. Cops' women can bond almost as closely as their men. When no one was around, Hilda and Hannah called themselves "The Bombettes."

Peggy was more than a little down. "Can you believe it? Our honeymoon's ruined."

Hilda said, "Cheer up. At least it took blowing up half the city to do it. You better get used to it, Peggy. Your husband's a cop."

Hannah said, "Thank God, all our men are safe. None of them even got more than bumps, bruises and a dunking. One policeman was badly hurt. Mickey said they didn't think he is going to make it."

The women cringed.

Mickey and his men worked into the night and when he got home he was dead tired.

Hannah had a nice dinner waiting in the oven. "Are you hungry, Michael?"

"No, sweetheart. I got something from the Salvation Army."

She turned off the oven. "Well, can you make it to the tub? You're filthy."

"I'll try," said Mickey.

Hannah could hear the water running as she gathered up his reeking clothes. *I won't even try to wash them. Maybe the rag man will take them.*

Mickey was asleep in the tub. She woke him. "Dry yourself off and go to bed, love."

She put on her nightgown and went into the bedroom. Mickey McGurk was snoring.

Another Distraction

Woodrow Wilson had another distraction to his south—Haiti.

The president sent the Marines to Haiti to try to restore order and essential services after a mob tore the sitting president to pieces a year earlier. They were still there fighting the Cacos.

The Cacos were a loosely knit group of brigands available to the highest bidder. That's how power was transferred in Haiti. You hired the Cacos and marched on the capital. They were on the march.

The Marines needed help fighting the Cacos so they organized the Gendarmerie d'Haiti, 2,500 Haitians led by 250 Marines, usually sergeants, who also held officer rank in the unit. The Marines liked the duty and the extra pay.

They earned that pay. The fighting was savage. Mike McGurk's old commanding officer, Major Smedley Butler, won his second Medal of Honor in Haiti. The Marines were there to stay.

Wilson's efforts to end the war in Europe were still futile as well. Britain was being bled white on the Somme.

The battle started on July 1 on both sides of the river. The British artillery launched the fight by firing 1,500,000 rounds at the German defenses. Those defenses were well prepared, their trenches three deep with massive numbers of machine guns, their artillery zeroed in on zones in front of their lines. The Tommies advanced in a line abreast into machine gun fire while taking artillery shells as they went. By the end of the first day, the British 4th Army had suffered 60,000 casualties. Mowed down were the remnants of the old regular army, mowed down were the Territorials, mowed down were the Pals Battalions recruited from the same trades in the same towns. The impact was devastating on Great Britain.

But there were many more such horrific days to come. By the

time the series of battles on the Somme came to a bloody end in November both sides had endured a total of more than 1,000,000 men killed and wounded.

Neither side was interested in talking peace.

If that was not enough for Wilson, Romania declared war on the Central Powers on August 27, 1916, and advanced fifty miles into the Carpathian Mountains against weak Austro-Hungarian forces. Most of Emperor Franz Joseph's troops were fighting on the Italian front.

The Italians, in turn, declared war on Germany the next day.

Romania's strike was ill advised. The Austro-Hungarian army might have been stretched thin but its friends weren't. On September 1, the Germans, Bulgarians and Turks invaded Romania driving its Army back deep into its homeland.

The next day the German military took dictatorial control of the German economy and most aspects of daily life in the Reich.

The world's leaders certainly weren't ready for peace. Wilson certainly wasn't willing to go to war. America stayed neutral, its mighty industries ever willing to supply the instruments of death at a reasonable or even an obscene profit.

At least one of Wilson's diplomatic efforts was still holding. The Germans had backed off unrestricted submarine warfare as he had demanded. The Kaiser, despite Navy pressure, was not ready to go back to it—yet.

Poking in the Ashes

It wasn't long after dawn on Monday when Mickey McGurk's phone rang. It took him a while to get to it in the parlor.

"Hello."

"This is Frank Hague, Mickey. I hope you got a good night's sleep. I want to go to Black Tom. Hans will pick you in a half hour and then double back and pick me up at City Hall. I want to see what happened with my own eyes. Be ready."

"Yes, sir."

Hague hung up.

Hannah walked into the living room in her bathrobe. "You've got to go, don't you?"

"Yep. Hans will be here in a half hour."

Hannah said, "You're still filthy. Get into the tub. I'll make some breakfast for you while you scrub."

"Germans. All they think about is cleaning. It's a wonder that you let me into bed last night looking like this."

"It's a wonder I let you into the house. Go," said Hannah.

Mickey had washed, shaved, dressed and was munching on a piece of toast dipped in egg yolk when Hans knocked on the door. Hans had cleaned up too.

Frank Hague, as usual, looked better than either of them. He pumped them for information on the short ride to Black Tom.

The railroad had armed guards blocking the causeway. They had to leap out of the way as Hans Mannstein rolled through. Hague didn't even look at them. Hague, who had never been to Black Tom, had never seen such devastation anywhere. Hans headed directly for Fire Chief Tom Boyle. He was easy to spot thanks to his white leather helmet. Hague was pleased to see that the chief's uniform was heavily soiled and he looked exhausted.

"Good morning, Chief."

"Good morning, Commissioner."

"What's going on?"

"Let's see. All the intact boxcars loaded with explosives are out of the yard. There'll probably be some live ordinance under the wreckage of the warehouses though. The boys from the National Guard will help us with that. We've got about fifty men watering down the debris. A couple of engines are standing by in case we have some re-kindling.

"When I got here just after one o'clock Sunday morning there were five companies working the job. I could see fire getting at some freight cars, fire on a couple of barges and fire in two of those warehouses. So I pulled the 4th and 5th alarms.

"The main water line was destroyed in the first explosion. We were all knocked down. We got up and began to pump water out of the river. Salt water is going to play hell with the engines, you know. That's when New York's fire boat arrived, thank God. We had forty or so men hurt last night but none badly and the rest of us were tossed around like medicine balls a couple times. But we're all right.

"We still don't know exactly where the fire started. I'm not certain we'll ever know. The fire probably had been burning for three-quarters of an hour before that ADT alarm went off. Those dumb railroad guys never did call us. The one guy who might have known something useful was the railroad police chief, Cornelius something or other. He got blown up, so no help there."

"Any chance of arson, Chief?"

"None, Commissioner," said the fire chief who had enough troubles and quickly changed the subject.

"But I got to say, those railroad engineers did one hell of a job getting a lot of those freight cars out of here. If they had gone up too, you would have had a lot more dead people. The cops got banged around too. They think that Doherty kid is dying."

"Doherty?"

McGurk interrupted. "James Doherty. From the 3rd Ward.

Works out of the 2nd. Been on the force five or six years. One of the first men on the scene."

Hague said, "Okay. I know who he is. I know his family. He's got some kids, doesn't he?"

"He does, Commissioner. One and one on the way. He married Theresa Butler."

"Yeah, I remember now. Her father is a pain in the ass. Doherty was lucky to get on the force."

McGurk said, "They weren't married then but it looks like his luck is running out now."

"I'll go to the hospital and see him."

"That would be appreciated, Commissioner."

Hague was looking around and started to move off. "Commissioner," said the fire chief, "I got to warn you. This is still a dangerous fire ground."

Hague smiled. "But not as dangerous as the neighborhood we grew up in, eh Tommy?"

"Probably not. But let me have a couple of boys take you around."

Hague said, "No. Keep them working, Chief; I'm proud of your fire department. The men did a great job. You did a great job. I knew you would when I gave you the job and you came through. I'm proud of you. I won't forget it. And to think just a couple of years ago, those firemen were a bunch of slobs sitting around playing pinochle."

"Those assholes are gone, Commissioner. Most of these men owe their jobs to you."

"Just so," said Frank who, meticulous in manner, immaculate in dress, leery of risking his health, plunged into the piles of debris. He shook hands and thanked each man he could reach. Soon they were coming to him forming a crowd around him.

Hague was no speechmaker. He just kept saying: "Thank you, boys. You did good. Real good. I won't forget you."

McGurk watched, smiling. *He's working the room. Good old*

Uncle Frank never misses a chance to nail down some votes.

That night, at supper, scores of firemen and cops were telling the story to their wives. "And Frank Hague says to me, 'Billy,' he says, 'You did a good job. Real good. I won't forget you.'"

"Does that mean you'll get a pay raise?"

"Ah, Annie. Leave it alone. The poor man has a lot more to worry about than me what with half the waterfront blown to bits."

"Thank God, you weren't blown to bits yourself."

Back at City Hall, Frank Hague was doing something he had never been seen to do before. He was reading the newspapers. Slowly, skipping over the big words, but reading nonetheless.

Mickey's friend, Jackie Farrell, did a grand job. First he writes that statement for me, then it turns out he's been feeding stuff to the New York reporters all night. That's what those reporters do. They go to the local guy and he sets them straight. Farrell's all right.

In the long career to come, this morning was probably the high point in Frank Hague's relations with the press. He came off looking like a prudent statesman who was justifiably angry at the incompetents who, through their negligence, had caused this unprecedented accident.

He probably liked best a front page story in the New York Sun. It told of the arrests for manslaughter and then went on:

"Jersey Justice scarcely ever moved so swiftly and so unexpectedly as putting the blame on the three officials. The first consequence came after the day's investigation of the earth-shattering explosions had established—so far as is possible in the time—these facts:

"The blaze was not of incendiary origin. Nothing adduced in the hunt for causes showed the least presence of a plot against the Allies to whom the immense store of ammunition was consigned.

"None of the numerous guards employed by the Lehigh had occasion for this kind of alarm for months."

That last bit's bullshit. But Farrell couldn't know that. I wonder what 'adduced' means?

The New York Time's coverage was less colorful than the Sun's but it was packed with facts. Facts close to unintelligible to the average man in Jersey City let alone Frank Hague. The Times' circulation was negligible there. It took a cop a half hour to find a copy for Hague.

Hague worked his way through the headlines on one front page story:

"Glass Damage Exceeds a Million;
Few Downtown Buildings Escape
Insurance Companies Prepare to Pay Heavy Losses, While Small
Property Owners Who Are Unsecured Suffer Heavily
—Strange Freaks of Blast Are Seen."

Too bad, thought Frank Hague, exhausting his store of sympathy for Manhattan's commercial community.

The New York newspapers were estimating the total damage at from $20 million to $30 million with the Times going with the lower figure, still a staggering sum.

The Jersey Journal said fifty were believed dead and twenty-one were hospitalized in Jersey City. Hague knew of three dead although the young policeman had just been given the Last Rites and was not expected to live out the day. The Journal put the damage at $75,000,000. But then the Journal was not considered a paragon of accuracy. That they managed to get out an "Extra" was a minor miracle.

Hudson County Prosecutor Robert S. Hudspeth called the explosions a "criminal conspiracy" and Governor James F. Fiedler was outraged too. He called the railroad companies' actions "barbarous." Both blamed the companies for negligence.

Hague was well pleased but was fast tiring of reading when

his secretary opened the door. "Commissioner, there is a long distance call for you from Washington, DC."

"Who is it?"

"He wouldn't say but he did say that he was certain that you would want to talk to him."

"Okay," said Hague, taking the receiver off the hook, "I want to hear you hang up, Terry. Don't try to eavesdrop. It'll cost you your job. Do you understand me?"

"Yes, sir," said Terry Lynch, a disappointed secretary. Hague waited for the click.

"Commissioner Hague here."

"Good day, Commissioner. Joe Tumulty here."

"I thought it might be you calling, Joe."

"First off, my condolences, Commissioner. I understand you have a few people dead and a large number injured."

"Yeah, lots of people got hurt but only three or four are dead that we know of. A young cop is dying as we speak."

"I'll pray for him."

"Thank you, Joe."

"That said, congratulations are in order, Commissioner."

"Congratulations? Jesus, Joe. Half the waterfront is gone, people are dead, most of the windows in the city are blown out. Black Tom is gone. I don't know what there is to be congratulating me about."

"Yes, you do, Commissioner. All that damage would have been there no matter what you did. I'm congratulating you for the way you handled Black Tom. It was masterful, Commissioner, masterful. From going to Washington to warn Congress of the danger to arresting those imbeciles for manslaughter, you did the right thing. Masterful, I tell you."

"Well, thank you, Joe," said a well pleased Frank Hague who was far from immune to flattery.

"The president joins me in this appraisal, Commissioner," said Woodrow Wilson's secretary and close political advisor.

I'll bet.

"Apparently those reforms you enacted in the police and fire departments paid off too. I'll wager this insures that you will be elected mayor come next May. That is, if we get through November successfully, of course."

"What do you mean, Joe?"

"I don't have to tell you that a catastrophe like this could cost everyone involved their jobs if it isn't handled properly. It could even cost Woodrow Wilson the presidency."

"Good God, Joe. How the hell could that happen?" Hague was perplexed.

"I'll get to that in a minute, Commissioner, if you will be patient with me. But first, let me ask you a question or two."

"Sure."

"Who is in charge of the investigation?"

"I've got Lieutenant Mickey McGurk and his squad heading up the investigation but they are just starting to dig into it."

"Can you trust McGurk?"

Hague's antennae were vibrating. "Completely. He's my nephew by marriage and I'm godfather to his son."

"Good. How is the investigation going?"

"Okay, I guess. There's not a hell of a lot to investigate. The railroads fucked up. Period."

"Very good," said Tumulty. "No possibility of arson, I suppose?"

"None."

"Very good. Tell me, how did the initial fire start?"

"We're not sure. Tom Boyle tells me...you know Tom Boyle?"

"I do. A competent man," said Tumulty.

"Anyway, Boyle tells me that we may never know how it started. The railroad guys didn't call the fire department. They tried to handle it themselves. An ADT alarm went off after the fire was burning for about forty-five minutes. When our guys got there, it was burning in three or four different places."

"Three or four different places, eh?"

Hague said, "Yeah, but it doesn't matter how it started; it was caused by negligence, Joe. Negligence. There have been lots of small fires at Black Tom, even explosions, this one just got out of hand. It was the fucking railroad that did it, Joe. You know how sloppy they are, the cheap sons of bitches. Won't spend a dime on safety, Joe. Not a dime."

"Indeed, Commissioner. Still, it is vital you totally control this investigation, Mr. Hague. You must control the information your people come up with and who learns what from them."

"Why is that, Joe?" asked Hague, who instinctively controlled everything he touched.

"No doubt you are correct. The railroad and its agents were negligent. That's what your investigation shows and should show. The different companies involved will help you on this. They will start blaming each other. In fact, that will start happening very soon."

"How come?"

"Liability, Commissioner. Liability. Many millions of dollars were lost at Black Tom and elsewhere. Someone has to pay and it won't be the insurance companies if there is still an unemployed lawyer anywhere on the Eastern seaboard. Black Tom will launch almost as many lawsuits as it did shells, Commissioner. Watch, the companies involved will even start suing each other."

Hague said, "I see. Yeah, I understand. In fact, if that cop dies, his family is going to sue the Lehigh Valley. John Milton will help them do it. But what does that have to do with the election in November?"

Tumulty said, "Nothing, sir. As long as Black Tom continues to be a regrettable accident caused by negligence. But let's suppose something else emerges. This is purely hypothetical, mind you."

Hypotheti—what? What in hell does that mean?

"What if your investigation uncovered a plot? A successful

plot on behalf of a foreign power to blow up Black Tom. All that damage, all those deaths and injuries on American soil. What then?"

Hague was appalled. "Dear God. I don't know."

"Since we are playing 'what if', I'll hazard that I do know, Commissioner. The president of the United States would have no choice but to ask Congress to declare war on that foreign power. The American people would demand it. The fact that America is not ready to go to war would be immaterial, Mr. Hague. Woodrow Wilson would have to go to war. Now, as a practical politician, do you think President Wilson could be re-elected some weeks from now on the platform, 'He Almost Kept Us Out of War?'"

Hague didn't even smile. "No, I don't," said Hague, who really didn't care.

Tumulty said, "Now, do you think, that the aftermath of such a gloomy scenario might even hurt your chances next May?"

Hague, who most assuredly did care about that, was silent. Tumulty laughed.

"But of course, all this is a mere exercise of our morbid imaginations. You have to deal with reality, Commissioner. And the reality is that Black Tom was caused by the criminal negligence of the railroad and others. Your investigation will prove that."

"It will, Mr. Tumulty."

"I know it will, Mr. Hague."

Hague asked, "Do you want me to keep you up to date on how the investigation is going?"

"No, Commissioner. Not at all. I will be more than content to leave those inquiries in your very capable hands. I shall be very busy preparing for the campaign. By the way, how is it going with your organization?"

Hague said, "Not bad. You know my organization isn't perfect yet, especially outside of Jersey City. But we are making progress. We'll be ready to go in November, at least in Hudson County. You can tell the president that."

"I will," said Tumulty. "It's going to be a hard fight. Hughes is very strong in the East. It would be a pity to lose New Jersey although I admit it almost always votes Republican in a big way. Of course, Roosevelt will be vigorously campaigning against President Wilson. He hates him."

I'm with Teddy on that. "I'll do my best, Mr. Secretary."

"I know you will, Commissioner."

Tumulty thought, *I don't think he knows 'Mr. Secretary' is an honorific reserved for cabinet officers. No chance of me getting into the cabinet. Not as long as the president is married to a woman who hates Catholics. Never been a Catholic in the cabinet anyway.*

"Now I must say 'goodbye.' Once again 'congratulations' but please think about what I have said: 'He Almost Kept Us Out of War' won't do."

"Right you are, Mr. Secretary."

Hague pondered what Tumulty had said. He went to the door and addressed Terry Lynch.

"Terry, is Mickey McGurk in the building?"

"He is, Commissioner."

"Get him up here now."

Hague asked, "Mickey, who else besides you are going to be looking into Black Tom?"

"The railroad, the warehouse company, the lighterage people for sure. The insurance people. Anybody who lost money. Lawyers and maybe cops from Trenton and Washington and maybe the Feds. Lots of people. Why?"

"Mickey, I want you to control this investigation. Tight as a drum. When anyone wants to know what happened at Black Tom, I want them to go to you. Tell them no more than you want them to know."

"Again, Commissioner, why?"

Hague tilted his head and looked at McGurk as if he was a moron.

"Mickey, Mickey." Hague shook his head. "Have you ever heard of a thing called an election? I hope so because we have two big ones coming up. My future—and yours—depends on how they go. Now I don't care who you put on this but everything comes back through you. There's going to be one record and you are going to keep it. We know now what happened at Black Tom but we don't know all the details. I don't want any of those details to come back and bite us on the ass on Election Day."

I should have known it. Frank Hague. Always thinking about politics. When the world comes to an end, Our Lord better be ready for the question, "What does this mean for the election, my Lord?"

"Do you understand me?"

McGurk said, "I think I do. Can you give me an example of a 'detail' I might keep under my hat?"

"Okay. Supposing you find out the cop on the beat was drinking and smoking with the watchmen and he threw his cigar butt into a boxcar full of TNT. Are you going to call a—what is it—a press conference?"

"Gotcha, Commissioner."

"Mickey. You run into anything out of the ordinary. Anything. You bring it to me first and we'll decide how to play it. Okay?"

"Yes, sir."

"Now. I want you to go over to the city and see your pal, Captain Tunney. Tell him what we got and find out if he knows anything we don't. Feed him everything we want him to know. You're aware he's got cops nosing around in Hoboken?"

McGurk said, "I do." *I'm the one who told you.*

"Make life easy for them. Tell them what's going on. No sense them digging too deep into this."

"Right," said McGurk.

"One more thing. I don't want anybody to know what you are doing."

"Oh. Got any ideas how I do that, Commissioner?"

"Sure, boyo. Use your charm. It works for me."

What Will Wilson Do?

In embassies and chancelleries throughout the world, men studied the speech Woodrow Wilson gave after accepting the Democratic re-nomination for president in September.

He excoriated the Republicans, lauded the Democrats and laid out his domestic agenda for the coming electoral campaign.

Then he got around to foreign affairs.

Wilson said, "In foreign affairs we have been guided by principles clearly conceived and consistently lived up to. Perhaps they have not been fully comprehended because they have hitherto governed international affairs only in theory, not in practice. They are simple, obvious, easily stated and fundamental to American ideals.

"We have been neutral not only because it was the fixed and traditional policy of the United States to stand aloof from the politics of Europe and because we had no part in either action or of policy on the influences which brought on the present war, but also because it was manifestly our duty, if it were possible, the indefinite extension of the fires of hate and desolation kindled by that terrible conflict and seek to serve mankind by reserving our strength and resources for the anxious and difficult days of restoration and healing which must follow, when peace will have to build its house anew.

"The rights of our own citizens of course became involved: that was inevitable. Where they did this was our guiding principle: that property rights can be vindicated by claims for damages and no modern nation can decline to arbitrate such claims; but the fundamental rights of humanity cannot be. The loss of life is irreparable. Neither can direct violations of a nation's sovereignty await vindication in suits for damages. The nation that violates these essential rights must expect to be checked and called to account by direct challenge and resistance.

It at once makes the quarrel in part our own. These are plain principles and we have never lost sight of them or departed from them whatever the stress and perplexity of circumstances or the provocation towards hasty resentment. The record is clear and consistent throughout and stands distinct and definite for anyone to judge who wishes to know the truth about it.

"The seas were not broad enough to keep the infection of the conflict from our own politics. The passions and intrigues of certain active groups and combinations of men among us who were born under foreign flags injected the poison of disloyalty in our most critical affairs, laid violent hands upon many of our industries, and subjected us to the shame of divisions of sentiment and purpose in which America was contemned and forgotten. It is part of the business of this year of reckoning and settlement to speak plainly and act with unmistakable purpose in rebuke of these things, in order that they may be hereafter impossible."

Then Wilson took Mexico to the woodshed claiming that his invasion of that country was "no violation of that principle" of national sovereignty. He bullied, cajoled, lamented and pontificated about Mexico but made no mention of when his troops would leave. Latin America trembled.

In Berlin: "So what do you think, Herr Minister?"

Arthur Zimmerman answered. "All talk and no action, as usual—except for poor Mexico." He thought for a moment. "It may be that there will be real opportunity for us in Mexico some day."

Making the Rounds

Captain Tunney's voice boomed out as Mickey McGurk walked through the door.

"Aha. The boy lieutenant from Jersey City. Sit down, son, sit down."

"Thank you, sir."

"Jesus. You got anything left over there to talk about?"

"Not at Black Tom, Captain, but the rest of the city is okay, mostly; we just lost a lot of glass."

"Ha. You lost glass. We had more plate glass broken in one square block than you lost in that whole rinky-dink town." McGurk ignored the insult.

"The sanitation department is hauling truckloads of broken glass away from the financial district. Every clown that can put a hammer to a nail is busy boarding up windows so the insurance guys don't jump out of them. The entire city is scared shitless wondering what is going to blow up next across the river. The mayor's unhappy. The chief of police is unhappy. I'm unhappy. You got any good news for me?"

McGurk said, "Well, there's nothing left in Jersey City to blow up. And the commissioner—you know, Frank Hague—is going to introduce an ordinance forbidding anybody from bringing munitions into Jersey City. The cops are going to seal off the city."

"Wonderful, I can hear that barn door slamming shut. The railroads aren't going to give up. They'll manage to get that bad stuff to the ships in the harbor. There's too much money to be made."

"Well, they're not going to move any more of that bad stuff through Jersey City," said McGurk.

"Why doesn't that cheer me up? How's that cop doing?"

"He died overnight, Captain."

"Shit. Give my condolences to his family, will you?"

"I will, thank you."

Tunney asked, "What about your investigation? Do you know what caused that first fire?"

"Not really. Maybe it was caused by sparks from the smudge pots the watchmen used to fight off the mosquitoes. Who knows? But the one thing we're certain of is that it was an accident."

"Yeah. That's what my people tell me too."

McGurk said, "In the end, it will be the negligence of the railroad, the docking company and the warehouse people. There's nowhere else to put the blame."

Tunney said, "Your boss was smart to charge those idiots with manslaughter."

"Yeah. And they won't be the last ones charged either."

"That's good to hear. My bosses want blood," Tunney said.

"I wrote up a report on our investigation so far, Captain. And I have a copy of what Commissioner Hague brought to Washington with him. The Lehigh Valley has had fires and explosions at Black Tom going way back. I thought you might like to look at both."

Tunney said, "I would, thanks. It will help with the report I have to send up to the mayor. You're pretty smart—for a kid. You know, it's funny. My first thought when I heard the explosion was that the Wobblies did it."

"The Wobblies? Why would you think that?"

"Why wouldn't I think that? We've been arresting them by the hundreds in the last couple of days. They're in up to their ass in the Third Avenue Railway strike. The cloakmakers' strike too. And they helped trash that wop newspaper, you know. I figured they wanted revenge for the arrests. And they're against the war to boot.

"I even had my people search police headquarters for bombs. They're great ones for the bombs. But then Jersey City kept blowing up and blowing up and I says to myself, 'That wasn't no

Wobbly bomb.' No, sir. Besides, I've got people close to the Wobblies and they say their leaders spent the night drinking and singing union songs. They were as surprised as anybody when the bombs began bursting in air."

"I'll bet," said McGurk.

"Thanks again for the report, Mickey. I appreciate it. Let me ask you for one more favor. If you run across anything that suggests that it might be arson or anything other than an accident, let me know at once. Okay?"

"Sure, Captain. In fact, here's your first piece of oddball information. Rumor has it, the railroad is going to claim that the first freight car went up because of spontaneous combustion."

"Spontaneous combustion? Is that possible?"

"Not according to my old chemistry teacher who fell down laughing when he heard it."

Tunney said, "Don't you love the railroads? What ever happened, it wasn't their fault. God's maybe. But not theirs. What a thieving bunch of bastards. Say, did you take my advice and make contacts inside those loony groups who want America in this war one way or another?"

"I did but there's nothing going on that you don't know about." Tunney didn't correct him.

Tunney said, "If I were you, I'd check with them again, you never know what they pick up. Most of it's nonsense but once in a while there's something useful buried in the bullshit."

"You think I might pick up something about Black Tom?" asked McGurk.

"Naw. I doubt that. But all that ammunition blown sky high might give those mutts ideas. You know, copycats."

"Nothing left to blow up in Jersey City, Captain."

"No, Mickey, but it's a big harbor. I'd appreciate hearing about anything you pick up."

McGurk's next stop was the Dougherty Detective Agency to find out the names of the four guards who were at Black Tom that night.

He was told politely but firmly that the client was the British government and there was no way Dougherty's people were going to give him the time of day without an order from a Federal court.

"It was an accident," he was told, "leave it at that."

Maybe the British Consul would give him more, but not Dougherty. The Union Flag was hanging outside the Consulate.

Too high to be pulled down.

After a short wait, Mickey was led to a small office where a tall, thin, impeccably dressed, youngish man rose to greet him. "Lieutenant, I am Charles Beauchamps. How may I help you?"

Mickey told him.

"Oh, dear, I am afraid I am going to have to disappoint you, sir. Any reports from that agency are highly confidential. Haven't even seen them myself. Wartime, you know. Everything's hush-hush. But if there was anything nasty in them, I think I should have heard.

"Still, if you feel you must see them, there might be a way. Go through your State Department in Washington. If your ambassador in London asks His Majesty's Government for a look see, it's possible he would be given access. He would pass the information back to your State Department and then you could ask your own people in Washington."

"Oh, that sounds easy," said McGurk.

"I am sorry I couldn't have been of more help, Lieutenant. I'm afraid protocol forbids it. You have my condolences on the death of that constable chap."

"Thank you, Mr. Beechum. His name was Doherty too, you know. Just spelled differently."

"Really? Well, I am sorry. Do you suspect the explosions at Black Tom were other than an accident?"

"No. Not at all. We're just trying to find out what caused the fire," said McGurk.

"Quite. Well, in any event, while we are very sorry all that ammunition was lost, His Majesty's Government was not directly involved."

"No?"

Beauchamps said, "It seems that most, if not all, of those munitions were consigned to Russia. Thankfully, ours passed though, without event, last week."

"Okay, Mr. Beechum. Thank you, for your time."

"Not at all, Lieutenant. Feel free to drop by for a chat anytime. Here, let me give you my card. I'd love to get your opinion on a number of things."

Am I being recruited to be a British spy? Would I get to hang around some limey Mata Hari? Too bad I'm a married man.

"Yeah. I might just do that. But I have to get back to police headquarters right now."

"Of course."

Mickey made his way back to Jersey City and changed into old clothes before heading to Black Tom.

"You look like a ragamuffin on Thanksgiving Day," said Hannah.

"And you look like an angel sent down from heaven to make me a nice lunch before I head back to work."

"You'll get a sandwich and thermos like everybody else but there'll be something nice waiting for you when you get home."

"I'll try not to dwell on that or I won't get any real work done this afternoon."

Mickey and Hans Mannstein were in the car heading Downtown. "Hans, let's stop by the White House Tavern before we go to Black Tom."

"Good. I could do with a beer myself."

The two Zeppelins were nursing beers and talking to the bartender who said, "What a night, Mickey, I thought we'd all be blown up before it was over. The blast knocked all the bottles down back of the bar. Broke them. Windows too. And it cracked the big mirror too." He pointed. "See?"

"I do."

"I tell you, it was a misery. It started off normal enough for a Saturday night. Good crowd. Everybody having a good time. Not even a fight. And then…"

The bartender clapped his hands together. "Boom! Lord, did we get busy after that. Everybody. Cops. Firemen. Engineers. Sailors. All manner of people. O'Shea woke up his wife and daughter and put them to washing and drying glasses. We were that busy. I had never seen the daughter before. Good looker…for an O'Shea."

"Tell me, Eddie. Before the explosion, were any of the watchmen in for a drink?"

"Sure, Mickey. They're always in for a snort and sometimes a half-pint."

"Who was here that night?"

"Let me see. It was a brutal night, the faces are all blurring together but I think Bozo Fitzpatrick was in just before everything went to hell."

"Fitzpatrick? Is that Mary's husband?" asked McGurk.

"No, a different Fitzpatrick. I don't know his wife's name."

Mickey described a different Fitzpatrick. "Tall—fairly thin—about fifty— gray hair— scar across his nose?"

"That's him. A good enough fellow," said the bartender.

Mickey said, "I know who it is. Have you seen him since?"

"Sure, he was in for lunch. Him and them other watchmen are helping with the cleanup."

"Thanks, Eddie."

Bozo Fitzpatrick was easy enough to find. He was concealed behind a pile of debris shirking work. Mickey told Hans to try to track down the other watchmen and question them.

"Hey, Bozo. How ya doing?" Bozo rose, sizing Mickey up.

"Fine. Yourself?"

"Never better. I'm Mickey McGurk. Do you mind if I ask you

a few questions? You're not in any trouble. I just have a few questions about the night of Black Tom." That's what they were calling it in Jersey City.

"I've heard of you," said Fitzpatrick, instantly wary. "You're one of them Zeppelins."

"Not today," said McGurk. "Just poking around in the ashes seeing if we can figure out what happened."

"Well, I can't help you with that. I'm just a watchman. I didn't see nothing."

McGurk said, "I'm sure you didn't. But you know, it's a funny thing, sometimes you see something and you ignore it. But then you remember it later when somebody asks. You know what I mean?"

"Yeah. But I still didn't see nothing."

"Bozo, why are you acting so nervous? Are you sure you didn't see anything—anything at all—before the fire engines came and you took off?"

Fitzpatrick had no intention of telling a cop—or anyone else—about putting out a fire underneath a boxcar and not reporting it. He pulled on his nose. "I'm not nervous. I'm just thinking."

"Good. Think hard."

It came to him. "Wait a minute. I did see something. But it don't mean nothing."

"What?" asked McGurk.

"I'm pretty sure I saw two guys in a row boat. Off the end of the wharf. But they weren't headed for Black Tom. They was going the other way."

"When was that?"

"I don't know. Maybe around midnight," said Fitzpatrick.

"What do you think two guys were doing in a rowboat around midnight?"

"I don't know. Crabbing, maybe?"

"You see any crab nets?"

"Too dark to see much."

"So you didn't call out or talk to them?" asked McGurk.

"No. No reason to."

"Okay. Anything else? Think hard."

Fitzpatrick pulled his nose. "No. Nothing. Just I saw one of those guys off a lighter walking ahead of me when I went for a drink."

"Did you recognize him?"

"No."

"Then how do you know he was off a lighter?" asked McGurk.

"Who else would be walking around the yard at that time of night? Say, Mr. McGurk, do you think we'll lose our jobs over this?"

"What do you think?"

Fitzpatrick pulled on his nose. "I think I better look for another job."

"Good thinking."

McGurk caught up with Mannstein. "What have you got?"

"Nothing," said Hans.

"Me neither," said Mickey.

They spent the rest of the day talking to watchmen, firemen and switch engine people. Nothing.

"Okay. Hans, let's call it a day. Tomorrow, I want you and Tony to contact your confidantes and see if they've heard anything about Black Tom."

* * *

Tomorrow came quickly. McGurk had breakfast with Fat Jack Lynch down in the 'Show.

"You gonna eat that that last piece of toast, Mickey?"

"No, Jack. Help yourself."

"Thanks."

McGurk said, "So, you don't know anything about Black Tom?"

"No, why should I? They don't hire longshoremen and they certainly have no use for a man in weights and measures. By the way, I'm sorry about Doherty. I know his family. Good people."

"Thanks. So no Irishmen work at Black Tom?"

"Sure they do. Some of them are going to lose their jobs because of this. Some of them got hurt. They're not happy," said Lynch.

"Any of them have any idea how the fire started, Jack?"

"Not that I heard of. Some sort of accident, they say."

"Okay. So I wasted my money buying you breakfast, did I?"

"Sure the pleasure of my company must be worth a hundred breakfasts, Mickey."

"At a minimum, Jack. Say, aren't the Brits going to hang that Sir Roger Casement today?"

"They already did. The miserable bastards. Everybody. The Pope. The Senate of the United States. Everybody begged them not to do it but they did it anyway." Lynch's jaw tightened. "But they'll pay for it, Mickey. They will."

"So you don't put any store in those Black Diaries with those homosexual escapades?"

Lynch said, "I had more than just a suspicion of that when I met him and that weird bunch in Manhattan before the war. But I don't see how sucking somebody's dick means you can't be a patriot. It's just British propaganda. Just like those stories of the Germans raping nuns and bayoneting babies in Belgium. Bullshit. Besides most of the fairies in Ireland are leprechauns."

"I think, technically, that fairies and leprechauns are totally different genres of mythical beings," said McGurk.

"You know, Mickey, sometimes I don't have any idea of what you are talking about. I think you stayed in school too long for your own good."

Mickey laughed. "You're probably right about that, Jack."

Lynch finished the toast. "Let's talk American politics, Mickey. They are of more interest to me these days. We have two big elections coming up and I intend to make my reputation working for your uncle's organization. I think you know I'm engaged to Maureen Corcoran, Al Murphy's daughter, and we're going to get married right after the elections. She's a wonderful woman Mickey and I love her. And, I might add, she's young enough that we just might have some more kids. If we don't, so what, I love her daughter, Gracie, as much as I love her."

"Good for you, Jack."

"I'm hoping for an even better job after the elections. I'll have a family to support then. When the time comes, Mickey, will you say a good word to your uncle about my work with you?"

"I can and will, Jack Lynch."

* * *

Hans Mannstein met with Tunney's men in the Clam Broth House in Hoboken. "So what's going on?" he asked.

"You mean besides half of Jersey City getting blown up?"

"Yeah, you guys hear any scuttlebutt on that?" asked Mannstein.

"Apparently some people got careless with some smudge pots. That's what I hear."

His partner chimed in, "Me too."

The senior New York cop stopped slurping his clam broth and said, "The Huns are happy as hell about Black Tom. They say it's like winning a big battle without firing a shot."

"Yeah? Well, we lost a copper. We're not so fucking happy," said Mannstein.

"We heard. Sorry about that. Did he have a family?"

"He did. One kid and another on the way."

"Tough." They finished their meal in silence.

As they were leaving, the junior cop looked at Mannstein and said, "You know, Hans. I never did ask you. Who do you want to win the war?"

"I don't give a shit. It's not my fucking war," said Hans Mannstein.

Peggy was with Tony when Hans talked to her.

"Look, Peggy, I know you are never going back to West 15th Street but could you talk to that Mena Edwards and see if you can pick up any scuttlebutt about Black Tom?"

Peggy looked at Tony who nodded. "All right. I'll give her a call. Say, you don't think any of those Germans over in the city had anything to do with Black Tom?"

"Nah!" Hans answered. "It wasn't sabotage, just stupidity."

Abie the Jew was sipping hot tea from an ice cream soda glass when Tony Aiello walked into the drug store in Kearny.

"Abie."

"Mr. Policeman."

Tony sat down. "You know Abie, I can't keep calling you 'Abie the Jew.'"

"Why not? I'm not a Jew anymore?"

"It's not respectful. It's like somebody calling me 'Tony the Wop.'"

"It's not the same."

"It is when some people say it," said Aiello.

"Such a philosopher. All right, so you want to know my last name? What's the matter, my dossier is incomplete?"

"Abie. Abie. Give me a break."

"All right, Mr. Tony Who-I-Won't-Call-a-Wop. My full name is Abram Aaronovich Ashansky. There. Happy? The man at Ellis Island, an Irisher I think, said I would do better in America if I was 'Al Shannon'. I don't think he could spell Ashansky."

"To hell with him, Abie. Ashansky is as good an American name as Shannon."

Abie said, "So you called me here to discuss names beginning with 'A'?"

"Well, Mr. Ashansky. Abie. Just checking to see if there was anything happening in your fruitcake community I should know about."

Abie sighed. "I don't think I'll ever get used to it. Poor people mocking the very people who would help them. The only people who would help them. No, Mr. Policeman, there's nothing I should warn you about. No, nothing. Of course, the anarchists are delighted all that dynamite blew up before it could kill workers in Europe."

"Did you hear anything else about Black Tom?"

"No. Just that they hope the explosions cost the capitalists millions."

"Any sympathy for our dead cop?"

"None. But let me say, I'm sorry for his poor family. Thanks to you, I have learned that not all policemen are bastards. Almost all, but not all."

"Well, thank you, Mr. Ashansky. Then let me make your day. Go tell your fellow Marxists and crazies that almost all that ammunition was already paid for—by the Czar."

"Truly?"

"Yes."

Abie the Jew smiled.

The Battle of Carrizal

What Wilson did not mention in his acceptance speech was the Battle of Carrizal in Mexico ten weeks earlier.

Troopers of the 10th Cavalry Regiment, the celebrated black Buffalo Soldiers of the old Frontier, were deep in Mexico along with thousands of other American soldiers trying to close in on the revolutionary brigand Pancho Villa who had raised hell in New Mexico.

General John "Black Jack" Pershing, the leader of the American expedition, was informed that Villa, who had been seriously wounded weeks before in a skirmish, could be captured at the town of Carrizal.

He sent about one hundred Buffalo Soldiers, commanded by their white officers, to investigate but, instead of Villa, they found four times their number of soldiers loyal to General Venustiano Carranza, the man Wilson recognized in 1915 as the legitimate president of Mexico but had bickered with ever since.

Because of an earlier slight to their honor, the Mexicans had orders not to permit the Americans to move any further south. This conflicted with the orders given to Captain Charles T. Boyd who talked it over with the Mexican commander, General Felix Uresti Gomez. The Mexican wouldn't budge.

Captain Boyd's orders didn't mention Mexican sovereignty and the Mexicans weren't the only ones with a sense of honor so he told the general he was coming through anyway.

The Buffalo Soldiers, erect in their saddles, weapons at the ready, advanced towards the Mexicans. Shots were fired. Then fusillades from both sides. General Uresti Gomez fell dead as did Captain Boyd.

When the wild melee was over, twelve American cavalrymen were dead and twenty-three men and their horses were captured. Mexico lost forty-five men. The rest of the two troops of the 10th retreated back to their base, the junior officer in charge himself wounded.

General Pershing was furious and asked Wilson for permission to attack the Carrancista garrison at Chihuahua. He was refused.

President Woodrow Wilson demanded that the American prisoners be released. His demand was described as "peremptory." That meant war if the Mexicans refused.

President Carranza, who had agreed to allow the expedition into Mexico to chase Villa, had been pressing Wilson to pull the troops out arguing that the Villa threat had diminished. He warned that the continued American presence would eventually force the Mexicans to defend themselves. Now it had happened.

The American press was in full bloodlust and Congress was not far behind. Much of the country was bellowing for Mexico to be punished.

The Mexicans gave in and the prisoners were released. That didn't end the uproar. There were reports that some of the American dead had been executed by their less disciplined foes after the battle.

Wilson downplayed the incident. In one speech he inundated his critics with a plethora of platitudes as was his wont. In another, to the New York Press Club speaking of Mexico, he said "force never accomplished anything that was permanent."

The Imperial German General Staff took note.

Kristoff

Captain John J. Rigney was enjoying a quiet morning at Bayonne Police Headquarters when the desk sergeant told him that an Anna Chapman wanted to see him.

"She said she was a friend," said the sergeant.

"Friend of my wife's but show her in anyway."

He rose to greet her. "Good morning, Anna. How are you?"

"Fine, John."

He pulled a chair away from the wall and put it in front of his desk. "Sit down and tell me what brings you in to see me on this lovely morning."

Anna fidgeted a bit in the chair. "I don't know where to begin... but I think my mother's cousin blew up Black Tom."

Not another one. This makes three. One Irish, one German, both drunk. God knows how many Jersey City has had.

Rigney looked dead serious. "What makes you think that, Anna?"

"He told my mother he did it."

"When was that?"

Anna looked at the captain triumphantly. "On the very night of Black Tom itself. When he finally got home."

"Was he drunk?" the captain asked.

"Well, it was Saturday night. But he wasn't falling down drunk. My mother said he kept saying, 'What have I done? What have I done?'"

What he probably did was wake up with some bohunk cow sleeping on his arm. Enough to send anybody over the edge.

"Okay, Anna. Let me make some notes here," he said, looking for some paper and a pencil.

Anna took this for complete vindication. Her mother didn't want her to go to the police and said she wouldn't say a word against her own flesh and blood.

"Okay. Now what's your cousin's name, address and how old is he?"

"He's not my cousin. He's my mother's cousin. His name is Michael Kristoff, 76 East 25th Street. I think he's twenty-three or twenty-four. He's from Hungary but he's a Slovak—like us. I don't like him."

Rigney looked up from writing. "Why's that?"

"He used to board with me. He was always late with the rent. He boards with my mother now. I think he's taking advantage of her."

Rigney asked, "Did your mother tell you anything else?"

"Yeah, she said he did it with two men in a rowboat and he got paid $500."

"Hmmm. A rowboat? Who paid him?"

"I don't know."

"Anything else?" asked Rigney.

"Yes. Momma said he quit his job six months ago and has been traveling all over the country and when he got back he had lots of money."

Rigney asked, "Is that all?"

"Isn't that enough? He blew up Black Tom."

"Well, Anna," Rigney said, "you know how fussy these lawyers are. We might have to get a bit more evidence before we can ship him off to jail and hang him. We'll keep an eye on him. Meanwhile, Anna, you stay away from him and don't tell anyone you came to see us. That's very important. He might get wind of it and ruin our investigation."

"I understand, John. Will you say 'hello' to Sheila for me?"

"I will, Anna. Take care."

Captain Rigney had no intention of wasting time on what sounded like a drunken drifter to him but he was a man known to hedge his bets. He recognized prudence as a virtue. He gave Kristoff's particulars to a new detective but didn't tell him about Anna's visit.

"Follow him around for a couple of weeks. See what you can find out."

"What do you suspect him of, Captain?"

"Nothing special. I just think he's a bit shady. See if he's up to something."

"Yes, sir."

The detective was back in two weeks. "Well?"

"Nothing, sir. He works at an oil company in Jersey City. He gets drunk on Saturday night. He watches his money, not a big spender. He sleeps in on Sunday. I don't think he has a girlfriend. I don't think he takes a bath once a week. He talks about when he was in the Army but nobody listens to him. He's not very smart, sir. If he's up to anything, I didn't tumble to it."

"Ah, well. Sometimes the old instincts are cockeyed. Thanks, Detective." Rigney didn't let it go. He decided to arrest Kristoff for "loitering" and turn him over to the Jersey City police.

Let them deal with him. We have enough creeps in Bayonne.

He told Lieutenant Mickey McGurk everything he knew about Michael Kristoff.

"What do you think, Captain Rigney?"

"Frankly, Mickey, I don't think there's a chance in hell that there's anything to it but I thought you people would like to come to that conclusion yourselves."

McGurk said, "My commissioner ordered me to make an absolutely thorough investigation. So far I don't think any of the half-dozen people who have confessed to blowing up Black Tom did it. Two of them, unhappily, didn't even know where it is."

Rigney laughed and shook McGurk's hand. "Well, good luck, Lieutenant. I'm sure the railroad will be delighted if you can pin it on someone else."

Kristoff was seated placidly in a holding cell. McGurk watched him for a minute or two before a turnkey took Kristoff to a small room where Mickey could interrogate him alone.

Well, he certainly doesn't look like much. Average height, average weight, blue eyes, red hair, brownish red moustache, ruddy complexion, high cheekbones, cheap clothes that look as though he slept in them, shoes that need new heels. Looks like a drifter.

Mickey had gone over all his notes from Black Tom and from the confidantes. He really wasn't sure what he was looking for. *Something to eliminate this nut, that's for sure.*

"You want me to go in with you, Lieutenant?" asked the turnkey.

"Nah, Phil. Just wait outside the door and don't let anybody interrupt me, okay?" Mickey didn't think anything would come of this but there was one thing in Rigney's notes that bothered him. Two men in a rowboat. That watchman had mentioned two men in a rowboat and a lone man walking out of Black Tom in front of him. No policeman liked coincidences.

"I'm Lieutenant McGurk. I want to ask you a few questions. Should I call you Mike or do people call you Christy?"

"Suit yourself."

"You seem to be pretty comfortable being in a police station, Mike. Ever been in one before?"

"Yeah. I had some trouble over in Rye last year. In September."

"Rye, New York? What kind of trouble, Mike?"

"They said I was carrying a concealed weapon. Not a big deal, really. I only had to do thirty days."

"A mere peccadillo, eh, Mike?"

Kristoff looked at him blankly.

"So, do you still have that gun?"

"No, it was more trouble than it was worth."

"Why did you have the gun?"

"I travel a lot and you can't be too careful."

"Tell me about your travels, Mike, especially the trips you took after you got out of jail."

Kristoff thought, *I'm supposed to stick to the truth as close I can but I won't tell him anything important.*

"Could I have a glass of water, Lieutenant?"

"Sure, right after you tell me about your recent travels."

Kristoff concentrated for a few moments. "Well, I was sitting in Penn Station over in Manhattan waiting for a train. I was going to visit my sister in Ohio. This guy comes up and introduces himself. He asks me if I want a job. I ask him what he has in mind."

McGurk asked, "What's this guy's name? The guy who walks up and asks you if you want a job while you're sitting there waiting for a train to take you to Ohio." *Rigney's right. He's stupid.*

Kristoff didn't blink. "His name is 'Graentnor' or something like that."

"What's his first name?"

"He told me but I forgot. I always called him Mr. Graentnor. Anyway, he offered me $20 a week to travel with him. That's good money so I told him I'd take the job. I had to go with him to a batch of cities. I carried his suitcases. Two of them. Heavy. Do the laundry. Buy tickets. That kind of stuff. You, know, like a valley."

You don't look like a valet, Michael my man.

"And then, when we got back, I'm supposed to go to work for him in a machine shop he owns."

"What does this Mr. Graentnor do?"

"He sells motors he re-builds in his machine shop," said Kristoff, who once worked in such a place.

Is he making this up as he goes along? "When did you meet Mr. Graentnor?"

"Early in January."

"When did you get back?"

"June."

McGurk said, "So this Mr. Graentnor pays you $20 a week to carry his suitcases and you travel all over the country with him for what, five months?"

"Yeah."

"An amazing story, Mike. What was in the suitcases besides clothes?"

"Books. Blueprints. Shaving stuff. Things like that."

"Blueprints of what?"

"I don't know. I can't read blueprints."

You'd be lucky if you can read anything, my friend. "Did you look through the suitcases, Mike?"

"Not really. The suitcases were always locked when he wasn't there."

McGurk asked, "What do you mean, 'when he wasn't there'?"

"Lots of times he'd take off and leave me in the hotel room. I didn't know where he went. I'd hang around the room or go down and sit the lobby. Sometimes I'd go for a walk and get something to eat."

"Where did you travel to?" asked McGurk.

"Oh, lots of places. Mostly in the Midwest. Chicago, Milwaukee, Minneapolis, Detroit, St. Louis. We went to Bridgeport and Philadelphia too."

"Okay, are you still working for Mr. Graentnor?"

Now Kristoff looked puzzled and thought for a few seconds before answering. "No, a funny thing happened. We were in St. Louis. He gave me a dollar to go the movies or something. When I got back, him and his suitcases were gone. He just left. So I packed my bag and I left too."

"Who paid the bill?"

"Not me."

"Have you seen him since then?"

"No, but I hope I run into him. I'd like that machine shop job. Twenty dollars a week is nice money."

"How did you get home?" asked McGurk.

"Same way I got there. Took a train."

Kristoff sat there, a pleasant look on his face, as if he had answered all possible questions about his trips. "Could I have that glass of water now?"

"In a minute. I only have a few more questions, Mike. So are you are back at work at the oil company in Bayonne?"

"No, they got pissed at me for leaving. I work for Eagle Oil Company in Jersey City now."

"That's near Black Tom, isn't it?"

Kristoff fidgeted in his chair. "Yeah. Why?"

Mickey ignored the question. "So what do you do when you're not working, Mike?'

"Nothing special. Drink. Try to pick up girls. Go to a party once in a while?"

"In Jersey City?"

"Nah. Women can't drink in the saloons anymore. You have to go across the river for that."

McGurk looked at his notes. Kristoff watched him carefully. "Did you ever go to a party at a brownstone on West 15th Street in the city?"

Kristoff hesitated. *Stick as close to the truth as you can but be careful.*

"Maybe. I went to a party somewhere around there once during the summer. Some German sailor I was drinking with in Hoboken invited me. I had a good time. Lots to drink. Good food. Pretty girls—not that they looked at me. Practically everybody there was German. I speak Slovak and a few words in Hungarian but no German, except to say 'hello' and 'goodbye'."

"So what did you do, sit in a corner?"

"Nah. I ran into two other guys who spoke English and we sat and talked about our time in the service. One guy had been a Marine. He'd been everywhere. The Philippines, Panama, Nicaragua. Me? I never got past Fort Hancock. Coast Artillery. The other guy had been in the German Navy. On a cruiser or something that got sunk in South America. Don't know his name either. The Marine told a very funny story about his people finding a big hotel in one of those dago countries full of Americans dressed up as generals. I tell you I laughed until I cried."

Yankee! Kurt Jahnke. Holy Mother of God.

Mickey McGurk was startled but his appearance gave nothing away. "I'll bet that was some story. What was the Marine's name, by the way?"

"I told you I don't know."

McGurk pressed him hard. "Was his name Jahnke, Kurt Jahnke or did they call him 'Yankee'?"

Kristoff looked frightened. *Jesus. How much does this cop know? Nothing, that's what he knows. He's fishing.*

"I told you I don't know his name. It was just a party."

"Did you meet anyone there nicknamed 'Whiskey'?"

"No and by the end of the night I didn't know my own name, either."

McGurk chuckled and immediately changed the subject. Sometimes that rattled suspects. But not Kristoff.

"Okay. Where were you on Saturday night, July 29th?"

"I don't know. That's a long time ago. Not easy to remember."

"Oh, yes it is, Mike. That's the night Black Tom blew up. Were you at work? Did you see anything? Did you go for a drink at the White House Tavern? Think back."

"Yeah. I remember now. I wasn't at work. We finished work by five o'clock. I wasn't even in Jersey City. I was visiting friends in Yonkers. We were drinking and I didn't get home until very late."

"How late?" asked McGurk.

"I don't know. Really late. I didn't get up until one o'clock in the afternoon."

"Really? Did you talk to anyone when you got home?"

"Yeah. My cousin. I board with her."

"What did you talk about?"

"Nothing much. This and that. I wanted to get to sleep."

"You didn't talk about the explosions at Black Tom?"

"I don't know. I don't remember. I was pretty drunk."

"Who did you visit in Yonkers and where do they live?'

Kristoff gave him a name and an address. McGurk wrote it down.

Without looking up he said, "One more thing, Mike, tell me about the rowboat."

Then he looked up. Kristoff's face was deadpan. He said, "I don't own a rowboat. I don't know nothing about no rowboat."

"Okay," said McGurk.

Mickey was wary of asking him any more questions. He had to think this through. He'd check his alibi and visit the Eagle Oil Company.

"Okay. We'll talk some more tomorrow," McGurk said.

"Can I have that drink of water?"

Mickey smiled and rapped on the door. The turnkey opened it. "Would you get Mr. Kristoff a glass of water? Then put him in a cell by himself. See if he wants anything to eat. If he gets bored, play gin rummy with him."

"Right."

McGurk started to leave. Kristoff's voice stopped him. "Lieutenant, can I ask you a question?"

Mickey faced him. "Sure."

"Why have I been arrested?"

Mickey had wondered if Kristoff would ever get around to that. "You're not under arrest, Mike. We're holding you as a material witness. You're in protective custody."

"But Lieutenant, I don't know anything. I didn't see anything. I don't even know what you are talking about."

"Ah, but that's the problem, don't you see? We have to hold you until we do know what we're talking about."

* * *

McGurk found Hans Mannstein and settled into the front seat of the touring car. "Hans, my lad, we're off to Yonkers, and back to Jersey City."

They arrived at the Yonkers address. "Hans, stay with the car would you? I don't like the looks of this neighborhood."

"Sure, Mick."

The couple at the Yonkers flat knew Michael Kristoff all right but insisted he wasn't there the night of July 29. "No, I tell you he wasn't here. He was here the Saturday before but he didn't show up that night."

"How can you be so sure?"

"Are you kidding? That was the night all hell broke loose in Jersey. The blast knocked a couple of jars of jelly off the kitchen shelf and made a hellava mess. Not only that but it loosened three of my windows. The putty fell off. It's a wonder the windows didn't go too. You think I'd forget that night? He wasn't here."

Hans was dozing when Mickey got to the Ford. "Alert watchdog you are."

"Just resting my eyes, Lieutenant. So what did they say? Did his alibi hold up?"

"Sort of. They say he was here but they seem fuzzy about the details. They were all drunk." McGurk didn't like lying to his friend. He didn't really know why he did it. He just did.

As they drove Hans asked, "What the hell is this about, Mickey? Who is this Kristoff guy? Why are we going to all this trouble? What's up?"

"Nothing at all, Jimmy. Just checking him out like I said. The Bayonne police said a relative told them he was at Black Tom the night of the explosions. I wanted to find out if he saw something."

"How could he see anything at Black Tom if he was in Yonkers?" asked Hans.

"He couldn't. Nah. I think he's just a mope. I just wanted to make sure."

They made their way back to Jersey City. "Hans, why don't you grab something to eat? I want to borrow the Ford. I have a couple of errands to run. I'll be back in an hour or two."

McGurk drove to the Eagle Oil Company and talked to a balding, blatantly bored clerk. "Did Michael Kristoff work until five o'clock on July 29?"

The clerk looked at McGurk and exhaled in exasperation. "I have the timecards in the back. I can look it up if you really think it's necessary?"

"It's probably not necessary but I want you to do it anyway."

"All right," he said. He got up and walked into a rear room muttering, "All these interruptions. It's a wonder I get any work done." He was gone a few minutes and returned.

"Your man didn't work at all on Saturday, July 29. In fact, he didn't come to work for three days before that either."

"Does he still work for you?" McGurk asked.

"I suppose so. He comes and goes as he pleases. I don't know why the foreman puts up with it."

A Place in the Sun

The Danes were not quite sure what to do with their islands in the Caribbean since the sweet days when African slaves cut sugar cane and made rum were long over.

The colony in the Virgin Islands which the Danes had held since the 17th Century was rapidly becoming a liability.

The slaves were freed in 1848 and the widespread production of sugar beets elsewhere undercut the need for sugar cane. Whites still controlled the land but the black population was impoverished. Denmark was pouring money into the islands, not taking it out.

Denmark actually tried to get rid of the Virgin Islands in 1864 after Prussia defeated it in a second border war. The Danes offered to trade the islands for South Jutland but the Prussians were having no part of that.

The United States had shown some interest in the islands as a naval base after the Civil War. The Danes were ready to sell them for $7,500,000, a sum close to the price paid for Alaska which was a vastly larger territory but with a less salubrious climate. The United States Senate balked and the deal fell through.

Negotiations between the countries went on and off for more than twenty years with one side or the other backing off.

Now the Danes feared Kaiser Wilhelm II, German Emperor and King of Prussia. The outbreak of war at sea had severely curtailed communications and trade between neutral Denmark and its island possessions.

The Americans knew the Germans could occupy Denmark anytime the whim took them. If that happened, the Germans also would win a foothold in the Caribbean, a base for their submarines. That was intolerable to Washington.

The Danes, a civilized folk, knew that they should sell the islands if for no other reason than to improve the lot of its people who were becoming more wretched. The only possible buyer was the United States.

The question was how to do this without infuriating the Germans. The Danish foreign minister told the American ambassador in Copenhagen that it was impossible for him to approach the United States on a sale. However, he said, if America was to show some interest in acquiring the islands such a sale might be possible.

Danish neutrality demanded that the negotiations be kept absolutely secret. They were. Ten months later, on August 4, 1916, a treaty was signed in New York transferring the Danish Islands to the United States for $25,000,000.

There was another cost as well. The United States agreed that Denmark could extend its political and economic interests throughout all of Greenland, its other possession in the New World.

Ratification by the United States Senate was swift. The people of Denmark voted in favor of the sale in a nationwide referendum. The only people who didn't have a say in the transfer were the Virgin Islanders themselves. Woodrow Wilson, the champion of self-determination, didn't ask them.

But the Virgin Islanders certainly weren't opposed. America had to be a better deal than far off Denmark. They even became American citizens—in 1927.

A Dark Cloud of Suspicion

Mickey McGurk got home late but his wife, Hannah, had supper in the oven waiting for him. He had little appetite but it grew some as he ate. Hannah was a very good cook. Mickey helped her with the dishes, the only man Hannah knew who would do that, but he was distracted. He looked in on their sleeping son for a minute and then went back to the kitchen where Hannah was sipping a cup of tea.

"Want some?"

"No. I don't think so." He sat down and looked at her, not smiling.

"Okay," she said, "what's wrong?"

"Nothing."

"Nothing?" She rose, poured him a cup of strong, black tea, and put it in front of him.

"Thanks," he said and took more than a sip. "Ah! That's good."

"You know, Mickey, what I like about you is that you are not the strong, silent type. You don't keep things to yourself, you don't pout and you don't hold grudges, at least where your family is concerned. You think it and out it comes. You don't know how much that means to me. That's not how you are acting tonight. You're not just quiet, you're brooding. Something is bothering you. Is it something about me?"

"No."

"The boy?"

"Absolutely not."

"The job?"

Silence.

So it's that damned job. I can't tell him how frightened I am when he walks out that door or how relieved I am when he walks back through it. I knew he was a policeman when I married him. I know he'll be one

418

until the day he dies. That's what I am afraid of.

"I thought you were working full time on that Black Tom investigation?"

"I am."

"So what's the problem? It's pretty cut and dried, isn't it? It was a really bad accident. The railroad was to blame and that's all there is to it."

Silence.

"It was an accident, wasn't it?" Hannah asked.

Mickey looked at her for a second or two and said, "Yes. Sure. Everybody agrees it was an accident."

"But?"

This is a hell of a note. I can't even talk to my wife about it. I can't talk to my best friend about it and he's a copper. I have to lie. I hate this.

"It's just that there are some loose ends. You know we want an airtight case proving that the railroad was negligent."

"Yes, you've told me that."

"The reason the case has to be airtight is that if we leave even a slight opening, the railroad's lawyers will drive one of their locomotives through it."

"So you have to make sure the case is perfect?" Hannah asked.

"No. No case is perfect. There are always some loose ends. But this time we have to work harder to tie them up."

"So you're worried about those loose ends?"

McGurk said, "Yeah, I'm worried. There's a lot of pressure on me. I've just got to think things through."

Hannah was satisfied. "Well, I'll leave you to it then."

"Nope. I'm off to bed with you. I'll let my brain work while I'm asleep. Sometimes you wake up with the answers."

No such luck. At breakfast, Hannah asked, "Well, did you come up with any answers?"

"Well, my brain is telling me to just keep plodding, tie up the loose ends as we find them and finish up the damned investigation and maybe, by then, there won't be anything left unanswered. The railroad was negligent, the railroad will pay. I'm sorry I'm in such a bad mood; I'll make it up to you when this is over."

"Don't fret, sweetheart. I understand. Will those men you arrested go to prison?"

"No. That was just to convince everybody we were serious. They'll never go to trial. These are going to be civil cases, not criminal ones."

"So then you'll be finished with Black Tom?"

"Right," he lied.

* * *

Mickey McGurk's office at police headquarters was just big enough for a desk, his chair, a lamp, a hat rack, a filing cabinet with a lock and two uncomfortable wooden chairs so his squad could be there at the same time. It was decorated with a photograph of Hannah and Francis on his desk and a calendar on the wall.

Mickey had two or three file folders on his desk. He was very intent on them. Every so often he would peck out a sentence or two with two fingers on an old typewriter that sounded like a small pile driver. As he typed, his suspicion grew. *Too many coincidences. Too many inconsistencies. Too many lies.* They added up to one big doubt that scared the hell out of him.

His office door was locked. Someone knocked on it.

"Hang on a second." He took the sheet out of the typewriter and put it in his pocket. The folders went the file cabinet which he locked.

When he opened the door, Tony Aiello said, "Good morning, Mickey. What the hell are you doing in a locked office?"

McGurk looked around before he answered, "Cooping. What did you think?"

"Oh. Didn't get enough sleep last night, huh?"

"Nope."

"Lucky you." Mickey just winked.

"You said you wanted to go over to City Hall. Are you awake enough to see the commissioner?" asked Tony.

Mickey slapped Tony on the shoulder. "If I'm not, I'm sure your driving will get the old heart pumping."

"Very funny, Lieutenant."

Lieutenant McGurk was ushered into Commissioner Hague's office.

"Do you mind if I lock the door, Commissioner? I don't think you will want to be interrupted when I tell you why I am here."

"I don't like the sound of that but go ahead."

Hague pointed to a chair in front of him. "Skip the small talk, Mickey. Get right to the point."

"Yes, sir. You told me that if I came across anything unusual about Black Tom I was to come directly to you."

"I remember."

"Well, I've come across bits and pieces of information that lead me to believe there's a chance that what happened at Black Tom was not an accident."

McGurk waited for Hague's reaction. Hague intertwined his fingers and pressed his lower lip together with his two index fingers. Then he spoke. "Arson?"

"Maybe."

"Who?"

Now McGurk paused, choosing each word carefully. "Could be German saboteurs. Three of them."

Hague exploded. "Jesus, Mary and Joseph! Do you know what you are saying? Four people dead. Hundreds injured. Millions in property damage. A railroad yard destroyed. Half of New York frightened to death. If there was ever a reason to go to war, that would be it. The Germans couldn't have been that stupid. Could they?"

"You wouldn't think so. But..."

"Who have you told about this?"

"Nobody."

"Not even your wife? Tony Aiello? Hans Mannstein?"

"No. Nobody. You were very clear on that. I was to come to you first."

"Well, thank God for that. What makes you think the Krauts might have blown up the place?"

McGurk pulled the quarter-folded sheet of paper out of his inside jacket pocket and put it in front of Hague who fingered the sheet. "Is this the only copy of whatever it is?"

"Yes."

"Good," Hague said as he tore the sheet into small pieces and handed them back to McGurk. "Put them in your pocket and burn them when you get a chance."

"Yes, sir."

"From now on, nothing goes on paper. Okay?"

Hague had calmed down. "Now tell me what was on that piece of paper, Mickey."

"Well, Commissioner, first let me tell you what we haven't learned at Black Tom. There are two things that really bother me.

"First, the top people in your fire department can't agree on how the fire started. When you are done listening to them you might conclude that the fire started in three or four separate places. Accidental fires don't start in three or four places but arson certainly might.

"Second, I'd like to know what the chief of the Lehigh Valley Railroad police was doing at Black Tom at that time of night."

"Wouldn't he be there because of the fires?" asked Hague.

"No. Cornelius Leyden was blown up in the first explosion. It simply wasn't possible for him to leave his home in Pennsylvania and get to Black Tom between the time when the fire was reported and the first explosion. He had to be there all along. Why was Van Leyden there? Why was the railroad police chief in a 'dead yard', a hundred miles from home on a Saturday night? Why can't I find anyone who can answer that question? That situation, by itself, raises suspicions. Now let me give you some background before I get to specifics of what else is bothering me. Okay?"

"No more background than I need."

"No, sir. After you went to Washington, you told me to team up with Captain Tunney in New York. He advised me to infiltrate any group that might give us trouble because of the war. Remember that Tunney had tumbled to the fact that the Germans were using Irish longshoremen to put chemical time bombs on British ships. So I developed sources in German, Irish and radical groups."

"Yes, I know. Why didn't you go after the British and the Allies?"

"No sense in it. They didn't have a reason to cause trouble; they were buying a lot of food, munitions and war supplies from us. They figured if we got into the war, it would be on their side."

Hague said, "They are right. Go on."

"So all we were getting were odd scraps of information. Seemingly useless at the time."

"I caught 'at the time'. What about now?" Hague asked.

"One confidante, a girl, went to some parties and dinners big shot Germans threw over in Manhattan and came up with three nicknames, 'Yankee', 'Christy' and 'Whiskey' among other things. I noted them although I did not have proper names to go with them.

"Then after Black Tom, I interviewed a watchman who I felt was holding something back. What he did tell me was that he thought he saw two men in a rowboat off Black Tom and another unknown man walking out of Black Tom just before the first fire was spotted."

"Not much to go on."

"No. There really was nothing to point to anything but

carelessness. Then the Bayonne police turned a guy over to me. A relative had claimed that he had told her mother that he bombed Black Tom. Supposedly he said he did it with two other guys in a rowboat. Got paid $500."

Hague's brow wrinkled. He asked, "Don't they call that hearsay?"

"They certainly do. Not very creditable."

"Don't you get a lot of false confessions?"

"We do, but this guy never confessed. The Bayonne police followed him for two weeks. Nothing."

"So why the fuss?"

"His name is Michael Kristoff. Then there's that bit about two guys in a rowboat that watchman told me about. Bayonne didn't know about that. What do you think a guy with a name like Kristoff would have as a nickname? Christy, maybe?"

"Thin."

"It is. But I questioned him and then checked out his alibi for the night of Black Tom. It didn't hold up. I don't know where he was but he wasn't where he said he was. When I was questioning him he told a lot of wild stories but he admitted to going to one of those fancy German parties and meeting a former Marine. They got to telling sea stories and the Marine tells a funny one about capturing a hotel full of Americans dressed up as colonels and generals. In Nicaragua."

"So what?"

"Commissioner, I was with the Marines who found those phonies. Me and my bunkmate helped escort them to the ship that took them to New Orleans."

He paused. "My bunkmate was a German immigrant named Kurt Jahnke. We called him 'Yankee.' Now I have to wonder why he was always taking photographs of the progress we were making on the Panama Canal. What do you think?"

"I don't like what I am thinking. Where is this Kristoff character now?"

"In a jail cell over at the station house. He's probably playing gin rummy with the turnkey who is the only one who gets to see him."

"Did you arrest him and book him?" asked Hague.

"No. I just put him in a jail cell and locked it. He didn't complain which is another reason why I am suspicious."

"You know none of this is hard evidence that would stand up in court?"

McGurk said, "I know. But you see where this might lead if serious people get to probing Mr. Kristoff and Black Tom in depth?"

"I do and I don't like it. If the Germans blew up Black Tom, America would have to declare war on them. There would be no way out of it. Wilson probably wouldn't get re-elected. Remember what I said about the slogan, 'He Almost Kept Us Out of War'? It might even hurt my chances to become mayor in May. Win or lose, if our investigation of Black Tom leads to war, that vindictive bastard will campaign against me. He's done it before and I lost."

Mickey struggled to keep calm. Really struggled. "Don't you think there might be things more important than your election, Uncle Frank?"

Now Hague appeared startled and struggled with the concept. Really struggled.

Finally he asked. "What do you mean?"

McGurk said, "America was attacked. Americans died on their own soil. Americans were injured. Millions in American property was destroyed. If Germany did that, do you think we should cover it up because it jeopardizes some political ambitions?"

Hague, who was not articulate but who was very quick witted, answered, "Of course not. But America isn't ready to go to war. Our Army is still chasing Pancho Villa. Your Marines are down in Haiti. We don't have a draft like those European countries. Who's going to fight the war if we have to go into it now?"

"I don't know," admitted Mickey.

Hague said, "On the other hand, if we can hold out maybe the war will end before we get pulled into it. I can't figure out what they are fighting about anyway."

McGurk said, "Being attacked on your own soil seems like a good reason."

Hague changed the subject. "How do we know that this Kristoff is telling the truth or if he is capable of telling the truth?"

Mickey thought for a couple of seconds. Hague did not interrupt him.

McGurk said, "Well, we could call in an alienist to examine him."

"What the hell is an alienist? Someone who works with immigrants?"

"No. An alienist is a doctor who specializes in diseases that affect the mind."

Hague said, "Oh, he deals with crazy people? That's the ticket, Mickey. This guy is probably crazy and we can chalk off his wild talk to a crazy man. Is there anything else bothering you?"

"Yes, consider the timing of the explosions. They go off in the middle of the night when they would cause the fewest deaths and injuries. Maximum damage with the fewest consequences. Maybe the incredible damage wasn't expected either. Think about that."

* * *

McGurk, choking down his misgivings, telephoned the physician he was told was the most expensive—and discreet—alienist in Manhattan.

"You want me to cross the river to Jersey City and examine a criminal?"

"That's about it, Doctor."

"Do you realize how much my fee would be, young man?"

"How much, Doctor?"

Dr. Hamilton Pearson didn't get rich ignoring unexpected opportunities. "I couldn't charge a penny less than $500 considering my time, expenses, and loss of practice."

"Done. When could you come?"

"How about this afternoon, Lieutenant?"

Mickey said, "I'll see you at two o'clock." And he gave the alienist directions to the station house from the ferry.

The doctor looked every inch a successful physician. Right down to his gray spats.

"It would help, Lieutenant, if you would tell me what you would like to learn," said Dr. Pearson. McGurk certainly wasn't going to do that.

"We just want you to evaluate his mental condition and estimate his intelligence. You might ask him what he knows about Black Tom. I want to know if we can believe what he says."

"I will." The examination took little more than an hour.

"Ah, Lieutenant. I don't think our Mr. Kristoff is really mentally ill although he does have delusions of grandeur. The stories he tells. However, I would say that he is of limited intelligence and is easily led. I wouldn't think he has much initiative himself. Yes, you could call him a bit feebleminded but not dangerously or criminally so. As for believing what he says, I conclude that Mr. Kristoff thinks his fantasies are true."

That's a big help.

"That fits in with our suspicions. What about Black Tom?"

"I don't believe Mr. Kristoff knows the gentleman. Or least what he had to say didn't make any sense."

Shit.

"Very good. I can't thank you enough, Doctor."

"I'll write up my report right after I get back to New York and mail it to you."

"That won't be necessary, Doctor. You told us what we needed to know. We'll not be troubling Mr. Kristoff much longer. Now about your fee, Doctor. Police stations don't deal with checks; will cash be acceptable?"

"Indeed."

"If you don't mind giving us a signed receipt?"

"Not at all. What should I put down as the subject matter?"

"Oh, 'Mental Evaluation of Michael Kristoff' and the date should do it." *That should cover our ass.*

The doctor followed instructions and handed the receipt to Mickey. "There you are, Lieutenant. Now don't hesitate to call if you need my services again."

"I will, sir." *This is the last you will be hearing from me, you overpaid quack.*

Hague was pleased with the alienist's evaluation. "I knew it. The guy's a nut. There's nothing there. Mickey, stay on your game. If you hear of any other investigator nosing around Kristoff, get back to me at once."

"I doubt that it will come to that. I'm practically writing their reports myself. Of course I don't know what the railroad is doing."

"I do. The railroad, the lighterage company and the warehouse people are busy suing each other. They're all accusing each other of negligence."

Mickey said, "Well, then neither you nor President Wilson have any problems with Black Tom." Hague ignored the sarcasm.

Hague looked at McGurk. "How about you, Mickey? Are you satisfied?"

"Sure," Mickey McGurk lied.

He knew who he had to see next.

Father McBride said, "You know, Mickey, every time the beadle says you're here to see me I want to hide in a closet."

"I thought we were old friends?"

Father McBride said, "We are, but you have a predilection for moral dilemmas."

"I have another one. But this one has to be discussed under the seal of the confessional," said McGurk.

Father McBride sighed and reached for his stole as Mickey got down on his knees. After Mickey finished his recitation of a variety of minor sins, Father McBride suggested they move to comfortable chairs. "There's no canon law that requires us to be in agony for a confession to be valid."

Mickey McGurk told Father McBride everything he and the commissioner had discussed plus he recounted the alienist's evaluation of Michael Kristoff.

"I see your dilemma. There's not much to go on now but if you and others dig hard enough and deep enough you might uncover a plot on the part of the Germans to destroy the munitions at Black Tom and, thus, Black Tom itself. That is a 'casus belli.'

"Now if the United States would declare war on Germany because of Black Tom would it be a 'just war'? Based on what you have told me, it would meet the three conditions set down by St. Thomas Aquinas."

"I thought you Jesuits didn't put much stock in Dominicans?"

"We make an exception for Aquinas. But other theologians down through the centuries have elaborated on Aquinas' basics for a 'just war.' If you dig more, you might prove that the damage caused by Germany was 'grave, lasting and certain.' The 'lasting' is a bit 'iffy' except for the deaths. The munitions have already been replaced, no doubt.

"There is one trump card in the argument though. If the people are against the war, the war is illegitimate. Do you think the people of the United States are ready now to go to war over Black Tom?"

McGurk said, "I don't know. But I think that discovering the death and destruction at Black Tom was caused by German sabotage at Black Tom might change public opinion overnight.

Remember what happened when those soldiers were killed and captured in Mexico? People were frothing at the mouth."

"Germany is not poor, powerless Mexico. But I see your point. Your dilemma deepens. Still I agree with Mr. Hague that America is not ready for war and the people don't want to go to war either. So whether Black Tom was caused by culpable negligence or deliberate intent the lesser evil is to go to court and not to war. We must always choose the lesser evil, Mickey, when confronted with a greater one."

"So just what court do we drag Germany into, Father?"

"There isn't one," said Father McBride. "Still, I think you are morally justified not to pursue those inquiries any further in hopes of serving the greater good. We ultimately may go to war but I don't think we must do it now." Father McBride had not commented on Wilson and Hague's electoral problems.

McGurk said, "I'm not so sure. But thank you for the discussion. I have a lot to think about. So what do I do now, say a Good Act of Contrition and wait for you to give me a penance and absolution?"

"Yep. For your penance say three 'Hail Marys' and take your next moral dilemma to somebody else. *Te absolvo...*"

Taking his leave, Mickey asked, "By the way, Father, who do you want to win the war?"

"That's easy," said Father McBride. "I want England to lose, I just don't want Germany to win."

Mickey headed back to the station house to cut loose Michael Kristoff. The desk sergeant intercepted him.

"Lieutenant, I got a guy here who wants to make Kristoff"s bail."

"Bail? We haven't even arrested him. I was about to let him go."

"Well, that's what he said."

"Okay, send him back to me."

Mickey sat behind his desk as a nondescript man walked in.

"What can I do for you, sir?"

"My name is David Grossman and I want to put up bail for Michael Kristoff."

"Oh, are you friends?"

"No. I don't even know the man but his co-workers down at Eagle Oil say he's a great guy and they sent me here to bail him out." Mickey didn't know Grossman worked for the Lehigh Valley Railroad who had hired him to watch Kristoff. The railroad had gotten a whiff of a rumor wafting west from Bayonne.

"The bail is $50. Pay the desk sergeant and I'll bring Mr. Kristoff to you."

Kristoff and the turnkey were playing cards. "Okay, Mike, everything you said checks out. You're out of here. We'll let you know if we have any other questions."

"Can I leave town?"

"Sure. Why not? Check with me when you get back."

Kristoff's relief was obvious. Mickey led him out to Grossman.

The desk sergeant approached. "What am I supposed to do with this $50 bail money, Lieutenant?"

"I don't know. Give it to your favorite charity."

"I know just the one," said the sergeant, putting the money into his pocket.

The Killing Fields

Woodrow Wilson had pressured the Germans into abandoning unrestricted submarine warfare after the French cross channel steamer Sussex was torpedoed with a substantial loss of civilians.

Admiral Reinhardt Scheer, the new commander-in-chief of the High Seas Navy, sent some of his Unterseeboots into the Mediterranean where there were many lush targets and others went to work laying mines. But the admiral remained an advocate of unrestricted submarine warfare. He was convinced Germany could win the *handelskrieg*, the "business war", at sea.

He secretly sent a force of seventy U-boats into British waters in the autumn of 1916. The subs sank 300,000 tons of British shipping in a few months. The British were alarmed, Wilson was not. It wasn't unrestricted submarine warfare; it just threatened to starve Britain to death.

In June, the Germans used phosgene gas for the first time, killing and blinding hundreds. The British and the French quickly retaliated, sending the gas casualties into the thousands. It was months before effective gas masks reached the soldiers on either side. Photographs of lines of blinded soldiers, their left arms on the shoulders of the men in front of them, horrified the world but didn't stop the gassing.

The British introduced a new weapon designed to win the bloody Battle of the Somme. The armored tank was impervious to small arms fire and its metal treads allowed it to grind down the barbed wire fronting German trenches.

Once inside those defenses, the tank, with a crew of eight serving two cannons and four machine guns raked the trenches with bullets. Thanks to the tank the British re-captured six villages.

The British were well pleased.

"There's nothing can stop those tanks, is there, Sarn't-Major?"

asked one Tommy.

His company sergeant-major, looking upwards at rain-swollen clouds, said, "No. Except maybe ... mud."

He was right. The British offensive ground to a halt in a morass of mud. Even the infantry couldn't move.

Germany began construction of the Hindenburg Line on September 23, a massive system of defense designed to protect her Western border.

The great Russian offensive stalled on September 30 on the Eastern Front. Four Russian armies had attacked along a 300 mile front and captured 350,000 Austro-Hungarian soldiers. The Germans pulled twenty-four Divisions from the Western Front and hurried them to the aid of their beleaguered allies. Crippled by the lack of reserves, the Russian attack was blunted. The Russians had suffered a million casualties. Morale plunged. Unrest spread back in Mother Russia.

Slovakia was ruled by Hungary and its men were drafted into the Austro-Hungarian army. Slovak casualties were heavy both on the Eastern Front and in Italy where at the Battle of the Piava River, close to 70,000 Slovak soldiers were killed. The people of Slovakia were outraged when village church bells were confiscated and melted down to make cannons. Nationalism, always warm under the surface, started to percolate in Slovakia.

Millions were dying in the killing fields of Europe and people were dying one by one as well. On October 15, the French executed Mata Hari, a Dutch exotic dancer. She was convicted of being a spy for Germany.

Well, That's That

The many investigations of Black Tom changed character as the days and weeks passed. The criminal investigations petered out. The civil suit investigations intensified. The goal of all the insurance companies was simple: collect premiums, deny benefits. *If it looks like your client is liable, move heaven and earth but find someone else to pin the blame on or find someone who, at least, shares some of the liability with your client.*

Mickey McGurk was at the center of all the investigations. Passing information. Withholding it. The insurance investigators amused him. Many of them were old coppers. None of them were inclined to do much legwork when they could have access to McGurk's file of past fires, explosions and mishaps at Black Tom. Nor were investigators employed by various lawyers more diligent.

He never heard the words he most feared: "Maybe it wasn't negligence."

Federal investigators had approached McGurk about Black Tom too. He found them to be condescending, arrogant and particularly inept. McGurk sensed that the way to control them was to defer to them. He would say, "No, I insist you work out of my office. I can use the squad room," or "I doubt that you gentlemen need any help from me but I do have some files if you think they could be of any use." They ate out of McGurk's hand.

Frank Hague was pleased indeed when Lieutenant Mickey McGurk read him a sentence from a story on Black Tom that appeared in the New York Times.

Quoting Bruce Bielski, chief of the Bureau of Investigations of the United States Justice Department, the story read: "There is nothing to justify action now by the Department of Justice. Our investigators seem to think that the explosion was an accident."

"I agree," said Frank Hague. "Let those greedy bastards eat

each other alive in court. Mickey, you did a terrific job. I owe you and I won't forget this. You should be proud of yourself."

Mickey McGurk wasn't so sure. None of his dark questions had been answered to his satisfaction. But he would go along with the decision to pursue them no further.

The Congress of the United States was adamant. Washington still thought Jersey City was an "appropriate port" for exporting expensive explosives. Not so, said Commissioner Frank Hague, the director of public safety for Jersey City, who pushed an ordinance through the city commission by a 4-1 vote banning the railroads from bringing munitions and explosives into his city.

Thus Jersey City's cops stopped incoming freight trains and checked them for things that go bang in the night. The railroads did not challenge the ordinance, neither did the Federal authorities. It was a pleasant interlude for the policemen, engineers, firemen and brakemen many of whom knew each other and enjoyed a chat. No explosives were found.

Black Tom itself was abuzz with activity. The cleanup job was massive. Long strings of gondola cars hauled debris away. Hundreds of laborers dismantled the piles of refuse that once were the heart of Black Tom. Frequently, unexploded shells were unearthed and everyone would scatter. Army ordinance people would examine them and announce the shells had no fuses and were harmless unless exposed to extreme heat. They were put in separate piles and carted off at the end of the working day.

Mickey had a vague uneasiness about Bozo Fitzpatrick, the Black Tom watchman who had noticed two men in a rowboat and a lone walker that night.

Does he know more than he says? Who has he talked to? Where is he? Is he a problem? McGurk decided to check.

The White House Tavern overflowed at noon. The owner was shrewd enough to put out a "free" lunch featuring a number of tasty but very salty items. Beer flowed freely and less than a quarter-barrel of it easily covered the modest cost of the lunch.

Lieutenant Mickey McGurk asked the bartender, "Have you seen Bozo around?"

The man standing next to him at the bar responded. "Bozo Fitzpatrick?"

"Yeah, that's him."

"Bozo's gone. Lost his job with the railroad. He's gone to Far Rockaway out in Queens. He has relatives there."

"Too bad. I liked Bozo," said McGurk.

The drinker said, "Well, you were one of the few. I have to think there's no work in Far Rockaway otherwise Bozo wouldn't go near the place."

"There is that," said the bartender.

Mickey thought, *Well, that's that.*

He was still having trouble sleeping, tossing and turning through the night. Hannah was very worried. "Mickey, you're going to ruin your health. Forget about Black Tom. Ask them to put you on some other case."

"I can't, my love. I've got to see it through to the end. I'll get to bed earlier."

"That's not the problem and you know it," said Hannah.

Work continued on clearing the debris from what was once Black Tom. Tony Aiello ran into what he now considered a friend at Black Tom. There he was, stripped to the waist in the warm sun, tossing metal into a gondola car.

"Abie! Abe Ashansky. How you doing, pal? You look like the strongman practicing for the circus."

"Life is a circus but I'm not the strongman. I'm a clown. One of many, but still a clown," said Abie the Jew. Abie wiped his hands on his work pants. They shook hands.

"It is good to see you too, Mr. Aiello."

"C'mon, Abe. It's Tony. Mr. Aiello is my father."

Abie took off the large handkerchief tied around his neck and wiped his brow. He was tan from the sun. "Of course. Tony. Yes. Hello, Tony."

"I thought we were friends, Abe."

"I'm trying, Tony. I'm trying. But I've hated policemen all my life. And now I find that one is among the few friends I have in this country. It's not easy, my friend."

Tony laughed. "Hey, Abe. I'll bet you'd win a popularity contest among those nutty radicals you hang out with."

"You'd lose, Tony. They don't like me much. I was trained as an advocate—a lawyer—I like to absorb both sides of an argument before I make up my mind or take action. Them? Don't bother looking, just leap. They argue, they split hairs, they quote sources more infallible than any holy book. Then they spit at each other and go off and form another group doomed at birth to split yet again. This is the curse of the radical classes. No. I'm afraid I'll never be more to them than a nudge."

"A nudge?"

"Someone who is a persistent annoyance."

Tony said, "That's stupid. You probably have more sense than all of them put together. They'd do better to listen to you."

"Like you listen to me? So now you're a Marxist?"

Aiello said, "No. But I have learned that at least one of you bomb throwers truly wants to help people like me and mine."

"Such a victory. No, I'm not laughing at you, Tony. Thank you. I treasure what you said. Now do you want to know what I have learned from you, my friend?"

"Sure."

"One. Some—not many—policemen are human beings.

"Two. Maybe America offers more than I expected.

"Three. Because of you I'm going to vote in this election for president. I understand that the smuck I'll vote for won't be elected. But who knows… maybe someday."

"Abie. Terrific. You're a citizen now?"

"Of course. You thought maybe I was going to stay a Ukrainian? Even the Ukrainians insist a Jew really can't be one of them. You people. You take anybody. Even us."

"Okay, Abie. You registered to vote?"

"I don't think so."

"Don't worry, I know someone who will take of that. Do you still live in Kearny?"

"No, I moved to Jersey City. That's how come I'm working at Black Tom. Besides it's easier to get to New York and the people who don't listen to me."

"Even better, my friend," said Tony.

* * *

Lieutenant McGurk made a telephone call to Captain John Rigney in Bayonne.

"Captain. Mickey McGurk here. Just called to see if you have any more lunatics you want us to certify?"

"What? Oh, yeah. That nut job Kristoff. As a matter of fact, Lieutenant, we do. I'd like to send you a couple of jitney loads this afternoon. Okay?"

"No can do. Our alienist retired on what we paid him to peep into Kristoff's brain."

Rigney said, "It must be nice to have money. Our department rents the bullets we store on our belts."

"Seriously, Captain. Have you heard any more from Kristoff?"

"Nope. I don't think he lives in Bayonne any more. I don't know where he is."

"Ah, well. You've got to admit his stories were entertaining," said McGurk.

Captain Rigney responded, "Did you ever hear such bullshit in your life?"

Thus it was that the three men of Jersey City's little bomb squad drifted back to routine police work. A quiet cajoling here, a brisk clubbing there.

They kept up their contacts with their confidantes and with the New York City detectives who still prowled around Hoboken but somehow, after Black Tom, the urgency went out of it. Jersey City had nothing left to destroy.

Mickey had lunch with Jack Lynch but they talked more about the upcoming presidential election more than anything else. The Irish in Jersey City were more interested in baseball and politics than the war.

"I tell you, Mickey," said Lynch, "I think the Democrats are going to do real good in the rest of Hudson County in November thanks to your uncle. I get around because of my job and it's obvious that the organization is getting stronger week by week. Even in places nobody's even heard of like Harrison and East Newark. It's amazing. It's like everyone knows he is going to be boss of the Democratic Party in this state and they don't want to be left out."

Irish-Americans, now that the wave of British executions was over, had banked the fires of hate that were always ready to flare up given the slightest puff of revolutionary leadership. That leadership was in prison perfecting its tactics. It would be heard from again. Still, if asked, the Irish wanted England to lose the war.

German-American enthusiasm for the war had been ground down by two years of blood-soaked combat where success was measured in yards gained per thousands killed. Communications with the old country were completely cut off. There were no letters. They didn't know whether their kith and kin were alive or dead. Dying for the Fatherland didn't seem to be so glorious now.

Friends of the Allies fretted that the alliance would run out of men and money before the Germans. Their hopes of American intervention rose as German U-boats submerged to attack neutral shipping. But just before President Wilson's exasperation would turn to resolve, the Germans would call a hiatus to unrestricted submarine warfare.

American public opinion was still firmly against the United

States joining in the slaughter. Mountains of munitions were still shipped by lighter from elsewhere in the Port of New York to waiting freighters anchored at Gravesend. The slaughter on both the Western fronts was being well fueled and went on unabated. Paid for in advance.

Now that things slowed down a bit, McGurk had time to read the newspapers. It was impossible to get away from the war. It was on the front page of every newspaper that had a wire service including the Jersey Journal.

He would shake his head when he read of the hundreds of thousands of casualties piling up on the Somme.

Why did they do it? Why do those stupid generals keep doing the same thing and getting the same results. It's pure murder. I'm glad I did what I did even if I hate myself for it.

Mickey had even talked to some old Civil War veterans who had braved withering fire at Antietem, Fredericksburg or the Wilderness. They too were stunned by the casualties on the Western Front.

Said one old-timer, "I'll tell you what, sonny, if it had been us out there facing them machineguns, we would have skedaddled."

Mickey had heard from some seaman returning from a trip to Russia that many of the Czar's soldiers on the Eastern Front were leavings the trenches and simply walking home. Their officers couldn't stop them.

Mickey didn't know whether that was true or not. He hadn't read it in the newspapers but then he knew that the news from Europe was heavily censored.

When will this stupid war in Europe stop? When they kill everybody?

He Kept Us Out of War

The campaign to elect a president in 1916 was as hard fought and bitter as any battle on the Western Front and revealed a nation split in half. In the end, 3,800 votes in a single state were all that separated victory from defeat.

Teddy Roosevelt wanted the Republican nomination but gave that up when he came in sixth on the first ballot at the convention.

The Republicans, still seething from the loss to Woodrow Wilson four years earlier, turned to a man who had been removed from politics for six years: Supreme Court Justice Charles E. Hughes.

Roosevelt turned down the Progressive Party nomination vowing to campaign hard for Hughes. Roosevelt wouldn't be party to re-electing Wilson by splitting the Republican vote again. There was always 1920.

Wilson, wildly popular with Democrats, was nominated for re-election on a forgettable domestic platform which culminated with the unforgettable slogan "He Kept Us Out of War."

Wilson was uneasy with that slogan; he feared America would be dragged into the war somehow and he would lose the election. It didn't happen.

The war in Europe was the key issue in the election. It was to be a referendum on Wilson's unwavering commitment to neutrality.

Ironically, Hughes' position was similar to Wilson's; stay out of the war for now while steadily strengthening the nation's armed forces for the inevitable.

That is not how the public perceived it, thanks to that indefatigable campaigner, Teddy Roosevelt. Teddy was colorful and always provided good copy for the wire services and newspaper reporters who trailed him everywhere.

Roosevelt, who despised Wilson and hated his foreign policy of neutrality, was an interventionist who wanted the United States to fight on the side of Great Britain and her Allies. He assailed Germany's supporters for committing "sabotage" in America.

Gradually the voting public saw Hughes as an interventionist too. The idea of joining the Allies had countless supporters. A large portion of public opinion had turned against Germany because of its harsh treatment of civilians in Belgium and France. British propaganda constantly fanned that grievance.

To every criticism, foreign or domestic, the Democrats answered, "He kept us out of war."

Said the Democrats, "The issue is plain: If you want war, vote for Hughes. If you want peace, vote for Wilson." This had great appeal because even many of those sickened by German behavior on land and at sea didn't want America to go to war. The slaughter sickened them more. It was their war, not our war.

Certainly many voters cast their ballots because of other issues raised during the campaign but none could ignore "He Kept Us Out of War." The polls closed East to West in America. The battle seesawed across the country.

Hughes carried all of New England except New Hampshire which went for Wilson by thirty-four votes. Hughes won all the Mid-Atlantic States. The old Confederacy was solidly for the Virginian, Wilson. Five counties in the South gave Wilson one hundred percent of their votes. They split the Midwest, Hughes taking the most populous states. Wilson was strong in the Mountain West and the West Coast, losing only Oregon.

It all came down to California where a powerful state Republican leader felt Hughes had snubbed him during the campaign and gave the candidate only lukewarm support. Wilson barely won California by 3,800 votes taking its twelve electoral votes which gave him a winning total of 277-254 in the Electoral College. The popular vote was Wilson 9,160,000 to

Hughes 8,548,000. But it was the electoral votes that counted.

Far in the future, another candidate would emerge victorious after being awarded Florida's disputed twenty-five electoral votes although the defeated candidate was more popular nationwide by more than a half-million votes.

Voters think they are casting their ballot for an individual candidate—say Woodrow Wilson or Charles Evans Hughes—but they are not. They are voting for a slate of electors who as members of the Electoral College are pledged to vote for either Wilson or Hughes when the college meets after the election. Not that they are required to vote that way, but they almost always do.

The number of electors in a state is the sum of its senators and representatives in Congress. Some thinly populated states have but three. If a candidate wins the popular vote in a state then his electors get to vote for him. Get a majority of electors—267 in 1916—and you became president. No state was irrelevant no matter how small. Big states were crucial.

California was decisive.

The Dress Rehearsal

The quadrennial Presidential election campaign traditionally kicked off on Labor Day with politicians marching in parades and giving less than sincere speeches about how they revered the working man. Traditionally the working man took such speeches with a grain of salt. One man they believed and revered was the labor lawyer Clarence Darrow. He said, "I have been a friend of the working man for fifty years. I'd rather be his friend than be one." No politician he.

The organization Frank Hague was building block-by-block, precinct-by-precinct, ward-by-ward, city-by-city had been hard at work long before Labor Day. It started work the morning after the polls closed at the last election.

Hague understood that politics in a big city was a fulltime business. His people filled needs and granted favors on a daily basis and collected political IOUs from those voters on Election Day. That was the basis of his strength. But in big elections, like the one in November, 1916, Hague needed to do more than just win. He wanted to rack up a huge majority in the county. That would be the basis of his strength beyond Hudson County.

To do that, the organization had to attract voters beyond its own ranks and those of its clients. Not one voter in a twenty was swayed solely by the planks in a party's campaign platform. Most would identify with one party or another. It was the others, independents, who would provide the makings of a landslide.

A good campaign had to reassure its hard core adherents that they had made the right choice, convince independents to join them and, if possible, persuade some of its foes to defect. The organization had to provide the bandwagon they would jump onto. It had to stage events that were as entertaining as they were effective. The organization would do this as often as possible in as many places as possible.

In an era when newspapers were the only mass medium, reporters would attend these events and write about them thus multiplying their reach. The press, in America, always treated political contests as horse races with the candidates as colorful jockeys. These political events were to take as many forms as the organization's leaders could devise. Some were dramatic like torchlight parades and mass rallies. Some were sedate like picnics, outings or the event that was staged in Pohlman Hall in The Heights designed to bolster Woodrow Wilson's vote. The Germans liked family events. German-Americans formed the majority in The Heights although other groups were growing in numbers.

* * *

The day was lovely. It was a warm day in October. The trees in the beer garden were golden and red, their spent leaves fluttering down, but they still offered some shade. Later in the afternoon the shadow of the building itself would cover the entire garden. The ladies would reach for a light sweater. The men's suit jackets would keep them warm.

Sophie and Otto Ganz and Amelia McGurk shared a table. Little Otto—Frankie—Little Frank or Francis ran around vigorously with his cousins.

Otto Ganz called out, "*Machen Sie nicht zu nahe an die Wand, Otto.*"

The little boy answered, "Ja, Opa."

The odds against a normal sized two and a half year-old falling over a four foot high brick wall were formidable but Mickey was glad his father-in-law was keeping an eye on the boy.

Mickey and Hannah were sitting with Peggy and Tony Aiello. The Mannsteins were nearby. The food was good and the beer better.

Frank Hague arrived around one o'clock with his entourage

which swelled the crowd appreciably. He headed directly for Mickey's table. His companions headed for the other tables.

Mickey called out, "Frankie, come here." He had to repeat himself but the boy finally ran over to the table. "Frankie, you remember your Godfather, Uncle Frank?"

"Yes, Daddy."

He reached out and shook Frank Hague's hand. "How do you do, Uncle Godfather?"

Everybody including the usually dour Frank Hague laughed. "I do very well, Little Frank. I have something for you." He handed the boy a silver dollar.

The boy's pupils dilated. He knew what a silver dollar was but he had never had one of his own. "Can I keep it, Uncle Godfather?"

"You can indeed, Little Frank, I'm that happy to see you again."

Frankie ran off to show his trophy to his cousins, whose reactions ranged from jealous to resentful. One seven year-old wondered if he could get away with snatching it. Seeing four policemen he knew within twenty feet, he decided against it. That was the last time he would let the cops intimidate him from walking off with an easy piece of change.

Hague moved on to the grandparents. "Amelia. We don't see each other often enough. Mr. and Mrs. Ganz, how nice to see you again."

Otto had stood and shook Hague's hand. "Mr. Commissioner, I hear good things about you and not just from my son-in-law either."

"Thank you, Herr Ganz. I hope you remember that not only next month but on Election Day next May." Everyone in earshot nodded.

"I will. I will."

Amelia said, "Aw, Frank. You look grand. How are you feeling?"

"Not as well as I'd like, Amelia," said Hague fingering the high collar surrounding his throat. "I'm prone to sore throats, even when it's warm."

Sophie said, "You should try some of that Vicks Vapo-Rub, Mister Hague. Maybe that would help."

"Thank you Mrs. Ganz. I will try that," said Hague who already had applied enough Vicks to grease the skids at the launching of a small ship.

"Now, if you will excuse me, I will say hello to a few of our other friends. I can't stay long. I've got to get to some other places before the day is done. It's going to be a tough election. Wilson needs every vote I can get for him."

Otto Ganz said, "I can remember when Mr. Wilson was no friend of yours."

"You have a good memory, Herr Ganz. But that's all water under the bridge. We're the best of friends now. Remember, 'He Kept Us Out of War'."

"Ja. There is that, so you have my vote," said Otto. Several of his friends murmured in agreement.

"Thank you, Herr Ganz."

Hague was not a comfortable campaigner. He was neither a glad-hander nor much of a speechmaker, and his syntax often collapsed just sentences after he opened his mouth. But he tried to look dignified, like a strong leader, and in that he succeeded. His passage through a room was more like royalty than a rising politician.

What Hague was superb at was organization. Where he learned its principles is unknown although they were unlikely to have been taught to him before his abrupt ejection from the 6th grade.

As usual, he started at the table immediately to the right of the head tables and worked his way around the garden counter-clockwise. As he approached a table, one of his people who had been sitting there chatting would join his group and impart some useful information.

Hague who had to be coached on names rarely forgot a face. "Mrs. Aiello, you look as beautiful now as you did at your wedding. That was a wonderful day. But I didn't get a chance to ask you then, Peggy, didn't we meet someplace before?"

Tony suppressed a giggle.

Peggy, straight-faced, said, "No, sir. But I do recall I saw you once before at some kind of gathering somewhere. A long time ago."

Hague said, "I'm sure that's it. I never forget a face. Well, thank you for the help you've been to my Zeppelins here. Nice to see you both again. Gentlemen."

"Sir."

Hague knew his organization rested on its ability to grant or withhold favors. His code to his secretary was simple. If he wanted something done, it was "Take care of this, Terry." If he wanted something delayed or doomed, it was "Look into this for me, Terry." Gratitude was showered on Hague; resentment was Terry Lynch's lot. Not a heavy cross to bear for an ambitious young man.

When Frank Hague left, the crowd thinned out quickly. But those who remained enjoyed the rest of the day. The organization picked up the tab. More than a few decided to vote for Wilson—and Hague next year.

* * *

On Election Day, Jack Lynch was heading to the polling place early with Barney Mollahan in tow. Barney, well into his eighties, was not steady on his legs. He had served in one of New York's infantry regiments in the Civil War and had been wounded at Gettysburg. He lived on a small Federal pension with a bit of help from his children who were growing old themselves.

As soon as they arrived, his poll watcher caught Lynch's eye and motioned him to a corner.

"Jack, I don't know what to do," said Barry Crowe, a pleasant man who avoided confrontation when he could.

"See that college kid over there nosing around? He's with something called the Honest Ballot Association and he's got a letter from the state attorney general. It says he has a right to be here. I don't want him here. I'm afraid he's going to spook the floaters."

Floaters were men from other parts of the city or New York who arrived to cast votes for other men who had died in the precinct during the year. In Jersey City, just because you were dead didn't mean you didn't vote. Good Democrats always voted.

"Let me handle it, Barry," said Jack Lynch, walking over to the young man.

"Good morning. I'm James Connolly, an investigator with the Hudson County Bureau of Elections."

"Good morning, I'm Howard Freeman, I'm got a letter from…"

Lynch put up his hand and smiled. "No need. We were told you were coming. We're both here to do the same job. To make sure this is a fair election. What have you found?"

The young Rutgers undergraduate didn't have much of an idea of what to look for and was glad to lean on his more experienced colleague. "Well, there don't seem to be any Republican poll watchers present."

"Really. That's odd. Let's check." They walked up to the precinct clerk.

"I'm James Connolly, from the Bureau of Elections; let me see the list of voters that have cast their ballots so far."

The clerk, who was Lynch's second cousin, said, "Yes, sir."

"Aha!" said Lynch who handed the list back. He turned to Freeman.

"The three Republicans in this precinct have already voted."

"Three? That seems like a small number."

"Not really. This whole assembly district is called the Horseshoe because of its shape. The state assembly crammed as many Democrats in it as possible. To reduce their influence in Trenton, don't you know."

"That sounds reasonable," said Freeman.

"The Republican poll watchers probably went to Weehawken. They say there's a lot of vote fraud up there."

He whispered in Freeman's ear. "If I was you, that's where I would go too. You're wasting your time here. I'll be here all day. Might make a name for yourself up there. Who knows?" Freeman's eyes brightened as he listened carefully to Lynch's directions on how to get to Weehawken. Those directions, if followed precisely, would put Freeman a block away from the Lackawanna Railroad ferry terminal in Hoboken.

"Thanks, Jack," said Barry Crowe.

Jack was on his fourth roundtrip to the polling place when a well built, well-dressed man walked in.

"I'm Harold Kramer from the Honest Ballot Association in Trenton. I'm looking for a young colleague of mine but he doesn't seem to be here."

Jack walked up to him. "Good day, sir. I am James Connolly, an investigator with the Hudson County Bureau of Elections. Can I help you?"

Kramer looked at him skeptically. "I wasn't aware that your bureau had investigators."

"Then you haven't kept up with the latest appointments. I'm here to prevent vote fraud."

Kramer laughed. "Do you really expect me to believe that?"

Lynch, annoyed, got close to Kramer. Very close. "Are you calling me a liar, sir?"

Kramer didn't back down. "Call it what you will. By the way, didn't the British execute you, Mr. Connolly?"

Lynch flared. "Now you mock the name of a brave man

besides calling me a liar. I think we should discuss this further — outside."

"Yes. Yes. Take it outside," said Barry Crowe, "I don't want the voters upset." The voters, election officials, ward heelers and other hangers-on, who formed an appreciative audience, were disappointed.

Kramer said, "You can't intimidate me, Connolly or whatever your name is. Indeed, we will settle this outside."

At the side door, he turned to Lynch and said, "I should warn you. I boxed for Princeton."

Lynch looked startled and said, "It will be a civil conversation, Mr. Kramer. I certainly wouldn't want to go toe-to-toe with you."

Kramer took five steps outside and turned around towards Lynch. Lynch head butted him in the face, and when Kramer's hands came up to his broken, bleeding nose Lynch kneed him in the testicles. No bolt-shot steer ever went down faster. Kramer lay in the fetal position, one hand on his nose, one hand on his crotch. Moaning.

A beat cop poked his head out the door. "What's going on here, Jack?"

"It's all over, Pete. This fellow came in, started an argument and demanded that we settle it outside. He used to be a boxer, I was very frightened."

The cop smiled and said, "I'll bet you were."

"But I defended myself and got lucky."

"Do you want to press charges against him, Jack?"

"Nah. I think he's learned his lesson, Pete. Don't stick your nose where it doesn't belong." Kramer just moaned.

* * *

New Jersey was Woodrow Wilson's home state but the Virginia-born president was a decided underdog. He won the state in

1912 with a bare forty-one percent of the vote, the rest split by two Republican candidates. This time there was only one Republican running. Woodrow Wilson would not win New Jersey without a miracle from his Presbyterian God.

Frank Hague, that rising Democratic power in Hudson County, did not care whether Wilson was re-elected or not. They were often political enemies. But it was important to him that Wilson carry Hague's county. Hague had city, county and state ambitions. He was indifferent to what happened nationally. That would change in time.

But the last thing Hague wanted was for a vengeful Wilson to campaign against him in Hudson County especially in Jersey City come May when Hague intended to become mayor. Wilson had bested him before in Hudson County and in much of Jersey City too.

When the polls closed across the country no one knew who had been elected president. It wasn't until California nodded his way that Wilson won re-election.

Frank Hague was pleased with the results. Wilson had carried Hudson County, thanks to Hague. *That'll keep him out of my hair.*

The president was buried in all other New Jersey counties except for two small rural counties that traditionally voted Democratic.

Frank Hague knew he was now the de-facto Democratic leader of New Jersey even if others, like H. Otto Wittpenn, wouldn't concede that yet. Wittpenn, an old enemy, would get his as soon as Hague was named mayor of Jersey City.

Black Tom was never mentioned during the campaign. It was yesterday's news. The dead were buried. The hurt healed. All the glass in Manhattan had been replaced. The damage to the Statue of Liberty and Ellis Island had been mended.

But Mickey McGurk had not forgotten Black Tom. He was still tossing and turning at night because of his decision not to probe deeper into the possibility that German saboteurs were responsible for the destruction.

Well, Wilson was elected and Frank Hague wouldn't care what Mickey did now. The commissioner was on record warning Congress of the dangers present at Black Tom. His ass was covered.

I'm not going to let those krauts get away with it. But who can I go to? Not the Feds. They already declared it an accident and they wouldn't want to embarrass themselves. Besides their boss is 'neutral'. New York and Trenton don't care. Who cares about Black Tom besides me?

The answer when he finally thought of it was obvious. *The railroad. The fucking Lehigh Valley Railroad.*

Wilson Keeps Trying

President Woodrow Wilson had been trying to end the war in Europe since it began but to no avail.

One reason Wilson wanted peace was because he became convinced America would be forced to enter the war unless it ended soon. She couldn't stay "neutral" much longer. The provocations by both sides were intolerable.

Now, less than two months after his re-election and more than two years after the nations of Europe had stumbled into this most horrific war, he was determined to try again.

The Battles of the Somme and Verdun were over. Both sides were exhausted but still bellicose despite numbering casualties by the million. The situation on the Eastern Front was as bad. The time was ripe.

So on December 18, he asked the Allies and the Central Powers to state their terms for ending the war. *This would start the peace negotiations*, he thought.

Wilson had this concept of the peace he would negotiate. It would be a "peace without victory." There would be neither reparations nor annexation of territory.

This was not the "peace" either side had in mind. They had lost too much already; the other side must be made to pay. Germany refused to disclose its terms.

His secretary of state had secretly assured the British that Wilson favored the Allies. Actually Wilson had come to believe that it was the British who were derailing his efforts because they wanted revenge and reparations. Nor was England going to neglect a chance to expand the British Empire.

The British and the French responded by suggesting terms that would require the complete defeat of their enemies.

Wilson then opened secret negotiations with Germany insisting he was a completely impartial arbiter who had the power to force the Allies to the peace table. The Allies were totally dependent on the United States for food, war materials and credit.

The Germans didn't bite.

Both sides were convinced they would win.

The new French commander-in-chief, General Robert Nivelle, was convinced of it. Nivelle, who had effectively used the "creeping barrage" at Verdun said, "Artillery conquers, infantry occupies."

Admiral Reinhardt Scheer was convinced of it. He was sure that his long range U-boats already sinking scores of ships could cripple Great Britain if Germany resumed unrestricted submarine warfare.

General Douglas Haig was convinced of it. Haig, who considered himself God's servant, had told the King that Germany would collapse by the end of 1916. Haig was promoted to field marshal on January 1. That did nothing to dampen his ardor for war.

Field Marshall Paul von Hindenburg, the new chief of the German General Staff, was convinced of it. Idolized by the German people, von Hindenburg was the de facto head of the German armed forces, events having reduced Kaiser Wilhelm II to a mere figurehead.

No one wanted "peace" but Wilson. The others wanted "victory" almost at any cost.

Wilson's latest attempt to mediate peace failed.

Meanwhile, the bulk of American troops in Mexico chasing Pancho Villa were withdrawn in January, 1917. Another failure.

The Coal and Iron Police

The Headquarters of the Lehigh Valley Railroad was a handsome five story, brick, Queen Anne style office building on a sloping side street near the river in Bethlehem, Pennsylvania.

Lieutenant Mickey McGurk stood across the street from it for a minute or two, admiring it. He expected something more sinister, maybe with bats hanging from the roof. He couldn't help it. No one in Jersey City thought of the railroads as benign even those who worked for them.

But here he was, minutes off the train from Jersey City, a bit early for his appointment to see the railroad's chief of police. He looked at the name he had written down: Dafydd Jones.

So a Welshman had moved up when Cornelius Leyden was killed at Black Tom. He had never learned why Leyden was there that night. *Maybe he'd find out from Jones.*

McGurk was carrying a cardboard portfolio containing all his notes, typed and handwritten, on Black Tom. His boss, Frank Hague, had told him to get rid of them. He would. He was going to give them to the Lehigh Valley Railroad in hopes that it would do something—anything—to make the Germans pay for what they did at Black Tom just five months ago. He had no place else to go.

Inside, a receptionist greeted him, told him Jones was expecting him and gave him directions to Jones' third floor office.

It said "Chief of Police" in gold letters arced across the frosted glass panel of the door. Mickey didn't know what to do—walk in or knock. He knocked.

"Come in," said a deep, strong voice.

Mickey walked in and saw a man behind a desk about twenty feet away. There was a conference table and six chairs against one bookshelf-lined wall and two wingback chairs separated by a small wooden table against the other. The man rose and moved towards Mickey.

He was short, well built, in his fifties and his thinning gray hair was parted in the middle. His face was devoid of hair except for a pair of bushy eyebrows. He was not smiling. He definitely was not smiling.

"Lieutenant McGurk?"

"Yes, sir."

"Come. Sit down. We'll be comfortable in those chairs. I'm Chief Dafydd Jones."

They shook hands, exchanging the expected "I'm very pleased to meet you."

"Would you like some coffee, Lieutenant?"

"No, thank you, sir."

The chief pulled out a pipe and stuffed it. "You smoke?"

"Sometimes but not now, thank you." said Mickey.

The chief lighted his pipe while peering at McGurk over the burning match.

"You know," he said, "you were pretty cryptic when you called. All I got out of you was you wanted to talk about Black Tom. I hope you'll be more forthcoming today."

"I will be when I know that the railroad is still interested in finding out what happened at Black Tom."

Jones said, "The railroad is very, very interested in Black Tom. We lost many millions of dollars there and we are the defendants in negligence suits that might cost us many millions more. Even the family of your dead policeman is suing us."

"I hope they collect."

"The Lehigh Valley Railroad does not like to lose money, sir," said Jones.

McGurk asked, "So you have a real interest in learning what really happened? If it was something other than negligence, would that command interest at the highest levels of your corporation?"

"If you have something to contradict the charge of 'negligence' I can get the chairman of the board down to sit in on this conversation."

McGurk said, "That won't be necessary, Chief. I am more than content to deal with you."

"Thank you," said Jones, leaning towards McGurk, "Now, tell me, young man, what do you know."

Mickey didn't mean to be dramatic but he paused for two or three seconds before he said, "German saboteurs destroyed Black Tom."

Now it was Jones' turn to be silent as he stared at McGurk. "Can you prove it?"

"No. Not really. But I have enough that when it's put together and you study it, you will come to the same conclusion I did. Then I expect the Lehigh Valley Railroad to use all its resources to pursue and find the evidence to prove the Germans did it. How you get them to pay for it, I don't know. But I suspect you people will find a way."

Jones puffed on his pipe. "I see you clearly understand how a railroad operates."

He got up and walked over to the conference table and sat down, as did Mickey.

"All right, Lieutenant, lay out your case."

Mickey did so with much clarity and completeness as he could. As he would put each piece of paper down on the table, Jones would pick it up and move it to his side of the table. He did not interrupt Mickey's presentation.

When it was over, an hour later, Jones said, "You'd never get an indictment with that material, let alone a conviction but I think you are right. Jahnke, Kristoff and that third man 'Whiskey', at the behest of the German government, set the fires that caused the explosions at Black Tom."

Mickey exhaled. He hadn't realized he was holding his breath.

Jones asked, "Why didn't you dig deeper into Black Tom yourself at the time?"

"Because my boss didn't want me to."

"Ah, yes. Mr. Hague. No friend of the railroad, I fear."

"You fear correctly."

Jones said, "Let's talk about what's to be done. You can be assured that the railroad will pursue this no matter how long it takes. You were right about that. Millions are at stake. Do you agree that our best lead is Kristoff?"

"Yes. But don't forget Mena Edwards. She lives in New York and I had no jurisdiction to go over there and question her after Black Tom."

"Jurisdiction is not something the railroad concerns itself with."

"Neither does my boss," said Mickey.

"Pardon me?"

"I'm sorry. Nothing. I didn't mean to get off the subject," said Mickey.

"Do you think Kristoff is still in Bayonne?" asked Jones.

"I'm not sure. His address is right there," said Mickey pointing to a piece of paper on the table.

"Yes," said Jones, "It's the same address we have."

McGurk was caught short. "What do you mean, the same address you have?"

"We picked up some gossip from Bayonne that he had told his cousin he had blown up Black Tom. I didn't want to bring it up until I saw what you had. We followed him after you turned him loose but our agent lost him."

McGurk said, "I take it that the David Grossman who 'bailed' him out worked for you."

"Yes," said Jones, "not our best agent it turns out. But we'll find Kristoff again and Mena Edwards too. Do you know where Jahnke is or this 'Whiskey'?"

McGurk said, "Probably on the West Coast. That's where they were coming from for the 'big party.' I presume they would hightail it back there. My hunch would be San Francisco."

"Makes sense."

They talked more about the case but the conversation began to peter out.

Mickey said, "Say, Chief, I'd take that coffee now if the offer is still open."

"It most certainly is and I'll join you."

They were relaxing in the easy chairs sipping their coffee. Jones had skillfully elicited information on Mickey's career with the Jersey City police. Now it was Mickey's turn.

"I see, Chief, that your badge says Coal and Iron Police; don't you work directly for the railroad?"

"I do. The railroad pays my salary. The Coal and Iron Police is a private police force but the state legislature gave us arrest powers throughout all of Pennsylvania. My force here is small and very limited in its expertise. We're good at spotting pickpockets at a railroad station but hopeless at preventing your young hoodlums from stealing our coal."

Mickey laughed. "I don't know. I got whacked more than once on the back of my legs."

"I hope it did you some good," said Jones who was not without humor. "No, my force—the Coal and Iron Police—will take what you have given us and expand on it. Do the leg work. But is likely—certain—that the railroad will bring in others with more skills than we possess."

"The Pinkertons, huh?"

Jones lost his sense of humor. "The time when we dealt with the Pinkerton Detective Agency is long past, Lieutenant."

"Wasn't it you people working with them that brought down the Molly Maguires?"

"That was long before my time, Lieutenant. But you know, Lieutenant McGurk, many people don't think the Molly Maguires were heroes."

"Really. I didn't know that," said Mickey McGurk.

Mickey rose to leave. "Thank you, Chief, for the hospitality.

And thank you for taking this case off my hands. I know somehow you will make those bastards pay. They killed two cops—one of yours and one of mine. I do have one last question. What was Chief Leyden doing at Black Tom that night?"

"I don't know," said Chief Dafydd Jones of the Coal and Iron Police.

As Mickey was leaving, Jones grabbed his arm. "Be at ease with yourself. You've done the right thing."

* * *

Hannah could see an immediate change in Mickey when he got home. He was affectionate, he was playful, he tussled with the boy. Mickey was his old self.

"So, what were you doing in Bethlehem, love?"

"Not much. I handed over a case that was of more interest to them than to us but I had a good time reminiscing with an old cop."

"That's nice," said Hannah.

* * *

Captain Hinsch received a $2,000 bonus for his work once the ambassador calmed down and realized that the Wilson Administration had no interest in the destruction of Black Tom.

Now his alter ego, Mr. Graentnor, turned to his target list and stopped at the Canadian Car and Foundry's enormous munitions assembly factory in Kingsland just across the Hackensack River from Snake Hill in the Meadows

More than one hundred other factories shipped powder, shells, shrapnel, and shell casings to that plant where 1,400 worked to turn them into 3" projectiles.

The Canadian owners, not as naïve as their American counter-parts, took security seriously. A six-foot high fence surrounded the property and the perimeter was patrolled by guards twenty-four hours a day. Canada was at war and feared sabotage.

But the threat came from within. Mr. Graentnor ordered one of his German-American operatives to get work at the factory. The man fetched up as the assistant employment manager.

"The man I will send you will say he was recommended by Captain Tunney. Put him to work in the place where you think he can do the most damage without killing himself," said Mr. Graentnor.

The day came just before Christmas. Russia had paid $83,000,000 for a huge consignment of projectiles. Some had already been shipped but most were stacked up inside the complex awaiting transport

"Okay, Wozniak. I'm putting you to work in Building Thirty, cleaning shell casings. You are going to have to be very careful. The stuff we use is flammable."

The inside of a shell casing was cleaned using a small belt-driven rotating machine. The casing was placed inside the machine and held there with a foot long piece of wood. Then a cloth, dipped into a pan of alcohol, was put into the shell as it rotated cleaning its sides. Then another cloth was used to dry the shell casing. The used rags piled up in front of the forty-eight work stations as the work day went on.

Employees were forbidden to bring matches into Building Thirty. No matter what, no matches.

On an exceptionally cold January morning, a blaze started in front of what turned out to Fiodoe Wozniak's machine and quickly spread.

One of the other workers saw that in the chaos someone threw a pail of something on the flames which grew higher. "I don't think it was water," he said, "and all the fire buckets held sand."

Within four hours, a half-million three-inch shells cooked off and destroyed the entire complex.

No one was killed in the fire thanks to Theresa Louise

McNamara who stayed by her switchboard despite the danger and plugged into each building shouting, "Get out or go up!" They got out.

Many of the chilled workers walked across the frozen Hackensack and through the Meadows looking for shelter on Snake Hill.

The Hudson County Insane Asylum shared the hill with the Almshouse, the county penitentiary, the Tuberculosis Hospital and the Contagious Diseases Hospital. The displaced workers obviously were desperate.

Panic swept Snake Hill. The nine hundred inmates of the asylum thought the world was ending as the shells burst in the sky. A pair of quick thinking doctors calmed them by handing out ice cream, candies and fruits, saying it was just a celebration marking the end of the war in Europe.

Office workers in Manhattan watched the pyrotechnics from their skyscraper windows. There was no panic there. Some said it was a much better show than Black Tom.

This time the authorities acted to find the man who had started the fire. It was quickly determined that Fiodoe Wozniak was that man. But when detectives arrived at his residence, the Russian Immigrant House in Manhattan, he was gone. He disappeared for a decade. Wozniak had been a conscript in the Austro-Hungarian Army before he came to America.

Frank Hague talked about the Kingsland fire with Lieutenant McGurk.

"I suppose you think it was the krauts that blew up that factory too."

"No doubt in my mind," said McGurk, as an unsettling feeling of guilt oozed into his soul. His was a sin of omission.

Blinker Helps Win the War

If you were standing directly in front of Captain William Reginald Hall, RN, it was difficult not to focus on his left eye, the lid of which moved incessantly as his face twitched.

Hence the nickname "Blinker", recalling the naval signaling lamp.

But if you were in front of "Blinker" Hall, you would do well to listen to every word he was saying. It is likely that he knew more about the enemy's intentions than anyone in Great Britain or the world for that matter.

After a long and distinguished seagoing career, Captain Hall felt his health required that he take a posting ashore. Fortunately for the Allies, the Admiralty offered Hall an assignment as Director of the Intelligence Division in October, 1914.

Two other events had occurred almost simultaneously. The Russians sank a German cruiser in the Baltic and recovered its code book which they passed on to the British. The Royal Navy, in turn, cut Germany's underwater cable to the New World.

Thus the German Foreign Office was cut off from its embassies and consulates in the Western Hemisphere, including the one in Washington, DC, except by diplomatic pouches which would move across thousands of miles of ocean in neutral ships making no more than twelve knots.

The United States, in its attempt to be fair to both sides, acceded to a German request to use the cable which linked our embassy in Berlin to the State Department in Washington. Our cable was obviously secure so German messages were handed to our Embassy for transmission. Almost all the messages were sent in the clear and yet no American read them. That would not be gentlemanly.

Captain Hall and his collection of eclectic and eccentric folk who peopled Room Forty in London rubbed their hands together and could hardly believe their good fortune.

The American cable ran from Denmark to a relay station in Porthcurno, England. That's where the Brits tapped into our cable. They were reading American messages from Berlin as well as those of the Germans.

When, in essence, you could read your enemy's mail—or especially that of a friend— the trick was to make sure that he didn't know you were doing it.

The Royal Navy received excellent intelligence from Room Forty and that, no doubt, helped the war effort. But it was the Irish who really felt the sting from Blinker's efforts.

His people tipped off the Royal Navy that Germany was sending a freighter with arms and ammunition for the revolutionary Irish in April,1916. A destroyer intercepted the disguised merchant vessel, the arms were destroyed, the Easter Monday uprising failed and Sir Roger Casement was captured and executed as a traitor.

But Blinker's early triumphs were as nothing compared to what he would accomplish after January 19, 1917, when the Germans had persuaded the American ambassador to permit them to send an encrypted message to their embassy in Washington.

It hummed through the cable until it reached the relay station in England where Blinker's people intercepted it. Then the message continued on to Washington.

The coded message was in blocks of four numbers each and it also helpfully designated the cipher that was used.

Room Forty had it partially decoded by the next day and fully decoded soon after that.

While Blinker's people were decoding it, the original message was passed on via a Western Union telegram from the German Embassy in Washington to the German Embassy in Mexico City. It was signed by Arthur Zimmerman, Imperial Germany's State Secretary for Foreign Affairs.

The message was explosive.

It announced that Germany would resume unrestricted submarine warfare on February 1. Should that provoke the United States into declaring war, then the German ambassador was to approach the government of Mexico and propose a wartime alliance with Germany. The hook was the return of Texas, Arizona and New Mexico after the United States and the Allies were defeated.

"We will make war together; we will make peace together," wrote Zimmerman. Germany also offered substantial help to Mexico to wage such a distracting war against the United States. That was the gist of the infamous Zimmerman telegram.

Blinker Hall knew this might be the catalyst Great Britain needed to draw America into the war on her side but he had to conceal how he got the Zimmerman message.

He couldn't allow our State Department to figure out that the British had intercepted its dispatches from Berlin as well. That might cause an irreparable breach of trust.

The tension grew even worse after January 31, when the Germans actually resumed unrestricted submarine warfare, sinking an American freighter that same day off the coast of Britain albeit with no loss of life.

For Woodrow Wilson, who had continued to walk that wildly swaying tightrope of neutrality since his re-election five months earlier, enough was enough.

On February 3, President Wilson broke off diplomatic relations with Germany. Speaking for two hours before a special session of Congress, Wilson detailed all of America's grievances including Germany's "relentless and indiscriminate warfare against vessels of commerce." He said we didn't want a conflict with the German government but war would ensue if Germany continued to sink American ships without warning.

The big break for Captain Blinker Hall came when a British agent in Mexico City managed to bribe a Western Union employee and got a copy of the encrypted telegram sent to the German Embassy there. Blinker now had a plausible cover story.

The British turned over the telegram, a copy of the cipher used, a German translation and an English translation to the American ambassador in London on February 24. At first, the wary Americans suspected that it was another elaborate British forgery. But it was sent on to Washington two days later. Wilson's administration released it to the press on March 1.

The Zimmerman Telegram caused a nationwide sensation. The Hearst newspapers, the Germans, the Irish, and the anti-interventionists branded the telegraph a forgery. The pro-British factions championed its authenticity.

The arguments ended on March 29 when Zimmerman himself gave a speech in Germany admitting the telegram had been sent. But he insisted the telegram was sent to the German ambassador not the Mexican government. Besides no alliance would be forged unless the United States declared war on Germany, something that hadn't happened. The naïve Zimmerman expected that explanation to put the issue to rest.

Arthur Zimmerman also thought Wilson was bluffing and that no action of Germany's could budge him from neutrality.

American public opinion, already anti-Mexican, turned anti-German overnight. The pious president, outraged by Germany and all her works, finally was ready to fight.

The United States of America declared war on the German Empire on April 6, eight days after Zimmerman admitted sending the telegram.

The declaration of war was the signal for German agents in America to flee if they could. Dr. Scheele decamped to Cuba. Jahnke and Witzke crossed the border into Mexico. Michael Kristoff enlisted in the United States Army on May 22 but was discharged in September for being tubercular and for having made false statements on his enlistment papers. He then vanished. The safe house on West 15th Street was abandoned.

The ever resourceful Captain Hinsch (alias Mr. Graentnor) chartered a schooner and with a crew of three, flying the neutral Dutch flag, sailed from a small harbor on the Jersey coast. He crossed the North Atlantic, rounded Scotland and dashed across the North Sea arriving safely in Germany.

Captain Hinsch had run the British blockade once again without incident.

The Home Front

The United States had declared war but the vote was hardly unanimous in Congress. The declaration of war passed in the Senate 82-6 with eight members not voting. It passed in the House 373-50 with nine members not voting. Opposition to the war was relatively widespread and open.

Military authorities expected a million men to enlist in the armed forces within six weeks of the declaration of war. Only 73,000 did so. The American Army alone would need millions of men. When war was declared, the United States Army numbered 121,000 men and the National Guard another 60,000. But enlistments soon picked up.

America would have to turn to conscription as it did during the Civil War. More than one expert remembered how the Irish had reacted in 1863. They ran amok in Manhattan killing blacks, destroying massive amounts of property and even burning down an orphanage. It took troops fresh from Gettysburg to get them under control. There were 4.5 million Irish-Americans in 1917. But the Irish didn't riot, they enlisted.

German-Americans numbered 8.5 million. Earlier, a German diplomat had claimed that a half-million of them were reservists in the Imperial Army. How would they react to conscription? The answer was a month or so away. Nothing serious would happen despite widespread resentment of the draft. Those German reservists would change sides.

If the American Army wasn't ready for war, American industry certainly was. It had been supplying the Allied war effort since 1914. It would quickly expand and almost effortlessly clothe and equip millions of Doughboys. All it needed was more labor and some of that was supplied by blacks who migrated from the inhospitable South to the less than hospitable North lured by the novelty of steady, decent paying jobs.

The war began to change America in other ways expected and unexpected.

The first noticeable occurrence in Jersey City after the declaration of war was the withdrawal of the police cordon that prevented the railroads from bringing munitions into the city. That ban had been in effect since Black Tom was destroyed in July. Traffic on the Central Railroad of New Jersey and at the other Lehigh Valley Railroad terminus north of the Gap picked up appreciably. Factories began to gear up for war work as a cornucopia of contracts poured out of Washington.

Public opinion was turning against all things German. It was only days after the declaration of war when Sophie Ganz said to her husband, "Otto, I think I will join the American Red Cross, liebchen."

Otto looked up from his newspaper and said, "Will you have to go to France?"

Sophie laughed and he smiled. "No. Maybe as far as Christ Hospital."

"In that case, enjoy yourself."

A clerk at the Red Cross was taking information for Sophie's application.

"Name?"

"Ganz. Sophie Ganz."

The clerk looked up and said, "Let me take you to our director." She knocked at and then opened a door. "Madam Director, this is Mrs. Sophie Ganz."

Sophie walked in and sat down. Madam Director was not smiling. "Mrs. Ganz. You are German?"

"Not any more. I'm an American."

"But you were born in Germany?"

"Yes, but I am an American citizen now."

"I see. I am sorry. We are not accepting any applications from Germans now. And we won't until we know where their loyalties lie."

"My loyalties lie with my country—America."

"We'll see. Perhaps, next year."

Sophie was thoroughly humiliated and said nothing to Otto until Sunday when another matron at Bethany Lutheran told all who would listen that the same thing had happened to her. Otto Ganz was aghast.

All over the city men and women were making decisions that would affect their lives.

Jack Lynch was asked if he intended to enlist, "Nah. I'm too old and too fat." Not so many of the younger members of Clan na Gael. Some of them rushed to join New York's 69th Regiment which was doubling its size. This was an Irish unit that had distinguished itself in the Civil War and now was led by Colonel William "Wild Bill" Donovan. One or two of those new recruits might have slipped a cigar bomb into the hold of a British ship. But that was then, this was now.

Detective Tony Aiello walked into headquarters and the desk sergeant said, "There's a guy waiting for you. Says it's important."

Tony saw Abie the Jew sitting on a bench outside his office. He called out, "Mr. Ashansky. How are you?"

"Wrong title, Mr. Aiello. It's Private Ashansky. I joined the Army."

"Good lord. That's something to talk about. Let's get a bite to eat. There's a peddler just outside. Okay?"

"It's about time you bought me lunch, Tony."

The cart was shaded by a bright multi-colored umbrella. "Two frankfurters with mustard and sauerkraut," said Tony.

"We don't sell them anymore," said the vendor. "How about two hotdogs, mustard and liberty cabbage?"

Abie shook his head. "So it starts," he said.

They sat on a nearby bench. Tony said, "So tell me."

"I've already taken my physical. You should see some of the sad cases they're taking. I leave on a train tomorrow for some camp in Massachusetts."

"You know, Abe, I thought you'd be the last person in America to go to war."

"Ironic isn't it? I flee to America so the Czar can't put me in his Army. And now it's Private Ashansky, and the Czar has abdicated. The reason I joined the Army is simple and I think, as a Marxist, it's logical. I hate this war. America can put an end to this war. Therefore, I should help her do it."

"Makes sense when you say it," said Tony.

"So are you going to enlist too?"

"No. I've been married less than a year and I'm not leaving her unless they drag me away."

"I don't blame you. I should never have left Rachel. You know, Tony, we are friends. You may be my best friend in America, if you can believe it. You're the only man here I trust. Now that I know you're not going to enlist in the Army, I want you to do me a big favor."

"Anything, Abie."

"Keep this safe for me," he said, handing Tony the key to a safe deposit box. "You know what's in it?"

"I think I do." *Rachel's dowry.*

"Yes. I'll write. We'll keep in touch. And I'll get the key from you when I get back."

Tony hesitated before he asked, "Abe, what if you don't come back?"

Ashansky said, "I'll be back. Lots of goniffs like them have tried to kill me and here I am. But I suppose it's a possibility. I doubt that Rachel, if she's still alive, will come to America looking for me. If she doesn't, then your future daughters will have a tidy nest egg. No? Tony, if you get drafted, give the key to your wife and tell her the story. If you trust her, I trust her."

"Will you go back to the Ukraine after the war to look for Rachel?"

"Yes, if I can. But I won't go back as a despicable Jew. I'll go back as an American citizen who doesn't give a shit whether anyone in the Ukraine likes him or not. That will feel good."

Elsewhere, Hans Mannstein told his fellow Zeppelins that he would be enlisting right after the municipal election. "You know how I used to tell everybody 'it's not my fucking war'? Well, it's my fucking war now."

"How'd your missus take the news?" asked a Zeppelin.

"She's furious with me. I'm sleeping on the couch."

"So, will you change your mind?"

"Not a chance. What is she going to do, divorce me?"

"Good luck, pal," said a Zeppelin.

Few people noticed little things like German dishes disappearing from restaurant menus. Or that nobody sang German songs any more. Attitudes towards German-Americans were changing. Hardening. But the Ganzs took notice.

"I hate this war," said Sophie. "I'm glad my grandson's name is 'McGurk'. I wish Billy's was too."

"Sophie! What a thing to say."

"Well, I do."

* * *

Frank Hague had no intention of offending German-Americans in any way. There were too many of them living in the 11th and 12th wards. To say nothing of the many thousands concentrated in the northern end of the county.

Of course, they had an unfortunate propensity to vote for H. Otto Wittpenn who had been both Hague's ally and enemy over the decades. But Hague was making inroads with the German-Americans in Jersey City, especially the younger ones. He intended to destroy Wittpenn for good in the gubernatorial election in November after Hague was elected mayor.

Hague's secretary, Terry Lynch, asked if he could speak to him one afternoon not long after the declaration of war. "I intend to work for you during the next couple of weeks until I drop, Mr. Commissioner."

You better.

"But when it's over and you are the new mayor, I intend to accept a commission as a second lieutenant in the United States Army."

Now that's a surprise. I didn't think you were the type to join up. "How come? You have a good future here with me, Terry."

"I know that and I thank you, sir. But I think I can be of much more use to you and to myself—if you will forgive me—if I accept a commission."

Okay. Now we find out what's in it for him.

"I don't know how long this war is going to last but I think there will be millions of men in uniform before it's over. When they get home they will be inclined to vote for young veterans like themselves. I hope—with your backing—to give them that chance. It will be like the Civil War. The Grand Army of the Republic dominated politics for decades afterwards."

They did indeed—for the goddamn Republicans.

"I like the way you're thinking, Terry. You're right. I am going to need people like you after the war. Thanks for giving me enough time to think of a good replacement for you as my secretary."

"I have a name or two I'd like to suggest to you, Mr. Hague."

"Don't bother."

* * *

Mickey McGurk's conscience asserted itself on the very day war was declared and demanded he do something to heal the open moral wound that was Black Tom. He went to see a Marine recruiter in New York bringing his Honorable Discharge and his medal.

The recruiting sergeant said, "McGurk, I can practically

guarantee you a job down in the Dominican Republic. We've been there for some time. The fighting has died down and in November we were ordered to reorganize their constabulary. With your prior service, your record as a police lieutenant and the fact that you speak Oxcart Spanish, we'd take you on as a sergeant and you'd be seconded to their National Guard and collect another salary as a second lieutenant. That's a real good deal."

"Not for me. It's France or nothing."

"Okay," said the sergeant. "You say you can't get into uniform until the middle of next month?"

"Right."

"Well, you might miss out on the first outfit that's going to France; they're forming right now believe it or not. But I'll ticket you for the next."

"Terrific." Mickey didn't think the war would end before then.

When Mickey got home that evening, Hannah could sense that something was amiss. Mickey said, "You know I don't like to keep secrets from you."

Hannah said, "I know and I love you for that."

"Well, I went to see a Marine recruiter."

Fear swept over Hannah.

"I'll be going back in the Corps after the election."

Now Hannah was angry. "You made a decision like that without even talking to me? Did you even give me or our son a single thought before you decided to go off and maybe get yourself killed?"

Mickey took her hands in his. She tried to pull away but he held them firm.

"I love you and Frankie beyond all reckoning. But this is something I must do or I won't be able to live with myself. It's that important to me."

Hannah, who had stopped pulling away, thought back and

remembered Mickey's restlessness. "This has something to do with Black Tom, doesn't it?"

"Yes."

"Tell me."

Mickey sighed. "I suspected—no, I knew—that German saboteurs had destroyed Black Tom and killed those people. I did nothing about it. I let everyone think it was just a big, bad accident. This has been grating on me for months."

"So you think you can go back into the Marines and punish Germany all by yourself?"

"Hardly. But I have to do my part. You wouldn't want to live with the man who sat this war out."

"Why don't you leave that decision to me?" asked Hannah.

"I can't. I've got to do it. I have no other choice," said Mickey McGurk.

"And what if you're killed?"

Mickey smiled. "I won't be anywhere near the front line. They'll probably put an old man like me in charge of the mules."

When he told Frank Hague of his decision, the commissioner didn't try to talk him out of it. He said, "Don't worry about Hannah and my godson. I'll take care of them."

"Thanks, Uncle Frank."

It is conceivable that Hague had had the slightest twinge of conscience himself.

Waiting on the Tanks and the Americans

French General Robert Nivelle was convinced in April, 1917, he could win the war in forty-eight hours by combining with the British Army to break through the German lines on a long ridge just north of the Aisne River.

The French poilus moved forward behind Nivelle's innovative "creeping barrage" which had worked so well at Verdun. They were in high spirits, convinced they were plodding towards victory after more than two and a half years of a bloody war which had claimed the lives of more than a million French soldiers, most of them infantrymen like themselves.

It wasn't a victory. The men thought it was a bloody shambles just like countless battles they had fought before. The morale of the infantry collapsed.

The failure shook the high command too, and on May 15 Nivelle was relieved of his command and replaced by General Phillippe Petain, the architect of victory at Verdun.

The mutinies started after 30,000 men left the front lines and moved towards the rear, just walking away from the trenches and the war.

Mutiny spread from division to division in Northern France until by the end of May it had affected almost half the French army. Unlike their counterparts in the Russian army who had butchered their officers when they mutinied, the French soldiers didn't harm theirs. They just refused to go back to the trenches and be slaughtered.

Mostly it was the infantry who mutinied; units farther back from the front lines didn't rebel as they had suffered fewer casualties. So there were cavalry units available to the High Command when it moved to suppress the mutinies. The troopers rounded up thousands of mutineers who were singled out by their own officers and NCOs.

Courts-martial were convened and mutineers sentenced. But the lenient sentences engineered by Petain angered many division commanders. Only 2,800 were sentenced to "hard labor" and 649 were sentenced to death. Of these, only forty-three were executed by firing squads. Petain decided to try to raise the morale of his troops from its nadir.

Petain promised his men more leave and an end to the continuous series of grand attacks. He told them he intended to wait for the arrival of the new, more reliable Renault tanks and the American Expeditionary Force. The front line infantrymen enjoyed rest periods, frequent rotation of units and the promised furloughs. The great attacks ended too.

Incredibly, the French were able to suppress knowledge of the extent of the mutinies and the Germans stayed on the defensive.

The British, however, were staggered by these events and, yielding to an inbred distaste for things Gallic, attributed them to the irredeemable defects of French character. They tried to encourage the French military to again take the initiative by launching the battle of the Third Battle of Ypres in Belgium. When the rains ended it almost four months later, the fifty British divisions and the attached seven French divisions had suffered more than 400,000 casualties.

The Unbossed

Frank Hague liked to walk the streets of his city at night, alone. Not only did it give him uninterrupted time to think but it was a nice check on how well his organization was performing its municipal duties.

The streets were clean. The cops were on the beat saluting him with their nightsticks. Fewer criminals plied their trade successfully.

Once in a while, Hague would stop at a fire box, pull the alarm and then take out his watch to time the response. If he thought the engine and truck came fast enough there were compliments enough to snuff out any resentment at answering a false alarm. But if the response was slow, the firemen faced a furious Hague who dished out reprimands and punishment. Once when a lieutenant talked back to the Commissioner, he got a black eye and a transfer for his insubordination.

Hague and A. Harry Moore were driven to the Episcopal Church of the Incarnation, not far from Bergen Square. Hague had an appointment with the rector at this fashionable, black church.

"Good morning, Reverend," said Hague, removing his hat.

"Good morning, Commissioner. My parishioners call me 'Father.'"

You mean like a real priest?

"A pleasure, Father," said Hague. "This is Commissioner A. Harry Moore, who may be known to you."

"Commissioner, welcome. I suspected this meeting might have political overtones so I took the liberty of inviting a young man to join us who, while lacking in years, is astute when it comes to things political. Gentlemen, may I introduce Fred Martin to you?"

Handshakes and greetings all around. The rector said, "I

understand you are Democrats and I must point out that most of my flock are Republicans and have been since the Civil War."

"We, like the church, encourage conversions, Father," said Moore, a Presbyterian.

"Touché, Commissioner Moore. Now if you gentlemen will excuse me, I will return to my more ecclesiastical duties."

While everyone was saying 'goodbye', Hague looked at Martin. Medium height and weight, straight dark hair, well dressed, his skin more yellowish than light brown.

What the hell am I doing talking to this kid? He's not old enough to vote.

Martin opened the conversation. "I take it you want to talk about the growing numbers of Negroes moving here from the South?"

"Well, yes," said Moore. Hague continued staring.

Martin said, "Almost none of them have ever voted but if you asked them, they would say they are Republicans. Their experience with the Democratic party down South has been, shall we say, less than positive."

"Can that be changed?" asked Moore.

Martin looked at Hague. "Are you interested in their party affiliation or their votes?"

Hague brightened and nodded his head almost imperceptibly. Martin caught the gesture. "Their votes, of course," said Hague.

Martin said, "I think I can get those folks registered and deliver those votes to you, Mr. Hague. But I will need help from you even if I am not a formal part of your organization."

"For example?"

"I think we have more crime here than elsewhere in Jersey City. Your policemen try but they can't tell good from evil. They have a tendency to arrive and club everyone in sight—perpetrator, victim and by-stander. It would be very useful to have a couple of Negro policemen hereabouts."

Hague had never given that a thought. "Negro policemen?"

Jersey City had none but New York did.

"Yes. Men from the neighborhood. Hard men, as you Irish say. Who know evildoers from churchgoers and would keep order."

Moore smiled. "Do you have anyone in mind?"

"Oddly enough, I do. A couple of big men who served out West with the 10th Cavalry.

Buffalo Soldiers. Mickey told me about them in Mexico. Tough boys, thought Hague. "They'd have to be loyal to me," said Frank Hague.

Martin smiled. "No, Mr. Commissioner, they—and the voters—would be loyal to me. I would be loyal to you."

"Fair enough," said Hague. "Is there anything my organization can do for you personally, Mr. Martin? You do realize that a Negro precinct captain would be impossible—at least for the time being?"

"Yes, sir. I realize that. I neither want political office nor do I want to work for the city. I've started my own business—in a garage but I hope to grow. You may have noticed that many Negroes have tight curly hair. I make a product that straightens hair temporarily. That's becoming popular among my people. One problem is that I have to use chemicals in large quantities which are not exactly compatible with public health. I certainly wouldn't want a problem disposing of these chemicals when my business gets larger."

Hague thought, *Every factory in the city is dumping shit into the river or someplace. I'm not going to bother this kid as long as he delivers those votes.*

"If I become mayor, I don't see that as a problem. Do you, Commissioner Moore?"

"Not at all. Good luck to you on your venture, Mr. Martin."

When they were driving off, Hague said, "I don't care what anyone says, that kid's Irish. There's a Mick in the woodpile there someplace." Frank Hague had made a joke of sorts but no one laughed.

Hague's organization was based on the city's twelve wards. He continued to build it from the bottom up. Individuals, families, buildings, blocks, precincts, wards, cities and the county itself.

His election strategy was simple: win. Tactics were, for the most part, devised by the ward leaders already known as the "Twelve Apostles." They, through their precinct captains and block captains, planned and carried out rallies in Greenville, card parties in Lafayette, parades Downtown, pinochle tournaments in Hudson City, and moonlight riverboat excursions to Rye Beach. Meanwhile continuously doling out favors and solving problems. The voters' gratitude would be cashed in on Election Day.

Sometimes this took considerable coordination among the ward leaders. Take the Great Torchlight Parade, for example.

The parade would start on top of the hill at Palisade and Newark Avenues, march down the length of Newark Avenue and cut over to City Hall where Hague and the rest of his slate waited to review it. Men from every block in every precinct in every ward would have to be staged along with bands and floats. Leaders sorted out their contingents. Torches had to be passed out but not lighted until the signal was given. Marshals had to prevent the men from drifting off to nearby saloons.

The women, children, the disabled and the elderly of the city had to take their places along the parade route under the eye of watchful policemen. More than a few of Hague's lesser known enemies slipped into the crowd to cheer. Hopefully, that would be remembered if Hague won. If he lost, no one would care.

The bands played and the men sang as they marched. A favorite was a new song introduced on Broadway just three or four years earlier. They bellowed, "When Irish eyes are smiling, sure they'll steal your heart away..." Their opponents wondered if that was all they would steal. The Torchlight Parade was a great triumph and was talked about for years.

Momentum was building and momentum is everything in local politics. Everyone likes to be with the winner.

Municipal elections in Jersey City were non-partisan as required by the commission form of government. So there were no Democratic, Republican or Socialist candidates per se. But candidates could band together under a slogan. Hague chose the slogan "The Unbossed" without experiencing the slightest sense of irony.

The electorate casts ballots for five candidates. They could split those votes any way they chose. Winning a majority took discipline. The organization was disciplined.

Hague's running mates were the popular A. Harry Moore, former Judge F. X. O'Brien, City Clerk Michael I. Fagan and Revenue Commissioner George Brensinger. Hague hoped Brensinger would help win the heavily German 11th and 12th wards. He was picked long before the outbreak of war.

Frank Hague was not much of a campaigner. His closest associates tried hard to keep his public speaking at a minimum. Sometimes they failed. Hague liked to speak at ladies' card parties. He knew he was popular with them for running the prostitutes and drug dealers out of town. Women, he also knew, greatly influenced their men's vote.

Hague would stand up and boast, "Jersey City is the moralist city in America." His audience would cheer wildly. The school teachers among them would wince. Hague's wife and his thirteen year-old son did not campaign with him. They were never seen in public.

The other men on his ticket handled the speaking chores very competently and Moore was very good at it as befitted a graduate of Cooper Union.

But the real work was being done day-by-day in the political trenches. Posters made. Envelopes stuffed. Voters visited. Favors fulfilled. Canvasses of the voters made, again and again. Tiresome work done tirelessly. Nothing was left to chance.

The New York newspapers ignored the Jersey City campaign but it was covered in detail daily by The Jersey Journal and The Hudson Dispatch which, while published in Union City, had considerable circulation in the Heights. Hague never read the papers. Moore did.

The ballot was a crowded one which favored the organization. At worst, some of their people might throw a vote to a cousin who was running but the other four would go the organization. Most would vote a straight ticket.

The organization's efforts were not frenzied like those of its opponents. The organization had it under control; it was simply a matter of making sure the vote got out on Election Day.

Jack Lynch was at his precinct's polling place when one of his block captains walked in. "I'm glad you're here Jack. I got a problem. Maybe you can help me."

"Let's see, Pat. What's up?"

"Well, old man Pringle is on his last legs. In fact, that's the problem, he can't walk at all. He's alert enough and he would vote if he could but I can't get him to the polls by myself."

"No problem. Go back and hold his hand, I'll be there in ten minutes." And he was, with two huge firemen and a stretcher.

Jack said, "How are you doing, old-timer? I understand you want to vote."

"Would that I could," said Matthew Pringle in less than a robust voice.

"Leave it to us," said Jack. The firemen strapped the old man securely to the stretcher and down the stairs they went.

The block captain said to Lynch, "I hope this doesn't kill the old man."

Jack Lynch said, "You couldn't kill that old bastard with a sledgehammer."

Fred Martin was talking to a small group of new voters, all black. He handed each one of them a four o'clock card with the names of "The Unbossed" on them.

"Now this is who you vote for, you hear? You don't vote for nobody else. Just them. If you vote for anybody else, I'm going to know it and you will be sorry. Do you understand?"

"Yes sir, Mr. Fred."

"All right. Now voting is a big privilege. You never voted down South and you wouldn't be voting up here if it wasn't for me. We vote right and maybe we can get those offays to do something for us. Help us."

"You sure do know a lot for such a young fella."

"Forget that 'young fella' stuff. We have to work together."

"Yes sir, Mr. Fred."

Lieutenant Mickey McGurk and the rest of the Zeppelins were at police headquarters. In civilian clothes. Waiting. Just in case.

But there was no real trouble, just the usual pains-in-the-ass with a snoot full drunks annoying the old folks. The beat cops handled it calmly and made sure the drunks voted too.

You could feel it in the air as the day wore on. The comments the voters made as they left the polls. The people on their stoops drinking beer and laughing. The organization was winning.

The "Unbossed" met on the floor below the Greenwood Social Club, the scene of a Hague victory years earlier. Hague, while not overtly superstitious, thought the place brought good luck.

The spacious room was staffed by dozens of party workers, some manning a dozen telephones, as results came in precinct by precinct. The results were tallied, ward-by-ward on big black-boards. Only tickets and candidates that Hague considered worrisome were counted. Dozens of others were ignored. It took most of the night to get the preliminary count but it was decisive.

The "Unbossed" had won, all five of them. A. Harry Moore led the ticket with 19,883 votes. Hague was second with 18,648.

It was traditional under the commission form of government that the candidate who won the most votes would be elected mayor by his peers. The new commission met immediately after being sworn in. Frank Hague was selected as mayor unanimously.

Hague was in his new, bigger, office by nine am. His desk with the special drawer was there too.

He received a telephone call minutes later from Joseph P. Tumulty, President Wilson's erstwhile secretary. Tumulty and Hague had been on friendly terms for many years despite Hague's differences with Wilson.

"Congratulations, Mr. Mayor. It was a long journey but you finished it famously."

"Thank you, Mr. Tumulty. As I once told you 'there will be other elections'."

"You did say that, didn't you?"

"What about you, Mr. Tumulty? Do you need any temporary assistance? I'm sure we could arrange something here in Jersey City."

"No. Thank you, Mr. Mayor. I'm fine. Lawyers never starve, you know."

"I can't believe that stupid son-of-a-bitch fired you. You get him elected and he fires you, the ungrateful bastard."

Tumulty's voice was jovial. "Language. Language, Mr. Mayor. After all, the man is president of the United States."

"What happened, Joe?"

"The usual, Frank. The President's second wife, Edith, can't abide Catholics and I'm a Catholic."

Hague sputtered, "The blacklegged... well, you know what I think of them."

"Not to worry, it won't take the President long to figure out that he needs me and then I'll be back right outside his door."

"How can you do it, Mr. Tumulty? How can you go back to a man like that?"

"I really have no choice, Mr. Mayor. He's my president and he needs me."

"You're a better man than me, Joe."

"I really don't think so, Frank." The telephone call ended amicably.

One election over, Hague immediately got busy preparing the next. His only formidable foe in the county was H. Otto Wittpenn who would be running for governor on the Democratic ticket in November.

What Wittpenn didn't know was that Hague had already made an alliance with Enoch "Nucky" Johnson, the unsavory Republican boss of Atlantic City and Atlantic County.

Hague's organization would be instructed to crossover and vote for Walter Edge in the Republican primary in September. With that unexpected support, Edge would win.

Then Hague intended to sit out the November gubernatorial election. His people would not vote for either man.

Wittpenn was doomed unless he could rack up the usual big Democratic majority in Hudson County. The organization's job would be to see that that didn't happen.

Hague also knew it would show everyone his ability to deliver the vote to whomever he chose. That's real power.

He also liked the idea that Johnson and he would split up the state, Hague's dominance prevailing in the northern part. Hague liked "Nucky" but he thought that the former sheriff of Atlantic County was too close to the rackets. It was one thing to accept "donations"; it was another altogether to be a working racketeer. Hague feared his partner would take a fall someday. But not until after November.

Jack Lynch had to wait until Hague finished his telephone call. He didn't mind. In fact, he was almost giddy with anticipation. Lynch was even pleasant to his brother, Terry.

"Congratulations, Mr. Mayor," said Lynch.

"Thanks, Jack. But I want to congratulate you too. Not a single bullet vote in your precinct. That's terrific work."

"Thank you, sir."

"Right. I've got a new job for you. As of now, you're the County Superintendent of Weights and Measures. But I don't want you to spend more than a day a week at that. I need you to really work your contacts in the rest of the county. To make that easier, I'm putting you on the County Democratic Central Committee. That'll give you more clout."

Lynch's mouth dropped open.

"Here's what's up, Jack. We are going to smash Wittpenn once and for all. Everyone in the organization is going to cross over and vote for Walter Edge in the Republican primary."

"Excuse me?"

"Pay attention. We're going to vote for Edge in the Republican primary and then in November we are not going to vote for governor at all. Without us, Wittpenn should lose," said Hague.

"Right," said Lynch, "I understand."

"Good. Any problems, Jack?"

"None, Mr. Mayor."

Hague clapped his hands and smiled.

"You know, Jack, your new job carries a nice raise with it. I know you're going to marry Al Murphy's Maureen. You might think about buying one of those nice brownstones Downtown. But don't move out of your ward."

Good Lord, he's all but promising me Al's job when the time comes. If I produce. Damn right, I'll produce.

"So have you thought about where you're going on your honeymoon?"

"We were talking about Atlantic City."

"Wonderful place. I might ask you to pay a short visit to a friend of mine there if you don't think Maureen would mind."

"She won't mind, Mr. Hague. She's a politician's daughter and she'll be a politician's wife."

Hague's last appointment of the day was an interview with Jackie Farrell of the Jersey Journal, his favorite reporter. The interview ran along the usual lines. Hague's plans for the city.

The problems, his solutions. Then Farrell asked, "How come the city commission picked you as mayor? Moore got the most votes and everyone thought he would get the job."

Hague looked at Farrell for a long moment. "Jackie, I'm going to tell you something. I don't want you to use it now. The 'Why' will be clear to you. Use it when the right moment comes and I'll confirm it."

"Okay, mayor, we're off the record for now."

"Harry Moore doesn't want to be mayor. He wants to be governor. He helped me become mayor; I'll help him become governor."

Hague helped A. Harry Moore get elected to three terms as governor and one as a United States Senator.

Over There

The 2nd Battalion, 6th Marines had driven back the enemy and were now holding a line anchored by Belleau Wood on the left and the ruined village of Bouresches on the right.

Major Thomas Holcomb's Marines had taken heavy casualties in their attack and they expected a counterattack very soon from the crack German troops they faced.

There was no time to dig trenches although some of the men scratched out shallow pits to give them some cover. One Marine from Virginia called them "foxholes."

Their sergeant major, John Quick, last heard of at Guantanamo Bay, had resupplied the battalion by driving a Model T truck chock full of ammunition and grenades right into the battalion's midst while under intense German fire. Thus he added a Navy Cross and a Distinguished Service Cross to his Medal of Honor.

Sergeant Mike McGurk was a section leader in a rifle platoon with two eight-man squads of Marines under him. He checked his men's positions and ammo supply. Then he returned to his own position. He filled his cartridge belt with five round clips for his Springfield '03 rifle and waited.

They came.

The Marines started picking them off at six hundred yards in the flat terrain beside the woods. McGurk flipped up his rear sight and set it for four hundred yards. He dropped into a prone position, a hasty sling tight around his left arm, the rifle tight into his right shoulder. His legs were at about a thirty degree angle to the left of his torso, legs spread apart with the inside of his boots flat to the ground.

McGurk picked out his target. A moving target was hard to hit but not if it was coming straight at you.

Sergeant McGurk held his breath, took up the slack on the

trigger, and squeezed. The rifle recoiled and the soldier in his sights dropped.

McGurk had worked the bolt and was swinging to his next target when he heard two blasts on his lieutenant's whistle.

The Germans had wavered and had started to fall back. That was the signal for the Marines to charge. McGurk rose to move his men forward.

That's when the bullet came for him.

Fired from a Mauser Gewehr 98 rifle, the 7.92 millimeter bullet hit the lip of McGurk's steel helmet, tearing it from his head. The bullet fragmented and a small piece plowed a furrow in the right side of his forehead and lodged there. McGurk was knocked over backwards senseless as Marines charged past him.

When he regained consciousness, a Navy corpsman was sewing up his forehead.

"Hey, don't move, Sarge. Sorry if this hurts. Can't help it."

McGurk said, "Doc, I can't see. My vision is blurry."

"Ah, you just got some blood in your eyes, that's all. I'll wipe them clean when I finish this."

"I've got a wicked headache too, Doc." McGurk also had a tender bruise under his jaw where the chin strap ripped off.

"Jesus, is that all you are going to do? Lie there and bitch? I'll get around to it."

The corpsman gave him the bullet fragment he dug out of McGurk's forehead and two aspirin for his headache.

"You know, you're probably going to get a wound stripe out of this but you are one lucky son of a bitch," said the corpsman.

"Luck of the Irish, Doc," said McGurk.

"Yeah? Tell that to Carney over there," said the corpsman pointing to a dead Marine not five yards away.

When the Armistice was signed and Sergeant Michael McGurk finally got home, he was lying in bed with his wife, Hannah. She ran her finger over the jagged little scar.

"Was it very rough in Belleau Wood?" she asked.

"I wouldn't know, love," said Mickey McGurk. "I was asleep through the worst of it."

They Never Quit

It was 1924 and America was fixated by Prohibition. Part of the country was trying to enforce it, a larger part was trying to evade it and in Jersey City it was mostly ignored.

Mickey McGurk had been captain of the Zeppelins for a year.

Frank Hague had been mayor for seven years.

The memory of the night of Black Tom was eight years old and fading.

McGurk walked into Hague's outer office and greeted his receptionist/secretary, Alice Patterson. Hague's friend, Mary T. Norton, was running for Congress and Miss Patterson was one of her top campaign aides. She was also a Democratic committee-woman from the 11th Ward. Hague incorporated women into his organization as soon as they got the vote.

"The mayor's expecting you, Captain," said Miss Patterson.

McGurk had a folded newspaper under his arm. "Good morning, Uncle Frank. I won't take up your time. I was just wondering if you read that story about Black Tom in the newspaper?"

Hague, who usually didn't read newspapers and had long ago forgotten about Black Tom, said, "No, I haven't. What does it say?"

McGurk said, "Well, the story is datelined Berlin, Germany. It seems that lawyers for the Lehigh Valley Railroad have filed a case there with the Mixed Claims Commission. They're accusing Germany of sabotage at Black Tom while America was neutral and demanding many millions of dollars in compensation."

Hague shook his head from side to side and said, "Goddamn railroads. They never quit, do they?"

"Nope," said Mickey McGurk.

Hague went back to plotting the next election.

It Took Sixty-three Years

The Lehigh Valley Railroad never quit.

The Lehigh Valley Railroad, in 1924, first pressed its claim of sabotage seeking millions in damages from Germany for the loss of Black Tom. It made its case before the German- American Mixed Claims Commission—eight years after the catastrophic explosions.

The railroad argued that German saboteurs destroyed Black Tom. The Germans said it was an accident relying on the railroad's earlier statements blaming it on "spontaneous combustion". The Germans prevailed and the commission ruled against the railroad in 1930.

But the railroad came back with what it said was "new evidence" and the case was re-opened. In 1939, the commission— in the absence of its German representative— ruled that the Imperial German government was responsible and ordered Germany to pay damages. This the Nazi dictator, Adolf Hitler, refused to do.

In 1953, a settlement of $50,000,000 was agreed upon. The railroad received its last payment in 1979. That was sixty-three years after Black Tom became a dead yard.

Most experts and historians agree that three German agents— Kurt Jahnke, Lothar Witzke and Michael Kristoff were the saboteurs that destroyed Black Tom although dissenters still argue that definitive proof of their guilt does not exist.

The German-born Jahnke was a naturalized American citizen and a former United States Marine who served in San Francisco, Pearl Harbor and the Philippines. He received a medical discharge from the Marines. Several successful sabotage operations were attributed to him on both coasts before America entered the war. Jahnke later had a career spanning decades in sabotage, espionage and intelligence work for Germany despite a brief falling out with the Nazis who suspected he was a Russian double agent. It ended for Jahnke in April, 1945, in Berlin when the Soviet Union's dreaded SMERSH captured, questioned and then shot him and his wife.

Witzke, a cadet in the German Navy who survived the sinking of the cruiser Dresden, escaped from internment in Chile and was teamed up with Jahnke on the West Coast in 1916. He was captured in Arizona in 1918 with incriminating documents on him. An Army court martial sentenced him to death as a spy. President Wilson commuted his sentence in 1920 to life in prison. President Calvin Coolidge pardoned him three years later. When he returned to Germany, Witzke received the Iron Cross, both First and Second Class. He headed up the totally unsuccessful sabotage efforts in England during World War II and faded from sight after that.

Kristoff, born in Slovakia which was then ruled by Austro-Hungary, had served as an American soldier and may have been involved in other attempts at sabotage before war was declared. He re-enlisted in the United States Army in May, 1917, but was discharged in September for being tubercular and for having made false statements on his enlistment papers. He surfaced in 1921 in jail in Albany, NY, serving time for larceny. Kristoff had used the alias "John Christie."

Except for minor brushes with the law, nothing more was heard from Kristoff until his death in a Staten Island, NY, hospital in 1928.

"I Am the Law"

Mayor Frank Hague's organization worked perfectly in the gubernatorial election in 1917. It did nothing and the Democratic candidate, H. Otto Wittpenn, lost. He came out of Hudson County with a 7,000 vote majority; markedly less than the usual 25,000. It wasn't enough to offset Republican majorities elsewhere. Thus ended the political career of the only man who was a threat to Hague's dominance of the Democratic Party in New Jersey.

Democrats won six of nine gubernatorial elections from 1917 to 1940. You couldn't win without Hague and he even made sure the Democrats lost one of the nine as well.

Hague, who hated the railroads, needed to squeeze much more tax money out of them. The railroads controlled both the state legislature and the State Board of Tax Appeals. The railroads were only assessed at 30 percent of their value for tax purposes.

Hague's instrument for changing this was one of the most respectable, old line men in Jersey City who was both a friend and an ally.

Edward I. Edwards, fifty-five, was a state senator, a lawyer, a prominent banker, a civic leader, a Democrat and a Protestant. He ran for governor in 1919 with Hague's backing. He came out of Hudson County with a large enough lead to win. Edwards appointed Hague allies to the state Tax Appeals Board and then the railroads got whopping tax bills. Their appeals failed.

Jersey City was always a heavily taxed city under Hague. The money was needed to support a huge municipal workforce. At its peak, there was one policeman for every 300 residents in the city. The property tax rate rose from $21 per $1000 assessed in 1917 to $53.13 per thousand in 1940. The property assessments rose as well. Never the less, the Chamber of Commerce supported Hague consistently.

Women got the vote in 1920 with the passage of the 19th Amendment and Hague, so to speak, promptly got the women. Ladies Auxiliaries were attached to all Democratic ward clubs. Democratic committee women were appointed. Hague's organization was a welcoming one.

A year later, Mary Norton, who Hague knew from her volunteer work in World War I, was elected to the Hudson County Board of Freeholders. She pushed for the construction of the Margaret Hague Maternity Hospital in Jersey City. Mary Norton was elected to Congress in 1924. She served thirteen consecutive terms until 1949. Her seniority helped Hague get much Federal assistance during the Depression.

Hague was an early supporter of Al Smith, governor of New York and a graduate of Tammany Hall, who had no disdain for big city bosses.

With Smith's help, Hague was elected vice chairman of the National Democratic Committee in 1924, a post he would hold for twenty-five years. Hague was also chairman of the Hudson County and New Jersey Democratic Committees.

A. Harry Moore, Hague's longtime ally, was elected to his first term as governor of New Jersey in 1926. His friend had come through. Moore would also serve terms as governor from 1932 to 1935 and from 1938 to 1941. Moore appointed Hague's son to the state's highest court because, as he told the press, "I thought his Daddy would like it."

Hague was an enthusiastic champion of Al Smith who won the Democratic nomination for president in 1928. Smith was the first Catholic to run for president. Hague's organization showed its muscle and its efficiency by staging a rally at the National Guard training facility in Sea Girt, NJ, fifty-eight miles from Jersey City. More 80,000 people made the trip. Fifty chartered trains traveled from Jersey City alone.

All was in vain though. Herbert Hoover defeated Smith thanks, in part, to the solidly Democratic but Protestant South which voted for the Republican. No surprise to Hague.

While Hague was strutting on the state and national political stages, his organization was perfecting what critics called his "machine." Unlike virtually all big city bosses who preferred to control from behind the scenes, Frank Hague ran for the city commission every four years and was named mayor for seven terms. In one election he got 94 percent of the vote. Critics could never claim he ruled without "the consent of the governed."

These ironically non-partisan elections were an excellent political litmus test. If rivals were on the rise, that would show up in these elections and, of course, be dealt with.

Hague's knowledge of his organization, the city and its people was encyclopedic. Hague was in his office every Election Day with a chart that showed every election district, who were the men and women in charge, who were their election workers, what the vote was in the previous election tallied hour-by-hour as well as the total vote.

When asked, he once pointed out the ten am vote was twice as large in one election district because that Election Day fell on a Holy Day of Obligation. He noted that a Catholic Church was across from the polling place. "We got them coming and going," he said.

Hague, of course, had more support that just his organization. Support he courted. He knew the Catholic Church could have brought him down overnight. At its height, the church probably claimed three-quarters of the white population of Jersey City as communicants. But Hague's open political agenda mirrored that of the church so no problem arose. He befriended other churches, the bar association, the chamber of commerce, veterans' groups, labor unions, fraternal societies, and clubs of all sorts.

To no small extent, Hague even influenced the local Republican Party. Democrats were known to switch their party affiliations so they could be appointed to boards that required bi-partisan membership. The organization even voted Republican at

Hague's command.

In 1928, a Jersey City policeman cheerfully explained to a state committee that while he had voted in the Republican primary in May, by September he had listened to the arguments and became a "strong Democrat" and as such had voted in the Democratic primary too.

Hague was the only one of the big city bosses who was able to dominate the other party statewide when he so chose.

Hague won the 1929 city commission election easily, and an urban legend current in the 1950s attests to the prowess of the organization.

According to the legend, the lights went out at a certain election district when the polls closed. Power was restored quickly and Hague won the district handily. Then, in 1943, the Hudson River was dredged and the ballot box from this election district surfaced. The ballots were dried out and counted. Hague had more votes in the river than he did in the stuffed ballot box. So went the legend which was believed as gospel by many.

The organization's prime job was to get the vote out and at this it excelled. A 1937 study said Jersey City had 127,000 potential voters, yet 161,000 were registered. The difference, of course, were those who had died or moved. The usually efficient organization was very lax in purging such names from the voters' rolls. "Floaters" were recruited to vote for them.

Hague protected himself legally by controlling the jury lists which, in the main, consisted of petty office holders, organization people, their wives and employees of municipal contractors. The organization could prevent or dictate a verdict and did. At least one political enemy was sent to prison for, of all things, vote fraud. He also controlled the bar association through allies who ran it.

In 1929, Hague donated an altar that cost $50,000 to the new St. Aidan's Catholic Church which was built in the heart of the city between Journal Square and Bergen Square. In that same year, he declined to answer questions asked by that state committee about his finances or about specific transactions that seemed far beyond the reach of a man whose salary was never more than $8,000 a year.

Hague certainly lived like a millionaire. In the 1930s, Hague occupied the ninth and tenth floors of the "Summit" at 2600 Hudson Boulevard which he owned. He literally could see most of his fiefdom to the East, West and South and a lot of it to the North. Ironically, the show piece of the ninth floor was a mahogany paneled library. He also owned homes in Deal, NJ, and Key Biscayne, FL, and rented a suite at the posh Plaza Hotel in Manhattan.

A great walker, Hague liked to visit Paris. He enjoyed golf and it was said he would have been a very good golfer had he taken up the game earlier in life. But what Hague really enjoyed was to bet on horses at the race track. His bets were often in the hundreds of dollars.

What paid for this lifestyle besides his modest salary?

Well, there was "Rice Pudding Day" when city employees and others kicked back three percent of their annual salary and thirty percent of any raise they received that year. That money was for the use of the organization and Hague.

Then there were millions upon millions in city contracts. Contractors have been known to kick back too. Ten percent was the most quoted number.

But it is most likely that a large chunk of his income came from protecting the "numbers" racket. Jersey City people were—and are—inveterate numbers players. You pick any three single digit numbers and bet, say a dollar, on them. If that number comes up as the last three numbers in the total amount of money bet at a designated racetrack that day you won $600. The odds are obviously against you but the odds are nowhere as bad as any modern day state sponsored lottery or gambling game.

So every day thousands of people spent a dime or a dollar on hope. Neither they nor Hague saw anything wrong with playing the numbers. The racketeers got rich and probably paid off Hague and his allies to keep the cash flowing. Undoubtedly, he had other sources of income too.

Hague was Al Smith's floor manager at the Democratic convention in 1932 but he quickly jumped over to Franklin Delano Roosevelt when the patrician New Yorker won the nomination. Roosevelt personally disliked Hague but he was an intensely practical politician too.

Hague persuaded Roosevelt to kick off his campaign in New Jersey with a big rally at Sea Girt. Hague's organization surpassed its 1928 logistical triumph. More than 100,000 people journeyed to Sea Girt. One hundred chartered trains left from Exchange Place in Jersey City along with fifty buses to make the fifty-eight mile trip. Each rider was given a box lunch.

Roosevelt's motorcade was met at the mouth of the Holland Tunnel, which opened in 1926, by little girls with bouquets of flowers. Roosevelt was joined by Hague and Governor A. Harry Moore.

The motorcade then leisurely made its way through the Democratic strongholds of Jersey City, Elizabeth and Newark with crowds cheering it on. The day was a triumph for Hague and his organization.

What Roosevelt said to Hague is unknown but from Sea Girt on, Frank Hague was FDR's political friend.

Roosevelt had hardly lowered his hand after taking the presidential oath when work started on Hague's crown jewel, the Jersey City Medical Center, much of it federally funded.

When completed, the Medical Center was the third largest hospital in the nation with its seven skyscrapers, some twenty-five stories tall. Built on Palisades bedrock, the Medical Center often had more staff than patients. It was socialized medicine, before the term was invented, in a city where socialism was anathema.

Everyone was treated there. If you were poor, there was no bill. If you weren't, the bill was minimal given the lavishness and the expertise of the treatment. You would be born there, be treated there, and, often, you would die there. It was Hague's answer to having been born on his mother's kitchen table.

As with everything, Hague exercised personal control when it came to the Medical Center and once flattened an intern when he determined the ambulance's response time was too slow.

There was even a nursing school which provided more good jobs for local women. In keeping with Hague's standards, no male visitors were permitted to go up beyond the first floor reception room at Murdoch Hall.

The medical bills, as were all other government benefits, were paid for with a vote on Election Day.

That some of the same materials used to build the Medical Center turned up in the construction of the Hague-owned "Summit" apartment house surprised no one. Few in Jersey City were even annoyed.

Hague, whose education ended at the 6th Grade, built three new high schools during his tenure as mayor and the Jersey City Junior College operated at night at one of the high schools.

The New Jersey State Normal School at Jersey City (now New Jersey City State University) opened in 1929 providing training for teachers.

The Jesuits gave education another boost a year later when they re-opened St. Peter's College (now St. Peter's University) which had been closed during World War I when most of its students joined the colors.

The governor of New Jersey laid the corner stone in 1931 for a very special school bearing his name, the A. Harry Moore School for Crippled Children (now the A. Harry Moore School). This school was one of the first in the nation constructed especially for children with disabilities. Governor Moore was instrumental in getting the necessary money for Hague to build the four and five story complex.

Hague was always looking out for the children. In fact that's how the infamous "I Am the Law" sobriquet was first hung on him.

Two boys under sixteen were hauled in for truancy to a police station where Hague happened to be. They told the mayor they'd rather go to jail than to school. Hague thought it would be better if they went to work but the authorities told him they were too young to do that legally.

Said Hague, "Listen. Here is the law. I am the law. These boys go to work." So they did.

After that virtually no liberal newspaper, that is to say any to the left of the Archbishop of Newark, would mention Hague without using the quote "I am the law." It might have been taken out of context but it was true. He was the law in Jersey City for thirty years.

Hague's Jersey City was slow to brand boys as juvenile delinquents. He even set up a Bureau of Special Services to deal with them. Boys of the authors' generation believed that was where two policemen, Bill Mc Laughlin and "Curley" Donchin, beat you to your knees "in loco parentis." No one knew anyone that underwent that treatment but all believed that's what happened.

If you persisted in misbehavior, an unsuccessful trip to the Parental Home in Bayonne was the norm before you were called to the serious attention of the courts.

Hague was influential in bringing the New York Giants top triple AAA farm team to Jersey City in 1937. Hague often threw out the first pitch at the Jersey City Giants' opener. All the schoolboys in Jersey City got in free on opening day.

Roosevelt's New Deal showered money on Jersey City for a "job program" with the Works Progress Administration. Roosevelt Stadium was built at Droyer's Point as was a stadium of the same name in Union City.

Norman Thomas, his Socialist enemy, said Hague ruled

during the Depression with "bread, circuses and punishment." The organization preferred to term it relief, outings and a police force that kept order.

Hague's record with labor was very mixed. In 1919, his police turned back fifty strikebreakers sent from New York to unload the SS Giuseppe Verdi at a city pier.

He was endorsed by Hudson County Central Labor Council in every election from 1913 to 1929. But this body represented American Federation of Labor unions most of which were building trades locals heavily populated with staunch Hague supporters. He was known to co-opt unions by having his people elected as officers, by bribing officers, or by offering valuable "favors" to union officers.

By 1936, it was estimated that eighty percent of the factories and businesses in Jersey City were "open shop" which meant that employees were not compelled to join a union.

Hague drew the line at the upstart CIO (Congress of Industrial Organizations) during the Depression and, in essence, banned the CIO as well as "communists and other radicals" from the city. Hague was the despair of civil libertarians but he managed to get 94 percent of the vote in the 1937 municipal election.

In November, 1937, the CIO, which did count socialists and communists in its ranks then, sent a wave of organizers from New York into Jersey City which seemed ripe for unionization.

Hague screamed that the city had been "invaded" and counterattacked. Thirteen organizers were arrested on trumped up charges and scores more were bodily thrown out of Jersey City by the cops.

The Chamber of Commerce called on all Jersey City civic and social organizations to rally around the mayor. The Chamber said, "We can solve our industrial problems without this foreign invasion."

An advertisement which ran in The Jersey Journal summoned

all World War I veterans to mobilize in Journal Square to show these "longhaired radicals from New York and elsewhere" that their presence would not be tolerated in Jersey City. A Catholic War Veterans leader suggested to an audience of eight hundred that they each bring a two foot length of rubber hose to the rally.

Hague himself was quoted as saying, "These strangers may well understand that the Stars and Stripes will continue to fly over our city...the red flag will never be hoisted while we Americans live in Jersey City." Hague, like the Roman Catholic Church, was a mortal enemy of socialism and communism.

Nonetheless, or perhaps because of that, Norman Thomas, six time nominee of the Socialist Party for president of the United States, decided to give a speech in Jersey City the next year.

Thomas, a Presbyterian minister until 1931, a "Christian Socialist", a pacifist, an anti-communist, a constant critic of the Catholic Church, an advocate of birth control, a graduate of Princeton and an urbane, well-spoken civil libertarian was the antithesis of Frank Hague.

The cops bounced him out of Jersey City twice in the same day. Thomas howled to Franklin Delano Roosevelt and J. Edgar Hoover, head of the FBI, claiming he was "kidnapped" by the police.

Hague did not deign to answer him. That was left to Daniel Casey who defended his cops saying Thomas' presence in Jersey City "had created a disturbance." He added, "The socialist leader's efforts and those of the communists and reds he represents to create disorder and violence in our community will be defeated just as was the efforts of the CIO to invade Jersey City."

The civil libertarians were now choleric denouncing what they called "Hagueism." Even Alf Landon, the Republican nominee FDR had buried in 1936, was sympathetic to Thomas.

The CIO had not been defeated, actually. The union sued over the arrests and the Supreme Court of the United States found in its favor in 1939.

A month later the CIO sat down with some of Hague's lieutenants at City Hall. When the union leaders emerged, they announced all was forgiven and then denounced the Republicans for trying to take advantage of the situation. The union stood firmly behind the Democratic Party, Hague's party. The Hague organization could be flexible when necessary.

In 1939, Governor A. Harry Moore appointed Frank Hague, Jr., thirty-four, as a justice of the Court of Errors and Appeals. While young Hague did not graduate from law school, he did pass the New Jersey bar examination.

Hague was an effective supporter of Franklin Delano Roosevelt when he ran for an unprecedented third and fourth term in 1940 and 1944.

He reluctantly complied with Roosevelt's request in 1941 to back Charles Edison, the inventor Thomas A. Edison's son, for governor. Hague threw one of his now patented soirees at Sea Girt drawing 120,000 people. Edison won and promptly forgave the railroads the millions they owed in back taxes.

World War II brought full employment and a relative boom times to Jersey City even as its sons and daughters marched off to war.

The trouble for Hague started when they got back. Strong employment and a solid social safety net woven by the New Deal meant that people no longer had to go to the organization for help. Returning veterans had the GI Bill which meant they could go to college, learn a trade, start a business, and buy a home without talking to their ward leader. No longer was getting as job with the city the compelling ambition of young men.

Young people wanted to move out of Jersey City and live in the suburbs or at the Jersey Shore. Now they had the wherewithal to do it.

The Irish had controlled the city for more than a generation and other ethnic groups were restive. Hague had not done much to satisfy their ambitions. The black population had grown very substantially and was all but ignored except on Election Day. The political caldron was bubbling.

Hague, who had always led from the front, decided to quit as mayor in mid-term in 1947. Like other big city bosses, he thought he could call the plays from the sidelines. He put his nephew, Frank Hague Eggers, in the mayor's seat.

Hague's last real organizational triumph was a rally in 1948 for Harry S. Truman. More than 200,000 people crowded the heart of Jersey City to see and maybe hear the Democratic candidate.

Meanwhile, a palace revolt led by John V. Kenny was underway. Kenny was a ward leader and the son of Hague's original mentor, the saloonkeeper Nat Kenny. The 1949 municipal election was fiercely contested.

Hague was speaking at a rally when he was heckled. Annoyed, he pointed at the offender and ordered, "Arrest that man." The nearby cop never moved. Hague was finished.

Hague died on January 1, 1956, sixteen days before his eightieth birthday. He rests in an impressive mausoleum in Jersey City's Holy Name Cemetery.

Black Tom is now an indistinguishable part of Liberty State Park which was formed in 1976 from land once owned by the railroads. Typically inadequate historical plaques there recall the night of Black Tom.

The skyline just across the river is dominated by the new Freedom Tower, built on the site of the Twin Towers of the World Trade Center destroyed by Islamic terrorists on 9/11, 2001.

But then everyone knew what happened almost at the instant it happened. Millions actually watched it happen on live television.

Not so Black Tom.

**TOP HAT
BOOKS**

Historical fiction that lives.

We publish fiction that captures the contrasts, the achievements, the optimism and the radicalism of ordinary and extraordinary times across the world.

We're open to all time periods and we strive to go beyond the narrow, foggy slums of Victorian London. Where are the tales of the people of fifteenth century Australasia? The stories of eighth century India? The voices from Africa, Arabia, cities and forests, deserts and towns? Our books thrill, excite, delight and inspire.

The genres will be broad but clear. Whether we're publishing romance, thrillers, crime, or something else entirely, the unifying themes are timescale and enthusiasm. These books will be a celebration of the chaotic power of the human spirit in difficult times. The reader, when they finish, will snap the book closed with a satisfied smile.